THE GRAVEYARD KILLINGS

WES MARKIN

Boldwood

First published in Great Britain in 2024 by Boldwood Books Ltd.

Copyright © Wes Markin, 2024

Cover Design by Head Design Ltd

Cover Photography: Shutterstock

The moral right of Wes Markin to be identified as the author of this work has been asserted in accordance with the Copyright, Designs and Patents Act 1988.

All rights reserved. No part of this book may be reproduced in any form or by any electronic or mechanical means, including information storage and retrieval systems, without written permission from the author, except for the use of brief quotations in a book review.

This book is a work of fiction and, except in the case of historical fact, any resemblance to actual persons, living or dead, is purely coincidental.

Every effort has been made to obtain the necessary permissions with reference to copyright material, both illustrative and quoted. We apologise for any omissions in this respect and will be pleased to make the appropriate acknowledgements in any future edition.

A CIP catalogue record for this book is available from the British Library.

Paperback ISBN 978-1-80483-779-5

Large Print ISBN 978-1-80483-778-8

Hardback ISBN 978-1-80483-781-8

Ebook ISBN 978-1-80483-777-1

Kindle ISBN 978-1-80483-776-4

Audio CD ISBN 978-1-80483-785-6

MP3 CD ISBN 978-1-80483-783-2

Digital audio download ISBN 978-1-80483-782-5

Boldwood Books Ltd
23 Bowerdean Street
London SW6 3TN
www.boldwoodbooks.com

To John and Elaine.

1

1980

Dean Maiden couldn't piss straight.

Hardly surprising.

Another job lost, another drink...

Another day in Thatcher's Britain.

He leaned his head against the wall above the urinal and worked on his aim. After all, he'd already sprayed his brogues twice this evening and didn't want to wreck them completely. He'd need them for the weeks – strike that – the months ahead in which he'd be scrambling around for work.

When someone slapped him on the back, he saturated his shoes again. 'Bollocks!'

'Head off the wall, Deano.' It was Ken Turner, landlord of The Dropping Well. 'Enough to be done without scrubbing your dribble off the sodding walls.'

'You'll be scrubbing the chuffing floor anyway,' Dean said, looking down at the puddles of piss.

'Just do as you're told and stop drooling down me bloody tiles.'

'All heart, Ken. After the day I just had!'

Ken raised his eyebrows, clearly interested. 'Go on.'

'Lost another job, didn't I?'

'That print shop in Bradford?' Ken asked, his tone of voice suddenly more serious.

Dean took a step back, shaking his foot and zipping up his fly. 'Aye.'

'Sorry to hear that, squire. Seems to be getting all too common round here.'

'You don't look too broken-hearted,' Dean said. 'You've got a pub chock full of wounded men out there. Taking their last pennies.'

'Piss off. I offer a service,' Ken said, unzipping himself. 'Trying to get all your bloody minds off everything.'

Dean looked at the filthy sink and decided against washing his hands. There was no value in putting his hands anywhere near it. He glanced down at his sodden shoes, then up at Ken, who had a smile dripping from his wide, sagging face. 'Bugger off.'

'Hey son, if I didn't serve you this medicine, then someone else would. At least you've got a pair o' lovely lasses to get home to. More than can be said for half that lot out there!'

Dean sighed. 'Aye. Until we lose the house and then Estelle buggers off to Greece with some tanned hunk.'

'You'll still have Penny.'

'Really. Seventeen now. She'll be gone soon enough.'

'Aye, she will.'

Dean shook his head and grunted. 'Ken, has anyone ever told you that you're a prize dickhead?'

'Just my wife, Deano. Just my wife.'

* * *

Dean staggered through plumes of smoke, nodding and grinning at the men he'd known for as long as he could remember, keeping up a brave face.

No one liked a whinger. And he wasn't the only poor sod in the pub with piss-stained brogues. Paranoia over employment and losing your bricks and mortar seemed to be at an all-time high. Ever since that witch had started running the country.

'Oi Deano! You can barely stand! I think you've spent enough time with Timothy!' Brian shouted over.

Timothy Taylor's Landlord. The beer of champions.

'Piss off,' Dean shouted back. 'Only just getting to know him.'

There was a new lass at the bar. She was young and pretty and reminded him of his daughter Penny. He couldn't envisage her working in a shithole like this but knew that it was probably only a matter of time. Money wasn't growing on trees these days, and she was almost eighteen.

He ordered another pint.

Jesus, 52p! Thatcher's Britain.

'One for yerself too, love.'

'Cheers,' she said, rustling in the till for his change.

'And if any of these barmpots give you any trouble, you call me over.'

She smiled. 'I will.'

He turned, leaned on the bar, drank back a third of the bitter in one greedy gulp and surveyed the crowds.

Most nights, when employed, he'd enjoy his time here immensely, flitting between groups of childhood friends. But tonight, despite the alcohol, he didn't feel like doing any flitting. If anything, he felt like crawling alone into a dark room with a bottle of whisky.

He took another large mouthful of Timothy, belched and then wiped his mouth with the back of his hand. He felt his watch brush against his cheek and looked down at his cracked Casio digital screen. The time was still readable. Just.

Shit. Penny!

His daughter was part of the team running a book club at St John the Baptist Church, which was scheduled to end ten minutes ago.

Ten minutes ago!

Bloody hell. He was supposed to be picking her up.

Knowing Penny, she'd have shrugged her shoulders and started walking already. *Shit!* It was dark and cold out there. The poor lass.

Penny would forgive him, but not his wife, Estelle. No chance.

Bad Dad would be back on the sofa.

Unemployed.

Piss on his shoes.

Sleeping on the sofa.

It was a day that really couldn't get any worse.

He finished his pint in one mouthful and staggered towards the door.

'Oi Deano,' Brian shouted. 'Where the bloody hell do you think you're going?'

Dean stuck two fingers up and exited The Dropping Well.

The icy rain whipped his cheeks. He sighed and lowered his face.

He'd be glad when this bloody day was over.

* * *

The heavy rain seemed to sober him, or at least give his thoughts clarity.

Although a clearer head just intensified his concern for Penny.

Determined to get to her, he broke into a quick jog towards his Ford Cortina.

Drenched, he climbed into his vehicle and ran a hand through his sodden hair as he felt the rain drip down the back of his neck.

The image of his daughter shrugging and setting off on a thirty-minute walk in this cold threaded through his mind again.

He hoped he was wrong, and that she'd asked someone else at the church to give her a ride back, but he knew, deep down, that she wouldn't have done that. Penny was the type of lass that didn't like to bother anyone.

Unlike me, Dean thought, turning the key and firing up the engine. *Her bloody old man.*

He caused bother wherever he stepped.

He popped the car into first and eased the vehicle forward, hitting his indicator to move out onto Harrogate Road.

An ambulance streaked past, sirens raging. Dean slammed his foot on the brake.

'Bloody hell,' he said, feeling a sudden burst of adrenaline. The ambulance had been going at some speed through rather heavy rain.

He took a deep breath and continued edging forwards.

Two police cars whistled past, sirens blaring, lights pulsing, but Dean was more resilient now after the ambulance and didn't feel a rush of panic.

'You boys want to slow down,' he said. 'You ain't stopping for man or beast at that speed.'

Half-expecting more emergency vehicles, Dean opted to wait for the sirens to dwindle. Not only did he want to avoid a collision, but he wanted to avoid the inquisitive eyes of the police. He'd had a fair number of ales already.

While he waited, Dean's mind clouded again.

In addition to the rain and the dark, there were several

drunken locals round here who didn't always behave the best. Granted, he knew most of them, and they'd know Penny was off-limits, but still, you should never underestimate a drunken man.

He thought about where she'd be right now. Further along on Harrogate Road, roughly at the point where it turned into Bond End.

Hang fire, Dean. You'll be with her in a minute or two.

Across Harrogate Road was the entrance to Mother Shipton's, pulsing under the blue police lights. Only last year, the Maidens had visited as a family. The petrified stone objects hanging under the lip of the cave had fascinated Penny. Dean hadn't been so fascinated with the objects, but rather with his daughter, who grew more beautiful by the day.

His fascination had been bittersweet.

The pride he'd felt had collided painfully with the understanding that she soon would be leaving them to make her own way in the world.

He sighed and continued to wait, but the sirens weren't stopping, and the blue pulsing caused by the distant flashing lights continued.

With his patience dwindling, he turned left onto Harrogate Road.

Up ahead, he could see that the police cars and the ambulance had come to a stop further up the hill, close to Bond End.

And then the blood froze in Dean Maiden's veins.

2

2023

Zac Livingstone felt ready to have sex.

At least, that was what he'd told himself, over and over, since this morning's offer.

In history, at nine thirty, Chrissie Greenwood's note had worked its way to him from one corner of the room to the other. It crossed various tables, greased many palms, yet arrived, still folded into a little square. Not surprising really. Chrissie was one of the most popular girls in school, if not *the* most popular, so no one would risk her wrath by unfolding and reading one of her notes. In contrast, Zac was one of the least popular boys in school, if not the least popular, so all eyes, *and sneers*, were on him as he had unfolded the note with trembling fingers.

Mrs Brown was sensitive to disruption, so when the pitch of her voice had changed for the first time in thirty minutes, everyone's eyes flew back to her. She may've been frightfully dull, but she had tendencies towards sudden maniacal behaviour which scared the students. So, all the Year II students had sat up straight, and regarded her attentively. This was fortunate for Zac because after reading the note from Chrissie he had immediately glowed red. Not a good look. And one he was glad had slipped beneath the radar.

The rumours that Chrissie Greenwood, who was said to have had more boyfriends than the Kardashians had Instagram followers, *liked* Zac, had started the previous day.

His best friend, Theo, had offered his usual cutting dose of realism. 'Unlikely; there's more chance of you being struck by lightning this afternoon.'

'It happens.'

'Okay, struck twice... in one day.'

Zac had considered researching it but decided against it. What would it change? Theo had thought the rumour was bollocks, and he was more than happy to keep dishing out reality checks.

And Theo still wouldn't have it. Even after he'd seen the note.

I'm ready. Knaresborough cemetery tonight. 10.15. Bring a condom.

'Bollocks.'

'Bollocks what?'

'Bollocks, you're getting a shag.'

'You read the note.'

'She didn't write that.'

'She did.'

Theo had been shaking his head so hard, Zac wondered if it might just fall off.

'Nah. One of her mates must have. It's a windup.'

'I *watched* her. We were eyeing each other up as she wrote it.'

'Pity that you're falling for it.'

Zac had snatched the note back. 'I'll let you know how it goes.'

'What goes? Get real, dickhead. If you want to have sex, you need to meet a female geek. A female geek that doesn't already know you, because they too, will be desperate to elevate their status and not lower it. That's why you wait till college. Geeks like me and you will clean up in college *because* the female geeks won't know you. I'm warning you now, this is bollocks. What's more... there are two problems here... well, three, actually.'

'Which are?'

'Ten fifteen is past your bedtime. Your mum and dad won't be best pleased about you wandering out on a school night. Second, where are you getting a condom? And finally, a graveyard? How the hell are you going to get it up in a graveyard?'

'All bases covered.' Zac had winked, turned and strutted away. Looking confident, but melting inside.

Yes, Zac Livingstone felt ready for sex... had done for a while now. But there was a big difference between feeling horny, *a lot*, and having sex, wasn't there?

Still, no one ever got anywhere by standing still. This was his time. Theo just had sour grapes that Zac's enormous leap had come first.

He made a mental note to be very unsupportive when Theo's time came too.

Zac scoped the local pharmacies but couldn't find one with a male behind the counter. Eventually, he chose a small pharmacy on Chain Lane, and waited until there were no customers. He crept into the shop, head lowered, face glowing, grabbed a packet of condoms, and went over to pay.

Most. Embarrassing. Moment. Of. His. Life.

Still, he was equipped. Getting out of his home was less diffi-cult. His mother always went to bed early as she liked to jog at five in the morning, and his father was away on business.

The third problem was an oddity: *how the hell are you going to get it up in a graveyard?*

For someone with no carnal knowledge whatsoever, where did you even begin with answering that?

He just assumed that he would be able to, being that he was *ready* for sex. And the entire process was natural, wasn't it? He didn't believe in ghosts or anything, so he didn't fear being interrupted by some long-dead grandmother six feet under.

* * *

Zac waited by the locked gates. The moon was full tonight, but the light, although welcome, didn't make the whole thing any less eerie. Also, the chances of being caught trespassing increased. He leaned against the stone wall by the knee-high 'Wetherby Road' street sign, nervously fiddling on his mobile. He wasn't focusing on anything in particular – his racing mind wouldn't allow that; it was simply an attempt to look less odd.

Ten thirty... and still no Chrissie.

Well done, Theo, seems you were right as usual...

'Are you coming or what?'

Heart crashing against the wall of his chest, he turned.

She was really here!

She wore leggings and a red crop top. She was also heavily made-up and had ample cleavage on show. Zac felt a surge of excitement, but also the butterflies swarming in his stomach. He hoped that in the moon's whiteness, the flushing in his cheeks wasn't obvious.

Instinctively, he tried the gate.

She laughed when it didn't budge. 'Over the wall, dickhead!'

'Yes,' he said, trying to sound confident and masculine, but knowing he probably sounded like a squeaking mouse.

'Hurry then, I'm freezing... need to warm up... know what I mean?'

Need to warm up!

Speared by a spike of adrenaline, he climbed on the street sign and hoisted himself over the wall.

When he dropped onto the other side, he saw her standing there, regarding him, hands on her hips, and he felt his entire body freeze over.

'Hi,' he said, again hoping she wasn't able to see how red faced he was.

She spun. 'Coming?' She jogged away among the gravestones, not bothering to use the path.

Despite his anxiety, he didn't want to let this opportunity slip. He chased after her, trying his best to use the path, forcing back the shock he felt every time he saw Chrissie trample over a grave.

Deeper into the cemetery, she turned and leaned against a crumbling headstone. She took a vape pen from her pocket.

He stopped before the grave, struggling to make himself right with this disrespect shown towards a burial site.

He tried to shake off his prudery – he was about to have sex in a cemetery!

Manners are going to be your undoing Zac.

She blew out a cloud of vapour and then offered him the vape. 'You want some?'

'I don't...' He broke off, realising he sounded lame.

'Sod that. Calm you down. Get you in the mood, right? Come here.'

Jesus! This was really happening, wasn't it?

He tried to strut, find that swagger he'd employed when walking away from his bitter best friend earlier. *All bases covered.*

Still, right now, he felt as if he was staggering... lumbering like a giant oaf.

Pathetic...

Several steps on the surface of the grave, he glanced down, fighting back a feeling of revulsion and self-loathing.

'They're dead, you know?' Chrissie said, laughing.

He nodded, cheeks suddenly on fire again.

Chrissie stepped away from the headstone and moved to within a metre of Zac. A cooling wind whistled through the cemetery, sending her hair across her face. She brushed it from her eyes.

Beautiful...

After another hit from her vape pen, she turned back to look at the headstone. Zac looked too, seeing that all but one word had worn away. *Elias.* The first name, perhaps.

She turned back and exhaled. Zac could smell the cherry scent of her vape. 'Bet whoever is down there's just dust and bones.'

Zac nodded. It was a rather obvious thing to say. Still, he wasn't standing here because of her sharp wit and intelligence. Chrissie was extremely popular and outgoing. She drank, smoke and had boyfriends. A lot of boyfriends. It seemed easy to be popular if you did such things.

Would having sex in a graveyard make Zac more popular?

As he was starting at such a low bar, he guessed it may have some kind of impact.

She came closer to him. He heard the night songs of birds in the trees. He felt a stirring below and glanced off into the distance at the thousands of graves.

How the hell are you going to get it up in a graveyard?

He'd suspected that the third problem identified by Theo was never really going to be a problem at all.

She pressed the pen to his lips. 'Taste it.'

He inhaled and felt light-headed for a moment. Suddenly worried he might just fall, he closed his eyes. She laughed. 'Are you nervous?'

Yes. 'No.' He shook his head, determined to look more confident.

'I don't believe you.' She put her hand on his face. 'But I don't mind... I like it. You're gentle. Different from most of the other dickheads.'

Oh, that sounded good...

She leaned in and kissed him. Her lips were soft. It shocked him, but she didn't press too hard, so he could keep himself steady.

This was the first time he'd ever kissed a girl.

He tried to let his head move naturally, in sync with hers, but was acutely aware that he'd no actual idea of what he was doing. Paranoid that he was doing it all wrong, he considered pulling back, apologising, when she gave a pleasurable moan...

And he felt his stomach light up inside.

In fact, he felt everything light up.

When her tongue moved in his mouth, the sensation became indescribable. He allowed his tongue to join hers in a slippery dance.

The light inside was now a raging fire.

She stepped back, fixed him in a stare that was exaggerated, but still very welcome, before throwing her vape pen down and pulling off her crop top.

His breath caught in his throat as he regarded the tight black bra, and her breasts pushed high...

'Did you get it?' Chrissie asked.

'Get what? Sorry?'

'The condom?'

He nodded, hoping he wasn't drooling.

This time, she didn't lean in, she pounced. The kissing became more forceful, her tongue thrusting in and out. When her hand started rubbing at the front of his trousers, where he wasn't simply just stirring any more, he suddenly felt as if he was going to explode.

She pulled one of his hands around her, onto her bum, and he let it rest lightly there for a moment, before she broke away and said, 'Don't hold back.'

He didn't know how to respond to such a request. This had already travelled far beyond everything he'd ever imagined. Squeezing one of her buttocks seemed like an option. Her moan showed he'd made the right choice.

She undid his belt.

Was this really happening...? Here... now... in a cemetery... on a—

Doubt tugged at him.

No, not now, Zac, not when you're so close.

She'd already undone the top button of his trousers, and slipped her hand down inside—

It was wrong.

This was wrong.

They were standing on someone's grave.

He pulled away.

'What?' she hissed.

Breathlessly, he looked around himself, desperate for a solution. He pointed over at a bench against a wall. 'There.' A large tree reached over the bench; its foliage hung down like the overgrown, mossy hand of a giant.

Chrissie glanced at the bench and then nodded down at his gaping trousers and his bulging underwear. 'I don't think you'll last until we get there.'

When she looked back up at him, Zac saw a sneer on her face. His stomach turned. Malice. Was that what he saw? 'I will,' he said.

'*No.* Now or never. Here or not at all.'

He looked at the crumbling headstone. *Elias.* At rest. *Dust and bones.* 'I... don't...'

'Have you changed your mind? Don't you want me any more?' The sneer and malice seemed to fall away now, and her eyes glowed with anger instead.

'No,' he said, trying to understand what he was suddenly feeling.

Guilt, perhaps? Over how he'd made her feel?

Or maybe he was now so far outside of his comfort zone that it was best to just choose to opt out instead of staying in.

Thinking back to the kiss, and his burning desire, he fought against his sudden reluctance. He couldn't remember ever feeling so alive and wanted to stick this out to the bitter... or rather... *glorious* end.

'No... I want you,' he said, feeling proud of himself for delivering the words in an assertive tone of voice. A tone that'd regularly evaded him in his life until now.

'Put it on then,' she said.

'Sorry?'

'Put on the condom.' She sucked on her bottom lip.

He thrust his hand into his pocket and yanked out the foil wrapper. With trembling hands, he tore it open, acutely aware of the instructions not to do so for risk of ripping the contraceptive. Instructions he'd read over fifty times since purchasing the packet.

Holding the prophylactic in one hand, he stared down at his gaping trousers and the bulge in his underwear.

'Hurry... now...' she said, the sneer returning.

He yanked his underwear and jeans down. He tried to kick them off, but his shoes were an obstruction, and he almost stumbled. Laughing, she put her arms around his neck to steady him and looked him in the eyes. 'Put it on.'

He flushed, looked down at her cleavage spilling out from the top of her black bra, and then looked at his erection.

When in Rome.

He reached down to work the condom on, squeezing the air from the tip as the instructions had advised.

After, he looked up.

'Good boy,' Chrissie said, drawing her hands away from Zac's neck, and then taking some steps back.

He creased his brow.

She continued backing away.

'Where are you going?' he asked.

She leaned over, picked up her crop top beside the headstone and slipped it back on.

He was about to take a step in her direction, but recalled, just in time, that his trousers were around his ankles.

Confused, he leaned over to pull his trousers up, but was interrupted by some voices behind him.

His blood ran cold.

No...

He glanced over his shoulder.

Noah Thompson and Sam Green.

Two idiots from Year II.

Sniggering and – worse still – filming him with mobile phones.

Panicking, he tried his best to cover his exposed crotch, but he was still quite erect, and so made himself look even more ridiculous when he winced.

It was all too late – Sam's phone was already pointing downwards at his nakedness.

'And what do we find out in the wilderness this evening, Sam?' Noah asked.

'Something small and timid,' Sam said. 'Vulnerable prey for the hungrier—'

Zac, feeling himself die inside, reached down and worked up his underwear and jeans.

The bastards were laughing hard now.

Including Chrissie.

Fastening his belt, Zac watched Sam turn his phone onto the headstone. 'Poor old Elias.'

'Some dirty little youth getting his game on over his remains,' Noah said.

'Turn it off,' Zac hissed, pointing angrily.

'The small, timid prey speaks,' Sam said.

Zac wasn't sure if he'd ever heard anyone laugh as hard as Chrissie was right now.

He looked at her with disgust.

She shrugged. 'Just a bit of fun, innit?'

Zac stumbled backwards.

He closed his eyes and saw his smiling best friend, Theo. 'I did try to tell you it was bollocks!'

After opening his eyes, he looked at Chrissie, trying to hide the sadness from his eyes, but knowing that it was on full show. 'I thought... I thought...'

'Thought what?' Chrissie sneered again. 'Really? Honestly? You think I'd touch that tiny little prick?'

Tears forming in his eyes, Zac panned his gaze darting over the three bullies.

What were they going to do?

Sam slipped his mobile into his pocket.

'That video,' Zac said, trying to stop his voice cracking. 'You can't do anything with that. I didn't give permission. I—'

'Look, dweeb,' Noah said and laughed. 'You gave us permission when you snogged my girlfriend and touched her arse.'

'I... I... it wasn't like that!' Zac said, pointing angrily at Noah.

Noah looked at Sam and then at Chrissie. 'Can you believe this?' He pointed back at Zac. 'Of course it was. We arranged it.'

Zac wiped the tears from his eyes. He wanted to say more, but his lips were quivering now.

'Don't cry, little man, we're going to turn you into an internet sensation,' Noah said.

Zac shook his head. 'No... no... *please.*'

'It's a grave, man.' Sam laughed. 'What the hell were you thinking? Getting your dick out on someone's grave? What were you planning to do? Knock one out? Certainly looked that way!'

Zac glanced at Chrissie. *No... I...* But wasn't it obvious? Chrissie had stepped back. It'd just be him, standing alone, on a grave, with an erection.

Chrissie would deny ever being here.

'I'm begging you,' Zac said, moving towards Noah.

'Don't worry. Maybe you'll attract some kind of weirdo who's into shit like this,' Noah said. 'You know, it may even be a blessing in disguise for a little virgin like you.'

Zac looked back at Chrissie who was still laughing hysterically.

He imagined the horror on his mother's face; Theo's face; *everyone's* face.

His life was over.

Completely.

Unless...

He stepped forward with one hand out, and the other balled into a fist. 'Give me your phones.'

Noah laughed. 'Who's going to make us? You? The graveyard perve with the little dick? This is getting embarrassing.'

Zac surveyed the floor, sighted a rock and swooped for it.

The bullies descended into hysterics.

'I bloody well will,' Zac said, shaking the rock in Noah's direction.

Chrissie came around the grave and had to steady herself against her boyfriend. She was laughing so hard.

With despair and anger racing through Zac in equal measure, he took a step towards them.

'You need to give me that phone.' He pointed at Chrissie with the rock in his hand. 'You... You... *bitch!*'

She shook her head, tears running down her face from the laughter. 'Yes... I admit it... but shit, is this worth it – so funny.'

Zac threw the rock. It caught Chrissie square in the face. Her head whipped back and up, and she fell.

Shit.

The two boys stopped laughing and looked down at her.

Chrissie was still.

3

1980

The police and ambulances may've called time on their ear-shredding sirens, but they weren't killing their flashing lights for love nor money.

Knowing that driving his car up to that chaotic buzz of emergency services was just asking for trouble, Dean Maiden abandoned his Ford Cortina beside the pub, and ran up Harrogate Road.

The thrashing rain slanted towards him, so when he was midway over the Knaresborough High Bridge, he stumbled, half-blinded, off the pavement and onto the road. Fortunately, there were no cars flying past, as was usual.

The road was now at a standstill from the commotion ahead.

Wiping his eyes, he jumped back onto the pavement, momentarily catching a glimpse over the side of the bridge at the slow-moving River Nidd below, where everything remained calm...

Unlike up here.

Dead ahead, near the turn-off to Bond End, which led along The Parsonage and down to St John the Baptist Church – where his daughter had been about fifteen minutes ago – something bad had happened.

Something very bad.

Two-ambulance-and-four-police-cars bad.

Adrenaline rushed through him.

Are you involved, Penny? Please, lass... please be halfway home already.

He shook his head as he ran.

It's the booze talking... Ignore it. She's got her head screwed on tight. Takes proper care of herself.

Not like him. An old, unemployed chuffing wino.

His heart thrashing further still, he pressed on, head turned down, away from the slicing rainfall. Passed another of his local pubs. *The World's End.*

It took his mind back to last Saturday. A glorious day. Sunny and fresh. Estelle and Penny. The food was great and his daughter's announcement that she was going to pursue her ambition to be a journalist, a proud moment.

Dean wiped the rain from his eyes. A multitude of people, some with umbrellas, some without, hovered outside The World's End, their curiosity piqued by what was happening up ahead. Some had even begun the walk up the hill, on the other side of the road, towards the emergency services.

Yet Dean was the only person running.

Why was he the only one running?

'Deano... *Deano*...' someone called from the front of the pub.

The voice was familiar, but he didn't care to put a face to it. His only concern was closing the ever-shortening gap to the scene of this accident to put his mind at rest.

Because that was the only conceivable outcome, really.

His mind being put at rest.

When he reached the first of the police cars, breathlessness struck. He leaned over, clutching his knees, gulping for air, while rain streamed down his face.

The beer bubbling away in his belly was demanding a way out, working its way up his throat. He swallowed it back.

'Dean?'

Dean looked up at his old friend from the school football team, Harry Rhodes. He'd been excellent between the sticks. To be fair, he could still save like Peter Shilton on a good day. He could also drink with the best of them – when he wasn't on shift with the local constabulary.

The grave expression on Harry's face almost stopped Dean's heart in his chest.

'Mate, Harry, what's...' Again, Dean felt the rising beer in his throat. He swallowed it back with as much might as he could muster.

When he glanced back up, Harry was looking behind himself.

'Harry?'

Harry turned back, his face even more ashen now.

'What is it? Harry?'

Harry brushed wet hair from his face. It was clear he was avoiding Dean's eyes. 'I don't know.'

A lie.

Straightening up, Dean reached out and firmly grabbed Harry's left arm. 'What's happened?'

'I don't know.'

Still no eye contact.

More lies.

A numbness spread down his arms.

Was he having a heart attack?

He tried to look around Harry, but the blurred combination of flashing lights and rain made it very difficult to see anything.

'A crash?' Dean said.

Harry shook his head. 'No crash, but—'

'Is someone hurt?'

Harry's eyes met Dean's for the first time, and how Dean wished they hadn't. The police officer looked as if he was about to burst into tears, and Dean knew that if he didn't get an answer soon, he'd be going into that chaotic stew of emergency services come hell or high water.

'Penny was walking this way!' Dean said. 'Listen to me. *Penny was walking this way!*'

Harry glanced behind himself again.

What was he looking for?

'Penny was *walking* this way. Aren't you listening?'

Harry met Dean's eyes again His sad expression was more apparent than ever.

'I—'

'Harry? Are you over there?'

Dean recognised the voice of the copper emerging from the blur of flashing blue lights. Mike Crawley. Another childhood friend. Another keen drinker.

Mike froze when he saw Dean. His eyes widened. It was a similar grave expression to the one Harry was wearing.

God, no, please no...

The nausea suddenly intensified, and he retched. He turned his head to one side and vomited. Then he staggered towards the front of a vehicle. With both palms against the bonnet, he emptied his stomach.

Penny?

He felt a hand on his shoulder.

'Dean... please, could you come this way?' Mike's voice.

'Penny?' he murmured, spitting out more vomit.

'Dean, *please*?'

Dean's sharp turn threw Mike's hand from his shoulder. 'You need to let me through.'

Mike stared into Dean's eyes. 'Could you come over here with me?' He nodded away from the scene back in the direction that Dean had come from. 'We need to have a word.'

'I've got to get my daughter! She's walking home alone. You're blocking the bloody way!'

'Dean. I need you to calm—'

'I'm calm. Just piss wet and desperate to get to my lass—'

'Dean, I'm sorry.' Mike's hand returned to his shoulder. 'I *really* am. But you need—'

'Sorry for what? What're you talking about?'

Harry came up alongside Mike now.

That same bloody grave look again.

That same struggle to meet his eyes.

Dean opened his mouth to speak, but nothing came out. He needed the bastards to move. Penny needed him. He sidestepped away from Mike's hand, swooped around the front of the police cars and darted away.

'Don't, Dean, please. Come back. You can't go in there. You *shouldn't* go...' Mike called after him.

Dean was now alongside the nearest ambulance, the rain thrashing his face again.

Mike's voice didn't drop in volume – he remained close behind him. 'It's too late! I'm sorry, Dean, *please* listen.'

At the back of the ambulance, a paramedic was pushing a gurney up a ramp.

Rain danced on a sheet drawn over a body.

A paramedic stared at Dean. 'Sir, please step back...'

Dean already had his hand on the sheet. 'Penny?'

Again, Mike's hand landed on his shoulder. 'I'm sorry, Dean. I'm *so* sorry.'

Dean stared at the paramedic, willing him to say that Mike was mistaken, but then the man's eyes lowered, sadly.

'Let me see her,' Dean said.

'It's not a good idea,' Mike replied. 'Trust—'

'No. I *want* to see her.' He stared at the paramedic.

The paramedic shook his head, struggling to raise his eyes to Dean. 'You really shouldn't.'

'Why? Why can't I see her?' His eyes darted anxiously left and right. 'Why?'

Dean turned his eyes back towards the road. In the flashing lights, he could make out the lines burnt into the road from locking tyres. He could also see the blood being diluted by the thrashing rain, and being washed away down the hill.

Washed away.

Penny.

His daughter.

Washed away.

He closed his eyes, saw himself with Estelle and Penny, sitting in a pub garden, enjoying the sun on a Saturday afternoon.

The name of the pub.

The World's End.

Dean Maiden turned and collapsed into Mike's arms, suddenly wanting nothing else but to die.

4

2023

What a shit show! Wasn't losing your virginity supposed to be some kind of landmark in the game of life?

'And also,' Rick, Zac's older cousin, had once said, 'sex is like a tap. Once you've turned it on... well... you get the picture.'

He'd had such high hopes. But the 'best night' and the 'tap' had never materialised – only this almighty shit show.

But should I be surprised? Really? Shit shows are often par for the course in my game of life!

Ten seconds after the stone had put Chrissie on her back, she moaned.

Zac, fearing he may've killed her, breathed a sigh of relief while Noah, her boyfriend, ran to her.

She moaned again.

Kneeling, Noah tried to move Chrissie's hands from her nose. 'Piss off... ow... shit.'

'I think it's broken,' Noah said, delivering the news rather unsympathetically.

Zac's heart dropped when he caught sight of the amount of blood on her face. The chance of getting that video recording off the bullies had diminished further – their desire to hang him out, make him that internet sensation, would've intensified further. His stomach turned.

What a shit show!

'You made me do that,' Zac hissed.

'You couldn't take a joke, dickhead?' Sam said, kneeling and picking up the rock that had struck Chrissie.

'It wasn't a joke.'

Chrissie moaned again. 'I need the hospital.'

Noah looked up at Sam. 'An eye for an eye.'

'Or a nose for a nose,' Sam said, smirking at Zac, and bouncing the rock from hand to hand.

Zac's blood ran cold.

Sam stepped forward. 'Don't move, bro, might be more dangerous if I miss.'

Zac turned and ran, sprinting over the graves. The fear of having his face smashed to pieces had trumped his earlier prudence over disrespecting these resting places.

Yes, Zac may've been a geek, but he wasn't out of shape, and he was doing a good job of keeping some distance between him and Sam, the school football legend.

Still, he wasn't resting on his laurels, especially when the threat to 'bash his face to cottage cheese' reached his ears, and he pushed his lungs to bursting.

The sight of another bench by a wall came into view. He planned to use it. Escape the graveyard.

And then what, smartarse? When that picture on the phone goes viral? Do you think your life will be worth living? The voice in his head sounded like Theo's.

Some best friend, eh? Piss off, Theo! Can't I at least save my bloody face first?

You'd do well to let him smash your face, Zac, so no one recognises you after the video drops online. You'll be known forever as that perve on old Elias's grave.

There was a heavy thud on his left shoulder, which made him wince.

The bastard had thrown the rock.

Sam was getting frustrated.

Which means if he catches you, he is going to beat the living shit out of you...

Zac veered left, to reach the bench sooner. Weaving around a few headstones en route caused him to trample on a few graves.

I hope there isn't a hell.

He'd danced around two more headstones and scurried over two more graves when something snagged on his foot.

He glanced down as he tumbled, one thought on his mind...

Night of the Living Dead.

Zombies in a graveyard.

Heart thrashing in his chest, not just from running, but from the sheer terror of what he'd just seen – or, at least, *thought*, he'd seen – he landed on his knees, gasped for air and turned over onto his arse to put paid to whatever his imagination had conjured up in the darkness.

But it wasn't his imagination.

His hand flew to his mouth.

'Got you, shithead,' Sam hissed.

Zac's eyes rose above to look at Sam, red faced and grinning above the headstone. Zac then pointed out the atrocity that'd just tripped him over.

Sam's eyes moved down, and his mouth dropped open. 'Jesus Christ. What's *that*?'

Zac shook his head. 'I don't know.'

No, this wasn't a horror movie. This wasn't *Night of the Living*

Dead. And this certainly wasn't a zombie. But it was terrifying all the same.

Folded into a foetal position was a skeleton. A stained, discoloured gown hung from it. There seemed to be little remaining soft tissue. Apart from the face, which had a dried waxy cover clinging tightly to the bones. It shimmered in the moonlight, rather like a damp bar of soap under direct light.

The long hair was coarse and faded.

Its hand, which although not blue and moving like those zombie hands in that film, seemed to reach out to him like the legs of a dead spider.

Zac realised it was this hand that had upended him and noticed with some disgust that one finger had snapped away and lay in the dirt. His hand dropped away from his mouth to tell Sam to call the police.

But the coward had already fled.

His eyes fell to the skull and then over to the headstone.

Estelle Maiden.

5

2023

Having already viewed the remains, Detective Chief Inspector Emma Gardner hung back out of harm's way.

Sandwiched between Chief Constable Rebecca Marsh and Detective Inspector Phil Rice, she'd like to say she was in good company.

But that'd be a lie.

Rebecca Marsh had once boasted to Gardner that on the day of her promotion, her superiors had praised her for being the most assertive and straight-to-the-point copper they'd ever promoted.

Assertive and straight to the point?

That was one way of putting a positive spin on being aggressive and blunt.

They didn't nickname her Harsh Marsh for the hell of it.

However, to her credit, Marsh could put on a show with the best of the top brass and was often careful in her choice of words – unless you were behind closed doors, and then it was more akin to the final scene in a *Rocky* movie. The best solution to this, or at least the only solution to this, Gardner had learned, was to keep the bloody door open.

Still, at least Marsh kept her less dignified outbursts out of sight. Phil Rice, meanwhile, seemed to thrive off causing offence in public. His narrow-minded attitudes would've raised eyebrows in the fifties, let alone today.

He'd even had the audacity to refer to himself as woke, because he ate different cuisines, acknowledged that women, overall, were now safer drivers than men, and because he appreciated that homosexuality wasn't a fashion statement any longer, but a response to biological drives.

'You sound so well read on the subject,' Gardner had retorted.

'Look. The world is changing. You move with the times and the attitudes.'

'Your tolerance is a thing of wonder.'

'You should try it more. Deep breath and accept. My psychiatrist taught me that.'

Gardner's eyes had widened in disbelief. 'Your psychiatrist?'

'Aye. And I made sure she was female, because of the gender pay gap.'

'Woke as they come,' she'd said dryly. 'My, did I have you wrong?'

Rice had nodded as if in agreement. 'Yes.'

Gardner had shaken her head, surprised by the slightest possibility that he really had taken that at face value. She'd followed up with, 'So, are you still seeing this psychiatrist?'

'No, I changed that one and opted for a woman under forty. I just find that after that age, they can get quite judgy... Always find that with women... you know? No offence, like.'

Unbelievable. She'd decided to kill the conversation before her sarcasm turned to irritation and then spiralled.

She did, after all, value Rice's assistance.

Despite Rice being far more anti-woke than he realised, he'd proven himself, on more than one occasion, to be an effective investigator, and lent support to that old maxim that 'You don't have to like the people you work with, do you?'

A tent had been set up over Estelle Maiden's grave, concealing the decades-old body which Zac Livingstone had stumbled over. The SOCOs were moving around it, ruthlessly picking at the scene.

'Shagging in a graveyard,' Marsh said. 'What an absolute—'

'Don't knock it until you've tried it,' Rice said.

Gardner looked at the smirking DI with a raised eyebrow.

'I *won't* be trying it, Detective Inspector,' Marsh said. 'And I don't want to be hearing about any of your *habits*, either. Nor does anyone in the incident room.'

Gardner couldn't resist smiling when Rice's face glowed.

'So, we're not convinced this is Estelle Maiden?' Marsh said.

'Estelle died in 1981, and the earth beneath this body is undisturbed. So, if it's her, and she was excavated – it was a while ago.'

Marsh looked around at the many graves. 'Well, if it isn't Estelle, and that body has come from somewhere else in here... it's going to be a long night.'

'Hopefully not,' Gardner said. 'I've asked Ray to look into Estelle Maiden. Someone has displayed that body there for a reason.'

'Bless Estelle's soul,' Rice said. 'I hope I'm as important forty years after my death.'

Marsh snorted. 'Fat chance. You're not even that important now.'

For Gardner, Rice and Marsh's acerbic exchange faded into the background as her thoughts returned to the folded skeleton. Yes, the earth was undisturbed, so unless it was Estelle, excavated many years ago, who the bloody hell could it be?

Someone connected to Estelle? Important to her?

And if that was the case, who would be peculiar enough to initiate such a reunion?

For information retrieval, Gardner knew of no one faster than Ray Barnett. There was also no one better to have in your corner if shit hit the fan and you found yourself in a precarious situation. The tall black detective sergeant was a fourth Dan in Ju Jitsu, and threw weights around the local gym for fun. He was also an avid reader of Batman comics and had even dabbled in some comic book artwork. Although this skill didn't come in handy as such, it did show that the world was composed of rather complex and unique individuals.

While Gardner waited for Barnett to come good on his mission to look into Estelle Maiden, she tasked some of the other officers with escorting the three male schoolkids away. Parents had already been contacted and, having been suitably disgusted with the details, had agreed to come to the station and sit with the minors while they made their statements.

Chrissie Greenwood, meanwhile, was in the hospital, having her broken nose seen to. She was yet to say anything, while Zac, the boy who'd found the body, had blurted out everything to Gardner.

Poor kid.

Gardner couldn't condone the violence against Chrissie, and considered it appropriate that Zac pay the price for impulsive aggression, but God, what a horrible thing to do to someone! Kids could be so cruel.

She'd reprimanded the two bullies, Sam and Noah, herself. 'You know that under the Sexual Offences Act 2003, recording a person doing a private act for the purpose of causing humiliation is illegal.'

Noah and Sam had looked as if they were going to throw up.

Not such big men now, are you?

She hadn't bothered to tell Zac that *engaging in sexual activities in public places* was also an offence. He already looked like he'd been through the wringer one too many times, and he knew well enough that he was in serious trouble for throwing that rock.

Although Noah and Sam had vowed to delete the footage, Gardner had seized their phones as evidence anyway. 'Part of a crime scene now, boys. And' – she'd moved her fingers between the two boys – 'if any of your friends find out about what you filmed here and what you did to Zac, then I'll make sure the consequences for today's palaver are a lot worse than they could be. Understand?'

They'd nodded, looking terrified. She didn't like wielding the axe with youngsters, but needs must. What they'd done to Zac couldn't become idle gossip. She imagined nothing would take a sledgehammer to a child's mental health faster.

'Losing a phone is like losing an organ to kids these days,' Rice had said.

'They need to start using them responsibly then,' Gardner had replied.

'I'm not arguing, boss. Totally agree. Surprised you didn't smash the bloody phone to pieces.'

Just at that moment, Gardner's own phone rang. Barnett.

She listened sadly to the tragic story of the Maiden family.

* * *

After listening to Barnett's information, Gardner approached the tent over the remains. She peered in at the pathologist.

'Anything else?' Gardner asked. 'Want to take a pop at age and gender?'

'You happy with best guesses?' she asked.

'Very.'

It was actually music to Gardner's ears. This pathologist's predecessor, Dr Hugo Sands, had despised giving out anything but cast-iron, undeniable facts. But Sands was old news, having been struck off a while back for some rather despicable behaviour.

'Looking at the pelvis, skull and long bones, I suspect female. Still, the forensic anthropologist will be far more accurate...'

'And age? Young, perhaps?'

'Yes.'

'Around seventeen?'

'I'm not going anywhere near that precise. But definitely younger than this Estelle Maiden would've been. Late teens to late twenties would be my range, looking at the teeth, the fusion of some bones and the skeletal features. I did some courses on this stuff. Although, like I said, I'm not an expert. Do you think you know who this is, then?'

'Just a gut feeling at this stage. Thank you.'

Gardner collared Chief Forensic Officer Fiona Lane. Gardner and Fiona had known each other a while, but it was only recently they'd struck up a friendship. Over the past few months, their friendship had evolved. They shared a love of live music and had visited Montey's in Harrogate frequently. Nights that often saw incredible amounts of gin and tonic consumed, while still costing less than the bloody babysitter.

'Expertise required, Ms Lane.'

'Of course, Ms Gardner. Although I can't promise you've come to the right place.'

'There's rarely a better place.'

'You're too kind.'

Using a map of the cemetery Barnett had just sent to her phone, identifying the location of one grave she'd requested, Gardner led Fiona through the maze of headstones.

'This is intriguing,' Fiona said.

'Just the obvious. I'm looking for the closest possible connection to Estelle Maiden. Still, it might be nothing.'

'Well, if it isn't, at least we get our steps up.'

Gardner paused, trying to orientate herself to the grave Barnett had circled. 'Bloody hell...' She turned slightly so that a row of trees was just on her left, and then cut down through another path of stones.

'Wait for me! These legs aren't what they once were,' Rice said, padding up behind them.

Gardner found the grave she was looking for and could see, immediately, that she didn't need Fiona's expertise to tell her the obvious. She felt a surge of adrenaline.

'The ground has been disturbed,' Gardner said.

'Very recently.' Fiona came up alongside her.

'What the chuffin' hell...' Rice said, reading out the name on the headstone. 'Penny Maiden. Age seventeen. Died 1980.'

Gardner knelt and looked closely at the ground. The soil had been scooped out then thrown back in quickly, so it now formed more of a mound than a flat surface.

'Going to take a lot of rainfall to get that ground flat again,' Fiona said.

'We need to get this grave excavated immediately,' Gardner said, rising to her feet and reaching for her phone as she turned and fixed Rice with a stare. 'Penny Maiden's not down there.'

'Okay, where else would she be then?' Rice snorted.

Gardner pointed off in the way they'd come. She knew this would sound ridiculous, but instincts were instincts, and right now, hers were positively screaming at her.

'On her mother, Estelle's, grave over there.' She pointed back to her resting place. 'Which means that plot is empty, or, God forbid, someone else has been buried down there.'

'Alive?' Fiona asked.

Gardner looked at her. 'I don't know.'

* * *

Gardner put the wheels quickly in motion. The ground had been disturbed, most likely to exhume Penny's body to display it on Estelle's grave, but another sinister possibility presented itself. If a body had been taken out of this grave, then was it beyond reason that another body could have been placed inside of it to fill the void? And who was to say that this person would be dead? The prospect, although conjecture at this stage, nauseated Gardner, and she hoped that she was just being overly cautious. Still, her rationale made the situation critically urgent.

However, it was, as the pathologist pointed out, highly unlikely that anyone could survive under there.

Survival times when buried alive ranged from minutes to a few hours. Unless the burial was very shallow, and tubes inserted to provide air, hope was at a bare minimum.

Also, machinery had to be discounted as an option to unearth. If, by some miracle, someone was still breathing, they soon wouldn't be under the force of a mechanical claw.

Grave diggers who worked this site were called in.

While they dug, Gardner explained her thoughts to the other officers present.

'Late 1980, a young girl, Penny Maiden, was killed in a hit-and-run accident on Harrogate Road. Partially up the hill, near Bond End.'

'Shit... I remember now. I was a boy,' Rice said, 'My dad worked that case. They never found who was responsible and the girl's death hit the area hard.'

'Awful. Every parent's nightmare.' Fiona sighed.

Gardner nodded. 'Not an understatement. Estelle Maiden died by suicide late 1981.'

'Yes... that's familiar too,' Rice said. 'What about her father?'

'Dean Maiden is still alive.'

'Lost his wife and child in one year,' Fiona said. 'Poor man.'

Rice nodded over to where the grave diggers were working. 'Wonder if he found out who ruined his life in the end.'

Ruined his life.

Her thoughts turned sharply to DI Paul Riddick. Her former colleague. Friend. Another man with a ruined life, who'd stopped at nothing, until the blood was on his hands.

Was Dean Maiden the same?

'Let's not get ahead of ourselves,' Marsh said. 'I mean – we've no confirmation that this body we found is even Penny's yet. Besides, how old is Dean Maiden now anyway? Into his seventies?' She nodded over to the grave diggers toiling. 'Looks like back-breaking work for someone in their seventies.'

'My money is on it just being a false alarm,' Rice said. 'It'll be Penny under there, and the ground has just been disturbed by wildlife.'

Gardner felt a surge of irritation and she opened her mouth to criticise his judgement. The ground had been more than disturbed – it'd clearly been dug up.

The loud voice of a grave digger caught their attention. They turned to see that one of them had their hand in the air. They'd found something.

'Good job for you that I didn't have time to take that bet,' Gardner said.

* * *

Gardner stood on some protective plates, looked down at the elderly corpse and sighed. Soil still covered most of his body, but the pathologist confirmed he was dead by brushing dirt from his face.

The shallow grave was only about a metre deep, so whoever had gone the full six feet for Penny Maiden, had refilled most of the hole before laying this victim to rest.

'I suspect he was dead before he went into the ground, or at least unconscious,' the pathologist said. 'This man didn't fight to get to the surface for air. I'll have to examine his whole body, but he looks like he's taken some kind of beating. There are bruises and cuts on his face.'

'The man is in his seventies,' Gardner said, and sighed again.

'Bloody hell,' Rice said, coming up alongside Gardner. 'It's Howard Walters.'

Marsh came up on the other side of Gardner. 'Seems that way.'

Gardner looked up at Marsh who, for the first time since she'd met her, appeared pale and disturbed.

'Out of towner here,' Gardner said, holding her hand in the air, and looking between the faces of her companions.

'Retired car mechanic, salt of the earth, everyone's favourite local, real do-gooder... Shit... Howard Walters was a bloody nice man,' Rice said. 'Which makes him a bloody nice murder victim,' Marsh said, sounding irritated. 'And which makes this an almighty pain in the arse.'

'What made this Howard so nice?' Gardner asked.

'Last I heard, he was taking underprivileged kids fishing,' Rice said.

'Let's not mention all the free car services he offered out from his business during the economic downturn.' Marsh grunted. 'The man's a local saint.'

'He's also Santa Claus,' Rice said.

Gardner stared at him with her eyebrow raised.

'At Christmas,' Rice said. 'At the church.'

'Going to be a vigil over this one,' Marsh said.

'And then the locals will have their pitchforks out,' Rice said.

Great.

Gardner looked between the body and the tent in the distance.

Penny Maiden. Victim of an unsolved hit-and-run. Dug up and returned to her mother.

She looked down at the dead man again.

Howard Walters. Local hero. Had you been driving that car? Living with a guilty secret? A secret that drove you into an altruistic lifestyle?

In which case, who found out?

Did you tell someone?

'Best get started then,' Gardner said. 'Does anyone know where Dean Maiden lives?'

6

2023

Right now, Detective Inspector Paul Riddick and Detective Sergeant Devon Dunn were struggling to see eye to eye.

Not the most ideal of situations on a two-man surveillance job.

Having already argued at length over Riddick's tuna salad, which had stank out Devon's vehicle, they'd since gravitated to music tastes. Being a pop enthusiast, Devon was desperate to warm up to this weekend's Eurovision Song Contest by listening to all the entries while they kept watch.

Riddick was having none of it. 'I've seen enough pantomimes and dipsticks dancing around in colourful outfits to last a lifetime, thank you.'

'I'm not asking you to watch it. I'm asking you to listen to it.'

'And that'll offer me a pleasurable experience... how?'

Devon nodded out of the window at the decrepit street. 'Might as well try it. No chance of lowering anyone's mood here, is there?'

'You really are down on Manningham, Ms Dunn.'

'We're sitting outside a drugs den.'

Riddick sighed. 'How about some Dylan? Look, I'll educate you.'

She snorted. 'Condescending prick. If I wanted to be educated by an old man, I'd see my grandfather.'

Riddick couldn't resist a laugh. 'I'm assuming, or rather, hoping, that he's under fifty? Preferably, mid-forties?'

'Of course not, but he'd listen to the Eurovision Song Contest.'

Riddick resisted making a quip about him being senile but held back. Not only was it poor taste, but he couldn't be sure whether her grandfather was senile. Such a slip could elevate a slightly frosty situation to one that was ice cold.

'Guess I'm just the old fossil then.'

Devon shrugged. 'Well, you bring it on yourself... Look, why don't we take it in turns?'

Riddick sighed. 'Whatever. Just trying to help. I thought Dylan would just open your mind a little... mellow you out?'

'I'm stuck in a car with a cantankerous old man with a chip on his shoulder. How's "All Along the Watchtower" going to help with that?'

Riddick sighed again. 'You're still pissed off about that tuna salad, aren't you?'

'In a vegetarian's car? Why on God's earth would the stench of dead fish piss me off?' She looked at him severely, which caused her blonde fringe to droop in front of her eyes. She whipped it back behind her ear with her finger.

'Claire wants me to lose weight. I'm on salads for the foreseeable. I'm certainly not having a salad with nothing on it. What do you want me to do – starve to death?'

'Try cheese? I like cheese.'

'Okay, listen to Dylan, and I'll bring us *both* a cheese board with all the trimmings tomorrow. Wait, look at this.' He pointed out the car window at the terraced house over the road.

Devon looked. 'The security light?'

'Yeah,' Riddick said. 'It just flicked on while you were giving me daggers.'

They both stared, waiting for some movement, but seeing nothing. False alarm.

'A cat, maybe?' Devon said.

'No, I think more likely a dog,' Riddick said seriously, forcing back a grin.

Devon looked at him. 'If I suggest a squirrel, and you laugh, does that mean we're friends again?'

'Certainly not. I couldn't be friends with anyone who watches the Eurovision Song Contest.'

'Oh, piss off,' Devon said, smiling.

The security light flicked off. Riddick returned his attention to the glowing front room.

'Not much activity tonight,' Devon said. 'So unlike Manningham. Last time we were watching this house, it was like a revolving door. The Ravens were selling more drugs than Boots. Maybe they've moved. Could our intel be bad?'

'Nah,' Riddick said. 'It shows our intel is good. If something big is going down, and word is out, people will steer clear.'

'I don't like it. Aren't you nervous?' Devon said.

'Yes,' Riddick lied. 'Pays to be nervous.'

'Don't believe you. Couple of the others back at the station think you've got a death wish.'

If I wanted to be dead, I'd be dead by now. Better I hang about and do some good. He looked up at the house again. *Obviously, that does come with risks.*

'Your friends talk too much. They've been watching too many movies. I'm not about to go running after armed smack heads. I'm not Charles Bronson.'

'Who?'

Riddick sighed. 'Dirty Harry, then?'

'Dirty who? Sounds like a pervert!'

'Ah, never mind.' *Maybe I am an old fossil!* 'Point is, we're careful. That's how it is now.'

'So, all those stories about you having a screw loose are bollocks, then?' Devon asked.

'Screw loose. Jesus! People hold me in such high regard. Hope you put those bastards straight – you've spent a lot of time with me now.'

'Of course.' She laughed. 'I told them I put you on the straight and narrow. Taught you we handle things in CID with more decorum.'

'Yes, Ms Dunn, I noticed that decorum. Clearly wasn't you I saw stumbling down that street half-drunk in that video post on Facebook the other night then?'

'Shit, really? I told Louise to delete that! Christ, I'll bloody kill her.' She reached in her pocket for her phone. 'She's a liability—'

'*Look.*' Riddick was pointing. '*Arthur.*'

Arthur Fields was standing at the door, looking out.

Riddick felt a twinge in his chest and stomach. A reaction he always felt when he saw Arthur. Sympathetic pangs, he called them.

'Now then, lad, what're you up to?' Riddick asked and sighed. 'Get back in fella. Up to your room.'

Out of harm's way.

Arthur stood there a couple of seconds longer, rubbing his head and looking confused, as he always did.

He disappeared back into his house and Riddick sighed with relief.

'Why'd he open the door?' Riddick asked.

'Dunno. Maybe he heard the cat, dog, squirrel or whatever it was.' Devon smiled over her nod back to the banter that had thawed the ice.

Riddick didn't smile. He was far from satisfied here. 'But he's not the one who should be investigating the noise. Where're the bloodsuckers who've taken over his life? They better be there. I want them tonight.'

'Poor lad,' Devon said.

You got that right, Riddick thought. *But not long to go now, Arthur. We've almost got enough on them... We'll get your life back to normal before you know it.*

Nineteen-year-old Arthur Fields had a diagnosis of autism, an IQ way below average and social anxiety that had brought him to his knees frequently. A kid of few words, but words that were often gentle and kind.

The first time Riddick had met Arthur, he'd come away likening him to a nervous animal in desperate need of help. He'd worried Claire with his words, 'You just want to put your arms around him. Shield him from all those wolves.'

He'd been with Claire less than a year, but she'd been his grief counsellor beforehand, so her detailed understanding of him had intensified their relationship. To the point that they were now living together. Knowing what she knew about the attachments Riddick formed with people, how could Claire not be worried about his friendship with Arthur Fields? After all, how did Riddick protect a man who had the mental age of a child from predators who had filled his home with drugs and guns?

Riddick had opted not to tell Claire that the worst predator of them all was, in fact, Arthur's own father, Keith Fields. The situation had already appeared hopeless – he didn't want to paint it as pointless too.

Suddenly feeling irritated, Riddick put on Dylan.

He waited for Devon to protest. She must have sensed that he was struggling with the idea of Arthur in that house again and spared him... for now.

She still looked at her watch though, refusing to hide her frustration.

'Keep the faith,' Riddick said. 'The Ravens are still in there.'

The stare she gave him suggested she didn't share this confidence.

This operation had been rumbling on for some time, and the end still didn't seem close enough for anyone's liking. Especially Riddick's, who wanted Arthur as far from these miserable, mean bastards as possible.

The Ravens were a drugs gang from East Bowling, and they were in the process of cuckooing Arthur and his home.

The term came from cuckoo birds, renowned for laying their eggs in the nests of other birds.

The Ravens were the exploiting cuckoos, selling their drugs from poor Arthur's nest.

Things had been progressing at a snail's pace until today's intriguing intel. The Mansters, Manningham's own drugs gang, would no longer endure these young upstarts on their patch. It surprised Riddick that it'd taken this long. A nasty piece of work called Nathan Cummings led the Mansters, and he wasn't renowned for his patience.

Today's information had suggested that tonight was the night.

Both gangs. One fell swoop for CID. It was an opportunity too good to miss!

However, a heavy presence here could scupper everything, hence the light two-man surveillance. Although, armed response was ready and close at hand. Once alerted, they could be here within minutes.

If the Mansters showed up for battle. Which was looking more and more unlikely.

Dylan was still going for it in the background.

'Did this singer just say it was getting late?' Devon said. 'He's not wrong!'

Riddick growled. 'Bob Dylan.'

Devon said, 'Bob bloody Dylan. Whatever. Activity here is at an all-time low. We've seen Arthur.' She looked at Riddick. '*Only* Arthur. What if all this is a dead duck?'

Riddick shook his head. 'No, my informant is adamant.' *And soon to be in pieces if he's wrong.*

'What if the Ravens have heard about the ambush, and went for a pre-emptive strike on the Mansters?'

Riddick carried on shaking his head, but he knew she was talking sense. Still... 'We've come this far. Let's just give it a bit longer.'

'But now that the smell of your tuna is vacating the premises, I'm getting hungry.' She pointed to a corner shop at the end of the road. 'And Khan's is looking very appealing.'

'No,' Riddick said. 'Besides, I hear the place is full of meat products – you wouldn't like it.'

'It will also be full of crisps, and I like crisps.'

'Bad for you. I really think not. Patience... please. I'll buy you a vegetarian pizza when this has played out.'

Devon sighed and regarded the house again. 'Can you believe Keith has allowed this to happen to Arthur, his son?'

'What's Keith going to do?' Riddick asked. 'He's not the man he was... not by a country mile.'

Devon nodded. 'Aye... didn't he used to think he was a bloody Kray twin or something?'

'And then some! He's now well into his seventies, living in squalor having pissed his fortune away, and smoking himself to death in a La-Z-Boy.'

'Couldn't have happened to a nicer man.'

'My sentiments exactly.'

'He loves his son, though.'

Riddick laughed. 'If he does say so himself! Part of the act. Gangsters, honour and family, and all that bullshit. I don't believe it. I know the man well. He's a monster. Let's hope he rots in that chair.'

Devon nodded out of the window. 'He bought him that house—'

'In Manningham? What a saint.'

She laughed. Then she looked at him apologetically. 'Sorry pal, but your miserable music has made me hungry.' She cracked the door. 'I'll be less than a minute.'

'I'd prefer you didn't,' Riddick said.

'Yes, and I'd prefer you didn't eat tuna in the car.'

'I outrank you, remember?'

She slammed the door before he finished his sentence.

Bloody hell – she was worse than he was!

He watched her walk down the dark road towards the glow of Khan's.

Dylan's voice grew louder.

'Not now, Bob,' Riddick said, killing the music, as he watched Devon entering Khan's.

You better get salt and vinegar... Ready salted doesn't do it for me...

He moved his attention back to Arthur's home. No movement. No security light.

His phone buzzed in his pocket. It could be a message from Claire checking in on him. He'd get to it when Devon was safely back in the car.

She came out of the shop, clutching a plastic bag.

He surveyed the empty street.

Get a move on... we don't want to get spotted.

Someone stepped out of the shadows behind Devon.

His mouth suddenly dry, Riddick cracked the door. 'Shit!'

He pounced from the vehicle, Devon's cries splitting his eardrums.

Looking ahead, he saw that a hooded figure had yanked his colleague's head back by her hair. His stomach somersaulted.

This was his fault. 'Police! Get your hands off her!'

The figure backed away. Thank God...

Riddick edged forwards.

The figure raised his hand above his head. He was holding something large...

Shit... no...

Tasting bile, Riddick broke into a run.

Too late.

There was a thud as the hooded figure brought his weapon crashing down.

The DS fell to the ground, face first. The figure turned to flee, but a large, Asian man had burst out of the shop.

Riddick, still sprinting, caught the glint in the shopkeeper's hand.

A knife.

God, it gets bloody worse!

The figure swung his heavy object again, striking the shop-keeper on the forehead. He spun and went to the ground beside Devon.

Riddick drew closer to the figure, who was lanky and moved like a gangly teenager. The weapon in his hand was a brick.

'Piss off or I'll do you too!' He threw the brick and Riddick swooped to one side, narrowly avoiding the same fate as Devon and the shopkeeper.

'Good shot, dickhead.'

The lad lifted his middle finger and turned to run.

Riddick went after him, but stopped when he drew alongside Devon. She held the back of her head. 'Devon—'

'Get after him,' she moaned. 'I'll call... back-up.'

He glanced at the shopkeeper. He'd rolled onto his back, but his eyes were now closed, and blood was bubbling out of his forehead and down his face.

Knowing that Devon had the shopkeeper's back, Riddick started after the fleeing lad, who was clearly young, agile and full of beans.

And then there was Riddick, who certainly wasn't in the best shape of his life.

It didn't take the unfit middle-aged alcoholic long to burn out and, when the lad drew him down a pitch-black ginnel, he started to lumber and gasp.

Claire had called it right with the diet. *Tuna salads for the foreseeable*, he thought, throwing himself onwards into the black.

Breaking out of the darkness and onto another street offered Riddick some relief. He sighted his quarry looking anxiously over one shoulder and jumped back into action with a sudden burst of confidence.

After picking up speed, he got within ten metres of the lad before he disappeared into another ginnel.

Shit! The lad certainly knew the lie of the land. Whereas Riddick was bloody fortunate to still be in the chase.

Riddick swung into the ginnel, cursing when he felt his weak left ankle buckling, but righting it at the last moment.

You're a disgrace, fella!

Still, he *was* gaining on his quarry and should probably be less harsh on himself.

Despite it being dark, he could still see the lad's outline, which was a relief. Otherwise, the idiot could've very well stopped, concealed himself and then ambushed Riddick in the same way he'd done Devon.

Riddick estimated himself to be within five metres of the lad...

The bastard turned right onto a street.

I'm going to get you, you little shit, Riddick thought, bursting from the ginnel as the adolescent darted out onto the road.

Unlike the mugger, Riddick checked there were no cars coming, which cost him a metre or two, before crossing the road and swerving around the corner after him.

The lad was heading directly for a large fence around a car park.

Shit...

Riddick didn't fancy subjecting his dodgy ankle to that.

The young man scurried up it like a bloody squirrel.

Impressive.

And a feat impossible for Riddick to repeat. Still, he tried to push it from his mind, lest it affect his confidence, and he threw himself at the fence at full pelt.

He impressed himself by making it halfway up at an admirable speed, before his left ankle stiffened. His foot skimmed the fence, but didn't land, and then he was falling straight down.

He didn't hear a crack as his foot twisted, but the shooting pain told him that the run was probably over. As were the next few months of pain-free walking.

Swearing at the top of his lungs, he worked his way back to his feet, eyes watering. He tried, tentatively, to put some weight on his damaged ankle, but winced and clutched the fence for support.

Aiming expletives at no one in particular, he watched the lad disappear.

Gutted, he hoisted his phone from his pocket and called in his location, and a description of a hooded male teenager for what that was worth.

Then he remembered Devon, turned from the fence, and limped away, cursing repeatedly.

* * *

It took Riddick a fair while to hobble back the route he'd just sprinted.

On the way, he spoke to Devon on his phone. She assured him she was fine. Whereas the shopkeeper was struggling. Rafiq Khan had recovered consciousness briefly, but Devon had failed to keep him awake, and he'd gone back under. An ambulance was on its way.

When Riddick reached the shop, the ambulance had arrived and the paramedic was wheeling the shopkeeper up a ramp.

Riddick limped over to Devon, who was sitting on the kerb beside another paramedic, holding a bloody rag to the front of her head.

He looked at the paramedic first. 'Is she okay?'

'She'll need an X-ray and stitches.'

He thumbed behind him at the shopkeeper. 'And him?'

'Too early to say.'

Bloody hell.

Riddick pointed at Devon. 'Get the all-clear before I speak to you again...' He sighed. 'I got clocked by a brick too, once. Not pleasant.'

She handed him the keys to her vehicle. 'How's your ankle?'

'Fine,' he said, turning and limping slowly in the direction of the parked car.

'Looks it,' she called after him. 'Don't think Dylan can help you with that.'

Despite feeling irritated with absolutely everything right now, he smirked at her quip. Deep down, he was relieved. It could've been so much worse for her.

Having been so worried about Devon, it was only now, as h

neared her car, that the disappointment and ramifications of the botched surveillance job hit Riddick full force.

The Mansters would be coming nowhere near Arthur's home and the squatting Ravens tonight. Not with all this commotion on the doorstep.

Don't worry, Arthur. I'll get you out of here. Like I promised. Just hang on a little longer.

He paused by a lamppost and held himself upright as he felt several flashes of extreme pain. He needed painkillers.

After taking some deep breaths and steeling himself, he completed the journey to the car. Only once he'd made it to the bonnet did he look up and see that the front door was standing open.

Adrenaline whipped through him.

The security light remained off... Someone had been in Arthur's house while Riddick had been gallivanting off down the street.

I'm so bloody stupid.

He limped across the road, breathing deeply. He put most of his weight on his right ankle but had to use his left ankle more than he liked in order to increase his pace.

The security light burst into life as he negotiated the short path to the front door. The overgrown garden reached out and dragged across his legs. He hobbled around some tangled shrubbery playing cat's-cradle with torn plastic bags.

Sweat ran into his eyes, and he paused at the open door to lean against the wall and offer his swollen ankle a moment's respite. He sucked in some air.

The pain was intensifying by the minute.

He had to let his breathing settle and wiped the sweat from his forehead as he did so.

It was only when he'd stopped making his own racket that he

heard whining. Riddick couldn't help but think of the dogs his father used to keep, weeping for attention behind closed doors, occasionally scratching at the wood.

Not prepared to wait while his friend Arthur could be in trouble, Riddick entered, leaning into the wall in the hallway to keep most of his weight on his right side.

He stepped through piles of unopened mail and takeaway menus, the whining growing louder as he moved deeper into the house.

'Arthur?' he called.

He paused.

The whining seemed to stop, but then kicked back up again. It was coming from the room to his left.

Riddick heard the young man's voice in his head from weeks ago. 'Ant Man. I wish I could get that small... imagine the places you could go... see... crawl into.'

Arthur was obsessed with Marvel superheroes.

To his shame, Riddick had used that. 'I just need you to be a hero a little longer. Just a week or so, Arthur. Can you do that? Can you be Ant Man?'

Leaning against the doorframe, keeping as much weight from his ankle as he could, Riddick opened the door and pushed it open.

The whining intensified.

Riddick gasped when he saw the lad on the sofa. No older than eighteen with a confused expression and a bloody hole in his chest.

One of the Ravens.

Practically a child, too.

Shit!

Riddick felt momentarily guilty for his relief that it wasn't Arthur.

Heart thrashing in his chest, he turned into the room, looking for the source of the whining.

At the edge of the room, there was another young man. Another Raven. He'd taken a bullet to the back of the neck.

Arthur was in the room's corner, curled up on his side in the foetal position, shirtless. The young man trembled, which sent ripples over his overweight back.

Alive.

But Riddick knew better than to feel relief just yet.

This whole situation had Nathan Cummings's fingerprints on it. And he doubted that the leader of the Mansters was done with his surprises just yet.

Riddick limped, unconcerned about his own pain, until he stood above his vulnerable friend.

'Arthur?'

The whining stopped, but the trembling didn't.

'It's me... Paul...'

A quiet, pained sobbing began.

Wincing, Riddick knelt down and placed one hand on Arthur's shoulder. 'You're okay now, fella.' He rubbed his shoulder. 'I got you.'

'Paul...' Arthur said, punctuating his sobs. 'Paul... I'm glad... so glad...'

'What happened, Arthur?' Riddick shuddered when he noticed the blood soaking into the carpet beside him. He reached into his pocket for his phone. 'I'm getting help...'

'They came...' Arthur stopped and whined again. 'It hurts... it hurts so much... I couldn't stop them.'

'It wasn't your job to stop them.' *It was mine.*

'Ant Man failed,' Arthur whispered sadly.

Riddick flinched. '*No*... you've done nothing wrong, Arthur.'

Nathan Cummings is the one in the wrong here.

And me, for chasing a boy I'd no hope of catching. I'm such a bloody fool...

Holding his phone in one hand and Arthur's shoulder in the other, he said, 'Turn over, Arthur.'

'What've they done to me? What've they done?'

Riddick eased Arthur over onto his back and took a breath so deep he wondered if his lungs would burst.

Mansters.

The word was carved into Arthur's chest. Each crimson letter oozed. Nathan Cummings had marked his territory.

Riddick looked into Arthur's eyes. He was little more than an infant and now he was more lost and in need of nurturing than ever before.

Because of Nathan.

And because of *him. Paul Riddick.*

I failed you, Arthur.

The sympathetic pangs in his chest and stomach that he always felt in Arthur's presence were now burning and painful.

I failed you.

I promised to be better... to stop all these sodding mistakes... and here I am again.

'I'm so sorry.'

The pain that raged through him far surpassed anything offered by his damaged ankle.

'I let you down.'

7

2024

Eighty-five-year-old Glenda Richards looked at her watch.

2.38 a.m.

Four minutes to go.

She glanced up at the locked entrance to Knaresborough cemetery.

Four minutes until I speak to you, my darling!

The timing had to be perfect.

Call it superstition. Call it plain madness. Call it what you want. It didn't matter.

She was determined.

And she'd get it perfect every year. Even after her artificial hips finally gave out, she'd find a way. Crawl if necessary! Although, a motorised wheelchair would probably be the better option.

The only thing that could be an insurmountable problem was the loss of her mind. Because that, and *only* that, could put a stop to this annual jaunt. (Although, some would argue that she'd already lost her mind.)

Still. *What did they know?*

This was it. This was Glenda's lot. All she had left. Her friends and family were gone. She'd not been able to conceive during her marriage to Patrick, and this had come years before all those fancy medical interventions. Often, she wondered if they should've adopted. If they could've had their time again, she'd probably try to talk him into it. But she wasn't one for regrets. No. This was her lot. And she was content.

An icy breeze pricked her through the gate, and Glenda felt grateful for her decision to double down on tights.

2.40 a.m.

Two minutes until she gripped that gate, pressed her lips to the gap and called into that gloom!

She stroked her watch. How she loved her gift from Patrick. Over fifty years ago! Engraved too.

To my Glen. Forever x.

And forever meant forever. So, until she went kaput, and they came together in the next life – this was how she kept it burning in her mind. This visit. This annual visit to where Patrick now lay.

Twenty years ago at 2.42 a.m. The exact moment Patrick had declared his love for her one more time before taking his last breath. The cancer had been cruel, but it hadn't stripped him of his final loving declaration.

And his determination in those last seconds forever fuelled her own resolve.

No, she wouldn't scale the wall of this cemetery at this ungodly hour. She was eighty-five and made of glass! But she'd whisper his name through the gate, into the darkness. She could tell him how much she missed him, and how much she longed to be with him.

And she'd do that until she, too, was gone.

2.41 a.m.

The watch was accurate to the second. She paid for a yearly service. An expensive one. She didn't want to lose any time.

She approached the gate, rubbing a tear from her eye with a gloved hand.

'Pat,' she whispered. 'I'm here.'

She looked at her watch.

2.42 a.m.

'I'm here, and I miss you so much.' She put her gloved hands to the gate. 'So, very, very—'

The gate swung open. She made a small gasping sound and pressed one of her gloved hands to her chest. *Odd.* Twenty years, and that had never happened before!

'Has someone forgotten to lock it?' she asked Pat. 'Or does it mean something else?' She pushed it all the way open. 'Should I come in?'

She knew Pat wouldn't want her walking around a cemetery in the middle of the night – especially not this one! It wasn't even a year since that poor man, Howard Walters, had been killed and buried here.

'Not a good idea,' she said, standing with the gate held open. 'A woman of my age.'

But she pushed the gate further open. Pat's grave was barely a minute from where she now stood.

This unlocked gate was surely a sign... wasn't it?

Could this be her last visit here? Was it in the stars for her to join him sometime over the next twelve months?

And if so, would that make her foolish for passing up this opportunity on so poignant a day?

She entered the graveyard and smiled.

Mindful of the many people around her laid to rest, she moved slowly, carefully and respectfully through the cemetery.

The streetlamps outside gave her enough light, but it was

gloomy, and no doubt uninviting to any others that may stumble on the open gate. She expected to be alone... and to stay alone... unless, of course, you counted the many thousands lying in the surrounding ground.

All around her fresh flowers patterned graves.

Gone but not forgotten.

Eventually, she sighted her husband's headstone, not too far ahead.

She gave him a little wave. It'd appear foolish to some, yet felt anything but to her.

Just to be close to him.

As she dropped her hand, she noticed two people sitting on the bench over by the wall.

She stopped and again put her gloved hand to her chest.

Keeping her eyes firmly on the couple, she took some deep breaths. They didn't move.

Now, Glenda. Keep yourself calm. Just a young couple seeking some privacy.

The rational explanation helped slow her breathing.

She squinted into the darkness, trying to find out more details, wondering if they'd noticed her. She raised her hand in greeting, but she didn't detect a response.

Trespassers.

Like you.

She spoke loudly. 'I'm sorry,' she said. 'Just here to see my husband, and then I'll be out of your hair.'

They didn't reply.

She squinted, hoping to see movement, but there wasn't any.

Remember Howard Walters?

Are you getting yourself into some kind of bother here, Glenda?

She looked behind herself. It wasn't too far to the open gate.

There'd be no running, but some quick steps might see her safely out of the cemetery.

Glenda doubted she was in any danger from this mysterious couple, but she couldn't hide from the peculiarity. Why sneak in here? Pat hadn't been the most romantic of men, but she couldn't remember him taking her on a date to a cemetery! Unless they were underage kids, desperate for alone time? Or, maybe the reason was the same as hers – bereaved relatives honouring the hour they'd lost someone dear to them.

Still, the situation was odd, so Glenda resolved herself to leaving this odd situation, and being content with giving her blessing through the gate as she'd done on every year previously.

She said, 'Sorry to disturb you.'

Sighing when they didn't respond or *move*, she turned and began the walk back towards the gate...

What if they're not okay?

This disturbing thought stopped her.

No... Glenda... this is none of your damned business. You're always sticking your bloody nose in.

She took several steps towards the exit before stopping again and turning back to stare at them, feeling more irritated than concerned now. 'Are you two okay?'

But unless they were playing with her, they clearly weren't okay... and how could she risk leaving two people in trouble? It just wasn't in her nature.

She approached, imagining Pat waggling his finger at her.

Ah, piss off, you old fool. I could never turn a blind eye. She smiled, nervously. *One of the many reasons you loved me.*

She worked her way further towards the bench, continually warning the peculiar couple that she was approaching.

Even though she wore her glasses, there were several trees sheltering this bench from the glow of the lampposts on the main road. Even now, merely metres away, the couple remained silhouettes.

'I'm sorry, there was an incident here last year... you may've heard about it? Someone died... and... look, I only came in because the gate was open, and... look... are you okay?'

Still no bloody answer.

Her thoughts came in Pat's voice. *They're taking the piss, Glen, love... couple of kids, going to scare the living shit out of you...*

Oh, Pat, stop it! What can I do? It could be a couple of kids taking the piss, but it could just as easily be a couple of kids hurt.

A metre from them, she saw that the two people were too tall to be children. She squinted in the darkness, willing them to move, but they remained motionless. Maybe they were just statues?

She waited. Nothing. They were completely unresponsive. And now, for the first time, she regretted her stubborn neglect of technology and wished she'd purchased herself a mobile phone.

She looked down at her hands. Her help would have to be the old-fashioned kind. She swallowed and edged forward, close enough to see.

They weren't statues.

God, how she wished they were.

The two people weren't really sitting side by side as she'd thought; rather, they were propped up against each other, their heads tilted back against the stone wall that ran behind them.

Tears in her eyes and a cold, painful sensation all over her ageing body, Glenda leaned in, trying to see them clearly, possibly recognise them.

It was impossible.

Their faces were completely covered in blood.

8

Gardner could hear her heart pounding against her ribs. The burning in her scar was merciless.

'Collette! Please, where are you?'

She looked right towards the closed door.

The screaming and shouting seemed to be quietening down outside now.

'Collette?'

She opened the door into a kitchen. The noise was louder again. It was coming from the other side of the high-rise. Gardner looked around the immaculate kitchen, and then let her eyes settle on the open patio door. A curtain whipped about in the breeze.

She clutched the scar on her chest and willed herself not to stop. She approached the curtain and drew it aside.

A small balcony. A few potted plants. A wicker chair.

A waist-high balcony.

Directly below, a crowd of anxious people had gathered on the estate's playground.

At the centre of the crowd, lying on the roundabout, was the body of her detective sergeant.

* * *

Gardner woke with a start, clutching the scar on her chest.

She bolted upright in bed, sucked deeply at the air as if she'd been drowning and was bursting free of the water, and faced reality.

Collette Willows had died almost two years ago.

And although the internal investigation had concluded otherwise, Gardner knew in her heart that it was because of the choice she'd made that day.

She wiped at her face, damp from both sweat and tears.

The door to her bedroom opened.

Rose, her niece, stood in the doorway, bathed in the landing light. 'I'm scared.'

'Okay, petal,' Gardner said, lifting back the duvet.

Gardner had adopted Rose after the girl's father, Gardner's brother, had gone to jail. The little girl closed the door behind her and scurried up onto the left side of the bed and into Gardner's arms. Gardner lay back, allowing the eight-year-old to put her head on her chest, and covered her with the duvet.

She stroked Rose's hair, soothing her – and herself – following her nightmare.

'I love you, petal.'

'I love you too, Auntie Em.'

Soon enough, Rose's breathing deepened, and she was at rest again.

But Gardner didn't immediately fall back to sleep. Not because of the nightmare. After all, this was nothing new. The nightmare was always with her, awake or asleep. Rather, she didn't fall asleep because she knew what was coming any second now... and anticipation of an event was the worst cause of insomnia.

And, sure enough, like clockwork, the door opened again.

This time, it was her seven-year-old daughter, Anabelle.

'I heard something,' Anabelle said.

That'd be your unsettled cousin who you hear about this time every night.

'Nothing to be worried about, pudding. I promise.'

'Can I come in with you?'

Gardner raised the duvet on the right side of the bed now.

Well, Gardner thought as her daughter hopped onto the other side of the bed, *who wants to be alone with their demons, anyway?*

She kissed both of her girls on the forehead and then slept despite being unable to move.

* * *

Gardner reached over Anabelle's head for her ringing phone on the bedside table.

How can she sleep through that and not her cousin creeping out of bed?

Seeing Marsh's name on the screen, she killed the call and sighed. A call this late could mean only one thing. She eased herself over Rose on her left, went out onto the landing and closed the door.

She called back. 'Ma'am, sorry, you cut off.'

'Emma...' The pause spoke volumes. 'I know you've your hands full, but we wouldn't call unless we needed you.'

Gardner sighed. Something terrible had happened.

After Marsh had explained and the call had ended, Gardner tried to ignore her thrashing heart and desperate need to get to the scene. She needed her focus here for a couple more minutes to organise her chaotic home life.

She darted up to the third floor and knocked gently on the first door.

Monika Kowalska, her Polish au pair, opened the door in her nightie.

'Sorry,' Gardner said. 'I really am. I know the nighttime is off-limits without notice, but something's come up. Can you look after Rose and Anabelle?'

'Yes.' Monika brushed jet black hair away from her blurred eyes. 'Something has happened?'

'Yes, work happened.' *At three in the morning.*

The au pair in her mid-twenties raised an eyebrow, trying to coax out more.

Gardner was in no mind to tell her that someone had bludgeoned a young man and woman to death and scare the shit out of her.

Gardner turned. 'I'm just going to grab my clothes from my room, and I'll be gone within minutes.'

'No problems.'

From the stairs, Gardner looked up at her lifesaver. 'And... sorry... Rose and Anabelle are in bed with me. Wholly inappropriate, I know, but could you... maybe... go in with them? I don't want them to worry if they wake.'

* * *

It was at moments like this that Gardner realised Monika wasn't an expensive extravagance, but an expensive necessity. She may have been giving her monthly pay packet a right beating, but at least she could keep working the job she loved.

Loved?

She rolled her eyes. She needed another choice of words, didn't she?

After all, she was about to look at two people who'd been snatched violently from their lives.

And *back* at that bloody cemetery, too!

Coincidence?

Who knew at this stage? After all, the murder of Howard Walters from last year was still unsolved, and so nothing was off the table.

9

It was past three in the morning, and Riddick couldn't sleep.

He tried not to move about, though, as it'd surely wake Claire beside him.

Claire Hornsby was his former grief counsellor, and one of the most caring people he'd ever met. It wasn't her beauty that had drawn him into this long-term relationship, but she still possessed that in droves. He glanced over at her and thought of their argument and the news she'd delivered this evening and sighed, before turning his eyes back to the ceiling.

Feeling the weight of anxiety on his chest, and the nightmares he'd surely experience if he did fall asleep, he closed his eyes and revisited his earlier meeting with Daz Horne in which he'd felt the stress momentarily lift. If he thought through it again, that fleeting moment of positivity might just return and trick his brain into some much-needed shuteye...

* * *

They didn't come more battle-hardened than Daz Horne. The excessive number of lines on his face – remarkable considering he was under the age of fifty – wasn't the only sign of this. The man had many stories to tell. In fact, Riddick was sure he could attribute each line on his face to one of his dramatic tales.

Daz was Riddick's sponsor in Alcoholics Anonymous. And was on the end of the phone every time Riddick teetered on the edge. Riddick was fortunate to have such a lifeline. And Daz should've been able to rely on him for respect.

But Riddick had never been the most reliable.

The disrespect had started following the botched surveillance job in Manningham eight months previously. Seeing Arthur Fields mutilated, a vulnerable teenager Riddick considered himself responsible for, had caused him to teeter. He should've called Daz immediately; he owed him that. But he'd bypassed making contact and had hit the bottle hard.

Daz had taken a picture of Riddick at his lowest. Unconscious on his doorstep. Then, after Riddick had sobered up, he'd used the photograph to make his point. 'Next time this happens, I won't be here to pick up the pieces. If you can't respect me enough to tell me you're spiralling, I can't help you.'

Riddick had promised that it wouldn't happen again. This ex-alcoholic was good for Riddick – better than DCI Anders Smith, his corrupt mentor, had ever been.

When you'd journeyed as far into the abyss as Riddick had done, hope, in any form, wasn't a resource to turn your back on.

Riddick sat at Daz's table nursing a lemon San Pellegrino. He looked up at Daz's carved features, and the eclectic mix of tattoos that coloured the sides of his neck.

'Tough day?' Daz asked.

Riddick had once said to Claire that Daz looked like a weathered stone and she'd liked the comparison. 'Stones are blunt impenetrable, and, in being so, reliable.'

'Join the club. Every day is a tough day,' Daz said and took a drag on his vape. 'The day that you think it isn't – is the day you take your eye off the ball.'

A stone, Riddick thought. *More like a brick wall.*

Daz pushed long black hair behind his ears and scratched a his stubble. 'It watches you... all the time... from the shadows.'

Riddick nodded. Daz wasn't telling him anything new. He'd heard this sermon countless times. Still, you couldn't really hear i enough. After all, the mind was remarkably resilient to change especially the mind of an addict. It was essential to be aware o your predator. And if you ever believed that you'd been reminded of this too many times, you were simply playing into its hands.

'When you take your eye off it... it comes,' Daz said.

'And you've the photo to prove it, too.'

Daz waved the comment away. 'The photo is irrelevant. A photo can be destroyed. Think of your scars instead. That's you reminder.'

'Everyone has scars.'

'Never a truer word,' Daz said. 'Everyone does. It's how you *handle* those scars that distinguish the person.'

Riddick nodded, sighed and finished his San Pellegrino. 'Th nightmares are relentless though.'

'Well, nightmares *are* relentless. They're supposed to be.'

'They've not been so bad in a long time. Not since... you know... not since...' He crushed the empty can with his hand.

'Say it.'

'Since I lost my family.'

Riddick winced over the sudden formation of a burning knc in his stomach, and let the can fall to the table. Squeezing his eye shut, he took deep breaths.

Daz allowed him a moment to regain control before asking, 'Are these nightmares different?'

Nodding, Riddick opened his eyes. 'They're about Arthur. His chest... carved open...' He shook his head. *The Mansters. Nathan Cummings.* He could feel the hate burning inside him. 'Arthur is innocent. He has the mind of a child. A *gentle* child, and Cummings puts him in the middle of a pissing contest with the Ravens. I should've stopped it before it got out of hand. I. Should. Have. Stopped. It.'

'Should this. Should that. Piss off, lad. I should be sleeping with Angelina Jolie and living in a mansion. Just knock it off. Shoulds are the worst way to treat yourself. And if anyone's reached their quota, it's you.'

'But I should...' He smirked. '*Must*! *Must* be accountable. *Responsible—*'

'Jesus wept, fella. You were following the bloody rules! You *were* responsible. In fact, for someone who has a problem with rules – you were, for once, doing the right thing!'

'I should've stopped Devon from going into the shop.'

'Ha. If I'd ever have tried to come between Hanna and a bloody snack... well, God help me. She'd have pulled out the last of my gnashers.' Daz smiled. Or at least tried to. Years of alcohol and heroin abuse had taken most of his teeth.

Daz looked down at the crushed-up can on the table. 'You want another?'

Riddick considered it.

'I was kind of hoping you'd say no,' Daz said. 'I only buy them because of you. And you've gone through a fair amount tonight. Won't be in Sainsbury's till the weekend.'

Riddick smiled. 'My wonderful host.'

'Your wonderful host on benefits and at your beck and call!'

Riddick nodded. 'And I appreciate it. I should phone more,

though. Feel like I'm always invading...' He poked the crushed can. 'And raiding your supplies.'

'Yes, you are starting to cost me money...' Daz said.

Riddick smiled. 'Seriously though, thanks. I just don't know—'

'Stop there,' Daz said, holding his palm in the air. 'It's what *I* do.' He moved his finger between him and Riddick. 'It's what *we* do.'

'So, let me repay you.'

'How?'

'I don't know... let me be *your* sponsor?'

'And what am I telling Carrie? That she's been overlooked for a copper with more baggage than a travelling circus? She's pulled me out of some tight spots. She's a rock.'

Like you're mine.

'So, nightmares are just nightmares, and shoulds are the Devil's food. And watch for the predator,' Riddick said, nodding. 'Any more conclusions?'

'How do you feel?'

'Before I came here tonight, I felt like I was being squeezed through a sausage mincer.'

'And now?'

'Like I'm coming out the end of it.'

'Interesting. So, you feel minced then?'

'Yes, but slightly better. Like there's a chance I can be put back together. You always make me feel like there's a chance, Daz.'

'Good...'

'But there's something else.'

'Go on.'

'You'll think I'm nuts.'

'After the sausage mincing analogy, how could I think that? Come on, spit it out.'

'I *keep* seeing them. Or at least I think I keep seeing them.

Molly and Lucy. I'll be walking around a supermarket aisle... and, well, you get the picture. An icy feeling in my chest, and it's them. Except... it isn't, is it?'

Daz shook his head.

'I see them in parks... outside schools. You name it. I *see* them.'

'I can't believe it's taken you this long to admit that to me.' Daz gazed down at the table and rubbed his temples. 'I see Hanna every day.' He lifted his eyes back up to Riddick. 'Every. Single. Day.'

Ten years ago, Daz had been driving his wife, Hanna, home from her office. She was a social worker, and they'd met after she'd come to his aid fifteen years earlier. After a lorry had switched lanes too quickly on the motorway, the passenger side of Daz's vehicle, and his life, had been torn to pieces.

'I'm sorry,' Riddick said.

'Don't be. I woke from a coma to a different world. A hollow world. I allow myself those moments. Of seeing her. Of missing her. Of longing for her. It fills the hollowness, reminds me how far I've come, and how proud she'd be. I use that when I look back at the predator and smile. One day I know you'll find that strength too.'

Riddick nodded. He couldn't believe that. The longing and the sadness just felt too painful to be anything but dangerous, and if he looked at the predator, he didn't believe he'd have the strength to smile at it.

But he wouldn't succumb. Not any more. Not now that he had Daz, and Claire. 'Okay, so to the real reason we're here?' Riddick said.

'Not again.'

'You love it!'

'Yes, but it's not Christmas.'

'You say that every time and then you still put it on regardless.'

'Yipee Ki-yay mother—'

'Don't,' Riddick said. 'Just put the movie on and let the maestro deliver the line.'

'Okay, but you can't watch it without another San Pellegrino in your hand.'

Their houses were close, so, following the movie, Riddick walked home, realising his mood had lifted slightly.

It was warm, and despite the late hour, people were out walking their dogs.

Riddick had always liked dogs and had recently discussed the idea with Claire – who wasn't averse to the suggestion.

Not a big dog, mind. Something energetic and cute. He liked schnauzers. They looked wise, and the salt and pepper colouring appealed.

Years back, Molly and Lucy had begged for a dog, while Rachel and Riddick stood firm. Time was at a premium when you'd little ones, and the poor thing would need walking... regularly. It was hard to commit to anything being a police detective with two small daughters. Dog walking had been out of the question.

Now those family responsibilities no longer existed, he was happy to entertain the idea.

He often tried to avoid thinking of his daughters, fearful of melancholy, but Daz's words were still very present.

I allow myself those moments... It fills the hollowness... I use that. I use that when I look back at the predator and smile...

One day, would Riddick be able to smile at the predator?

Damn it. Yes. I will.

Thank God for Daz.

He really made you feel that anything was possible.

As he neared his home, he checked his phone and re-read some messages exchanged with Arthur earlier in the day.

Bacon and egg for dinner... again...

Do you eat anything else, mate? Think of your arteries!

Does Ironman worry about that?

He's got bigger worries! The shrapnel in his heart?

Riddick smiled. Arthur's wounds had taken a long time to heal. Let him enjoy his fry-ups. *For now. I'll be clamping down on them one day...*

Since the incident, Riddick had been in continual touch with Arthur. Their friendship had blossomed. In Arthur's more excitable moments, he'd ask rapid-fire questions about superheroes.

When this happened, Riddick would try his best, despite often failing, to answer them. He saw the barrage of questions irritated most people, including Arthur's own mother, Roni, but Riddick embraced them. They amused him and reminded him that Arthur was here and recovering.

Riddick arrived home and was surprised to see Claire sitting at the dinner table.

It was approaching ten o'clock. He'd expected to see her in the lounge, watching a crime drama. He recalled the beginning of their relationship when they had watched every single episode of *Inspector Morse* together.

'What you smiling at?' she asked.

'Happy memories.'

'Care to share?'

He told her as he approached. She looked as scrumptious as ever in a silken blue nightie. He placed his hands on her shoulders, and she reached up to put her own hands on the back of his and looked up at him.

She offered a smile, but he was concerned that it was a forced one. 'What're you looking all serious about?' Riddick asked.

She broke eye contact but continued to rub his hands 'Preoccupied.'

'Do you need a cup of tea while you tell me why?'

'Paul, sit down, please.'

Shit... this did sound serious!

He smiled nervously as he sat opposite her and took her hand over the table.

'You seem in a better mood. Daz is good for you.'

Not what he was expecting... but a good point. 'Probably more down to the fact that I just watched *Die Hard*.'

She smiled again – it seemed genuine this time.

'He's a legend,' he said.

'I hope you tell him that.'

'Of course I do. He keeps a regular supply of San Pellegrino for me. Not going to put that at risk.'

She continued smiling for a moment, nodding over his humour, but then she looked down, sighing.

Here it comes...

'Eight months ago, I thought you were going to die...'

'But I didn't, did I? Thanks to Daz... and *you*. Especially you So, why the serious conversation?'

'Because you're not happy.'

'I am.'

'You're lying.' She fixed him with a stare.

He lowered his head. 'Okay, most of the time.'

'Most... really?'

Riddick sighed and shrugged. 'Some. I try, but' – he pointed a his head – 'there's a lot that goes on in there, you know.'

'Shit, I know that, Paul.' She reached over and took his hand. 'And I knew that when I signed up, but the problem is that *some* isn't enough any more. Especially when that *some* doesn't seem to be with me...'

He looked at her. 'Of course it's with—'

'Paul, it isn't.'

Riddick's face flushed. 'If you'd just let me finish!'

'Don't get angry.'

He took a deep breath. 'I'm not angry. Frustrated.' This wasn't the first time they'd had this conversation, but Riddick was certain they'd turned a corner of late. 'Why tonight? What's brought this on?'

'Sometimes... I don't know... sometimes, you're just not here with me. And, I know, I get it. God, I get it, Paul. It must be hell sometimes. The things you've lived through. The things you live *with*. But if you're not here with me, then what's the point?'

Riddick closed his eyes. He'd been in a good mood. A better mood. And now this. *What do I say? What do I do?* 'I love you, Claire,' Riddick said. He tried to feel the words, and he did. He was *sure* he did.

'I think you do... in your own way. But you're still a prisoner. We've been together a year, Paul, and I *can't* free you. And although Daz is doing a bloody good job – I can't help but feel like I'm failing miserably.'

'That's rubbish!' Riddick said, squeezing her hands. 'You, fail? I haven't known warmth in my life since... since...'

'Yes, but that's the point, isn't it? That bloody *since*! I can't be the follow-up. The sequel. The not-quite-as-good-but-watchable.'

Riddick released her hands. 'Please...' He put his hands together as if to pray. 'Please, tell me what to do. I don't want you to feel like this, and I do love you... I really do.'

'I don't think there's anything you can do,' Claire said. 'Everyone has to grieve, and that's your right.'

'So, I'll keep it away from you, I promise.'

'You already do! That's kind of the point. You internalise it. I guess if you just talked about it, let it out more, things could be more natural. Things could move.'

'I'll find someone else to speak to. I'll get this sorted out. Yes, I've had a difficult few weeks. Nightmares and such. But I felt I was coming out of it today.'

'Good, I'm glad.'

Riddick took her hands again. 'So, this time, I work on not going back. I work on staying out of it.'

'You must. You really must because...' She broke off.

'Because what?'

'It isn't just about you and me any longer.'

'I don't follow.' But he did, and his blood ran cold as Claire uttered her next words.

'Because in seven months' time, you're going to be a father.'

* * *

Recapping the events of the evening hadn't helped. It was half past three in the morning and Riddick felt more awake than ever.

Still, finding out you were going to be a parent was no small thing. He sighed and slipped from his bed, careful not to wake Claire.

He swooped for his phone and exited the bedroom onto the landing.

As he descended the stairs, he thought back to his reaction to Claire's revelation earlier.

Following a stony silence, he'd tried to cover his shock with positivity, but she wasn't born yesterday.

'Tell me what you're really thinking, Paul.'

He'd tried to swerve the question, but she was persistent, asking again and again. Eventually, he'd said, 'I can't go through that pain again.'

'The pain of raising children?'

'No... the pain of losing them.'

Her face had spoken volumes. Pale, drawn, completely full of despair.

But how else could he feel?

After Molly and Lucy had been murdered, how could he feel any confidence going into parenthood again?

At the bottom of the stairs, Riddick's phone vibrated.

Devon?

He answered, 'What's wrong?'

'Promise not to go ape over this?'

'It's three thirty – what's going off?'

'And not stitch me up?'

'Talk to me Devon.'

'Nathan Cummings is about to be arrested.'

10

Parking in the Lidl car park, a stone's throw from the Knaresborough cemetery, Gardner recalled with clarity the experience here eight months previously.

Seeing Penny Maiden's skeletal remains curled up on her mother's grave.

Unearthing the body of local hero Howard Walters.

A peculiar case.

Her peculiar case, and one in which she'd failed.

She exited the car park, an icy sensation kicking up in her stomach, and approached York Road. Marsh's words from earlier looped through her head. 'Barely out of their teens... blunt force trauma to the head and faces... would be unrecognisable to their families... pulverised... if it was appropriate, I'd suggest a stiff drink.'

Poor Glenda Richards.

An eighty-five-year-old woman having to discover that. To her, they'd be kids. Shit, to someone of Gardner's age, they were kids!

Blunt force trauma.

Howard Walters' life had been knocked out of him with a

single blow to the back of his head. It was possible that Howard could've died from a fall and a bang on the head. However, these two current victims... *pulverised*? It sounded as if someone had gone at these youngsters with some venom.

She crossed York Road, usually busy and dangerous, but not now. It was eerie in its late-night silence. A good thing, really, Gardner was in a world of her own – lost between *then* and *now*.

Two *pulverised* youngsters.

A decaying victim of a hit-and-run.

And Howard Walters. Owner of Howie's Garage near Aspin for forty years. A pillar of the community, supportive of disadvantaged youth. Following retirement, the childless widower had kept Howie's Garage going, so he could share his mechanic skills with young people who were yet to fall on any fortune in life. Under his guidance, the young people would repair cars for the locals for slight cost but Howard wouldn't keep a penny for himself.

His other love in life had been fishing, and again, he was happy to share this expertise with those needing direction and interests. Howard had been a generous man.

Someone without enemies was rare, but it happened, and it made for difficult investigations.

And, in this instance, a complete nightmare from day one.

The community had showed up in large numbers for Howard's vigil. Those who spoke had demanded justice for his murder. Over the coming weeks, they became frustrated. Gardner had tried to explain in press conferences that justice didn't always work like that, and that the wheels could turn slowly. It had sparked outrage. Especially as she wasn't one of them. She was a southerner. From a place where life was cheap.

The press, fuelled by nasty freelance journalist, Marianne Perse, had revelled in the community's frustration and irritation with the outsider.

On this occasion, Rice had stood tall for Gardner. He'd worked the community angles as best he could when that road became closed off for her. Unfortunately, his abrasive attitude had got the better of him, and he'd provoked the press too.

Or rather, 'fed' the press, because sometimes you can't help but fee that the press wants to be provoked.

Again, as in some previous cases, information had seemed to leak from Gardner's team, and when the working theory from the incident room became public knowledge, the heat on the case really went up.

The working theory was that Howard Walters had been behind the wheel of the car that killed Penny Maiden in 1980.

To be fair, it was an obvious leap, and one that nearly anyone with a brain cell would lean towards.

After all, what other reason could there be for putting Howard in Penny's grave, unless he was linked to the victim?

But it was a theory *unspoken* in a loving community. Until the sodding leak had revealed it!

In the here and now, Gardner shook her head as she passed the major incidents van and several vehicles belonging to forensic and other police officers who'd opted to park on York Road. There was, of course, room for her. But she preferred to keep her car separate from the building chaos, so she could disappear as and when with no fuss.

Her mind wandered to that backlash eight months ago.

It'd been overwhelming.

The suggestion that Howard had skeletons in his closet was too much for some of Knaresborough's population, and even those with sense had soon been swayed by the words of Marianne Perse

Gardner had met no one who enjoyed stoking fires as much a Marianne, who never rested until she'd created a raging inferno.

Eventually, pressure from above had forced Marsh's hand an

Gardner, the southern alien, was off the case. Rice, local but displaying little patience with sensitive individuals, was also off the case. Marsh had instructed them to go nowhere near it. Gardner had questioned the ethics behind this instruction. And Marsh, indignantly, had questioned Gardner's desire to stay in Knaresborough, threatening her with a move back south.

A year ago, Gardner would've ripped her arm off to come good on such a threat.

But now that she'd settled, and her children had settled, she wanted to stay.

Marsh had handed the investigation to Detective Sergeant Ray Barnett and provided him with a small team.

Poor Ray.

Gardner reached the gate, which was propped open and being dusted down by SOCOs. She logged in with a young, fresh-faced officer, and then suited up.

As she entered, she glanced at the crumbling wall. She doubted it'd taken many kicks to get that lock to break out of it.

She was still some way from the activity, so as she began her journey down the path that wound between the graves, she thought back again to the working theory she'd had on Howard's death.

There had only ever really been one person with clear motive for Howard's murder.

Penny Maiden's father, Dean.

11

2023

After Gardner had delivered the news of his daughter's excavation, Dean Maiden reached for the oxygen mask hanging by his bed, and placed it over his face with a withered, trembling hand.

'Do you want me to get someone?' Gardner asked.

Dean shook his head as he sucked in more air. It dislodged tears from his eyes, which ran down his face, making the many crevasses in his seventy-five-year-old face shimmer. Gardner had always wondered if you could cry if one of your eyes was made of glass. Now she saw that you could.

She made a note to find out how Dean had lost an eye.

Dean removed the mask. 'I'll be okay in a moment.' He then replaced it on his face for more oxygen.

It'd been over forty years since Dean had lost his daughter in very tragic circumstances. Gardner wondered, briefly, what happened to the devastating sense of loss as you crept into your final years, and your own body started to fail. Did the loss intensify, and come back to fill your remaining days and hours with despair, or did it numb and blur like all the rest of your faculties?

She thought of Anabelle and Rose, praying to God that she herself would never have to find out. A tear crept into her own eye.

She looked at Rice next to her, who was looking around the sterile room.

In fairness, the nursing home had tried to give it some character. They'd hung up colourful pictures of the Viaduct, Mother Shipton's Cave, the flowers in the castle grounds in full bloom, but nothing could hide the reality of the place they were in. It was a place people were brought to die.

Dean lifted the mask away and hung it back by his bed. He shook his head, dislodging more tears. 'What a vile thing to do... How could they... *anyone...* do that?'

'I don't know, Mr Maiden.'

'So *vile.*'

'I agree.' *It's also a vile thing to bury an old man – potentially alive.*

'I mean...' He looked at Gardner. His eyes had already been bloodshot when she'd come in, but they were worse now after the sobbing. 'Is nothing sacred?'

Gardner regarded him sympathetically while she tried to weigh him up. *Someone obviously felt passionately about what happened to Penny, and potentially wanted to avenge her. Maybe reuniting her with her mother celebrates the sacredness of your daughter's life. Maybe it was you?*

But the more she looked at Dean, the more she couldn't help but feel that the digging up of a corpse, and then the burying of another one, was beyond this man in his current state of health.

It surprised Gardner when Dean pulled back his duvet, moved his legs over the side and stood. Rubbing the small of his back, the old man walked over to his window. Then he opened the curtains to stare outside.

Dean was clearly still physically in control of himself, but did he have enough *control* to dig up a body, and then bury another?

'Can you think of *anyone* who might have a reason to recover your daughter's body?'

Dean thought a while, and then shook his head, sighing. 'I haven't got the imagination to think of any reason...' He turned back. His stare was uneven, because of the immovable glass eye, but Gardner could still feel the weight of his gaze. 'Can I see her?'

Stunned by the question, Gardner exchanged a look with Rice.

'I don't think that's a good idea,' Rice said. 'It's been a very long time.'

'*Please.* Just her face... Just once. I wanted so much to touch her face... *after*... but they never let me. If I could see her now... then... just once, maybe, I could touch her...'

'I'm sorry, Mr Maiden,' Gardner said. 'That can't happen.'

He sighed again, looked back out of the window and rubbed tears away with the sleeve of his pyjamas. 'She wanted to be a journalist. She'd have been good at it, too.'

Gardner again exchanged glances with Rice who moved his fingers in a small circle to suggest that they should get on with quizzing him about Howard.

Not yet... not just yet.

Dean continued, 'There isn't a day that goes by in which I don't think about her. But I don't mind so much any more. Want to keep her alive in here...' He pointed to his head. 'Fresh. Forty-odd years and I can still picture her as if it was yesterday.'

'I'm sorry that whoever killed Penny was never caught,' Gardner said.

'Me too,' Dean said.

She glanced again at Rice, saw the impatience in his eyes, inwardly sighed, and then told Dean about Howard's body found in Penny's grave.

'Howard Walters?' Dean said, the brow above his good eye rising.

'Yes,' Gardner said. 'Did you know him?'

'Of course I did.' Dean shook his head, still looking stunned. Fake? 'Spent my whole life here, in Knaresborough, same as Howard. But we were never *good* friends. Passing acquaintances, really. Wait a moment.' He glanced at Gardner again. 'You don't think that I... well... that I'd something to do with it?'

'I didn't say that.'

If your current state of health is genuine, it'd be hard for me to think that... Unless, you employed someone to help you?

'No. But I can tell. You're thinking that maybe Howard was the one who hit Penny, and this is my elaborate attempt at revenge.'

'Not so much an elaborate attempt as a raging success,' Rice interjected.

Gardner glared at Rice who looked away.

'It's too early for these conclusions,' Gardner said, turning her attention back to Dean. 'But what're your thoughts on the possibility that Howard was involved in what happened to your daughter?'

'My thoughts?' His voice rose slightly, which caused him to cough.

Gardner stood up. 'Do you need your oxygen?'

Dean held his hand up as he coughed once more. 'No... I'll be okay.' He took some deep breaths. 'If he killed Penny, this is the first I've bloody heard of it... and... well, good riddance, if it's true. Although, the bastard got to live his whole bloody life first!'

Gardner sat back down while Dean returned to the bed. He sat down on the side and reached for his oxygen mask, but he didn't use it just yet.

'What was your relationship with Howard like?' Rice asked.

'Relationship! Ha! What did I just say? I knew him by name. *Acquaintances*. Knew who he was. He fixed my car a few times.

Don't recall ever being friends with him. Not my cup of tea really...'

'Explain...'

'Ah... nothing really...'

'No, please,' Gardner said. 'Go on.'

'He was a bit of a ladies' man, is all. A few of us noticed tha roving eye. Then, one day, I saw him chatting to my Estelle dow The Dropping Well while I was off buying a round. She was a giggles, like. I didn't like it one bit. Told her so. I guess I was eve more down on him after that.' He put the oxygen mask on an took two breaths and then removed it. 'But I didn't kill him.'

She looked at Rice, feeling somewhat frustrated. *Ladies' ma roving eye. Wasn't the man supposed to be a pillar of the community?*

Rice shrugged.

When she looked back, Dean was on his feet again, rolling hi shoulders. 'Have to keep stretching out, or I'll just seize up. Lik the chuffin' tin man.'

'Howard was a *very* popular man in this community,' Rice said

Dean nodded. 'Not denying it.'

'Yet, he's a womaniser?' Gardner said.

'Maybe the women in question liked the attention.' Dea shrugged. 'Look... just telling you what some of me and my mate saw back then. Always flirting with the ladies. Like a dog with tw dicks! I bet he ruined a few marriages! Maybe, if you help a fe kids out in later life all the sins of your youth are absolved? Wh knows?'

Dean Maiden clearly had no time for Howard, but if he was hi killer, why bother filling them in on this? He wasn't behaving like man with something to hide.

'Whose marriages were ruined?'

'I said "I bet". I might be completely wrong. Just telling yo what we all thought. You can just tell sometimes, you know, wit another fella? Besides, even if he did ruin a marriage or two, well, many people from back then have already kicked the bucket! So, if someone had been hankering for revenge, why leave it so long?'

'Maybe something came to light?' Rice asked.

'Maybe,' Dean said.

'Has something come to light, Dean?'

Dean snorted. 'What you saying?' He coughed and then pressed the oxygen mask to his face again.

'You said you thought he made advances towards Estelle. Do you think she reciprocated in any—'

Dean tore his mask away. 'Watch your tone, fella. You don't speak of the dead that way... and you certainly don't speak of Estelle that way.' He glared for a moment and then sucked hard on his oxygen mask.

Gardner nodded at Rice to instruct him to stop, and then looked back. 'It's okay, Dean.'

He stared at Gardner desperately. 'She wouldn't. Estelle would *never*,' Dean said. 'And, for what it's worth, I don't reckon that Howard is responsible for Penny.'

'What makes you say that?'

'I'm sure I saw him in The Dropping Well that night before I left, and all hell broke loose.'

Gardner creased her brow. 'Are you certain about that?'

'It was forty-odd years ago...'

'Does that mean you're not?' Rice asked.

Dean thought about it. 'No. I guess I am. *Yes*. There isn't a second I don't remember from that night. And, if it ever threatens to fade, the dreams kick up to give me some rather vivid reminders.'

I hear you on that one, Gardner thought.

'So, if it was him, he'd have had to have hit Penny in his car before coming in for a pint – and who in their right mind would do that? Whoever did it will have put the pedal to the floor and left.'

Gardner made notes. It wasn't enough to write Howard off as the potential driver. This was a memory from a very drunken, emotional night almost half a century ago – although, it did cast a shadow over her working theory. Frustrating to say the least. If Howard wasn't the driver, then the whole investigation just became a lot more complicated.

'I have to ask you, Dean, as to your whereabouts over the last twenty-four hours,' Gardner said.

Dean laughed. 'You can have twenty-four months if you like! *Here.* In this bloody place.'

'We'll need to get confirmation of that.'

'I'm sure you'll get as much confirmation as you'd like from the front desk.'

And Gardner didn't doubt it.

12

2024

If you didn't know that you were approaching the scene of a brutal murder, you'd be forgiven for thinking that this was a young couple, deep in love, stargazing from the bench, carving out forbidden time...

But Gardner knew.

So, as she approached the bludgeoned victims, the icy sensation that had started in her stomach rose into her chest.

The team had set up halogen lights so the damage done to these poor individuals was on full display. Gardner stopped metres from the carnage. A tingle ran down the scar caused years ago by a knife which had burst one of her lungs like a balloon.

Whoever had done this had done so in a frenzy, smashing their faces beyond recognition.

The forensic pathologist, Robin Morton, who'd also been present in the cemetery eight months ago, was inspecting the victims. She saw Gardner and then came over, unhooking her facemask. 'The bodies were positioned like that *after* they died.' Robin cracked her knuckles.

'When?'

'Not long ago. Couple of hours at most.'

'Jesus, the parents. The poor parents,' Gardner said, shaking her head.

'They've been attacked with some anger.'

No shit.

Fiona Lane, Chief Forensic Officer, came up alongside Gardner and nodded a greeting.

Gardner smiled at her friend, but neither found the motivation for a quip in the shadow of such brutality.

Fiona pointed at a white-suited SOCO approaching holding a bag. 'The murder weapon... a rock. We know where it happened, too.' Fiona led her over some plates to an old patch of gravestones. She pointed to the ground. 'The drag marks begin here and lead to the bench. We've also recovered two empty bottles of Budweiser.'

'Foul stuff. Wouldn't be my choice of a last drink,' Rice said, joining them.

Gardner didn't give his humour any attention.

'We've got a lot more than last time we were here,' Fiona said.

'Good news,' Gardner said. Trace evidence and DNA had been in short supply eight months back. 'Great work.' She tried to sound positive, but she was struggling to shake the cold sensation inside and the tingle in her scar.

'Their names are Vivianne Gill and Ralphie Parks,' Rice said. 'We've got their driver's licences. Both nineteen.'

Nineteen. So young.

'So we've addresses for them then?'

'Yes,' Rice said. 'Vivianne's address is in Oxford and Ralphie's is in Hull. They both live away at university. They're both from Knaresborough though, and both are back home on term break. I've already retrieved the addresses for both sets of parents.'

Marsh came over. 'Thoughts?'

Gardner only had one thought right now. 'Tragic.'

'Yes. Tragic. Three murders in this cemetery in one year. The first unsolved. We're about to enter a world of pain. Let's clear this one up pronto before tragedy becomes a full-blown disaster.'

'Right now, I'm leaning towards this cemetery being cursed rather than the crimes being linked,' Rice said.

'Agreed,' Marsh said. 'Until further notice, Emma, you work this case with Phil, and leave Ray on the other case.'

Gardner forced back her irritation at being frozen out by that brief discussion and conclusion. 'I think it's best that we don't close off any avenue. It's a murder investigation.'

'Don't I bloody know it? Unfortunately, so do the press – who are *already* gathering. Remember how this played out eight months ago? For God's sake, you two, don't go near them. Leave it to Joe.'

Joe Bridge was the press officer.

Gardner, still stunned by how violently these two young people had been yanked from the world, struggled to hold back her frustration. 'It sounds like you don't bloody trust me.' Snapping at a superior was often a bad move. Snapping at Marsh was *always* a bad move.

Marsh narrowed her eyes.

Shit... Gardner braced herself.

Marsh snorted and turned away, calling over her shoulder. 'Stay away from the press.'

'Bloody hell,' Rice said. 'I can't believe that.' He looked at Gardner in disbelief. 'Did she just spare you?'

'I can't believe it either,' Gardner said. 'Maybe she's going away to meditate over the best torture methods?' She looked over at the bodies and then up at Rice again. 'Okay... so how do we get past the wolves, then?'

13

Avoiding the wolves was easier than she'd expected.

The press officer, Joe Bridge, had the complete attention of the assembled reporters. He was good at that.

'Nice move, partner,' Rice said, after they'd slipped away.

'Partner?' Gardner said with an eyebrow raised as the prepared to cross York Road. 'Try assistant.'

'Well, boss, I'll take that. To be finally accepted. Better tha nothing.'

Gardner snorted. 'Accepted... *tolerated*... and let's be clear, that only because I got glimpses of a beating heart under that obnox ious coating—'

'DCI Gardner?'

Gardner rolled her eyes.

Freelance journalist Marianne Perse emerged from behind tree alongside the outside of the graveyard wall. She wore Burberry Kensington Heritage trench coat, and her hair wa freshly cut.

It was always freshly cut.

It seems parasites could make a lot of money.

'Officer Bridge is over there answering questions, Ms Perse.'

'But *you're* over here,' Marianne said, smiling.

Rice clapped. 'If I'd realised that such astute observational skills paid so well, I'd have changed career long ago.'

Gardner looked at him and shook her head. Best not to antagonise her. Antagonised, Marianne was like a wasp.

'Two people dead, DCI Gardner? Young we're hearing. Could you confirm their ages?'

Gardner clutched Rice's arm. 'Just cross.'

They started over the road.

'We're hearing murmurings that the deaths are suspicious,' Marianne called after them.

'*Murmurings*,' Gardner said to Rice. 'Where the bloody hell do they get this stuff from?'

'They've plenty of *little birdies*.'

'You're telling me – there's one somewhere in our station that needs poaching for starters.'

They reached the other side of the road.

'Where did you park?' Gardner asked Rice.

'Walked. Had a glass of wine. Date night.' He smirked.

'Date night with *who*?' Gardner screwed her face up in disgust.

Rice smiled. 'Yes, amazing, eh? Now and then, someone says *yes*; sometimes, if I'm lucky, more than once.'

'Stop there, I'm begging you. I'm worried that famous kimono we've heard about comes into the story...'

Behind them, Marianne Perse's voice grew in volume. 'Are the murders connected to the discovery of Penny Maiden's body and the murder of Howard Walters?'

'Has she just crossed the road and followed us?' Gardner asked Rice.

Rice looked over his shoulder. 'Looks that way.'

'For fu—'

'Can I be honest, boss?'

'No. I'm not in the mood for honesty. Let's just get away from her.'

Gardner increased her pace, hoping to put more distance between them and this vile reporter.

'She's attractive...'

'*Please!* I said no honesty. Plus, when has she ever had a nice word to say about you? Where's your self-respect, man?'

'Aye, but—'

'I get it,' Gardner said. 'If you were limited to women who were nice to you then I guess you'd be limited to nothing...'

Rice sneered. 'Funny.'

They turned onto Chain Lane.

'DCI Gardner, are the murders connected?'

Marianne was persistent, that was for sure.

Gardner felt the irritation surging through her. *Don't bite, Emma.*

'If they're connected, will you be allowed to lead on Howard Walters' murder again?'

Allowed! Really? Sodding upstart.

Gardner turned. 'Chasing me down the flaming street? Are you the bloody paparazzi? Piss off before I lodge a complaint.'

She saw Rice looking at her, wide eyed.

Wasn't a bite... just a nibble...

'It's just with how fractured community relations became last time, I thought it prudent to ask. After all, might it be wise to allow someone with a better understanding of the town to step in?'

Better understanding?

'Piss off. Haven't you got lives to go off and ruin?'

Yes... she'd bit. Shit.

Marianne smirked. 'I don't know what you mean.'

You know exactly what I mean...

'DI Riddick?' Marianne said.

Don't go there, Emma. 'Go and see Officer Bridge, Marianne.' She narrowed her eyes. 'Last warning.'

'Wow. You're sounding more and more like him every day, DCI Gardner.'

Gardner flinched. *God, she really was throwing down the gauntlet.*

'Abrasive, closed, inappropriate...' Marianne continued.

Finding her voice again, Gardner said, '*You're* the one chasing us down the street.'

'For the truth.'

'Truth? You're only interested in truths that destroy!'

'If you're referring to DI Riddick, the man was an alcoholic and he was working.'

'Where's your evidence?' Gardner asked, pointing her finger at her. Forget nibbling, forget biting even. She now had the urge to take great big chunks out of the woman.

Marianne shrugged. 'I was close to taking a dangerous officer off the streets, you know that don't you, DCI? How close I was. He knows too, doesn't he? Next time, I'll out him.'

'Such a pleasant young lady,' Gardner sneered.

'The people have a right to good police officers.'

'And they've got them and, for the record, for *your* record, DI Paul Riddick was one of the best.'

'Was?'

'Still is,' Gardner said, knowing what had caused the slip of her tongue, but not wanting to give anything to this vulture. She narrowed her eyes.

'So, you've seen him recently?'

Not for the best part of a year.

She turned away, recalling the moment they'd parted. Her anger, and his despair. Learning that he was a murderer had left their friendship in tatters.

Better he was gone. Yes, life was far less colourful and far more predictable, but it was safer. And you couldn't put a price on safety.

She looked back. 'Are we done, Marianne?'

'Three dead in this cemetery. Is there a serial killer on the loose?' Marianne asked.

'Speak to Officer Bridge.'

'So, you're happy for me to tell the readers that they're in no danger?'

'Officer Bridge.'

Gardner turned and crossed Chain Lane to walk alongside Rice.

As they entered the car park, she chanced a look behind her and was glad to see that Marianne had given up.

'Thanks for the support,' Gardner hissed at Rice. 'If you even attempt to say you enjoyed watching that, I'll have you on report!'

Rice nodded. 'Hated every second, boss.'

'Good.'

f DS Devon Dunn's definition of 'going ape' included driving at breakneck speed to a nightclub in Manningham with gritted teeth and an axe to grind, then Riddick was doing his best to fulfil it.

But this was Nathan Cummings.

The spiteful bastard who'd carved Arthur's chest.

And if Nathan was in as much bother as Devon claimed, then Riddick wanted to be part of the final showdown.

Very much so.

It was almost four in the morning and the streets were quiet. Most of the drunken revellers had returned home, or simply passed out in shop doorways.

Riddick parked opposite the club.

There were two Volvo V70 response cars close to the entrance; an ambulance was just behind. A paramedic was attending to someone Riddick didn't recognise sitting on the kerb. A uniformed officer lingered there and another officer was in dialogue with a large, suited man at the front. A bouncer?

Riddick approached the first of the two response cars. Inside, he could see a uniformed officer. In the backseat was Nathan with a bandage around his head.

'Sir?'

He turned to see Devon. 'You're not part of the response.'

'Neither are you.'

He smirked. 'Guess I went ape.'

'Figured. That's why I'm here, too.'

'To keep an eye on me? Well, no need, if everyone here has done their job right... and Nathan finally gets what he deserves, I'm simply here to smile.'

She lowered her head.

'What?'

'This one won't stick, sir. I'm sorry.'

Riddick narrowed his eyes, recalling a smirking bastard, Nathan, smoking and celebrating outside the courthouse with his lawyer. A free man, while poor Arthur was recovering from a skin graft.

Riddick nodded at Nathan in the response car. 'Looks like they're trying.'

'They're failing. The bouncers are all vouching for him.'

Riddick shook his head. 'I also bet their pockets will be full of cash before the night is through. Bet the CCTV went down in the club too?'

'Yep. Blew a fuse... *apparently*.'

Riddick screwed his face up and eyed Nathan sat in the car. 'Coincidences always fall his way, don't they? Tell me what *really* happened.'

'Nathan didn't want to queue for his drink... seems someone didn't take too kindly to being shunted out the way.'

'I take it this stupid someone didn't know who Nathan was?'

'Seems not.'

Riddick nodded over in the direction of the ambulance and the injured man. 'Did our naïve spokesperson for social justice throw the first punch?'

'According to the bouncers, Nathan, the bar staff *and* some witnesses...'

'Nearly everybody. Another dead end then.'

'Nobody's going to piss off the Mansters around here, though, are they?'

'Seems not,' Riddick said. He nodded at Nathan's victim who was being patched up. 'And what did he have to say? Will his statement get us anywhere, you reckon?'

'No. He's changed his tune. Now taking full responsibility. Provoked Nathan himself and displayed threatening behaviour. *Apparently.* Someone must have got to him.'

'Either that, or he just opened his bloody eyes and saw who he was dealing with.'

'Can't blame him. He probably wouldn't have lived to see the inside of a courtroom.'

'That's the problem, isn't it? That's *always* going to be the problem. Wait here.'

He broke away from Devon, went over to the vehicle and tapped the glass. The officer wound his window down and Riddick showed his ID.

'Sir?' the officer said.

'Hop out, son. I just need two minutes.'

'We're about to cut him loose.'

'Not before I've had my two minutes, you're not.'

The officer stepped out and let Riddick take his seat in the front of the vehicle. He closed the door and wound the window back up.

Riddick looked in the rear-view mirror at the bastard sitting behind him. There wasn't a mark on him.

'Did he even lay a hand on you?'

Nathan smirked. 'Not all wounds are visible, you know?'

Riddick stared at him, his eyes narrowing.

'Should I be worried, *Paul*?'

'Yes... especially if you use my first name again. In fact' – he jangled the keys in the ignition – 'why don't you test me on that one? Fancy a drive?'

Nathan snorted. 'Easy Detective Riddick...'

'So, what've you been up to, Nathan?'

'You don't know? Well, I was forced to defend myself—'

'*No.* Not that bullshit. Handbags at dawn in a seedy nightclub? Who gives a shit? No... what've you been up to, in general, Nathan?'

Nathan shook his head. 'I ain't a clue what you're on about.'

'The Mansters?'

'The who?'

Riddick laughed. 'You've been lying for so long, I bet you're even starting to believe it yourself!'

Nathan lifted his hands to show that he was cuffed. 'This is persecution.'

'It's a welcome sight.'

'A temporary one.'

'Maybe so, but it doesn't end tonight, does it?'

'With you involved, probably not.'

'It seems that we're both getting to know each other quite well.'

Nathan sucked at his bottom lip and then sighed. 'But, as I keep telling you, I'd nothing to do with what happened with poor Arthur.'

'Shut up, shithead.' Riddick glared at him. 'Arthur didn't speak for months afterwards. Just moaned in pain. And cried. He's like a child, you see. What you did... you might as well have done it to a little kid.'

'You really aren't listening, are you? Wasn't me. Do you even have any evidence?'

Riddick took a deep breath, trying to settle his surging anger.

Nathan laughed. 'Let it go. You're like a dog with a bone.'

Riddick clenched the steering wheel and looked at the keys. How good it'd feel to drive away with this bastard, somewhere they could be alone, somewhere he could get the truth out of him. Inadmissible in court? Yes. The end of his career? Yes.

Cathartic? Most definitely.

'You ready to let me go yet? I've got things to do...'

The bastard was *all* smiles.

Riddick jangled the keys again. 'What about our drive?'

'Nah, you're all bark. You'd have made your move by now. How long has it been now since what happened to Arthur? Best part of a year? Time to give it up, old man.'

Riddick's fingertips twitched against the keys in the ignition.

Five minutes.

Five *lonely* minutes.

It was all he needed.

And was what he craved.

Sensible, Paul, be sensible. Think about the fact that you're now going to be a father again...

Riddick saw Nathan looking out of the window at Devon and wetting his lips with his tongue. 'You still knocking about with that lass? Any joy yet, mate? If not, I—'

Riddick turned the keys. The engine roared to life. He hit the indicator and glanced in the rear-view mirror at Nathan's paling face. 'Are you ready for my bark?'

He moved the vehicle forward slowly.

'Okay... okay... you've made your point!'

The officer knocked on the window and threw a confused look at Riddick.

'I want you to say it,' Riddick said.

'Say what?'

'What you did. I want to hear you admit to what you did to Arthur.'

'Nothing! Why would I?'

Devon was now knocking on the other window. She looked even more panicked than Nathan.

'Last chance,' Riddick said, increasing speed, moving away from his colleagues. 'Last *bloody* chance.'

'Okay, okay, it was me.'

Riddick hit the brake and watched Devon and the other officer chasing up behind. 'They really worry too much about me.'

'I'm not surprised,' Nathan said. 'Now what you going to do?'

Riddick shrugged. 'Nothing I can do. Yet. Your word against mine. Still... at least I know I'm on the right path. I'll be in touch...' He cracked the door open.

He stepped from the car and handed the keys to the officer as he patted him on the shoulder. 'You shouldn't really leave these in your vehicle...' He gestured over his shoulder at Nathan. 'He's free to go. He's like a baby lamb. Doesn't get any more innocent.'

He turned and smiled at Cummings.

You dickhead.

15

Gardner drove to Castle Ings, the steep road connecting the Waterside to the town, while, alongside her, Phil Rice made the necessary phone calls to ready family liaison officers for the two bereaved families.

She pulled over by the Parks' residence and waited for Rice to finish. 'Keep you fit walking to and from your home on this road.'

'Try racing up it, pushing a hospital bed.' Rice grunted. 'Never again.'

'Yeah, I caught the bed race this year – didn't really get it, to be honest.'

Rice shrugged. 'What's to get? You run around town pushing beds on wheels, then swim through the Nidd, before getting completely pissed. You southerners are always looking for meaning in everything!'

Strange folk, Gardner thought, opening the car door. Stepping out, she took care not to trip and roll down the sharp incline.

It was past four now, and the houses were dormant. She put her finger to her mouth to tell Rice to be quiet, knowing full well what a foghorn he could be. Then she approached the house the needed, rang the doorbell and gave Rice another warning glance.

Best behaviour.

He issued a belch behind the palm of his hand.

Are you serious?

'Excuse me... red wine and a stomach ulcer.'

It surprised her when the light in the lounge went on.

'Someone's on the couch, then. I don't envy anyone who married.'

'Not everyone lives in perpetual misery, you know.'

The hall light came on, lighting the glass panels around the front door. Gardner readied her identification.

A middle-aged man in a dressing gown opened the door brushing tangled hair from his face. His eyes were bright red.

The stench of marijuana was strong.

She willed Rice to keep it to himself; now wasn't the time.

Gardner introduced herself. 'Max Parks?'

'No, sorry...' His eyes rolled back slightly. He was complete out of it. 'I mean, this *is* his house, yes, but I'm not Max... Wow police... sorry... what's this about... is it serious?' He rubbed h face. 'Maybe I should leave?'

Best you don't go driving off anywhere in that state... 'Sorry, wh are you? And where are Max and Evie Parks?'

'I'm Kieran—' He broke off before giving his surname. H suddenly looked as if he was coming around. 'Sorry, what's th concerning?'

Gardner felt her irritation levels soaring, but Rice got ther before her. 'We're the police. Answer the questions, please.'

'Sorry, I'm Evie Parks...' There was a middle-aged woman the lounge door, partway into the hall. She was also wearing dressing gown, and her hair was also dishevelled. She was rubbin at her face as if she'd just been woken too.

Gardner exchanged a look with Rice. *Husband out of town, perhaps? An affair?*

Evie approached the door. Her eyes were also red. 'What's this about?'

Gardner tried to show her identification again.

'I heard,' Evie said. 'Sorry... please tell me why you're here.'

'It's a serious matter, I'm afraid, Mrs Parks. Is your husband not home? Is he close by?'

She looked confused. 'He's upstairs, of course. Asleep.' She looked at her watch. 'It's four in the bloody morning.'

'I'm here,' Max said, coming down the stairs, fastening his own dressing gown. 'I hope this is good. It's rather late.'

He squeezed himself between Kieran and his wife.

On the stairs was another woman. 'Is everything all right?' she asked.

What was going on here?

Gardner looked at Rice. She detected a ghost of a smile on his face.

Were Ralphie's parents swinging?

If the news she was about to break hadn't been so bloody dire, she may have laughed over how surreal the situation had become.

'I'm sorry, Mr and Mrs Parks, but we really need to speak to you alone.'

'Why? What's happened? Whatever you think we've done, just say it!' Max said. 'We've nothing to hide.'

Another couple came down the stairs.

Clearly not, Gardner thought.

* * *

Afterwards, Rice asked Gardner in the car, 'Have you ever been to a swingers' party, boss?'

'I have now,' Gardner said.

Rice laughed to himself. 'At least they won't struggle for an alibi.'

Gardner shrugged; she wasn't in any mood for it.

'Surely, boss, you can see the funny side of this. Honestly, I thought I'd walked right into a comedy sketch.'

Gardner interrupted him with a loud sigh. 'We've just had to tell two people that their only son is dead... Not sure I'm in the mood to giggle over a middle-aged couple's journey of sexual discovery.'

Rice sighed. 'Suit yourself, boss. Still... Suzie will be relieved that they knocked back an FLO. We'd have to do a serious risk assessment before putting her in that one! Mind you, they didn't look as if they'd be in any mood to drop their keys in the fruit bowl for a while now!'

'Knock it off, Phil. If I wanted stand-up, I'd go to a professional. Do your job and tell me what your thoughts are.'

'Quite a common reaction, despite the uncommon context. They're stunned and in denial. They'll want to formally identify; first thing, I imagine.'

'Not happening,' Gardner said. 'Their faces. No parent should see that. We'll do it with dental records.'

'Notice how they thought the sun shone out of Ralphie's arse? A glowing character reference from a pair of swinging stoners. I'd take it with a pinch of salt. I mean, just imagine being their kid! If he knew what they were up to... I mean... wow. It'd put me on a rebellious train.'

'Let's hope they kept it discreet,' Gardner said. *Not that it'll matter much to Ralphie now, anyway.* 'They said they thought Ralphie was at Vivianne's.'

'Yes, and they're adamant he still is. That's some heavy denial. Being stoned out of your brain doesn't help.'

Gardner looked out of the car and up at the lit lounge window. 'They'll be on the phone to Mary and Ryan Gill right now.'

'Good job we sent Ray and Lucy there. Don't imagine that the swingers would've delivered the news with any subtlety.'

'Give Ray or Lucy a ring please – if they're done, I want to know if they got anything different.'

'Well, let's hope so,' Rice said, searching through his numbers. 'If it's just more of that fairy-tale bullshit – a couple destined for a life together, couldn't be happier, and preferred to stay indoors than mess about with drink and drugs, blah blah – then we're going to have very little to go off.'

While Rice made the call, Gardner looked down at her notes.

V&R since Year 10… adoration… university hard… V lovely… settled R… both well-mannered… homebirds/not roaming… some friends, nothing significant… no knowledge of sex parties… not aware of any connection with Howard and Penny.

Beside her, Rice finished the phone call. 'Interesting…'

'Sex-party interesting?' Gardner said.

Rice smiled, looking satisfied that Gardner was finally showing some of her sense of humour. 'Nothing can ever be *that* interesting, but you're going to want to get over there now.'

16

Nathan Cummings was on three promises tonight.

Usually, he'd choose his lady based on mood, but the come-down from cocaine (he'd had to chuck it before being cuffed), had left him feeling lethargic, so he opted for the closest option.

Angel.

The fact that she enjoyed powder as much as he did meant he'd be able to recharge at hers, too.

The walk was just ten minutes, a shortcut through ginnels and the old park, quicker than waiting for a taxi. Driving hammered wasn't an option; the filth would relish pulling him over. Following his rendezvous with Angel, Nathan would get on the phone to his man, Harris. The dickhead who'd challenged him back at the club would be at the hospital by now, having his nose put back together. Nathan always went for the nose because there was no quicker way of making a mess of someone. Problem was that the long night of agony that came with resetting a nose may give the fool second thoughts on keeping his mouth shut. The last thing Nathan wanted was the police asking more questions over the inci-dent. Be better if Harris could have a quick word with him just to

ress the necessity to let sleeping dogs lie. Always best to be sure.
Harris had a way with words. He also had a way with a lighter too,
if someone was struggling to walk the correct path.

Nathan scaled the fence so he could cross the park. A couple of
young teenagers recognised him in the distance and turned and
fled.

He thought then about another nose he'd like to break.

DI Paul Riddick wasn't Nathan's first experience with the filth.
He'd been leader of the Mansters for a good number of years now
and attracting the attention of the holier-than-thou pigs was par
for the course.

But Riddick was different.

It wasn't so much the devious look in his eye, which suggested
that the threat of aggression was anything but a bluff, because that
was nothing new to Nathan either. He'd met rough coppers before,
and had received his fair share of backhands. No... it was more
than a devious look in his eyes... something more akin to a feeling
you had in his presence.

Here was a man living close to the edge, but charging purpose-
fully to his end.

Like a suicide bomber.

Strange comparison, he knew, but it was the only one he could
think of.

Riddick was a genuine threat to Nathan and he was going to
have to find a solution.

There was a scratching sound behind him. He turned.

Unmoving swings. A stationary roundabout. *Nothing.*

Dotted around the railing he'd scaled were a couple of trees
and Nathan wondered if a squirrel had scurried up the tree.

Fairly sure he was alone, he turned back. He wasn't too
worried; very few people alive would take a chance on the king.
That man in the club tonight had been an anomaly. He'd failed to

recognise Nathan in time and the price for his foolishness was drastic change in appearance.

This time, he heard a creaking noise.

He spun and saw the roundabout rotating.

Riddick? 'Really? You sure you want to do this?'

He paused, pretending to wait for a reply, but trying to wor out where the frustrating pig was concealing himself.

There was only one option, really. A tree a stone's throw fror the roundabout. He wouldn't have had time to get anywhere else.

You want to play, filth... let's play...

He knelt down and slipped a flick knife from his sock. One c the bouncers had hung on to his knife before the coppers ha arrived. Nathan would've preferred a gun, but going to a clu armed with a piece was just asking for jail time. Knives were mor discreet, and people were always more willing to help you out wit them than a loaded gun. He pressed the button on his flick knil and listened to the snapping sound. Admiring the silver glint i the moonlight, he approached the creaking roundabout an stopped it with his foot.

'How do you think this is going to play out? You're in my terr tory now.'

He circled the roundabout.

'No CCTV... no witnesses...' He stopped himself short c saying: *Just like on the night I carved open that imbecile's chest.* Yo never know. The copper could be recording him.

He approached the nearest tree. 'I suppose I could simpl lodge a complaint about you following me. Harassing me.' Ye That'd be more appropriate for a recording. Maybe just a sligl tease? 'Maybe I could lodge a report with that pretty officer yo like. Devon, isn't she?'

He threw himself around the tree, thrusting his knife.

The tip of the blade met only air.

When he turned, he'd realised that his ambusher had skipped all the way around the tree to assail him from the back.

He was too late.

He saw a long metal bar arching through the air, and then everything went black.

17

The contrast between the Gill household and the sexually liberated Parks' residence couldn't be any starker.

The air was thick with melancholy, and as Gardner waded through it, she felt it was appropriate. The Gills had just had all the joy sucked out of their lives.

Gardner glanced right at Rice as she sat next to him on the sofa, noting the sad expression on his face. She focused on it, desperate to store it in her memory bank; to see him expressing emotion was like seeing a rare animal travelling to the UK for a zoo appearance.

Mary Gill was over at the mantelpiece, adjusting the position of three framed photographs. All three were of Vivianne at different stages of her life.

Ryan Gill remained seated on the couch, looking purposeful, engrossed in his phone.

Was he sending messages, alerting the world to the loss of his only daughter?

Or was he falling foul to social media, looking for support?

Whatever the reason, the discovery in his daughter's bedroom had left everyone dumbfounded. It'd been completely unexpected, and so significant that Gardner had asked Lucy and Ray to take a step back while she handled it.

Lucy and Ray waited outside beside the growing number of vehicles – one of which was a forensics' van, in which sat the duffel bag full of ecstasy tablets that had been recovered from Vivianne's wardrobe.

'Shit. Viv has her performance tomorrow,' Mary said. 'Karen needs to know.'

'Karen?' Gardner asked.

'Her piano tutor for five years. Someone will have to stand in for her. Karen's going to be disappointed. I hate to let her down – she's been a godsend.'

Disappointed? Understatement of the year! Gardner nodded sympathetically at Mary. *You're in shock. You want to continue to play the organised mother. Your role. Your connection to the past. You'll not be relinquishing that in a hurry.*

They'd already quizzed the Gills on the drugs, who claimed to be completely unaware of their existence, which seemed reasonable. After all, why grant Ray the opportunity to have a quick look round if they'd had any idea?

Regarding the drugs, the conversation had rarely deviated from Ralphie Parks. He was to blame in the eyes of the parents. Vivianne was perfect. Ralphie had now ruined her life.

'But the bag was in Vivianne's wardrobe, Mr Gill. Surely, she must have known?' Gardner asked, returning to the conversation that had only recently ended in a spell of silence.

Ryan lifted his eyes from his phone screen. They narrowed. 'She mustn't have known what was in it. Maybe he just asked to leave it in there.'

Maybe, Gardner said, making a note, *or maybe not.*

'I'm not bloody having it,' Ryan said, raising his voice. 'Do you hear me? There's absolutely no way, absolutely no way, that Viv had anything to do with those drugs. It's him... absolutely... and anyone that knew them both will tell you this.'

'His parents spoke highly of him, though,' Rice said.

Ryan snorted. 'Those bloody parents – they can't see what's in front of their sodding faces. They're lost in their own world.'

That's one way of putting it, Gardner thought. 'If the drugs did belong to Ralphie, he's obviously heavily involved in something. They've been together for' – she looked down at her notes – 'over four years. How would Vivianne not know what he was mixed up in?'

'Listen,' Ryan said, leaning forward. 'Viv was a beautiful soul. A. Beautiful. Soul. She'd do anything for anyone, even that lout!'

Keep his secret then, perhaps?

Mary had circled around to the back of the lounge, and she was now adjusting an arrangement of candles on the back table. Gardner recognised them as a set she herself possessed. Fake candles. To be switched on, giving the false appearance of a flickering flame. 'Such a mess. Viv can't handle mess... never could. Need to get all this in order.'

Gardner felt a wave of sadness. There it was again. The shock. The denial. Gardner had seen it before many times. The bereaved looking for that possibility, that element of doubt, anywhere they could. Mary was staring at the flickering false candle arrangement as if it was the beating heart of her dead daughter.

'He's a monster,' Mary said.

'Ralphie?'

Mary nodded. 'She told me things. The idiot told her she'd put on weight. Made her feel shame.'

Ryan turned and looked at Mary. 'You never told me this.'

Mary shrugged and continued staring at the candles. 'I kept

elling her she was better off without him. She agreed to stop alking to him for a while at university. But it didn't last.'

Ryan turned around. His eyes were wide as he pointed to his head. 'He was in her head, you see. I should've dealt with him when I'd the chance... but I didn't.' He lowered his eyes and muttered, 'He was *bad news*, but we tried to do the right thing.'

'We didn't want to push her away,' Mary said.

Ryan sighed. 'You hear all these horror stories about coming on too strong...' His face dropped. 'But now I'm living in a horror how. I *should've* stopped it.' Ryan had cast his phone away and was now clenching his fists.

Gardner decided against more questions. This was a very troubled audience, and Lucy and Ray had already put the parents through it earlier, too. They'd enough to go on concerning Vivianne's last movements, which would get careful consideration in briefing.

Daisy Langford, the FLO, was in the kitchen, preparing hot drinks for everybody; she'd been gone for a short time now, and Gardner resolved to leave when she returned.

Ryan suddenly looked up. His face was the palest it'd been since she'd arrived.

'Mr Gill?' Gardner said.

Ryan stood up. His paling face contorted into a horrified expression.

Gardner and Rice stood.

'I'm going around there! I'm going round to *that* vile house. I want to know what's going on!'

Vile house.

So, were the Parks' nocturnal activities common knowledge?

'That's not such a good idea,' Gardner said.

'Not a good idea? You're in my house, telling me my daughter is

dead, and I know for certain, as you will soon enough, that it
because of that little bastard!'

Gardner wasn't inexperienced with bereaved parents and the
erratic mood swings, but that didn't make it any easier to deal with
She saw Mary make a sudden move for the lounge door.

'Mrs Gill,' Gardner called out.

The door suddenly swung inwards and collided with Mary.

It was Daisy, entering the room with a tray of hot drinks – sh
must have prodded the bottom of the door with her foot. The doo
bounced back off Mary and hit Daisy. The drinks flew everywher
Both Daisy and Mary gave brief cries and Gardner was quick t
barge past Rice to assist.

Gardner sighed with relief when she realised no one had bee
hurt. An unexpected miracle on a day where this family had expe
rienced no miracles at all. She looked at the tea all over the floo
and on the doorframe.

'More mess,' Mary said. 'An awful sodding mess.'

Gardner reached out and touched Mary on her shoulder. 'I'
sorry.'

'The mess, look at the mess,' Mary exclaimed, her voice fillin
more and more with frustration.

Gardner felt her insides crumbling. 'Maybe you should just s
down?'

Mary's eyes darted left and right, no longer interested in th
spilled tea. She seemed horrified, looking everywhere. 'I *have* t
clean up.'

'I think that can wait for the moment.' Gardner's own daugh
ters came into her head, and she tried desperately to force th
images away, knowing they'd make her emotional.

Mary, meanwhile, yanked herself back from Gardner's touc
and continued to look in all directions. The mess was just a
excuse, an escape route from the hell she found herself in.

But there was no escape route, was there?

Not really.

Gardner took a step forward. Mary looked at Gardner, tears in her eyes, and then flung herself into her arms, trembling with anguish.

18

1980

Forehead burning, Dean Maiden stumbled backwards, trying to blink out the blood running into his left eye. The back of his foot caught the bottom step, and then he was on his arse on the second step. 'Stop!'

She didn't.

Her nails flashed again. His cheek burned.

'Stell!' He raised his hands to protect his face.

'*Why?* How could you? How? You *knew* the time she left. You weren't there for her.'

He cried behind his raised hands. The tears stung the open wound on his cheek. 'I wish I could go back... God, I wish, I wish... It's all I want... all I can think about.'

'Drinking... Everything is gone... gone. Because of your drinking.'

Lying back on the steps, he let his hands fall away and determined that maybe it was for the best if she just bashed him out of this sodding world.

There was a loud knock at the front door.

He groaned and eased himself up into a sitting position, wiping at the blood and tears in his eyes.

Estelle now had her back to him, watching as the front door opened.

Keith Fields came into their home, smoking.

'How dare you!' Estelle hissed.

Dean reached out to grab her arm. 'Stell!'

He missed completely, but she didn't move to the visitor as he feared she might.

Keith breathed out a cloud of smoke, turned to close the door behind him, took another long drag and then strolled over to them.

The man was tall and wiry with dishevelled hair and yellowed jaundiced eyes and looked like a factory worker weathered by poor conditions. Still, despite this, he dressed like the richest man in town. Because he was the richest man in town.

The suit he currently wore probably cost more than Dean could earn in a year in a print factory.

'I came to pay my respects again,' Keith said, opening his arms, offering an embrace.

'Once was enough,' Estelle hissed.

The visitor lowered his arms and shrugged.

'Stell, come on, please,' Dean said.

Estelle took a backward step and gripped the banister of the stairs. Dean's heart fluttered when he saw her knuckles glow white. *Keep it together, Stell.*

'I *wanted* to say that the service did young Penny proud,' Keith said.

'We'd like you to leave now.'

The arrogant prick shrugged and took a long drag on his cigarette. After he breathed out, he narrowed his eyes. 'So, I can pay for her funeral, but I cannot pay my respects?'

'Leave. Now.'

Dean could see the fury on his wife's face. He could also see the irritation in Keith's. The combination of both could be explosive. 'Stell, it's better that—'

'Don't be a spineless pig,' Estelle spat, turning her wide eyes onto Dean.

He felt his heart sink. How right she was. He regarded Keith and that ghost of a smile on his smug face. Nothing would've given him greater pleasure right now than striking him down... Of course, it'd probably be the last thing he ever did.

And Estelle would be next.

Unacceptable.

'Stell. Stop, please.'

'Quit talking! Not unless you want me to flay the flesh from your bones.' Estelle turned her gaze back to Keith. 'You said you wouldn't come to the service.'

'I kept my distance. It was lovely.'

'You'd no right—'

'It hurts me what happened.' Keith touched the centre of his chest and his face sagged.

'Bollocks,' Estelle said, pointing at him again. 'You couldn't care less. What more do you want from us?'

'Nothing. I don't want anything.'

Dean knew this was the truth. This man had their silence already. There was nothing else he could take from them.

'I'm just here to tell you, that if you ever need me, you can come to me. I'm here...' He paused, took a large drag. 'Come to me first.' He released the smoke.

He was threatening them.

'You've made your point,' Estelle said. 'Now, piss off.'

Dean flinched. *Stell, for pity's sake!*

'Time is a healer,' Keith said. 'But it can also be a bad influence. Just come to me first, okay?'

'You're a broken record! How many *bloody* times?' Estelle said.
'Do you want me to express gratitude or something?'

'Stell!' Dean interjected. 'Enough!'

'It's okay,' the bastard said, that ghost of a smile flickering
across his face again. 'It's been a trying time, a horrible time. I just
wanted to bring clarity to a muddy situation, that's all.'

'No, Keith,' Estelle said, taking her hand from the banister to
point at him. 'You bring the Devil to every situation.'

Dean knew he had to put a stop to this. He stood, and with a
shaking hand took Estelle's arm.

'Get off me!' She shook her husband off. 'Touch me again and
I'll claw your eye out.'

Their visitor chuckled. 'Sorry,' he said, holding up his hands.
'Shouldn't laugh, but she always was a *card*. Look at what she's
already done to your face!'

Estelle continued pointing at Keith. 'Maybe you should know
better then? Coming here – how dare you!'

Dean saw Keith's eyes narrow again. She was throwing down
the gauntlet.

Insanity. 'I'm sorry, she's tired...'

His wife glared at him. 'Show some balls, man.'

The gangster took a cigarette packet out of his pocket, opened
it and stubbed his fag out on the inside of the lid. He dropped the
butt in and took out another. After lighting it and filling his lungs a
few times, he said, 'One last thing.' He reached into the inside
pocket of his jacket and pulled out a bundle of notes, proffering
them in Estelle's direction.

'No more,' Estelle said, shaking her head. 'Keep your filthy
money.'

Keith shook his head wearing an expression of disbelief.

Dean reached out and took the money.

While maintaining eye contact with Estelle, Keith said to Dean, 'What do you say?'

'Thank you,' Dean said, feeling disgusted with himself.

'You've got to be kidding?' Estelle said, keeping her eyes on Keith.

'He gets it,' Keith said.

Dean raged inside. Angry, disgusted, torn... but getting them-selves killed – what did that solve?

'It must have been tough Dean, for you to see her that way,' Keith continued.

Estelle hissed, 'Have you no shame?'

'Just trying to empathise.'

'I didn't see her,' Dean said, his balled fists quivering. 'She was covered and...' He squeezed his eyes closed. He saw his daughter's blood on the road... *washed away in the rain...* He opened his eyes. 'Leave... please.'

The monster lingered between them, smoking, amused by something. Eventually he said, 'Well, if no one is going to offer me a drink, then I may as well be off.'

Thank God.

Dean looked at his wife, gave her a quick nod to suggest it was almost at an end, and that she should just hold on a moment longer, but then he saw a change come over her. Her face seemed to suddenly set itself into a determined expression, and a bright-ness, an excitement almost, seemed to come into her eyes.

'You've been here all this time,' Estelle said, looking back at Keith. 'And you've not even offered me a fag.'

Stell...

'You're a card,' Keith said, smirking, reaching into the packet for another cigarette. 'Do I say that enough?' He winked at her.

She touched his arm. 'Just a drag will do.'

Keith and Estelle had some history. Some fumbling behind bike sheds at the local comp. A shared fag or two. The thought always disgusted Dean. What he was witnessing right now disgusted Dean.

What the hell are you playing at?

'Stell—'

'Dean, man,' Keith said. 'The lady wants to smoke.'

Estelle took the cigarette from Keith, and Dean felt his stomach turn over.

'Stell, no—'

Keith held a finger up to Dean. 'Hush, man. *Hush.* She needs this.'

Keith watched Estelle put the fag to her lips and take a long drag. The end flared, and then she pulled the cigarette from her mouth. She tilted her head back, just as Keith had done moments before, and exhaled the smoke upward.

Keith chuckled. 'What a lass you are, Stell. Always said that about you. We're from the same stock. We get knocked down, but we *always* get back up, eh? I always wonder if things could've ended differently between me and you.'

Dean felt like his insides were melting. Especially when he saw her eyeing him up, before taking a second drag. But this wasn't what it looked like. It was so obvious Keith must have known he was being toyed with.

Still, why would he care?

He probably felt he'd nothing to lose in this situation.

Whatever Estelle's intentions, Dean needed to put an end to it. 'Shall I walk you to your car?'

It sounded ridiculous, but it was suddenly all he had.

The idiot looked at him and snorted. 'Why would I need you—'

Estelle lunged. There was a sizzle, closely followed by a scream. The smell of scorching skin filled Dean's nostrils.

'Get off! Bitch!' As Keith stumbled back, Estelle moved with him, keeping the fag pinned to his face.

Dean yanked his wife away with both hands and watched, in horror, Keith's retreat as he clamped his hand over his left cheek.

Estelle stepped forward, wide eyed. 'I asked you nicely... many, many times.'

Jesus! We're dead. Dead! He'll kill us right now!

Keith dropped his hand, revealing the black and blistered spot on his cheek, which would likely scar. He gritted his teeth, showing signs of discomfort.

Dean looked at the wounded man's fists clenched at his side.

The monster started to edge forward.

Estelle's smile grew wider. 'Come on,' she taunted. 'Believe it or not, you were such a gentle boy back then... what happened to you?' She waved him on. 'Come on. Show me the real you. I never really met him.'

Keith took another step, but her words had struck home somehow. He looked confused. Still, Dean had seen enough. If he was going to hurt Estelle, it'd have to be over his dead body.

He stepped between them.

It snapped Keith out of his confused stupor; his eyes widened.

Dean clenched his fists and watched Keith take a deep breath. His eyes were twitching and watering. Surprisingly, the bastard smiled again, even through all the discomfort he must surely be feeling.

'You think you know me well, Stell,' Keith said. 'Just maybe you don't know me as well as you think.'

'Every time you look in the mirror and see that scar, remember this moment, and remember Penny, because I won't forget, and neither should you.'

'I'd stop while you're ahead.' He took another few steps back. 'I could still change my mind on how this all ends.'

Keith turned and left the house, clutching his cheek. He left the front door open. Estelle then turned to Dean. 'You're pathetic.'

'I know.'

She put her arms around him and rested her head on his chest.

'I thought you were worried about him killing us.'

'No, Stell, I was only worried about you. I couldn't care less what happens to me any more.'

She gripped him tightly and cried.

19

2024

Eight in the morning and Gardner was grateful for caffeine and the socially acceptable high it offered.

She looked around her busy incident room at everyone else doing the same – it seemed she wasn't alone in her gratitude.

Wielding an unopened cereal bar, Lucy O'Brien came over. 'I brought a spare, boss.' She winked. 'I noted the jealousy in your eyes when you watched me eating one of these the other day.'

Gardner smiled. 'That better not be true. There's nothing worse than a food gawker. My ex used to do it to me when I ordered the sticky toffee pudding in the restaurant, and he was on a diet. Always ended up with his fork in it.'

O'Brien put the cereal bar down on the desk just in front of Gardner. 'I thought it was one of the ten commandments. Nobody should ever have to share their sticky toffee pudding.'

Gardner looked down at the cereal bar and felt warm inside. She was starving, and overrun by children and crime, and Lucy had shown awareness and kindness. 'Okay, but turn away – we've one minute, and I don't want you to watch me wolfing it down. I'll put you off lunch.'

Lucy took a step back, smiling. 'You wouldn't.'

Bloody hell, was she flirting?

Surely not!

Gay and single, yes, but she was twenty-something, and Gardner was... well... a depressingly higher number than that!

Add to that, she'd almost got Lucy killed a while back when he'd asked her to look after Rose, and her sociopathic brother had turned up and given her concussion.

The argument against flirtation was heavily stacked here...

And why even the interest, Emma? Since when were you gay?

She threw one more smile at Lucy – *nice eyes, though* – turned and wolfed down the cereal bar.

When she turned back, she counted her officers. Ten. *Where was the eleventh?*

It took her a moment to figure out it was Ray Barnett – another of her crew subjected to a rather late night. Overslept? Shit, there was a bollocking she was in no mood to be issuing.

She glanced at Rice, who was still fiddling with the incident board, which he'd been doing for a couple of hours now and nodded. She then clapped her hands together.

'No one complains about being tired,' Gardner said. 'I've been up *all* night.'

'You look fresh as a daisy,' DS Will Holbeck called out.

'Good genes,' she said and grinned. 'But park your sarcasm, Will. I'm glad you've grown in confidence since your promotion but keep it to yourself or I'll have it back!'

A rumble of laughter. Quick ice breaker and they were all reacquainted.

Now to bring the mood back down and introduce the job.

She sidled over to the incident board and pointed out the photographs of the victims under the randomly generated operation heading. *Operation Red Cascade.* 'Vivianne Gill and Ralphie

Parks. Both were nineteen. In a relationship since fifteen, both a
different universities. Discovered bludgeoned at quarter to four i
the morning in Knaresborough cemetery by a Mrs Glend
Richards. Mid-eighties.' She pointed at a picture of the elderl
lady. There were sighs and murmurs of shock. 'Obviously not
prime suspect, but we'll still do due diligence on interviewing he
Brad, you can...' She looked over at DC Brad Ross.

He looked gutted, and she clearly heard him murmur, 'Really
under his breath.

She thumbed at the plastic wallet attached to the board behin
her. 'Once it's assigned, it's assigned. Done randomly by th
computers. Suck it up.'

They all giggled – apart from Brad, that was.

It was all bollocks, of course. There were no randor
assignments.

'Won't take you long, Brad. So, murder weapon is this rock..
She pointed to a picture. 'Early doors on pathology as per; I'n
hoping for something, *anything*, by this afternoon.'

When she paused for breath, the inevitable irritating whisper
began. 'Anything you want to ask me?'

A few hands went up.

'Look, at the moment, it's not being treated as connected.'

Her colleagues exchanged looks.

'Until we know otherwise, Ray's investigation into Penn
Maiden and Howard Walters stays separate – although Ray
helping with Red Cascade in the initial stages.' *Should he decide*
turn up today!

Hands were still up.

'We leave it,' Gardner said. 'As soon as we get a sniff of some
thing otherwise – that's the decision.'

'Was it your decision?' Holbeck asked. He was never one to b
silenced.

She smiled. 'No, the computer again.' She flashed him a raised eyebrow.

Another laugh.

'Wind your neck in, Will!' Rice said.

You can talk, Gardner thought. She then considered Will's suggestion that she was behind this call. *Of course I'm not. But I'm too shattered right now to really assess how I feel about it.*

Gardner introduced the other characters in the collage of photographs. Mary and Ryan Gill. Evie and Max Parks. Her audience particularly enjoyed listening to Rice's description of the swingers' party. He embellished it, but she didn't rein him in. It was good for morale.

Afterwards, she regained their focus easily with a cough. She'd got the measure of her predominantly male crowd over the last eighteen months. They knew who was in charge.

Gardner explained the different reactions to the tragic news by all parents and then moved onto the recovered batch of ecstasy tablets. She nodded at Lucy.

'The pills are printed with the image of a unicorn head. They're bad news. Super strong MDMA. Been a spike of hospitalisations in Yorkshire. I spoke to someone I know in CID earlier and they reckon it's coming in through the gangs in Bradford.'

'Nothing new there,' Rice said. 'Shit's been flowing into Harrogate and Knaresborough from some of these sewers for as long as I can—'

Gardner's stare cut him off.

'Boss,' he said, and went back to his board. He was becoming more and more adept at reading a bollocking before the words came out. He valued his newfound position as assistant SIO, and God knows, Gardner considering pulling it regularly. But every time she came close, he hauled something out of the bag...

Would he haul something out of the bag on Operation Red Cascade?

She wouldn't be surprised.

'Okay, well done Lucy. And, as you've pointed out, we're already in close touch with CID over this,' Gardner said. 'This feels like county lines to me.'

She turned and regarded Matt Blanks, their HOLMES 2 operative, who, over the last year or so had experienced a change in persona. Gone was the shaggy hair. Cue the smart suits, styled hair and clear skin. Stumbling out of adolescence so late into your twenties was nothing new, but suddenly becoming the snappiest dresser in town – well, that was something else entirely.

'Matt, could you make a note to draw together all local county lines incidences in the last five years or so. Let's see if anyone off our cast list' – she threw a thumb behind her head – 'makes an appearance.'

Matt nodded.

'So back to the victims. We managed some early calls. Vivianne was on her way to a first-class degree from Oxford according to a wowed tutor. While Ralphie Parks was causing problems at Hull University with his behaviour. Spot the difference?'

Will's hand went up.

'It was sarcasm, Will,' Gardner said.

Some more laughter.

'Maybe there's truth in what Ryan Gill is saying,' Gardner said. 'Maybe Vivianne didn't know about the drugs, or maybe she was being manipulated? Either way, seems the Gills had a view on Ralphie, and we've yet to find much to the contrary.'

'If he was that bad, how could they stomach it?' Jeff Oats, a usually restrained, quiet DS, raised his voice slightly. 'If my daughter was involved with someone like that, I'd quickly be putting a stop to it.'

Murmurs of agreement travelled across the room.

Gardner recalled Ryan's words... *You hear all these horror stories about coming on too strong...*

Still, Oats had a point. And four years was a long time to suffer in silence.

Had Ryan finally lost control? Confronted them in the cemetery?

Surely not? His own daughter? An accident, perhaps? Had she got in the way of her father and the wayward boyfriend? Had Ryan then damaged his own daughter's face to pull the wool over their eyes?

At this juncture, nothing could be ruled out. And as was often the situation in cases like this, the parents would have to come under scrutiny.

She pointed at the map of the cemetery on the board and the images of the local area around it. 'So, no CCTV in the graveyard, but we need to scour the local area for movements from Vivianne, Ralphie and our potential murderer. Some door banging – because we need to find out where our two were before they ended up dead. Too soon to say without doubt, but the pathologist believes it was at least a couple of hours before she saw them, but not much longer. So, we're thinking they died between twelve and two. They told their parents that they were at each other's houses for the evening. Were they in a bar, or taking a romantic stroll by the river? And how'd they end up in a bloody graveyard between twelve and two?'

Rice was nodding. 'Yes, they're nineteen, not like they've got to hide out for a shag.'

'If the parents are religious...' Brad said.

'Are you not listening? The Parks were having a sex party. They probably wouldn't even think twice about asking—'

'Don't even go there, Phil,' Gardner said, holding out her hand. 'Not if you're meaning to be humorous.'

He shrugged. 'Might be worth consideration.'

'Maybe so, but we'll do the considering on that one *later*.'

Rice nodded.

'Everything we have so far is on HOLMES.' She nodded over at Matt. 'Including this...' She reached down onto the table and picked up a photograph. There was already Blu Tack on the back, so she stuck it up next to the other cast members.

This was the last item on her agenda and she'd deliberately left it until the end.

This way, she'd kept the focus on the tragic loss of life, and hopefully stoked the fires of duty in her crew. What came next might become a distraction.

Sensationalism.

Gossip.

Most were leaning forward, squinting, trying to see the picture. Those middle-aged and over struggled, but Brad saw him. 'Bloody hell, is that—'

'Sebastian Harrington,' Lucy finished for him.

'Aye. The Tory tosser in the flesh!' Rice said.

Sebastian Harrington had been a Conservative MP throughout the seventies, eighties and nineties. He cut a divisive figure in these parts. Hard-headed during Thatcher's reign, there were many who struggled to forgive him for some particularly difficult times. On the flip side, as was always the case with politics, there were some who admired his rather savage approach to getting things done, and now credited the prosperous nature of Harrogate to his bullish approach to leadership in those years.

'He's Ralphie Parks' uncle. On account of him being Evie Parks' older half-brother.'

'But he's seventy-odd,' DC Cameron Suggs said. 'How old is Evie Parks?'

'Fifty,' Rice said. 'Sebastian and Evie's late father, Bart Harrington, liked to have affairs with much younger women. When Sebas-

ian hit twenty-five, Lorraine Petch, who was only twenty-four at
he time, became pregnant with Evie.'

'He had an affair with someone younger than his own son!'
Holbeck exclaimed.

'You sound surprised,' Rice said. He was pointing at the picture
of Sebastian, a tall, distinguished looking man with a neat crop of
white hair. 'You don't know about people like this?'

Gardner looked at him. He was allowed his political stance. No
argument there. *But stereotyping*? He knew her golden rule on that
one. He shrugged.

'Actually,' Lucy said. 'In fairness. He's been working at the
youth centre down at Stockwell.'

Gardner looked at O'Brien.

'My friend's son, Jake. He's fifteen – used to get into a bit of
bother. Says Seb – that's what they all call him – is a good laugh.
Comes and helps man the club. Has some skills on *Mario Kart*...
apparently.'

Gardner smiled at Rice, who looked stunned.

See?

'Must be a guilt thing,' Rice hissed. 'Over all the lives he shat
on. Happened with my dad when he started to lose his marbles.
Suddenly he was this gentle giant who'd hug you goodbye. The
man never hugged a single person until he finally realised what a
prick he'd been—'

'Anyway,' Gardner said, cutting him off. 'First stop for me and
Phil today is to talk with Sebastian Harrington. Obviously, the
press – and a certain Marianne Perse – are going to enjoy themselves immensely now we've a minor celebrity involved. I think it's
best to get the measure of him and rule him out as early as possible. Meanwhile, we all need to get ourselves focused and active.
This isn't a random killing. There's anger in this murder, and the
motive will be key. Let's build up a picture of our victims' lives both

in Knaresborough and in their university homes. The gangs and county lines will be a clear focus. We've their mobiles and we'l use the cell towers and any CCTV footage we can to build up thei last movements. Social media is to be hit hard. And the school Let's get as much of a background as we can. Tasks, as per, are or the board. Let's reconvene at six.'

20

Riddick had a go at building bridges.

After bringing Claire tea and toast, he showed her pictures he'd researched earlier of suggested nurseries online.

However, simply by trying, he became paranoid that his sudden enthusiasm seemed forced.

And, sure enough, it wasn't long before she asked to be left alone.

She'd his number, all right. Paul Riddick, self-indulgent to the max, wasn't ready to commit to a new life.

So, he needed to change. Change fast and change *hard*. But when fighting off the urge to drink sapped so much of your will, where was he going to find the energy for this?

He sighed.

Claire was the best thing that'd happened to him in a very long time...

Shit! If he messed this up, he really did want shooting.

Later, after he'd driven to HQ and was in his office, he turned his attentions back to Nathan Cummings. Unfortunately. The man was foul and made of bloody Teflon.

By 10 a.m., he'd already made two very significant life reso-
lutions.

Come what may, I'll be the best father to our child, Claire. But first...
I'm going to put an end to that bastard Nathan Cummings if it's the last
thing I do.

His thoughts were interrupted by a knock at the door. DCI
Kerry Bradley walked in. Kerry led this unit of CID that dealt only
with Bradford, and the ever-growing problems of drug-trafficking
and county lines. From Bradford originally, she'd personal experi-
ences of loss due to this crime epidemic, which made her driven,
although to most of her underlings, *driven* was simply a synonym
for *obsessed*. She barely slept, and kind of expected the same from
the rest of them. Many found her overwhelming. But Riddick liked
her – probably because she valued him immensely.

Probably because he was cut from a similar cloth.

Kerry rarely greeted people, and got straight to the point, so
her sudden entrance was unsurprising. He was, however, rather
taken aback by a dark look in her eyes.

'Is everything okay?'

'What the hell did you do last night?'

Riddick sat up straight in response to the attack. She'd obviously heard about him playing silly beggars in another officer's car.
'Made it clear to Cummings that he wasn't invincible.'

'And how did you do that? By killing him?'

His mouth fell open slightly.

'Paul?'

'What? I... no! What's gone off?'

After she'd explained that someone had ended Nathan's life
with a blunt instrument, he closed his eyes and leaned back in his
chair.

This wasn't good.

Yes, Riddick could cross off his resolution to put an end to Cummings – someone else had saved him the bother. But doing it after his little stunt in the police car?

Not really the best time, thank you very much.

Things were about to get very messy.

21

On the way to former Tory MP Sebastian Harrington's home in Harrogate, Gardner picked up a call from Barnett.

There were very few excuses for missing a briefing, but she'd a lot of time for Ray. He was usually a safe pair of hands, and a key player in navigating those crucial turning points that came so rarely in an investigation. Bollocking him would be awkward, although necessary.

Make it good, fella...

'Boss, I've been at the hospital.'

Strong start. 'Are you okay?'

'Not me, boss... Two nineteen-year-olds. Charlotte Hughes and Adam Briggs. Admitted to hospital just before midnight last night. Ecstasy tablets... both collapsed. Mainly down to dehydration. They're out of the woods and expected to make a full recovery.'

Despite being on her hands-free, Gardner pulled over at the side of the road. 'I'm glad.' She looked in her rear-view mirror to watch Rice pull up behind her.

'Is this the bad batch?'

'Sorry, boss, bad batch? News to me.'

Of course. He hadn't been at the briefing...

'Were they unicorn tablets?'

'Yes.'

Gardner took a deep breath. 'Why were you there?'

'I couldn't get back off to sleep following our interview with Mary and Ryan Gill, so I was researching emergency calls logged yesterday evening. An ambulance crew picked these two kids up round 11.45 p.m. for suspected drug overdose. As they were the same age as the victims, and we'd discovered the bag of ecstasy, I went to look. Sorry for not being at the briefing, boss, but the lad, Adam woke up. Nice lad. He'd taken two of those unicorn tablets from the bag recovered from Vivianne's room.'

'They're a bad batch. CID have confirmed it. They've caused a spate of hospitalisations.'

'Makes sense. Poor kids. Breaks my heart to see them do this to themselves.'

Gardner nodded sadly. She couldn't agree more. 'Where did the ambulance pick them up last night?'

'From a party. A catch-up of old friends. Students on break from university. There were fifteen there in total...'

'Ralphie and Vivianne were there, weren't they?'

'Yes. And the address isn't too far from the cemetery either.'

'Well done, Ray. Did you ask Adam about Vivianne and Ralphie?'

'Yes, but he was rather out of it, and still is, to be fair. He simply says that *everyone* was off their heads. Most of the evening is a blur to him. He remembers dancing, before lying on the sofa. He has no concept of time.'

Gardner sighed. No point in the next question, but she tried anyway. 'So, no idea when our victims left the party?'

'Afraid not...'

Gardner thought.

Everyone was off their heads.

Holier-than-thou, Vivianne! A potential first from Oxford and piano recitals. No chance that bag couldn't possibly be hers, could it? Yet here they had a rogue boyfriend, recreational drugs...

Who were you, young lady? Were you led astray, or maybe there's a twist in the tale... maybe you did the leading?

Gardner probed Barnett further, but it was clearly now time for legwork.

'Brilliant work. Let's get this wrapped up. Go to that address and take Lucy; she'll be good with the youngsters. Get names, addresses, the lot. Start piecing together the entire evening from the moment Vivianne and Ralphie got there. When we've the names and addresses of everyone that was at the party, contact HC and have everyone prioritise talking to the revellers involved. A statement from *everyone*. I don't care how blurry it is – they can rack their brain cells – the ones that are still functioning, that is. If we're watertight until the moment they left that party, the rest will fall into place. I'll join in after I've spoken to Sebastian Harrington.'

'Sebastian Harrington? The Tory? What the hell has he got to—'

'Lucy will fill you in.'

After the call, Gardner sat up straight in her car seat, positivity surging through her. Not only had she been spared the need to bollock Barnett, but he'd just delivered a golden lead.

Smiling, she glanced at the passenger seat, forgetting for a moment that she was alone in the car. Rice was following her in his own vehicle.

Turning her eyes back to the road, she sighed, admitting to herself that it hadn't been Rice she was offering a smile.

No.

That smile had been for someone else.

An absent friend.

Someone who, like her, so relished the chase for the truth.

Enough, she thought. *It's better this way, Emma.*

You know damn well it is.

22

'Of all the bloody things,' Kerry had said, clutching her forehead. 'Threatening to drive him off somewhere in a sodding response vehicle! And now he's bloody dead!'

'I didn't know he was about to be killed.'

'Ah... that's okay then.'

After Kerry had listened to his side of the story, she told him to stay put until the investigative team tasked with Nathan Cummings's murder showed up to grill him on his whereabouts following the confrontation.

Riddick didn't stay put.

Of all the foolish things...

He shook his head.

You can't bloody help yourself, can you?

He alternated between bashing the steering wheel and rubbing at his sweaty forehead as he drove.

After he strayed slightly into the opposite lane and was forced to swerve back at the sudden appearance of a gung-ho biker, he hit his forehead instead. *Calm down, you pillock; an accident is all you bloody well need!*

He *should've* stayed. Had he anything to worry about, really? He'd returned home immediately following the witnessed argument with Cummings. Automatic Number Plate Recognition would pick him up, and his alibi, Claire, would solidify his innocence. Besides, there wouldn't be any forensic evidence linking him to a murder...

Still, he couldn't spend the whole day under investigation. Tied down. Frustrated. Begging to keep the badge.

No, all of that bloody soap opera would have to wait.

Because he knew who'd killed Nathan Cummings.

And he didn't like it.

Not one little bit.

23

Gardner had researched Sebastian Harrington early doors. She'd seen the cold figure in grainy photographs and listened to his bullish tone in recorded comments. A staunch believer in privatisation and free-market principles, Sebastian had been a very vocal, and rather aggressive, flag-waver for deregulation in the eighties.

Her research had churned up countless images of him clapping over-enthusiastically to Thatcher's most famous line on being stubborn, 'The lady's not for turning.' She'd burned her ears with some of his most well-known rants. Many seemed to condemn the idea of society, and that social responsibility could hold back progress and drive back Britain.

Still, O'Brien's anecdote in the incident room regarding her friend's fifteen-year-old son Jake had stuck with Gardner, and so she wasn't as shocked as she would've been when confronted with a man who appeared to have completely changed his persona.

Sebastian had the gated drive, the Victorian-esque décor and the ridiculous amount of living space that no family, no matter how big, needed. Especially considering that Sebastian was a

hildless widower. He still dressed sternly in a tight tailored black
uit and sported perfectly cropped white hair.

But as soon as he shook their hands, the sternness in his
presentation seemed to melt away, and he moved his eyes warmly
and enthusiastically between Gardner and Rice. He shook their
hands, not too firmly, and kept hold of Gardner's. 'Thank you.
Everything we have, we owe to people like you.'

A strange opening statement, and one that Gardner didn't
understand fully, nor really know how to respond to.

'Thank you, sir.'

'Enough with the sir. Seb please.' He still had Gardner's hand.
'You're the heartbeat. What you do... you keep the people safe in
their houses, the children happy in their schools. Both of you.' He
took his hand back from her. 'All of you.'

It'd be easy to consider his compliments well-rehearsed fluff,
standard from most politicians, but he simply sounded too
genuine for that to be the case.

'Nice of you to say so, sir – wish everyone shared that view...'

'They do,' he said. 'They *really* do. Sometimes, you know,
things just get lost in translation.'

*Is that what you think was happening to you in your earlier years,
when you were condemning the ideas of social responsibility? That your
ideology was getting lost in translation? Or did you come to realise that
you were wrong?*

He led them into a wide hallway, adorned with expensive
framed art.

'Tea? Cake?'

Considering Barnett's earlier discoveries regarding the party,
Gardner was keen to just get a move on. 'We're okay, thank you,
Seb. It's maybe best we sit down.'

'Sounds serious...' Sebastian said.

Gardner and Rice exchanged a glance.

Does he actually know about Ralphie yet?

'It is,' Rice said.

'It's not about my nephew, is it? About the trouble he's in?'

No, he doesn't. But how can he not? Why wouldn't his sister hav *contacted him?*

'Can we sit please, Seb?' Gardner insisted.

'Of course,' Sebastian said, leading them into a large lounge 'Unfortunately, despite my best efforts, the boy has a waywar nature. An attraction to poor behaviour. I blame my father, Bart holemew. He was drawn to misdeed, too. Ralphie has those gene I have to say I dodged that bullet! Always been a goody two-shoe myself!'

Sebastian pointed down at a large chaise longue covered wit floral patterns. Gardner and Rice sat. The former MP didn't. H hovered in front of them, suddenly looking rather pale.

'Please sit, Seb,' Gardner said. 'There's something we need—'

'Listen, and you've heard this right from the horse's mouth. I'm not coming to his aid again. I just can't. I've told Evie, *no*. So, if it about that, you've my word. He must learn the hard way. The we of patience has run dry. Now, I must insist on cake. Really, I mus Not just for you, but for me, too. All this stress over Ralphie ha worn me down, and I need the sugar. Also, it's carrot, you know And it comes with tea. That, too, is non-negotiable. Will that sui you, DCI Gardner?'

Gardner nodded. 'Yes, please.'

He turned an inquiring eye to Rice.

'Go on then, thanks.'

'Great!' He clapped his hands and then went to his kitchen.

'Jesus wept,' Rice said after Sebastian had exited. 'He mus have been visited by three ghosts on Christmas Eve.'

'It's four,' Gardner said.

'Four what?'

'Ghosts, you dickhead.'

'It's clearly three. I read it at school. The ghost of Christmas Present—'

'I'll stop you there. Save you time. It's four. His best friend, Marley.'

Rice looked irritated. 'That doesn't count.'

'Why not? He wasn't alive in the version I read, so he was a ghost.'

'Whatever. Still, it's bullshit. I reckon Harrington's putting all this on. Ask anyone in Knaresborough or Harrogate. No way that man can change.'

'He's very convincing.'

'He's a politician. He's skilled at it. And he's desperate. Look at this place.' He opened his arms up and gestured around at the cavernous living room with its curved ceiling, and small, but still expensive-looking, chandelier. 'Nothing would make you lonelier faster. Everyone is always nice when they need a friend.'

'Bloody hell – it's a shame you don't need one then. Bloody thaw you out.'

'Very funny.'

'Now, listen... I'm breaking the news to him gently.'

'Maybe find out more about what's depleted his sugar levels first?'

Gardner shook her head. 'You really think everyone is completely thick apart from you, don't you?'

Rice paused and looked thoughtful. 'Do I have to answer that?'

Fortunately, Sebastian returned. He placed the china in front of them, poured them both a tea and then nodded down at the carrot cake, which was served on two small dishes with spoons. 'Made it myself.' He did look rather proud as he sat on the sofa opposite.

'Apparently you're a dab hand at *Mario Kart*.'

Sebastian lifted an eyebrow. 'Who told you?'

'A child at the social club has a relative in my team. Speaks very highly of you.'

Sebastian smiled. 'Really? Nice to know.' He took a sip of tea. There was suddenly a glow in his face that hadn't been there prior to exiting the room.

Still, she was about to bring his moment of happiness crashing down. Needs must. 'So, what was the issue with Ralphie that was causing your anxiety?'

'Ah... so his latest misdemeanour. Isn't that the reason you're here?'

'You said he was in trouble?' Gardner flipped open her notebook.

'He'd been caught stealing on campus. *Again.*'

Gardner was confused. 'Again?' They'd already completed a thorough background check on Ralphie – there'd been nothing on his record about stealing. 'How many times had this happened? What was he stealing?'

Sebastian sighed. 'It's happened twice... that I know of. From the newsagents on campus for the first time. The second time the bookshop. I had a word with the powers that be at Hull University after the newsagent fiasco, and they stopped the investigation.'

'So, you influenced them?' Rice's tone was sharp.

Sebastian looked unfazed. He'd have suffered far worse attacks in his career. 'It was a request, not a demand.'

'But they interpreted it as the latter,' Rice continued.

Sebastian shrugged. 'You'll have to ask them.'

Gardner looked at Rice. *Give over Phil. This man has stood up in the Houses of Parliament. He's looking at you like you're blowing kisses.*

'They said that as long as it didn't happen again, they'd keep it under wraps. It was genuinely a polite request.'

'Sounds inappropriate.'

'Ruining his academic career sounded worse. Besides, I told Evie, Max and Ralphie himself, that I wouldn't be doing it again. He'd had his last chance. But he didn't listen. This time, textbooks, too! I mean. Ridiculous! Not the rebel's first choice.'

'Maybe he did it to sell them?' Gardner said.

'He doesn't need the money. No... he's just attracted to trouble, that one. I'm not the first person to say it, either. Of course, it could all just be a cry for attention.'

'What makes you say that?' Gardner asked.

'Have you met his parents?' Sebastian asked.

Swingers. Self-absorbed. Gardner nodded.

'Still. It'd never work. That cry for attention. The parents just run to me, anyway. Well, no more. They were warned. No. The boy must learn, and if it costs him his university place – then so be it.'

'Sorry, but could I ask when you found out about this *second* incident?'

'About three days back... but she's contacted me *many* times since. Begging and begging. I won't relent this time.' He took his phone from his pocket. He showed the blank screen. 'Look – switched off. Has been for over twenty-four hours. It's either that or block her! I can't cope any more. Just a moment. Let me switch it back on and I'll tell you when it started. Wait... here we go.'

The phone went into a frenzy of beeping. 'Insane. She's so incessant. There's a voicemail here from four in the bloody morning!'

Gardner and Rice exchanged a look.

'Seb, please put the phone down. There's something you need to know.'

'Sorry... wait... all these text messages. Let me just... Look. Five in the morning! Let me read it to you, show you what I have to suffer.'

'Seb... *please.*' Her tone was insistent. 'Put the phone down. I've some bad news.'

Sebastian lifted his head, simultaneously moving the phone to his side. The paleness from earlier had returned to his face. 'You're not making much sense.'

'I'm so sorry, Seb. There was an incident late last night at the Knaresborough cemetery involving Ralphie. I imagine that's why your sister was phoning late.'

'A cemetery... What's he done now?'

'I'm really sorry to tell you this, but Ralphie is dead.'

Sebastian shook his head from side to side, his eyes falling. 'There must be a mistake...'

'I'm afraid not,' Gardner said. 'Both him and his girlfriend, Vivianne, I'm afraid.'

'I saw something about it on the news. Potential murders... but no names... no names.' Sebastian's hand went to his mouth. 'God. I switched my phone off. I'm a bloody fool. A bloody, bloody fool.' He squeezed his eyes shut and lowered his head.

24

1980

Dean struggled to walk. Although the drink played some part in his, it wasn't the complete story. It was the unbearable weight of grief that was most to blame.

Penny had only been gone two days – it wasn't her funeral until next week – and yet, Dean already felt he'd suffered for an entire lifetime.

Keith, suited and smoking, as was always the case, was leading him into an industrial estate.

Dean looked up at the peeling name in red paint above the workshop.

Howie's Garage.

Not that Howard Walters was here any more. He'd a new place up near Aspin. Quite a prosperous one at that, too. His old workshop was yet to fall into new hands. Such was the sign of the times that so many places stood empty.

Keith rolled the shutters up, turned and put a hand on Dean's shoulder. 'Are you having second thoughts? I can't have you regreting this.'

'Regret is the least of my concerns right now,' Dean said.

'Aye... I can imagine.' Keith smoked; the tip of his cigarette flared.

'I *think* I need this.'

Keith pumped out a cloud of smoke. 'Aye. Yes. I imagine you do. Shit... it's all I'd be able to think about. But, you know, even if you don't do this, I'll make sure it's done, anyway. And the money for your daughter's funeral, your mortgage payments, *everything*... it's all covered. And there will be work for you too, Dean, when you feel ready. A great tragedy this. An awful one. But neither of us is to blame. Once we put it right, and then we all move on. In silence. It's all we can do.'

Move on? How is that even possible?

Dean nodded just so the bastard would take his hand back from his shoulder.

Still lumbering like a bear, Dean followed Keith carefully into Howie's Garage. The light was dim. He kept his eyes on the ground, but still struggled to avoid clipping the strewn engine parts as he moved.

The smell crept up his nostrils and clawed at the back of his throat.

Engine oil. Fuel.

He stopped, closed his eyes, and was back standing in the swamp of emergency vehicles, looking down at that gurney. Penny's pale face, her half-opened eyes... *No, that's not right. She's been covered, hadn't she?*

He opened his eyes and took a deep breath.

'Do you need another minute?' Keith said.

Dean took another deep breath. 'No. I *do* need this.'

'I know. Which is why I called you... which is why I wanted to help...'

Nothing to do with helping yourself, eh, Keith? Dean thought. *Give me closure, quickly, so that when the police fail to find the killer, I don continue hounding them and hounding them... keeping the whole sorry thing alive for time immemorial... keeping the pressure on you... because if it ever came out that it was one of your men driving that vehicle... well... what would that do to you?*

Better to get it all tidied away now, eh, Keith?

But don't worry, I'm taking your scraps. Your money. This vengeance.

It seems I'm as weak as Stell always thought I was.

'You know that your Estelle will also come to appreciate this closure,' Keith said. 'I remember that lass well... a fiery one! So, I know that she'll come around to what you're about to do in time. And the money. Everyone always comes around to the money. I'll visit after the funeral, of course – see if there's anything else that can be done. A copper investigation that rattles on and on forever is good for no one, least of all you two. Justice needs to be swift. I'm sure she'll be seeing things a lot more clearly in a couple of days.'

Would she though? Could anything ever be clearer than her current hatred for him? Despising him for drinking, while their daughter lost her life several hundred metres away?

He continued to follow Keith to the back of the dim unit, wondering what the closure offered to him this evening would feel like. Would his soul be forever leaden with his actions?

Probably.

But would he be able to look into Penny's eyes in that photograph at the funeral?

He hoped so. God, he really did.

Dean could hear something deeply unpleasant now. And, when Keith opened the door at the back of the unit, he quickly realised that it was the sound of pain.

He shivered.

Keith led him out into a small, walled-off area that served this unit and four adjacent ones. The walls were high and topped with barbed wire.

Safe from prying eyes.

The pained moaning now made Dean's skull throb, and he kept his drunken head lowered as he moved, stepping over cigarette butts and bottles. There was a powerful stench of piss, but Dean was rather glad of it. It helped mask the smell of engine oil and petrol.

They stopped at a huddle of three men, all with their backs turned. One twisted and nodded at Keith.

Keith smiled at Dean. 'All yours, fella.'

Surreal.

Two days ago, Dean may've been out of work, but he'd had a family who loved him.

Now, he was all alone, on the verge of cold-blooded murder.

The huddle parted slightly, and Dean saw Neil Clark kneeling.

Blood and tears were causing Neil to blink continuously, but he couldn't reach up and clear his eyes, because a rubber car tyre pinned his arms to his side.

The stench of fuel was suddenly strong again.

Dean felt a cold pressure on his chest.

Neil wasn't just blinking from tears and blood; his eyes were streaming from the petrol they'd doused him in.

Dean looked at Keith, who was still smiling.

'It's called necklacing. I read about it. Common in South Africa. It's effective and sends a message. The little shit deserves nothing less – wouldn't you agree?'

Dean couldn't answer any question; the cold pressure on his chest seemed to intensify.

He imagined Stella's response. *Barbaric, Dean. This is barbaric.*

The weeping and moaning continued. Neil was muttering something, rather incomprehensibly.

'What's he saying?' Dean said, forcing the words out.

'He's begging for his life.'

But he's taken everything from me. Everything. How can it be barbaric? And how does he dare weep and beg for his life? This man... driving out of his mind on drugs... out of his senses...

'And hit my little girl... my little girl.'

Neil looked up at him. Blood dribbled out of his mouth. He said something, but again it was incomprehensible.

Estelle's voice crept into his head. *And you, Dean, are you any different? Driving pissed... It could just have easily been you that hit a little girl.*

'No... no... *no!*' Dean said.

He felt the eyes of Keith and his men turn on him, but he still couldn't shut Estelle's voice up. *You're no different from the man you're going to burn alive. No different. Do what needs to be done, but then turn the flame on yourself.*

'Give the word,' Keith said. 'And I can end this for you—'

'No,' Dean hissed. 'I want to hear him say it! I want to hear this bastard admit to what he did.'

Keith snorted. 'Look at the state of him! You won't get a word of sense. Pickled. Pickled on the shite he was supposed to be selling.' He leaned over and spat on him.

Dean closed his eyes. It barely felt like a day since his daughter had started secondary school. Wonderful times! Long-term employment. His relationship with Estelle had still been passionate. Penny had been full of ambition and energy.

He'd cracked it.

Or so he'd thought.

Life was good at its lies – making you believe the unbelievable.

Until the reality... no employment, high mortgage rates and a government that couldn't give a—

'It has to be *now*,' Keith said, pushing something into his hand.

Dean opened his eyes and looked down at the Ronson Varaflame lighter.

Neil wailed.

Penny's killer was so young. In fact, he probably wasn't much older than Penny had been. Dean stared into the beaten kid's swollen eyes. 'You killed her... my daughter...'

Neil was neither shaking his head nor nodding.

'He's a mess,' Keith hissed. 'Put him out of his misery.'

Dean lit the lighter but kept his eyes on Neil's. 'Admit it... Admit it...'

The lad dribbled blood. His head slumped back down.

'Please...' Dean said. 'Tell me the truth.'

'Now!' Keith said. 'Or *I* do it.'

Dean took a deep breath. He leaned forward and brought the naked flame closer towards the tyre...

Keith, and his men, moved backwards. 'Make sure you move back, quick, too... *after...*'

An inch away from the tyre, the vapour from the fuel stung Dean's eyes. He closed them and he was back in that swamp of emergency vehicles again.

Except this time, his daughter was covered on that gurney.

This was the truth.

Lines burnt into the road from locking tyres.

Blood being diluted by the thrashing rain.

And his daughter, Penny, being washed away down that hill.

Washed away... forever.

Penny.

His daughter.

Washed away.

Don't Daddy. Don't.

Dean stood, turned and pocketed the lighter. 'It's just not me.'

Keith nodded. 'That's okay. I get it. Stand back.'

Dean walked away and when he reached the door back into the unit, there was a whoosh, and everything glowed.

He was halfway into the unit before the screaming died away.

Like his daughter.

Washed away.

25

2024

Riddick came out of the lift on the fifth floor. He walked down the corridor, then turned on to another. Ahead, he sighted the flat he was after and approached.

The door was ajar.

He hovered outside for a moment, listening to the television blaring away inside, and smelled the stale tobacco.

Riddick prodded the door with his foot. The door swung open and he stepped in. 'Knock knock.'

There was a chesty cough, followed by the sound of spitting and then, 'Who's there?'

Riddick entered and closed the door behind him. He'd been here before, so he headed past the bedroom door on his left, the tiny kitchen on his right, to the lounge up ahead. En route, he screwed his face up over the black mould on the wall.

At the entrance to the lounge, he regarded Keith Fields sitting in a tatty La-Z-Boy. He was just in the process of stubbing out a roll-up in an ashtray already piled high. The old gangster grinned exposing his rotting teeth.

'Still alive then,' Riddick said.

'Ticking over, yes.'

Riddick raised an eyebrow. 'Ticking is an exaggeration. Intermittent pulsing by the looks of you.'

Keith looked more and more emaciated every time Riddick saw him. His face, lined with wrinkles caused by constant smoking and drinking, seemed to fold in on itself. That burn mark on his cheek was still clear as day, though. Rumours were that he'd stubbed a cigarette out on his own face after losing a bet. The burn had then become infected and by the time the doctors had it under control, it'd eaten away a chunk of his cheek and left a large hollow in his face. Riddick doubted he'd done it to himself, but Keith was happy to keep the story alive – machismo had always been important in his role.

'To what do I owe the pleasure?' Keith said and laughed. His laugh was chesty and caused another fit of coughing.

Riddick rolled his eyes and walked over to the archaic television set on the floor. It must have been from the late seventies. He pulled the plug out.

'Oi. I wanted to know what the banker was going to offer! The bastard would've dealt, I'm sure. Looked weak as piss.'

'You know, it's best to close your front door and lock it, especially when you're a burned-out former gangster with more hits out on him than Billy the Kid.'

He grinned again. 'No one would dare.'

Riddick looked around the dishevelled lounge. There were a couple of pizza boxes in the corner, and empty beer bottles strewn around. 'I think you're right. It does look a major health risk for the assassin.'

Keith laughed and then coughed again. This coughing fit went on for some time, forcing him to lean forward in his La-Z-Boy as he hacked up phlegm into the overflowing ashtray.

'Nice. Thanks for that... Jesus, how the mighty have fallen, eh?'

Keith leaned back and winked. 'Appearance isn't always the reality, eh?' He pounded his chest. 'Still working just fine in here.'

'Working with what, though? Cholera? Tetanus? Look, I'm pretty sure you've black mould in your hall. I suggest getting it looked at.'

'I smoke fifty a day,' Keith said. He thumped his chest a second time. 'I lined these lungs, young man. No shite getting through that barrier.'

Riddick sighed. 'Always nice to catch up and listen to your suggestions on healthy living... but that's not why I'm here. You messed up, fella.'

Keith snorted. 'You think? I used to have an empire.' He reached over to the table for his tobacco and his papers.

'Well, that's one word for it.'

'I lost it to outsiders. Worst thing they ever did was open our bloody borders. Look at it. Foreigners marching around, now – stealing our industries.'

'Dealing drugs, eh? What a wonderful, sustainable industry. Did you pay tax on that?'

'Not my point.'

'No, you're telling me the European Union ruined your life. I assume you voted Brexit?'

'Who didn't?' Keith said, pointing in his direction.

'Quite a few people, I believe. Anyway, how is Brexit going for you?'

He looked around his room. 'Slowly.' He laughed again and finished with a cough.

'Nathan Cummings died last night, Keith.'

Keith continued rolling his cigarette. He chuckled and coughed away from his loose tobacco. 'With news like that, please do come around as often as you like. How did he cop it?'

'Kind of hoping you'd tell me. You arranged it, after all.'

Keith looked up at him with his jaundiced eyes, regarded him, and then said, 'Ha! I think you need glasses, son. Have you not noticed I'm at the bottom of the toilet?'

'Yes... and it all feels a little too... what's the word? Yes... *obvious*. It all feels a little obvious. Contrived...'

'Don't know what you're on about. I know that I'm not skulking in the shadows, stalking prey, or paying Russian hitmen. I'm in a La-Z-Boy coughing my guts up.'

'You shouldn't have done it, Keith.'

Keith leaned over and spat in the ashtray again. 'You always were a card, Paul. But I didn't do it. Why the concern, anyway? Did you like him or something?'

'Between you and him, I'd rather take *you* to lunch... so make of that what you will. But, Keith, it isn't your place to go around killing.'

'I'd never do such a thing,' Keith said, looking up and winking.

'You're no stranger to it. Is there something you want to confess to me?'

'Not you, no. Your old boss, though. Good ole Anders. Now I'd be happy to bend his ear on a few things.'

Riddick felt his blood running cold. *Don't bite. He knows all about the close connection you had to Anders.*

'Do you still visit him?'

'Visit him...? What're you talking about? He's dead and you know it.'

'His grave, son. Do you still visit his grave?'

'Never visited it once.'

'You're lying.'

Yes... he was.

'We'd some good times, Anders and me.'

Riddick forced back the irritation. *Don't bite.*

'He once told me you were like him.' He pointed at Riddick.

'Said he'd big plans for you. Told me to watch this space. Never came to much though, did it?'

Riddick struggled to fight off the adrenaline, and a growing sense of nausea. 'Corruption really wasn't my bag. He died disappointed. And alone, might I add.' Another lie. Riddick had been there when he'd taken his last breath. 'I imagine you will too.'

'Newsflash: we all die alone. Anyway, are you sure that corruption isn't your bag? A little birdie told me something you got up to of late.'

The nausea intensified. *Surely he can't know about Ronnie Haller?*

Not so much that the man took his family from him, everyone knew that, but rather...

Does he know I had him killed in prison?

'Bloody hell, son. That got you, eh? You look like you've seen a ghost.'

'What the hell are you talking about?' Riddick raised his voice.

'Easy there, son... just that you got all macho with Nathan Cummings in a cop car, rather like you're doing now.'

Inwardly, Riddick breathed a sigh of relief.

Keith continued, 'You best be careful that they don't start looking at you!'

'Was this little birdie the same birdie that you had kill Nathan in the park last night?'

'Ha!' Keith said. 'Look, I get you're pissed off because *you* wanted to kill him.'

'No. I'm just pissed off because I don't like you' – he pointed at Keith – 'and I don't like folk taking the law into their own hands.' Inside, he felt the hypocrisy in his claim, but stood straight and tried to keep it from his demeanour.

Keith lit his cigarette, took a long pull on it, tilted his head back and exhaled. The smoke rose in an upward trajectory. 'Two final thoughts, son.'

'Call me son again and I'll break you before you even get to the first thought.'

Keith smiled and nodded. 'First – I'm a little old man without a pot to piss in. How the hell am I going to get up off my haemorrhoid-ridden arse and hack down Bradford's most wanted? And it's not like I can afford a hitman, is it?' He paused for another longer drag on his fag. *How did that not make him cough, when a mere snort or laugh would antagonise his chest?*

'Second,' Keith continued. 'Like you, I'm glad he's dead. And, to be honest, I wish it had been me. I'd have gutted him like an animal. Have you forgotten that the bastard carved open my boy's chest? Ah... but how could you forget?'

Riddick flinched.

'Because you were there, weren't you? And if you'd been doing your job properly – it'd never have happened, would it, *son*?'

Riddick stepped close to Keith and hit the roll-up out of his hand. It flew across the room.

'My final thoughts, you murderous old bastard.' He gestured around him. 'First... this, *all this*, is a ruse... a disguise. You've not topped. A man like you never stops. Second... yes, I remember.' He placed his hands on the arms of the La-Z-Boy and leaned in, so the bastard could feel his breath on his face. 'Not a day goes past that I don't think about Arthur... about what Cummings did to him. So, don't misunderstand me here' – he leaned in closer to whisper – 'regarding Nathan, good riddance. You've taken away my problem. However, this is now an issue for you.'

'How so?' Keith said, trying to maintain eye contact with Riddick despite the proximity of their faces.

'Because *you're* now my problem, Keith. You put Arthur into that life... *you*—'

'I bought him a house. More than his bitch of a mother ever did—'

'That'll be the mother who loves him dearly... treasures him That's more than money could ever buy.'

'She babied him. I tried to give him independence.'

'You fed him to the wolves.'

'Bollocks.'

'He's with his mother now... and that's where he'll stay, free from you.'

'Or?'

'Or I'll put an end to your world' – Riddick stood up straight again and looked around – 'in all its glory. No more. What you do blows back on your son. Everything stops now.'

Keith was shaking his head, sneering. 'You know nothing.'

'I know *that*' – Riddick pointed to smoke rising from the corner of the room where the fag had landed before – 'is a major problem.'

'Shit,' Keith said, stumbling to his feet.

Riddick left the flat with one thought on his mind.

I should've just let him go up in flames.

26

With this new information provided by Sebastian, Gardner opted to revisit Ralphie's parents. Fortunately, this time, there was no sex party. Max and Evie Parks appeared more crestfallen, and more in keeping with what you'd imagine bereaved parents to look like.

Gardner didn't start the interview with Sebastian's claims, though; instead, she began by quizzing them over the drugs recovered in Vivianne's room. They were steadfast in Ralphie's innocence.

'So, you believe the drugs must have belonged to Vivianne, and that Ralphie didn't know of this?' Rice asked.

'I never said that! I only said that I don't believe they belonged to Ralphie,' Max said.

'But if they didn't belong to him, then they must have been Vivianne's.'

Max shrugged. 'I don't know. That, or someone else she knows perhaps?'

Evie, who'd offered little so far, decided now to weigh in. 'I always knew there was something with Viv. You know, I was fond of her and all, but come on, no one is that good, are they?'

No one is that good! Maybe not in the eyes of people who threw sex parties in the house in which their son was staying, but Gardner had met plenty of people who she'd defined as 'very good'.

'So, what're you suggesting?' Gardner asked.

Evie shrugged. 'Maybe she led Ralphie astray?'

'But Vivianne wasn't in Hull when Ralphie committed those offences.'

Evie's eyes widened.

'Those?' Max said.

'Yes. The theft from the newsagent and then the bookshop.'

Max shook his head. 'There's only one outstanding offence. The bookshop. The newsagent accusation was rescinded because it was bollocks. Who've you been talking to?'

'We're the police, you know?' Rice said. 'We can access important information. Wouldn't it be wise for you to share everything with us?'

Gardner looked at Evie. 'We've been talking to Sebastian. Your brother.'

Evie shook her head and looked down.

Max guffawed. 'Well, that explains it! Have you done your research on Seb?'

'Again,' Rice said, 'I'd like to point out that we're the police.'

'I don't like your tone, officer.'

'And—'

'Max,' Gardner said, cutting off Rice, 'would you be able to tell us about your son's offences please?'

Max wasn't finished. 'Seb has a god-complex! Wikipedia. Seriously. Just have a look.'

'The offences?' Gardner pressed.

Max sighed and then described the incidences, playing down

his son's poor behaviour. 'Boys will be boys, you know. I mean, I've got a few stories I could tell. I'm sure we all have...'

Boys will be boys. I'm sorry, Gardner thought, *I don't view the world through the same lens as you.*

'Is there anything else regarding your son you'd like to share with us?' Gardner asked.

'Like what?'

'Misdemeanours?' Rice said.

'Look, *we* didn't hide this from you. The newsagent one was bollocks. He just forgot to pay for his magazine. Happens! The second one, which is also bollocks, is under investigation, so we'd assume you knew about that, anyway.'

'If he only forgot to pay for his magazine,' Rice said, 'then why did Seb need to get involved?'

Max waved his hand. 'All that old bastard did was speed the process up in the first instance. Outcome would've been the same, anyway!'

'In which case,' Gardner said, looking at Evie, 'why be so insistent that he helped again? Especially if you're so certain, Max' – she looked back at him – 'that the second investigation is flawed too?'

'What's so difficult to understand? Just for speed. Get the bloody thing out of the way,' Max said. 'But, no! The old man is a fake. Can't even help his own nephew out. Claims it's best for him to learn from his mistakes. What mistakes? Forgetting to pay for a few bloody books? He can take his holier-than-thou attitude and stick it up his arse!' Max said. 'All he did was drag out an unnecessary situation that embarrasses the whole family!'

Following the interview, Rice and Gardner chatted in her car.

'Arrogant tossers,' Rice said. 'Pompous.'

'You can't help but feel that they're more concerned about how this situation reflects on them rather than the loss they've actually experienced.'

'No wonder their kid went off the rails. Makes me angry.'

'I know. I could tell. Try and keep your emotions in check, Phil.'

'Aye. Shit. Anyway, dare I say I preferred our time with Tory toff Seb?'

'Carrot cake will do that.'

Rice laughed. 'Yes... he certainly lowered my guard with that one. But still, there was something else... You know, it takes a lot to change my mind about someone.'

'Really?'

He rolled his eyes. 'But I did. By the end of our chat with Seb, I felt his sense of guilt in the room. It was tangible. Do you know what I'm saying?'

'Yes. Seb seemed more devastated by this boy's death than his own parents.'

'I know... Strange, huh? That man back in that gated bloody property is desperate for atonement, while these two are desperate to hold on to their privileges and hedonistic lifestyle above all.'

'You know, you really seem to be getting more thoughtful and sensitive. Have you started reading?'

Rice laughed again. 'Yes, I finally learned.' He then shrugged. 'Just takes people a long time to get to know the real me. I'm quite guarded.'

Gardner laughed. 'Okay, let's end the conversation before you tell me about your immense love for fluffy animals, and romcoms.'

'Actually—'

'Please, I beg of you.'

She checked in quickly with Barnett. The host of last night's party had been identified as nineteen-year-old Ethan Williams.

'd kicked off around 7.15 p.m. and Vivianne and Ralphie had been
n attendance.

'Ralphie brought unicorn ecstasy tablets with him.'

In her head, she could see Max Parks' face dropping when he
inally heard this. *The shame.*

'He just gave that up?' Gardner asked.

'No. While I was in his kitchen talking to him, I spotted a
couple of loose tablets on the table. He'd overlooked them. He
wanted to make it very clear they belonged to Ralphie, and he'd
never touched them himself.'

'Did you believe him?'

'No. You should see the state of him. He'd clearly sampled
hem. However, he was fairly convincing when throwing Ralphie
under the bus.'

*How did you get the drugs, Ralphie? Are you connected to county
lines and the supply chain in Bradford? Is this what cost you your life?*

'It was Ethan who phoned the ambulance for Charlotte
Hughes and Adam Briggs after they passed out on the sofa. The
call went in at 11.35 p.m. and the ambulance arrived nine minutes
later. Just prior to this, everyone apart from Ethan left. Vivianne
and Ralphie among them.'

'Okay... how far is the cemetery from there?'

'About fifteen minutes.'

'So, it roughly takes us into our two-hour window for the time
of death. Okay, good work, Ray.'

Barnett explained how he'd allocated the list of attendees
Ethan had given him, to members of the team. 'We'll work through
the names. Someone will surely be able to tell us the movements
of the two victims after they left, and tell us if anything untoward
went off at that party.'

'What? Apart from the excessive drug use?'

Barnett laughed. 'Yeah, apart from that. Ethan, himself, claims to have seen nothing out of the ordinary, and that Viv and Ralphie were just behaving as loved-up as usual.'

'Well, let's hope that all this MDMA hasn't turned their brains to Swiss cheese. We need their memory banks. And go easy on them, Ray...' Gardner imagined that there would be a number of anxious and blurry-eyed teenagers, strangled by an MDMA come down, opening their doors to Barnett and co. over the next hour. None of them would be the wiser to the deaths of their two friends – not unless they'd something to hide.

'Yeah, lesson learned. Ethan cried for almost ten minutes after I broke the news to him. I'll go gentle.'

Gardner took some names and addresses down in her note book, and offered to lend a hand, then bid farewell to Barnett until the evening's briefing.

After the call, she filled Rice in. 'Okay, hop in your car, and follow me.'

Her phone rang. She saw it was Monika, her au pair, and looked at her watch. The kids would still be at school so this call was unusual. Her mouth went dry. 'Monika, is everything okay? Are the kids okay?'

'Yes...'

Gardner took a deep breath, relishing a moment of relief.

'There's someone here to see you,' Monika said. 'James Wright?'

James Wright? 'I don't know who that is. What does he look like?'

'Older... white hair... smartly dressed.'

Gardner's moment of relief was gone. Instead, her heart started to race. 'You didn't let him in, did you?' She looked at Rice as she asked this and saw the concern in his expression.

'What's wrong?' he mouthed.

'Sorry,' Monika said. 'He insisted.'

She gulped, pressing the phone tighter to her ear. 'Monika, I don't know—'

'He's your schoolfriend. He showed me a picture of you with another woman... younger. Says that all three of you were close...'

Schoolfriend? What schoolfriend? And why would one of my school-friends be up north?

Something was really off here.

'Listen, Monika. I need—'

'He seems nice?'

'Just listen. I don't know who James Wright is. It's best you just get out of the house until I'm there.'

Silence. *Shit!* She was scared. 'Monika?'

'Err... yes?'

'Out of the house.'

'Okay.'

'I'm coming home.'

27

Every second of every single day, Riddick felt his destructive needs.

But it wasn't every day that he felt them intensifying so quickly.

A definite cue to seek help.

First, he'd try fish and chips and fresh air in a quiet park to gather his thoughts. But if that failed, then he'd have to seek Daz.

He sat on a park bench and watched a man throwing a ball for his cocker spaniel, owner and dog looking blissfully happy. Over to his right, a young mother was holding a toddler's hand as they wound their way up the path towards the play park. Again, they seemed content.

Happy... content...

Why were such states unavailable to him?

After casting his chips aside, he rubbed at his throbbing temples with greasy fingers.

Stop being ridiculous! You don't know what's going on in any of their lives; you can't be sure that everything is perfect.

He resisted the urge to stamp his feet and shout. Such was the frustration he felt over being such a self-pitying, pathetic bastard.

He had a partner who loved him, for Christ's sake! Who was pregnant with his child!

Another chance at life, you ungrateful dickhead.

He clenched his fist and gently thumped his skull. *Stop it with this bullshit. This paranoia...*

Taking a deep breath, he closed his eyes and leaned back, and let the sun warm his face. Then he counted his breaths. A method taught to him by a doctor.

Five minutes.

Five more minutes.

You get back up, you go back to Kerry and those investigating Nathan's death. Apologise to them, say you'd some kind of panic attack when you heard about Nathan. Provide a statement, tell them that starting that car to intimidate him had been a mistake. You take your medicine for that one.

Then... then, you go home, and you build that life... because Paul, just because you had your last life taken away from you, doesn't mean you're not worth another.

Does it?

A series of images burned through his rationalisations. Ronnie Haller lying dead on the prison shower floor. Arthur Fields, his chest carved, looking into his eyes – asking him why he'd not protected him. Then, and this was the one that brought the shortest and sharpest intake of oxygen, Gardner turning her back on him when she'd found out what he'd done.

He opened his eyes.

Ahead, the dog walker was looking grumpily around for a missing ball. The mother was nursing her crying toddler who'd slipped and grazed their knee.

After rising to his feet, he reached into his pocket, opened his phone and clicked onto to his phone book.

He went down to G.

His finger hovered over *Gardner*. His phone rang, cutting off his intention.

Roni Fields.

Arthur's mother.

He answered the phone. 'Roni?'

Roni was crying. She sounded beside herself. Riddick couldn't understand her.

'Roni, what's wrong?'

'Paul... Paul...' She coughed his name out between sobs.

Riddick jogged towards the car park. 'Where're you? Home?'

'It's Arthur... my baby.'

'What about him? Is he okay?'

'My baby... my baby.'

Riddick's jog turned to a sprint.

28

There was only one thing on Gardner's mind as she drove to her home.

James Wright... old schoolfriend... who are you really?

Monika wasn't outside her house.

Where are you? I bloody told you...

Heart thumping, Gardner tried her front door. It was open.

She saw Monika on the bottom step, trembling. 'He's gone.'

'When?'

'It must have been when I phoned you in the kitchen,' Monika said, rising to her feet.

Why would this mysterious visitor have disappeared before he'd arrived back? Unless he'd simply been here to put the shits up her?

Mission accomplished.

Without closing the front door, Gardner moved forward and put her hand on the young Polish woman's shoulder. 'I'm sorry if I scared you on the phone. I just wanted you to get out.'

Monika nodded. Gardner could feel the poor woman's entire body quivering under her hand.

Gardner had many years of experience locking away her nerves and anxiety from public view, so she didn't physically shake like Monika.

Of course, that didn't stop her insides feeling like they were dissolving into jelly. 'What happened, *exactly*?' She tried to keep her tone gentle after terrifying her with her panicked response earlier.

Monika told the story of James Wright up to her decision to let him in. 'He was nice. Polite. Smartly dressed. White hair. *Older*... than you, but not really old. He said he was your schoolfriend – told you. He sounded *just* like you.'

'Sounded like me?'

'Sounded like. What's the word? Accent. He had the *same* accent. Southern, like you. And rural.'

'West Country?'

Monika shook her head. 'I don't know that. I just know he sounded like you.'

Gardner recalled an evening a while back when Rose had run from the house because she'd been desperate to visit her father in jail. A non-starter, of course, but the mind of a young child could be anything but rational. A man, thank God, had intercepted her before she'd made it to the busy road.

A white-haired man who'd been polite, older, smartly dressed and with her accent.

This didn't feel like a coincidence.

She'd considered the meeting peculiar, but she'd been at the backend of a difficult investigation and Riddick had gone off the rails, so she'd not reflected on this incident a great deal. Until now.

She tried desperately to recall the conversation but caught only fragments. She remembered the man saying he was looking at properties up here and he'd simply been in the right place at the right time regarding Rose.

James Wright?

Was this his real name? She was certain he'd not given his name last time.

Regardless, she'd be researching the hell out of 'James Wright'.

Gardner forced herself from an anxious mode into a rational one. Fear wasn't conducive to the truth. It'd send you down one blind alley after another. 'Let's get you a hot drink, Monika,' Gardner said, leading her au pair towards the kitchen. *Or something stronger if need be.*

There was a knock at the door.

Heart in her mouth, she broke away from Monika and turned, noticing she'd left the door ajar.

Gardner held her breath as the door opened inwards, slowly.

'Lucy?' Gardner sighed with relief.

'Boss?' O'Brien looked concerned. 'Are you okay?'

Gardner nodded. 'Yes. How did you know to come here?'

'I just heard from DI Rice. He said that you were vague and told him to stay put. He said you looked stressed.'

'Yes...' Gardner smiled, noticing as she'd done earlier, O'Brien's eyes. 'I'm fine.'

O'Brien now looked embarrassed. 'Boss... I'm sorry... if I shouldn't have come.'

Feeling overwhelmed by this surprise visit, Gardner moved towards O'Brien, locking onto those interesting eyes. 'No. Thanks Lucy. I appreciate it. You caring.'

And she did. This was the first time in a long time that anybody had really shown any concern for her. Her ex-husband had been useless. There had been Riddick... at least until his demons just got too much for him, for them both.

'I just thought, after last time, you know, with what happened with your brother... I panicked. Thought it was maybe something to do with that.'

'It's not,' Gardner said, placing a hand on O'Brien's upper arm. *At least, I don't think it is.*

She pulled her hand back and broke eye contact with her, momentarily.

Right now, she needed her head back in the game – to find out who'd infiltrated her private world.

'Someone came round here,' Gardner said. 'They claimed to know me, but I've never heard of them.'

'Are they dangerous?'

'I really don't know. It must have something to do with my past as he came from my neck of the woods. When Monika went to phone me, he left.'

'Sounds like whoever this is, is playing games. Boss... I think—'

Gardner held up the palm of her hand to cut her off. 'I'll contact Marsh, don't worry. But I'm not having my kids back here without me, so I won't be at the briefing. Not until I know what's going on.' She looked at her watch. 'The school day is almost over.' She looked at her watch, wondering if Monika was in any fit state to pick them up. 'Jesus, if I can't sort this out quickly, then I'm going to have to find somewhere for Rose and Ana to stay—'

'They can stay with my sister, boss. She's got a massive house and two kids of her own.'

'Thanks Lucy.' Gardner smiled. 'But you should probably ask her first.'

'Don't need to. It's a given.'

'Thanks, you're a gem, but still, I wouldn't want to impose. It'll be fine, I'm sure.' *Besides, last time you helped, you took a blow to the back of the head from my bastard of a brother. Not putting you in danger again.*

After saying goodbye to O'Brien, Gardner went into the kitchen.

The kettle was boiling, and Monika was sitting at the kitchen table, still pale and shaken up.

Thirty minutes until the kids finished school. She'd make Monika a hot drink before phoning Marsh, try to calm her down before picking them up.

Beside the kettle was a photograph, and she recalled Monika's words on the phone before:

'He showed me a picture of you with another woman... younger.'

Heart freezing in her chest, Gardner steadied herself against the work surface. She produced a small gasp, as she grabbed the photograph. She stared at it, but the world around her was swelling, and she closed her eyes.

She took several deep breaths, opened her eyes and turned with the picture in her hand. 'How did this get here? Is this what he showed you at the door?'

Monika's eyes widened. 'Yes. I took it from him. I was going to make him a drink, so I put it by the kettle. I completely forgot all about it.'

Gardner closed her eyes again and leaned back into the work surface.

'What's wrong? Emma?'

But she didn't reply. She was too busy reliving one of the worst moments of her life.

Directly below, a crowd of anxious people had gathered on the estate's children's playground.

At the centre of the crowd, lying on the roundabout, was the body of her detective sergeant.

She opened her eyes and looked at the women in the picture again.

Both her, and DS Collette Willows.

Smiling over glasses of Prosecco.

29

Riddick pulled up at Roni Fields' home in Boroughbridge. The street was quiet. Calm.

He felt anything but.

Exiting the car, he looked up at the house. What was going off? Roni's call had been desperate.

He began by hammering on the front door. No response. He tried the handle, but the door was locked. He pounded again. 'Come on... come on...' He knelt down, opened the letterbox and shouted in, 'Roni! Arthur! It's Paul...' Still no response.

He hopped backwards, lining himself up to charge. He held his breath.

The door opened.

Roni Fields hadn't looked well since the night Arthur had been cut by Nathan, but some colour had returned to her cheeks over the previous months.

Riddick's heart sank when he saw that the colour had gone again.

'What's going on?'

She backed away, turning, and Riddick tracked her down the

hall to the staircase. There, she sagged against the banister, as if every ounce of strength had literally drained from her body.

He touched her shoulder. 'Roni, speak to me.'

She shook her head. 'It's my fault.'

'What is?'

'There's blood. And his eyes... there's something wrong with his eyes.'

Riddick staggered backwards as if she'd hit him in the stomach. 'Where?'

'Bedroom...'

Riddick broke into such a hard sprint that he stumbled several steps up.

'I wasn't watching,' Roni called after him. 'This is my fault. I wasn't bloody watching.'

After getting back to his feet, he scurried to the top of the stairs. In the hallway, he sighted Arthur's bedroom door, slightly ajar...

He couldn't shake off images of that night in Manningham. *Arthur alone in the room's corner, curled up on his side in the foetal position, shirtless. Letters carved into his chest. Oozing.*

Yet, he'd lived.

Then... *but what about now?*

Riddick barged into Arthur's room. 'Arthur!'

He saw the blood first. His hand flew to his mouth.

A moment of relief burst from the terror, like a single ray of light in the gloom, when Arthur coughed, moaned and then murmured something.

Riddick was quick around the side of the bed, looking down on his friend. 'Arthur, it's me, Paul.'

Arthur groaned. His eyes were closed.

Mouth gaping, Riddick looked down at the young man's bloody chest. *Not again? Surely not again.*

When Riddick looked closer, he saw Arthur was bleeding from a multitude of fresh scratches, not knife cuts or old wounds. 'Arthur, who did this?'

Arthur groaned again.

Riddick looked at Arthur's right hand. His fingernails were long and bloody. Skin had built up beneath them.

Have you done this to yourself?

Why? Why'd you do that?

He shook his head and glimpsed Roni looking on from the doorway. 'Why didn't you call an ambulance?'

'Look at his eyes.'

Riddick leaned over the murmuring nineteen-year-old and placed a hand on the quivering boy's face. 'Arthur... it's me. Paul. Look at me.'

He continued to groan.

Riddick tried again, raising his voice this time.

Arthur's eyes burst open. They darted back and forth, taking in their surroundings, before finally settling on Riddick's face.

His pupils were large and dilated.

'What's wrong, Arthur?' Riddick said. *What the bloody hell has happened to you?*

Arthur opened his mouth to speak, but simply emitted a small moan like an injured animal. Drool ran down his cheek.

'Look in the side drawer,' Roni said.

Riddick opened the side drawer. It was empty apart from a small sandwich bag. He grabbed it, held it up, and his breath caught in his throat.

Unicorn ecstasy tablets.

Super strong. Dangerous. The scourge of Bradford. Nathan's batch.

The world is better off without you, Cummings.

Still, Nathan or no Nathan, CID had been too late in stopping unicorn from hitting the streets. It was now in Boroughbridge, and his good friend was in trouble.

Riddick shook the baggie. 'Where did you get these, Arthur?'

Arthur was clearly struggling to comprehend anything, so Riddick raised his eyes to Roni again, directing his question to her.

She shrugged. 'I found him like this. The bag of tablets was next to him. But isn't it obvious?'

Riddick looked back down. He guessed it was. Who else? 'When was the last time he saw his father?'

'I didn't know he had done.'

'Do you know how many he's taken?'

Roni didn't answer.

'How many?' he said, louder this time.

Roni shook her head, crying. 'I don't know.'

'Do what you should've done before, Roni, and call a bloody ambulance.'

While Roni did that, Riddick kept talking to Arthur, trying to bring him back to his senses. 'Hey, Antman, keep it together. World is going to go to pot around here without you on the ball.'

Roni came back in, tears coming down her face. 'Keith... that bastard... I was in that world with him for so long. Will they put me in jail when they see those? Who'll look after Arthur?' She nodded at her son. 'Will they put him in jail?'

Riddick looked at the bag. There were a lot of tablets in there. Enough to charge someone for dealing.

Riddick left two tablets out on the bedside table, so the paramedics could take them and know what the lad had ingested.

He then pocketed the bag. 'Never mention this bag. Okay?'

Roni nodded. 'Thanks, Paul—'

He held up his hand and shook his head. Being thanked made him want to throw up.

30

While Monika went to collect Rose and Ana from school, Gardner gave Marsh everything she knew about James Wright – although that was most probably not his name. By the time the call had ended, Gardner realised, with great dissatisfaction, that she knew barely anything about the man.

It was a shame Monika hadn't thought to look outside at the vehicle he had arrived in, but Gardner wasn't disappointed in her. The poor girl had been anxious, and not everybody was born with an investigative nature. *It's probably more of a curse than a gift*, Gardner thought.

Marsh, more reassuring than usual for obvious reasons, promised to call in favours and get to the bottom of this sooner rather than later.

Sitting in the kitchen in front of an open laptop, Gardner reached over and picked up the photograph that 'James Wright' had left behind. A selfie of her and Collette enjoying drinks in The Cloisters.

She remembered the night well. She traced her friend's smiling face with her finger. 'Hey you.'

Willows may've looked happy in the photograph, but she hadn't been. The photograph had been taken on the evening that Willows had ended one of her relationships, to a woman that Gardner had been fond of, too. Willows had been chock-full of anxiety; full of paranoia that she wouldn't find the comfort and happiness she craved.

She was dead a week later.

Gardner nudged a tear from the corner of her eye. 'I'm so sorry.'

Willows had been a feisty officer. Although she never challenged authority, she'd always stood her ground. It made a refreshing change. Because of stale expectations in the force, most officers were subservient early in their careers, which didn't make for effective detective work where inspiration, personality and fiery obsession often heated the cauldron of success.

Willows didn't just bring unpredictable energy into her job, she courted it in her personal life too.

Two years before her own death, Willows had a fling with a fellow officer, Lorraine Pemberton, who was already in a long-term relationship. It was a relationship that'd had a significant impact on Willows' life. She'd finally accepted her sexuality, something she'd always struggled to do due to an upbringing by a religious and overly puritanical widowed mother. Unfortunately, Willows underwent extreme trauma when she watched Pemberton die in the line of duty.

The manner of Pemberton's death had been awful, not unlike Willows' own a couple of years later, and she struggled to hold down a stable relationship from that day forth.

Gardner closed her eyes and thought of the day she lost her friend and colleague.

While investigating the murder of Nirpal Sharma, a gangster in Tidworth, Gardner and Willows had found themselves at a twelve-storey high-rise estate, interviewing a man that used to run drugs for Nirpal. Gardner had been hoping that the man, Nigel Harnett, may have an inkling who wanted Nirpal out of the picture.

Nigel claimed to have been clean for a while. But he'd known something. Made clear by his subsequent assassination that had happened while a staged knife attack on the estate had distracted Gardner. A man called Lewis Petrich had marched into Nigel's flat, cut his throat and then had thrown Willows from the balcony.

Eight floors up.

Gardner touched Willows' smiling face again as a tear ran down her own face. 'God, I'm so sorry.'

Petrich had been caught. So had his boss, Rob Mitchell. Both had been sent to jail.

Gardner hoped that they were both still there, and she'd asked Marsh to confirm it for her.

Despite Gardner blaming herself for being duped into leaving Willows alone, an internal investigation determined otherwise. She disagreed with the internal investigation, so her boss, Superintendent Joan Madden had seconded her up north to get her head straight.

In fairness, the secondment had worked. Gardner had realised her marriage was a sham and found a new lease of life. She'd even found herself, after several glasses of wine, contemplating staying...

Using the laptop, Gardner went to Willows' Facebook page, and scrolled through the many posts from friends and family.

Happy heavenly birthday, Col!

Make sure you're partying up there... hard!

Love you, honey... still miss you... Mum x

Gardner wiped another tear away from her eye.

She scrolled down to Willows' last post – two days before she died.

It was a gif of a movie star looking smug with the caption: When your boss tells you that you've talent!'

Willows' last shout-out to the world, and it was about how good a conversation had made her feel that day. Gardner had been praising her on her ability to spot the smallest of details on the investigation they'd been currently working.

Two days before I led you to your bloody death...

Gardner welled up, although it wasn't the first time she'd seen it, and it wouldn't be the last.

She heard the front door open, and her excitable children bundling in. Quickly, she wiped at her eyes, not wanting them to see her distress.

Fortunately, she heard her children storming up the stairs, desperate to hit their toys, no doubt.

Monika came into the kitchen.

'Can I just have a minute please, Monika? I'm going to go through some photos. I wondered if you'd look with me.'

'Sure,' Monika said, coming to stand behind her.

Gardner clicked on Willows' photographs on her Facebook page and cycled through them.

Willows with friends, partners, family members, in beautiful locations...

'There,' Monika said. 'That's him.'

Gardner leaned in and looked closely at the picture of the older man with his arm around Willows' shoulders.

Yes, Gardner recognised him too... it *was* that man from all those months ago on this estate. The house hunter; the hero in the right place at the right time for Rose's late-night wander; the liar.

Who are you?

She lingered the cursor over the image to see if Willows had tagged him.

She hadn't.

Willows' mother had blamed Gardner. *Understandable.* Consequently, Gardner hadn't been at Willows' funeral.

If I'd have been there, would I have seen you?

Willows' father had died when she was a child.

Maybe you're an uncle? A family friend?

She took a screenshot and reached for her phone to call Marsh back.

31

Kiera McLeod shook her head in disbelief as she watched Sebastian Harrington jog past Harry, a ten-year-old boy, with the ball at his feet. She chuckled to herself when the seventy-plus former MP sent the ball past Jake into the back of the net.

Sebastian reeled away in celebration, pointing at his head, suggesting it was all in the mind, a celebration made famous by a Premier League footballer.

The kids thought it was hilarious.

They loved Sebastian, and Kiera was glad.

Jake and Harry were examples of two boys that came to the Stockwell youth centre who hadn't had the best start in life. Both with single mothers who worked flat out. Fathers nowhere to be seen. They lived on the breadline while many of their peers at school lived lives of Riley.

She'd never met a politician like Sebastian; driven beyond words to spend time with children who'd drawn the short straws.

The day he'd offered to volunteer seven months ago had been a significant moment for this youth centre. A male role model in his seventies who was so gracious with his time, wisdom and money, was priceless.

Kiera found it truly shocking that there were people in this town who'd spit on the ground at the mere mention of his name.

Of course, she wasn't from Yorkshire originally, and had only moved from Scotland five years back with her husband, so she couldn't really hold court over the opinions of those that had been here their entire lives.

Even so... *really*?

How could this man really be the monster some thought he was?

* * *

Afterwards, Kiera and Sebastian sipped tea while the kids socialised in the hall. Some played table tennis, while others boogied along with CGI dancers holding Nintendo Switch remotes.

Kiera noticed he was quieter than usual. 'Has scoring goals taken it out of you, Seb?'

He laughed. 'Not the player I was – must admit. Once upon a time, I'd calves like Jack Grealish.'

'In fairness, you looked pretty handy out there.'

He smiled and turned away. When he looked back, she could see a tear in his eye.

'Seb, are you okay?'

He nodded. 'Have you heard about what happened at the cemetery last night?'

'Yes.' How could she not? It was all anyone was talking about. Although the names of the victims were yet to be made public.

'One of them was my nephew,' Sebastian said.

Kiera put her hand to her mouth.

'I've had some shocks in my time, but that one... well... has to be the biggest yet.'

Kiera took her hand from her mouth and put it on Sebastian's arm. 'I'm so sorry. That's awful.' She tried to force back tears, but inevitably, some broke free and ran down her face. 'Holding all this in while you're here... You need to be with your family.'

Sebastian guffawed. 'My family? Those that are left don't like me all that much. And to be perfectly frank, they're not too like-able either. My presence would make the situation worse.' He sighed. 'If that's even possible.'

Kiera squeezed his arm. 'I'm so sorry about everything. I can't imagine what you're going through.'

'Thanks, but I'll be okay. I wasn't that close to Ralphie. His parents ensured that.'

'I bet you cared, though.'

He nodded. 'Tried to.' He looked off into space. 'He was a right handful, that one.'

'You're the bloody best there is with a handful!' Kiera said, nodding at Harry and Jake, now going toe to toe on *Mario Kart*. 'You've brought a lot of smiles to a lot of faces.'

'It wasn't the same with Ralphie. I could never get through to him. The young man had everything he ever wanted. Sometimes, when they never want for anything, it's so difficult to talk sense into them. Maybe I should've tried harder.'

'I bet you tried as hard as you could.'

Sebastian sighed.

Kiera made him another cup of tea and brought it over. She was curious to know what had happened regarding his nephew, but knew such a question would be insensitive, so she just gave reassurance. 'They'll find whoever did this.'

'They know it's something to do with drugs, but that's as much as I know. I expect I'll hear from them again soon.'

Kiera smiled. 'If you ever need anyone to talk to.'

Sebastian smiled back. 'Other than these kids, you're the only person I do talk to. And I wouldn't have it any other way.'

32

Sitting beside the hospital bed, Riddick looked down at Arthur's bandaged chest, imagining what would've occurred if his young vulnerable friend had possessed a knife rather than just sharp fingernails.

He grimaced and shook his head.

Understandably, Arthur's mother, Roni, was a mess. Five minutes ago, she'd gone in search of coffee and something sugary and was yet to return.

Slumping back in his chair, Riddick considered the unicorn batch that had hospitalised about nine teenagers in the past month alone. A baggie of which now sat in his jeans' pocket.

The drug was potent and it was only a matter of time before someone died.

It'd be wishful thinking that the death of Nathan Cummings would stem the cancerous flow around Yorkshire. It was in the hands of many gangs now. The Ravens themselves had dealt the same product before the Mansters had closed them down.

Riddick took Arthur's hand, and the young man opened his eyes. 'Paul?'

'Aye... it's me, fella.' He ran his other hand through Arthur's hair. *Thank God you're okay.*

'Where am I? Mum... where's Mum?' Arthur's eyes swung around the room. Riddick was pleased to see that his pupils were no longer wide, bottomless black pools.

'Hospital. Your mum will be here shortly. You're okay, buddy... promise.'

'My head feels like a football. Kicked until there's no air left in it.'

Riddick grinned. It may not always be intentional, but Arthur always brought smiles to people's faces. 'It's all that scrapping with supervillains.'

'Really?'

Riddick smiled again over how convinced Arthur sounded.

'Not true!' Arthur realised.

Riddick patted the hand he was holding. 'It's something you swallowed, matey... Something that was bound to make your head feel like a deflated football. Can you remember taking anything?'

'Just medicine.'

'Well, this certainly wasn't medicine, because this stuff doesn't do you any good. Where did you get it?'

Arthur looked up at the ceiling, thinking. 'Sometimes I feel like there are things hopping up and down in my head. And they won't stop.' He touched the centre of his head with the hand that Riddick wasn't holding. 'Here is where it hurts most *when* it hurts. And it hurts like a son of a bitch.'

Riddick smiled again over the vocabulary he'd assimilated from American movies.

'So, you'd a bad headache, yes?'

'Yes and I took some medicine.'

'Which wasn't medicine...'

Arthur squinted. He looked confused for a moment, but then

seemed to catch up. 'Yes... I think... I thought they were... what do you call them...'

'Paracetamol?'

'Them the ones,' Arthur said.

'I need to know where you got them from.'

Arthur rubbed at his nose. He squinted again. 'My jacket pocket. My *leather* one.'

'You always carry around paracetamol in your jacket pocket, Arthur?'

'No. I did think it was lucky. But they say lucky comes in threes. And I was on two already today.'

'Which were?'

'Mum won five pounds on a scratch card.'

Technically, her luck then. 'And the other?'

'John, next door, let me stroke his dog. He doesn't usually. But today, he'd a muzzle on.'

Riddick nodded, smiling once more. 'How do you think the tablets got into your jacket pocket?'

'I don't know. I didn't think about it,' Arthur said. 'I should've done, sorry.'

'Where's your jacket been?'

'*Everywhere!*' Arthur sounded momentarily excited. 'It feels so good on my skin... but... I haven't had it for a while.'

'What do you mean?'

'A long time, but I only started wearing it again the other day.'

'How come?'

'I'd forgotten about it, but it was in one of the boxes Mum brought back from Manningham. I used to like the feel on my skin. She dug it out last week.'

Was it possible that one of the Ravens back in Manningham had used Nathan's jacket while they were cuckooing his home, and left some tablets in his pocket?

The explanation made more sense than Arthur receiving the tablets as a gift from his father. Keith was many things, but supplying his vulnerable child with ecstasy to play with seemed a little farfetched.

'Did anyone else ever use your jacket, Arthur? While you were back in Manningham?'

'Maybe.' Arthur closed his eyes. 'I can't remember... but my head is really hurting again.'

'We'll ask the doctor for something. Some proper medicine. You shouldn't have taken those tablets, Arthur, without knowing what they were – promise me you won't do anything like that again?'

'Am I gonna die?'

'Nah. No one around here is allowing that. Especially, me and your mum. Grim Reaper getting nowhere near you, boyo.'

'Grim who?'

Riddick nodded. 'Never mind. But you'll be fine.'

'Good. Because Mum would be sad if I died.'

She would, yes, Riddick thought, nodding again. *And how selfless of you.* 'And you, Arthur – I'm sure you wouldn't want that, anyway.'

'No, Paul, not at all! I don't like the dark, I don't like it at all. And I think it's gonna be dark when you die.'

Riddick squeezed his hand again. 'What gave you such a headache today, anyway? Can you remember anything else apart from the scratch card and John letting you stroke his dog?'

Arthur looked like he was giving it some thought. 'No. It's blurry. *So* blurry. Like when you're watching TV and it goes funny and twitches.'

'Glitches?'

'Yes. There were things dancing in my head. Been like that

since I woke up this morning. But, when it just got too bad, I took the medicine... *bad* medicine.'

Riddick nodded. 'One last thing. When was the last time you saw your father?'

'Not for a long time.'

'You telling the truth?'

'Yes. I'm scared to see him. He's mean. Last time he swore at me, you know?'

'Yes, I know,' Riddick said. He'd also called Arthur an imbecile.

This had been over two months ago. Seems Keith was in the clear.

'You think he'll apologise?' Arthur looked desperately at Riddick.

'One day, I'm sure.' Riddick nodded, although hopefully not; the idea of Arthur staying away from Keith forever was a very appealing one.

Just before wrapping it up, Riddick had another thought. 'What did you do yesterday, Arthur...?'

'Shopping! Groceries.' He licked his lips. 'A pasty from Greggs. Then, TV... then... more twitching... sorry *glitching*.' He rapped his knuckles against his forehead. 'I wish it worked better in here. I've always wished that.'

Arthur struggled considerably with his short-term memory. Still, he often managed to surprise people with things he'd stored in his long-term memory. He could still remember what he'd eaten on his fifth birthday – and loved to remind everybody. 'Jelly and chips... on the same plate!' But then ask him what he ate yesterday, and his expression would go blank.

Roni came back into the room. She saw that her son was awake and rushed over. She stroked his face, kissed him on the forehead. 'Oh, my boy.'

Afterwards, when Arthur drifted off for another sleep to

recover his energy following his experience, Riddick turned to Roni outside and asked, 'What did you do yesterday?'

'We went shopping, nothing special. Watched a movie, went to bed early. Very normal.'

'When did he start wearing his leather jacket again?'

'A couple of days back. I dug it out of his boxes of belongings we brought back from Manningham.'

'Yes, that's what he said.'

'Why?'

Riddick sighed, thinking about the bag of unicorn pills in his own pocket. 'It seems he brought back a souvenir from those dark days in Manningham.'

33

Gardner joined the briefing online with a headset on.

It was hard to interact with a room of people from her kitchen, so after a brief introduction, she handed the reins to Rice.

He did a sterling job. Probably because he thought he was being heavily scrutinised by Gardner. He wasn't; her mind was elsewhere.

Marsh wasn't in this briefing, so Gardner continually glanced down at her phone, desperate for her superior to get in touch.

She hadn't expected it to take long to identify the man. The image had been clear. Anyone who'd the balls to march into someone's home and scare the shit out of someone surely had to be in the system somewhere.

Her headset couldn't keep out the sound of her young children pounding around the house. She turned the volume up and tried to focus.

Barnett was currently going through the list of all the guests he'd spoken to at Ethan Williams' house party. 'Grace Grosvenor had to leave the room three times to throw up while I was interviewing her.'

There was tutting and groans from many. A number of Gardner's team had children in their late teens – she was sure that the thought of them consuming unicorn-emblazoned ecstasy tablets was firmly on their minds.

'The story was fairly consistent among the guests,' Barnett said. 'Including the fact that Ralphie and Vivianne were there and enjoying each other's company. Most of these kids deny taking anything, despite them looking worse for wear and being very vague in their recollections. There were a few who openly admitted to taking the drug, and then spending the evening in a haze. No one seemed to tell me where the victims went after although a lad called Toby Brundle offered one interesting inconsistency. Apparently, Vivianne and Ralphie had an argument.'

Gardner unmuted. 'I thought they were enjoying each other's company?' She hit mute again to prevent interference.

'That was in the house,' Barnett continued. 'Following the incident with Charlotte and Adam passing out on the sofa, the guests left. About 11.40 p.m. They all went off home in several directions. Toby walked towards the cemetery, so I quizzed him over who he was with. He said he walked alone. When I asked him about Vivianne and Ralphie, he said he hung back and let them go ahead because they were having an argument, and it'd be awkward to walk with them.'

Gardner unmuted again. 'And what was the argument about?'

'He wasn't specific. Claims he couldn't hear what it was they were arguing about.'

'Did he seem like he was hiding something?' Gardner said into her mic.

'Well, to be fair, he's hiding *less* than the other kids I've spoken to. But yes, apart from the argument, the story feels too loose and vague...'

'Manufactured?'

'Potentially. Although, most were probably that out of it, they mightn't remember much of what went off… hence, the vagueness.'

Using a large map on the screen, Barnett highlighted several routes that the students took in order to get home. He also high-lighted several routes to the cemetery.

Gardner spoke. 'Lots of streets, and a lot of doors – how many have we pounded on?'

'Not enough,' Rice said. 'I'll get onto it.'

At that point, Ana came into the room and ran over to Gardner. Gardner checked she was on mute and killed the camera link. She pulled off the headset.

'Okay, sweetheart?'

'Mummy, something's wrong?'

'How so, honey?'

'Moni, she seems sad. I saw her crying in her room.'

Gardner was unhappy about Monika's breakdown in the pres-ence of her children but wasn't about to turn into a raging bull over it. She'd had one hell of a day, and unlike Gardner, hadn't been desensitised into a lump of stone by decades in the force.

'She's not been feeling well, Ana. Can I ask a favour?'

Ana nodded.

'It's a big girl favour, are you okay with that?'

Ana stood up straight.

'Could you take Rose up to your bedroom and play with that new LOL campervan until I finish at this meeting, and then I'll get you some supper?'

'Yes,' Ana said, sounding overwhelmed with excitement.

Once Ana had left to enact her 'big girl' duties, Gardner turned back to the screen, and hit the mic and switched the camera on.

Rice was currently going through the pathologist's report, which Gardner had already seen. Both victims had high levels of MDMA in their system and had indeed suffered death by blunt force trauma. The rock. It was still too early for any significant DNA results.

It was at that point that Marsh came into the room. 'I've just got off the phone to CID. The unicorn tablets recovered from Vivianne Gill's house have been linked to a Bradford-based county lines outfit called the Mansters.' Marsh looked around the room. 'They're sending over an officer tomorrow to brief us. The leader of this group has just been found murdered in Manningham, so it seems we've a lot to learn.'

Gardner sighed. *CID? Tomorrow?* She should've been the one filling her team in on this information after being briefed by Marsh. Instead, she was stuck here, behind a computer screen, panicking.

And what was she panicking over, anyway? She still didn't really have any clue.

James Wright?

Who the bloody hell do you think you are?

* * *

Straight after the briefing, O'Brien phoned Gardner.

'Lucy?'

'I've spoken to my sister, Cathy – she's fine with having Ana, Rose and Monika.'

Gardner stood. 'I said that—'

'Listen, *boss*... please. Tilly and Poppy are going to love it. They're the same age.'

Instinctually, Gardner wanted to cut this plan down, dead. She absolutely hated the idea of taking advantage of someone else. Especially someone who was showing an interest in her that was pushing past the professional. How may this be viewed further down the line? Would someone suggest she was using O'Brien? Exploiting her?

She took a deep breath and reflected for a moment.

Deep down Gardner knew this was her best, and only, option.

How else was she getting out of the house and back on the case?

'Okay...'

'Thanks, boss.'

'Why are you thanking *me*?'

'For not leaving us to the mercy of Phil. Sorry... did I really just say that?'

Gardner laughed. 'I heard nothing. Thanks Lucy. I'm going to pay Cathy though.'

'You can try; she won't take it.'

'It's the law,' Gardner said.

'Well, that's your speciality. Wait till you see the size of the house. Jude is always away working, and Cathy is always with the kids. She loves kids. Believe me, you're doing her a favour.' Gardner thought about O'Brien's eyes lighting up over her acceptance of this plan.

'Have you given Cathy all the details about why I need her help?'

'Yes. She's fine with it. They're minted and their security is like Fort Knox. Plus... I'll stay there too.'

'Shit, I just feel like—'

'Boss, it's fine. You want me to collect you all?'

'No, I'll drive them, but I'll have to get straight back off. I'm behind on my own investigation!'

'Sorry, boss, I thought you were coming to stay too?'

'No. I really can't, Lucy.'

'I don't think that's a good idea. What if he comes back? At night? When you're alone.'

I'm counting on it. Then I can find out who this dickhead really is. 'It'll be fine.'

34

___

Despite his earlier warning to Kiera at Stockwell youth centre that his presence would make the situation worse, Sebastian succumbed to the urge to give his condolences to his sister.

He stared at the front door a while before he summoned up the courage to knock on it.

Expecting her to look dishevelled and broken, he was surprised to see that she was smartly dressed, with perfectly styled hair and make-up. He kept his surprise in check, acknowledging how different people responded when confronted with significant loss. After giving her a sad look, he said, 'Evie. I'm so sorry.'

Evie looked him up and down, her top lip curling up slightly. 'What do you want?'

Her reaction was unsurprising. They hadn't been on the best of terms before Ralphie's death. She'd be happy to make the brother she disliked accountable in some way.

Still, he tried. 'Is there anything... *anything* at all... I can do?'

'Where were you yesterday? All night?'

'I'm sorry. My phone was off.' He took a step forward. 'But I can help now.'

'Help how? He's dead.' Tears sprang up in her eyes. She wiped at them, smudging mascara across her face. 'Ralphie's dead. So what actual use are you any more?'

Sebastian took a deep breath. Here it was... the blame. But had Sebastian's refusal to make the thievery charges go away at Ralphie's university contributed to his death? Really? He doubted it had anything to do with it.

He exhaled. 'Please... Evie, if there's anything—'

Max stepped alongside her. He was also dressed smartly and looked freshly shaven. 'Ha! You?'

'Max, I'm—'

'Piss off,' Max said and slammed the door in Sebastian's face.

He sighed.

Yes, they'd experienced trauma, but their brutal words were hardly out of character. They could be in the best of spirits, and he'd still get it both barrels.

He turned and sighed again.

Maybe this was it for him and his sister?

After all, with Ralphie gone, he'd been left with no route back in.

* * *

Sebastian drank another cup of tea and tried his best to read a book, but just couldn't focus.

He considered some light exercise in his personal gym, but opted against it, deciding he'd be pushing it following his goal scoring exploits earlier.

Finally, he settled on watching television. He made it partway through a classic episode of *Bergerac* before falling asleep.

He awoke suddenly with an urge. And, whenever confronted with this urge, it needed to be settled immediately.

His legs felt heavy as he climbed the winding staircase to the third floor, his decision to play football with the kids at Stockwell Road Park threatening to backfire. He wondered if he'd be bedridden in the morning.

In his office, he wandered over to his shelf and ran his finger over the spines of his many photo albums, most in sets, before withdrawing a blue, tatty one that didn't belong in any set. Before sitting, he stroked the other albums again, thinking of all those glorious images of his late wife within them.

He sighed, sat down and opened the photo album to the first page.

The pictures were of people that weren't related to him but who meant so much to him. They brought tears to his eyes, and he cried long into the night.

35

Riddick smoothed the cold sides of his pint glass, wetting his fingertips with the condensation.

Even though he was staring down into the amber liquid, his mind remained locked on that image of Arthur in his own bed.

Covered in blood. Moaning. His eyes deep black wells.

He looked up from the drink he craved and glanced around the Black Bull, busy with an early evening rush of smiling folk.

Riddick lifted the glass to his lips.

One man at the bar, half-pissed, raised his bottle, took the volume up a notch and declared to all, 'Here's to a night off putting the kids to bloody bed.' He looked up. 'Thank you, lord.'

I'd give anything to experience that with Molly and Lucy again.

Anything at all.

He took a large swig of beer, rolled it around his mouth, enjoyed the taste, and then swallowed. After the bitter, icy liquid slipped down his throat, he sighed.

'Stop!'

Riddick opened his eyes. Daz was hovering over the table with his face screwed up. 'I'm too *bloody* late.'

Riddick set down his pint.

Daz looked as if he might suddenly swing for Riddick. 'Daz—'

'Couldn't you just bloody wait?' He plonked his palms down on the table and then suddenly deflated, hunched over.

'It's Birra Moretti Zero,' Riddick said.

Daz lifted his head slightly, an eyebrow raised. 'Zero?'

'Yes, alcohol free.'

'Still—'

'I know. Before you start, I know it's still not good enough.'

'It's a trigger,' Daz said. 'The taste.'

Riddick couldn't deny it... *Shit*, it'd tasted good! 'I know. I just said that.'

Daz held up his hands and gestured around the public house. 'And there's no bigger trigger than being in this bloody place. And sod you for putting me in the situation. You're not the only pissin' alcoholic around here. Anyone else, I wouldn't have come.'

'You don't sponsor anyone else.'

'You surprised? Sponsoring you is like sponsoring ten men – all with twenty-tonne chips on their shoulders.' Daz had inflated again, and his tone of voice had picked up. 'We need to get the hell out of here, Paul.'

Riddick looked down sadly. 'Nothing in here can hold a torch to the real things triggering me.' Riddick held up his hand. It trembled. 'Look at the state of me. *Before* I walked in here, I might add.' He let it flop back down on the table next to his beer-flavoured water.

'Shakes are good.' Daz tapped the side of his head. 'Shakes remind you to start thinking!'

'Sod thinking. Thinking makes it worse for me.'

'Well, I guess it depends on where you direct that thinking.' He pointed at the pint. 'You need to think about the damage *that* causes. And not come to a place that'll ruin you... *us*.'

Riddick nodded. 'I agree. That's why I called you.'

Daz reached over and clutched the back of Riddick's hand. 'Good. I see that now.' He'd calmed. 'So, let's get out of here and talk somewhere else. Preferably a place that the Devil hasn't dressed up to look like heaven.'

Outside, they chatted in Daz's car. 'I can smell that bloody beer.'

'Sorry,' Riddick said.

'Talk to me then. What's triggered you?'

Riddick began by describing the confrontation with Nathan Cummings the previous evening, followed by this morning's revelation that the drug-dealing scumbag had been murdered and Riddick was facing interrogation.

'And you just buggered off?' Daz said, his eyes wide.

Riddick nodded, moving into a description of his confrontation with Keith Fields. Then, he moved into the most dramatic incident – seeing Arthur covered in blood. 'It was like I'd fallen back through time. Like I was living through that whole horrific night all over again. I thought I'd lost him *again*.'

'That's awful,' Daz said.

Riddick forced back tears and then moved on to explain that Arthur had taken unicorn ecstasy tablets.

Afterwards, Daz patted Riddick on the leg. 'You know what I think?'

'That's why you're here, isn't it?'

'Indeed. You, fella, need a career change.'

Riddick smiled. 'It's crossed my mind.'

But would it really make a difference?

Badge or no badge, if he sensed injustice, would he really sit it out? How do you get it out of your blood?

'Seriously, well done, mate. For holding back.' He nodded at the Black Bull through the windscreen. 'Kind of... Many have relapsed over far, far less than what you've gone through today. Reaching out to me was a good move.'

'Bloody hell, get this on tape! Some praise!'

'Yes, and well-earned praised... but I haven't finished yet, so don't get your hopes too high.'

'Shit, here it comes.'

Daz sighed and shook his head. 'Running from your superiors, Paul? Jesus, that's a new level. And now I'm lost for words.'

'Unusual.'

'Precisely.'

'They might hang me out.'

'You didn't kill him...' Daz fixed him with a stare. 'You didn't, did you?'

Riddick tutted. 'Come on. He was a vicious, sadistic piece of shite, but no, I didn't kill him. He was a civilian, and I shouldn't have confronted him in the car.'

'Sounds like you conducted yourself more calmly than I did yesterday when a traffic warden ticketed my car because less than an inch of my left wheel was touching a double yellow. But then, I guess I'm not a cop... *thankfully*.' Daz sighed. 'Jesus. Running from HQ. Do you think they've got a picture of you on their board right now with a large red line around it?'

'They'll know I didn't kill Nathan. Not only will they have clocked ANPR by now and seen that I went home last night before he was killed, they'll probably also have contacted Claire to get an alibi. She's not picking up my calls to confirm. Still, Kerry, my super, will be pissed off. Along with those trying to get to the bottom of Cummings' murder. They've tried ringing... tonnes of times.'

'And you've not answered?'

'Been rather busy.'

'So, you out of a job you reckon?'

Riddick shrugged.

'Okay,' Daz said, taking a deep breath. 'Any more bombshells before we attempt to solve this situation?'

Riddick held his finger up to gesture one. 'Sorry...'

'What is it?'

Riddick took the plastic bag full of ecstasy tablets out and put them next to Daz's handbrake.

Daz's mouth hung open.

'That,' Riddick said.

'You think? Bloody hell, Paul... you've got me knocking on heaven's door tonight.' He touched his chest. 'Yes... it's flapping all over the shop.'

'I couldn't have the spotlight on Arthur. A baggie of drugs will do that to you. The lad is frail as it is.'

'So, instead, we get pulled over and go to jail?'

'I was going to flush them in the Black Bull toilet, but I got distracted.'

'Yes, I noticed. Well, you're not going back in. Let's find a McDonald's.' Daz started the engine.

* * *

After disposing of the drugs in the McDonald's toilet, Riddick and Daz ate burgers while chatting in the car park.

Riddick was calming down. Daz always brought him back. A combination of warmth and good humour. There were very few people that managed that. In fact, he could recall only one right now.

He remembered the perky southern DCI in her bright yellow raincoat standing awkwardly over the lifeless body of a teenager behind the Knaresborough Castle keep. A fish out of water, but a brilliant detective.

It'd been the first time he'd met DCI Emma Gardner – the most compassionate friend he'd ever had.

And he'd betrayed her with his lies and behaviour.

His head dropped.

'Okay, you ready? Back to HQ?' Daz asked, scrunching up the little cardboard box that had held his Big Mac, and throwing it into the door pocket.

Riddick nodded. *Time to face the music.*

36

After sending the children off 'for an adventure', Gardner took a phone call from Marsh.

'We've identified the person on the Facebook picture you sent me.'

Gardner took a deep breath.

'Neville Fairweather,' Marsh continued. 'Ring any bells?'

Gardner exhaled. 'No... but at least it confirms that the name James Wright is bullshit.'

'Yes, indeed... but...' Marsh sighed.

Not like her to be lost for words. Something is up.

'Ma'am?'

'Emma, how sure are we about this being the man? Is your au pair absolutely convinced?'

Gardner clenched the hand that wasn't holding the phone into a fist. 'Her jaw was on the kitchen table when she saw his picture... Plus, I saw this man on my estate, around a year back. You're not questioning my recall too, are you?'

Marsh snorted. 'Okay, Emma. Shit day, I know, but pipe down, love.'

Love? You condescending piece of... Gardner pounded the back of her sofa with her fist.

'It can't be Neville Fairweather who came around today,' Marsh said. 'Not unless he can teleport! He's in Turkey on some kind of business trip. He left two days back. There can be no error. It just can't be him. Yes, he's from your neck of the woods. You were right about that, but he definitely didn't visit your home today. Your au pair must have it wrong.'

Gardner suddenly felt like every nerve in her body had burst into flames and she was on her feet. 'It's a mistake. Can you double-check, ma'am?'

'No mistake. I've confirmed it with both UKVI and Border Force. You want the documentation? Is my word not good enough for you?'

Gardner bit back some venom. Marsh, although an almighty pain in the arse, was on her side. She'd be patient, but only for so long. 'No, ma'am. I get it.' She paused. 'Can you at least tell me what you know about this Neville Fairweather?'

'Not much, despite there being quite a lot to know. He keeps a low profile. He's a powerful man, minted to the eyeballs, big-shot property developer, entrepreneur, philanthropist, provides an intravenous line to charities... you name it... he's there. He's like the man you don't recognise on all the photographs of the great and good, the one that holds the cards, that pulls the strings...'

That fakes his own international movements...

'But Neville Fairweather isn't your man. I'm sorry, Emma. God, I wish he was.'

'Still, he sounds powerful...'

'So, is our Home Office. He hasn't fooled them.'

'Doesn't mean he's not pulling strings... as you just said so yourself.'

'Look, Neville isn't a threat to you anyway. Looking at a profile of him, he's more likely to pay for a safe house and an armed guard for you than stalk you. The man, according to the press, is a saint. He also donates to Labour and is as socialist as they come, apparently. Although I've always wondered how people so wealthy could be socialists, but, that's beside the point.'

'So, what's his connection to Collette Willows?'

'I've yet to find one.'

Gardner sighed.

'Emma, you need to stay on guard. At least we know that your stalker looks like Neville. We'll find out who they really are soon enough.'

No, you won't, because it was Neville Fairweather.

She went over to her computer and googled him.

The first image was of him drinking champagne with Elon Musk.

Bloody hell.

An absolute dead ringer for the man who'd stopped Rose from running out onto the road...

And a dead ringer for the man with his arm around Willows on her Facebook image – the one that had sent Monika into a flutter...

Who was this man, who could fake his absence from a country?

He must be powerful.

And when power was involved, the risks and the dangers intensified.

Terrified as she was, she had to suck it up. She had two small children to worry about. Neville Fairweather had picked the wrong target.

'Talk me through your precautions, Emma.' Marsh's voice broke her searching.

She explained how the children had gone to stay with O'Brien and her sister.

'Why don't you go to a hotel?'

'No, I'll get my children out of harm's way, but he's not putting me on the run,' Gardner said. 'Besides, whoever it is has been watching me for a year. If he was going to do me a mischief, he'd have done it by now.'

'Do you want time off?'

'No.'

'You sure?'

'Yes!'

'Kind of hoping you were going to say that. But, if you're in briefing first thing tomorrow, there's something you need to be prepared for. Another shock...'

'After today, you think you can shock me, ma'am?'

'Yes, I do.'

She was right.

37

Riddick couldn't believe that Daz was still sitting in the station car park. He climbed into the passenger seat. 'It's been over three hours, mate! I told you I'd get a taxi home.'

Daz held up a battered Dean Koontz paperback. 'I've been just fine. And wanted to make sure you were too. Knew my chances of a phone call later would be slim.'

'I think you're just worried about letting me off the leash again.'

'Leash! I wish. I'm more bothered about you shaking off that bloody muzzle.'

Riddick snorted.

Daz eyed him. 'Go on then. What happened?'

'Something completely unexpected, actually.'

'What? *Unexpected?* In the life of Paul Riddick – I just can't believe it!'

Riddick shook his head. 'And this is why I wouldn't have phoned.'

Daz mimed zipping his mouth.

'Good,' Riddick said and then explained how he'd been spoken to, severely, regarding his conduct with Nathan Cummings, but he was in the clear following the murder. As he'd suspected, ANPR, combined with Claire's alibi, had been enough. A small murder team was working through a list of suspects, which Riddick, thank God, wasn't on. 'So, no big red line around my name on the board, as you thought.'

Daz laughed. 'My bad. How could I ever have thought something possible with someone so squeaky clean?'

'I'm on a warning regarding conduct, but nothing else. They bought the excuse that I left HQ this morning because I was anxious.' He sucked in a deep breath. 'They knew how badly the Arthur Fields incident has affected me – the guilt and whatnot. They could see how Cummings' death may've brought it all rushing back. As long as I see the counsellor again, they'll keep it under wraps.'

'Bloody hell, when did employers get so sympathetic?'

Riddick nodded. 'Different world these days. Where mental health is concerned, *nobody* wants to end up being the bad guy. Buys you some leeway.'

'So that was the unexpected occurrence?'

'No... but what I'm about to tell you stays confidential...'

Daz threw his paperback on the back seat, laughing. 'Jesus! You couldn't write this! I just drove you to McDonald's to flush away a batch of ecstasy tablets and now you're worried about trust!'

'Keep your voice down!'

'Get to it then, fella.'

Riddick told him about the ongoing Bradford county line investigation and the unicorn batch of ecstasy tablets.

'The shit that you brought into my car?'

Riddick nodded. 'Stuff was super bloody strong. Put a fair number of kids in the hospital – including Arthur. And now it's ended up in bloody Knaresborough. Two other kids were hospitalised last night.'

'Knaresborough's burgeoning drug culture? Not sure I can see it.'

'You should. Where there's money, there's *always* business and corruption.' He sighed. 'I'm gutted. Having that shite on my stomping ground depresses me. Thing is, I've been asked to go there tomorrow morning. Back to the place and people I used to work with. I had problems there... many problems...'

Riddick rubbed his temples, recalling that look on Gardner's face on that fateful day when she'd discovered that he'd paid money to have Ronnie Haller murdered.

There'd been such disappointment in her eyes. And loss.

Their friendship in flames...

Except, had it just been friendship? There had been times when he'd suspected more.

Would he again be forced to see her disappointment and face that loss?

'Your problems are with you, Paul, not the place and people,' Daz said, interrupting his reflections.

'Say it how it is.'

Daz shrugged. 'What's the point if I don't?'

Riddick also shrugged. 'Aye. But even though you're probably right, it'll still be a frosty reception. I'm not particularly well liked.'

'I'm sure they'll appreciate your expertise.'

'They're in the middle of a murder investigation. I doubt they'll be appreciative of much.'

'Murder?'

'Aye. Two nineteen-year-olds beaten to death in a graveyard with a rock. Both of them with this drug in their systems. One of them, the lass, Vivianne Gill, had a duffel bag full of the unicorn-covered bastards at her place.'

'Shit.'

'You can say that again.'

'Someone must think highly of you if they think you can put the pieces together.'

'Believe me, no one thinks highly of me.'

'I don't believe that.'

'You should. There's someone there that did use to have my back, like. But I turned that into a shower of shit, as per.'

'Who?'

'Don't sound so surprised!' Riddick smiled and grabbed Daz's thigh. 'Yes, before you, sweet cheeks, there was someone else...'

Daz brushed his hand away, laughing.

So, Riddick told Daz all about DCI Emma Gardner.

And his sponsor looked captivated.

But who wouldn't be when the storyteller spoke with such passion?

* * *

On the way back home, Riddick tried ringing Claire for about the tenth time today.

And, for about the tenth time, she didn't pick up.

He shook his head. Pregnant and having to provide him with an alibi. She'd already been pissed off with him; he imagined she'd now be seething.

That was what happened if you hooked up with the human wrecking ball.

After thanking Daz, and promising to check in with him tomorrow, he approached his driveway, protecting his eyes from the spitting rain.

Claire's car was gone.

As he unlocked his front door, dread weighed heavily on him.

He'd cocked this up, hadn't he?

As he wandered between dark, empty rooms, dread quickly became a familiar resigned feeling.

Yes. You made a mess of it in Knaresborough, and now you've made a mess of it here too.

When he'd determined that she wasn't there and seen that some of her bags and clothes were missing from the wardrobe, he returned to the kitchen and found a note by the toaster.

He noticed first the kisses and the term of endearment at the bottom: *Love you, C xx*

Hope?

He read the letter.

Yes... some hope.

She was staying with her sister to collect her thoughts. She requested privacy and suggested that she'd be the one who'd get in touch.

He vowed to respect her request.

Then he traced her last words with his finger. *Love you, C xx*

Riddick opened his mouth to return the endearment but couldn't.

He closed his mouth, unsure as to the reason.

38

For most of the night, Gardner dwelled on two men who were causing her great anxiety, her mind flitting between both in equal measure.

When she'd arrived in Knaresborough, she'd been a fish out of water, vulnerable following the death of her colleague and partner, Willows and tasked with taming a room full of middle-aged Yorkshire policemen. It had been inevitable that she'd turn to someone.

Her mistake had been choosing DI Paul Riddick, a broken and grief-ridden alcoholic.

Still, it was a simple mistake to make when the alcoholic was also the most caring and compassionate man that she'd ever met.

But his compassion was his curse. The lengths he'd go to for the truth could be terrifying. And on those times when he'd pushed himself to the edge of sanity, the ground would crumble, and those around him would also fall into the darkness...

Yet she could've forgiven him all this. She could've been there for him through any moment he'd needed her. His near-suicidal behaviour, his relentless drive to stand for vulnerability, against those who sought to abuse it, no matter the cost.

She could've taken it all.

Every painful drop...

But for *that* one thing.

Because there had to be a limit, didn't there? There just had to be. And if becoming what you'd always despised wasn't a limit then what was?

Riddick had paid for the assassination of his family's killer and for this, there could be no redemption.

And you lost me, Paul, the moment you lied to me. Our reunion is professional. I need to know Ralphie and Vivianne's connection to this drug racket and that's all.

She looked at the time and groaned. It'd be another exhausting day tomorrow.

But it didn't stop her fingers flying over the keyboard as she relentlessly researched Neville Fairweather, looking for the truth behind the man who'd just turned her life upside down.

It was exactly as Marsh had said. The man was special. Or, at least, perceived to be by the press who praised his charitable nature and investment in society. Pictures of him shaking hands with people such as Bill Gates, Barack Obama and many others were in abundance.

Neville had been in her home today. There was no doubt about that. Monika had been frightened, but she wouldn't point out this man unless it was him, would she? Besides, Gardner could *still* see him, clear as day, rescuing her daughter on the edge of this estate.

A few times she went downstairs to check all the doors, peer out the window for any signs of activity and pour herself a glass of wine. And each time, her mind wandered back to Riddick.

She recalled standing outside Riddick's home, months after his betrayal, just before his relocation to Bradford.

Her one moment of weakness.

She'd seen that the man who'd lost everything – including himself – had found something again.

A woman.

There had been jealousy. Yes. She wouldn't deny it. But it'd been for the best. He'd got his new start, and now she'd have hers.

So, when he'd tried to contact her, and he'd tried many times – she'd ignored him.

She went back to the laptop and rubbed at her temples, realising that she'd done the best of a bottle now.

Let's keep it professional tomorrow, Paul. Let's get to the truth, quick and easy. You go back to your second chance, and I'll come back to this enigma... Neville Fairweather.

She flicked through a multitude of pictures featuring Neville fulfilling his duties as a member of the great and the good.

Who the bloody hell are you?

She stopped dead.

It was a picture of Neville cutting a ribbon, unveiling a new park in Harrogate from many years back.

The man standing next to him was Sebastian Harrington.

39

1981

Dean staggered into the disused industrial estate.

He closed his eyes before he reached Howie's old garage.

Whoosh...

The sound of Neil Clark's execution was as clear in his memory as it'd been that night. It had been one year, but the burning of that man still glowed fiercely.

He opened his eyes and continued staggering. Ten pints of Timothy Taylor's did that to a man. But even in his inebriation, he could tell nothing had changed.

The place was still desolate, and the glow from some lamp-lights was still weak. These were still desperate times. Nobody was affording the rent on these units and selling them was a fantasy. Right now, with the state the country was in, especially the north, they couldn't even afford to bulldoze them.

Thatcher's Britain. Northerners left to rot.

He stumbled into some shutters. He laughed. No need to worry; no one was here.

When his drunken laugh fizzled away, a question came through his mind: *Why are you here, Dean?*

It was the clearest thought he'd had in hours, and the clarity took him by surprise.

His inability to answer it wasn't surprising, though, and his thoughts began to spin wildly again.

All he knew was that the place was a symbol of the darkness in his past. And tonight, it was like a magnet pulling at him.

Whoosh...

Neil Clark.

He may've only been a year older than Penny, but he'd been driving that car, and had fled like a coward.

True, Dean, but did he deserve to burn trapped inside a melting rubber tyre?

'Don't answer,' he said, out loud, slurring his words.

Your last thread of sanity may just rely on it.

As he approached Howie's Garage, he looked at the peeling name above the shutters.

Despite the times, Howard had done a good job with his new place in Aspin.

The man was a hound with the ladies, though. No question. He recalled a time when he'd caught him flirting with Estelle. Dean clenched his fists.

Not that it mattered much any more. Dean's relationship with Estelle was at an end, anyway.

As he drew nearer, Dean realised that the shutters of the unit were raised about a metre. A thin puddle of light spilled out from under it. Something he'd failed to acknowledge before because of the surrounding streetlamps and his pissed state. Rather than concern, he was filled with curiosity.

He smirked. *Clearly, I'm pissed as a fart.*

Closer still, he heard some quiet voices coming from inside.

That's your cue to leave...

Except, the strength of Timothy Taylor really was in his veins.

Besides, what was it Estelle always used to call him before she'd packed off and left?

Spineless?

Okay, Stell, I'll show you spineless.

He ducked under the shutter and into the garage. It was exactly how he remembered it!

Scattered engine parts, that same smell of burnt engine oil... except this time, there were two figures silhouetted at the rear of the garage.

Another cue to leave...

Instead, he bent down and picked up a piece of metal and brought it closer to his face. A spanner.

Adrenaline bubbled beneath his alcoholic-induced confidence.

He thought back to his last argument with Estelle, when she'd confessed her affair. 'I'm leaving you for someone with a backbone.'

So, it's backbone you want?

He set off, staggering around the debris, almost going over two or three times. Considering how unsteady he was, he did an admirable job of getting closer without giving the game away. Close enough to recognise the sharp dresser with the dagger-like nose, anyway.

Keith Fields.

The other man, however, was clouded by the smoke coming from Keith's cigarette.

Dean threw his spanner from hand to hand as he continued his approach.

When the spanner didn't land in the other hand, he glanced down in time to see it clanging off the ground.

Shit.

When he looked back up, Keith was coming quickly out of the smoke and shadows. 'Dean?'

Dean swayed, grinning. 'My old buddy.'

Keith threw his cigarette to one side. 'What're you doing here?'

'Good question!'

Keith inched forward, balling his fists. 'One that needs answering... *now*.'

Dean held up a finger. 'Wait... just let me...' He looked down again and, despite the blurriness, he sighted the spanner. He knelt and scooped it up. As he rose back up, he stumbled and went to his knees. The thud sounded worse than it felt. 'This is becoming rather undignified.' He looked up at Keith and pointed the spanner in his direction. 'Who're you here to kill tonight?'

Keith's eyes widened. He clenched his fists.

'You wouldn't hit a man while he's down, would you?' Dean said.

Keith had turned to look at the other man in the smoky shadows. 'Give me a moment. I'll deal with this.' He then turned back.

'Guess what? The divorce papers came through today,' Dean said. 'My life is a mess.'

Keith snorted and said, 'I wouldn't see it like that. You're probably better off without her. In fact, I think you realised that and headed out to celebrate.'

Dean glared. 'I knew you'd see it like that. What did you always call her?'

'A card.' Keith nodded down at the spanner in Dean's hand. 'Okay, this is getting embarrassing. What're you intending to do, Dean?'

'Depends.'

'On what?'

'On whether anyone is in danger?'

Keith smiled. 'Well, no one was in any danger until you turned up...'

'Hilarious. I want you to apologise, Keith.'

'Ha! Really? For what?'

'The fact that my daughter is dead because of you.'

'She's dead because of Neil Clark.'

'Who worked for you.'

'We can't be held responsible for everything our employees do.'

'He was out dealing your drugs... high on your crap... that—'

Keith knelt with a finger to his mouth. 'Be quiet, Dean. We dealt with the problem, in-house. For you. You were paid well, and I offered you the scumbag who ran down Penny, and you may have turned it down, but you were still there. You were still complicit.' Dean gritted his teeth as he recalled the whooshing, followed by the screams of agony. He felt both anger and regret tearing at him in equal measure. He shook his head, unset his teeth and murmured, 'No... no...'

'I think the law would say that you were.'

Dean glared at Keith. 'The police were happy to stop investigating, weren't they? Did you pay them off too?'

'I think it's best you call it a night.'

'What if I kick up a fuss? Force them to investigate again? It'll blow back on you.'

'And you? You'll be in jail for Neil Clark.'

'And you think I really care?'

Keith nodded and thought for a moment. 'I'm not sure you do... no... which worries me. It should also worry you.'

Dean laughed. 'You think much worries me after what I've been through? What you put me through!'

Keith sighed and stood again. 'Okay. I'm going to assume that the drink is doing the talking tonight. If you go home now and sleep it off, this needn't go badly. Then, we'll chat in the morning about the importance of discretion again. I think you'll see it differently in daylight. You need to get back on the rails quick smart, or it'll destroy—'

Dean threw up.

It splashed down his front and onto Keith's shoes.

Keith skipped back a few steps.

Dean held up his hand to suggest that was his lot, but then retched again. Four times in total. There was a lot of sick. The stench of beer was pungent.

'Jesus! You're disgusting! Piss off.' Keith turned.

Dean allowed the rest of the vomit to dribble from his mouth, before spitting out any remaining chunks.

He rose to his feet, watching the bastard walking away, back into the shadows. He then looked at the spanner still in his hand.

He charged, suddenly determined to break open the bastard's head; however, his own vomit took him into a skid. Despite losing his balance, he got in a swing, striking him in the back.

Keith wailed, while Dean hit the concrete with his knees again. The spanner slid away from him.

Dean watched Keith lean against an upright piece of car-repair equipment as he groaned, while, ahead of him, the mystery man stirred in the shadows.

Keith staggered forward, eyes narrowed. He pointed at the scar on his cheek that Estelle had given him from the cigarette. 'First, this, and now you try to brain me? You, my son, are out of lives.' He knelt and picked up the spanner Dean had foolishly relinquished.

Keith drew back the weapon and Dean, for the first time since arriving at the industrial estate, felt fear. Keith's intentions were clear.

Still, would Dean change anything about this confrontation?

No way!

He grinned at Keith who was tensed and ready to strike. *Standing up to you was one of the best things I ever did.*

The spanner flashed, and the world burned white. The pain in the upper left side of his face was extraordinary.

The second blow sent him over onto his side, and he felt his own vomit against his cheek.

Then, the flashes came in quick succession.

One... two... three...

'*Stop!*' someone shouted.

Four...

'Keith, stop! That's enough. Damn it. You've knocked his bloody eye out of his head...'

Dean recognised the voice.

Unbelievable.

What was *he* doing here?

It was his last thought before everything went black.

40

2024

The photograph of Sebastian Harrington and Neville Fairweather together had sent Gardner into a spin. She'd spent most of the night online searching for another stronger connection between the two than this one solitary image but had come up empty-handed.

Neville was supposed to be some holier-than-thou socialist, so he certainly wasn't making donations to the Tories... none that were on the record, anyway.

Maybe their appearance together opening a park in Harrogate was just a simple coincidence? Except wasn't Neville from Wiltshire? Meaning he'd very little business up here attending grand openings...

Just before heading off for the morning briefing, Gardner called an old friend.

DCI Michael Yorke sounded out of breath.

'Bit late for a run,' Gardner said. 'Incident rooms don't prep themselves.'

'Week off. Been getting some lie-ins.'

It was five in the morning.

'How's Pat and the kids?'

'Grand. Rose and Ana?'

'Same. Sorry to interrupt your run, sir.'

'Bloody hell.'

'Sorry, *Mike*.'

'I've already told you that you'll be looking down on me from an ivory tower one day.'

'Ha! I heard that SEROCU were sniffing around you.'

SEROCU were the South East Regional Organised Crime Unit, and rumours were that their Chief Constable Riley Robinson, the face and dinosaur of the unit, was due for retirement.

'They can sniff all they want,' Yorke said. 'I'm deliberately dousing myself in Brut to throw them off the scent. And don't worry about interrupting my run. Rosie runs with me now.' Rosie was Yorke's Cockapoo. 'And she was stopping to, well, answer a call of nature. Although that's looking anything but natural...'

'Shall we cut the pleasantries, then?'

He laughed. 'Why not? We usually do.'

'I need your help, Mike.'

* * *

Feeling somewhat reassured that Yorke was going to investigate Neville Fairweather, despite him having some time off, Gardner refocused on the way to HQ.

En route, she contacted Rice to go through some updates on Operation Red Cascade so far, which were few. She also asked him to press ahead with assigning tasks. The pounding of *more* doors that littered the route between the party house and the graveyard, the most pressing of tasks.

She'd deliberately kept Riddick to the back of her mind this morning, but in doing so, the thought of him now reemerged like a ten-tonne truck. So, when she arrived in the car park at HQ, she looked around for his car, before realising she'd no idea what he currently drove.

Chest tightening under the anticipation of seeing him, she buzzed herself into HQ and opted for the stairs. Every time she turned a corner, or someone ahead of her turned into her path, her breath caught in her throat.

By the time she was in her office, she still hadn't seen her former colleague.

She sighed, but then rolled her eyes over this expression of relief. She was going to have to see him sooner or later.

There was a knock at her door.

Make that sooner.

She sat bolt upright in her chair, gulped and said, 'Come in!'

Rice poked his head around the door.

Bloody hell.

She took a deep breath.

'Just checking in, boss. You ready for the briefing?'

She nodded.

'He's here, you know?'

She stood. 'Paul?'

'Yes, of course... who else, boss? You okay?'

The fact that I'm considering running for the back door would suggest not. 'Have you spoken to him?'

'No. He's waiting in the incident room. I saw him walking in though...'

'Okay.'

'He still looks like a pompous, arrogant twerp—'

'Phil, please.' She rubbed her temples.

'Well, you know how I feel and—'

'Yes,' Gardner said. 'I *know* how you feel about him. In fact, everybody in the department *knows* how you feel about him. Shit, everybody in North Yorkshire *knows* how you feel about him. You make it sound like some closely guarded secret. What's your point anyway?'

Rice looked taken aback. She realised she may've gone in too hard.

Ah well. It was good for some people. Rice was one such person.

'My point is...'

Seems he hadn't viewed her question as rhetorical.

'That I think it's best we find out all we need about Mansters and unicorn pills and then send him packing!'

'Thanks for your thoughts on the matter.'

'Well, I'm just saying.'

She closed her eyes. 'Well, thanks for *just* saying.' She sighed and then opened her eyes again. 'Now piss off and offer him a cup of coffee. No one is being rude on my watch. And if you wind him up, Phil, so help me God—'

The door closed. He'd gone.

Rude bastard.

41

Riddick was answering another pointless email from HQ on his phone when he sensed someone hovering above him.

He didn't need to look up. He could tell who it was by the smell of cheap aftershave.

'Phil,' he said, still punching out his email. 'How do?'

'Fine. Can I've a second, please?'

Riddick stopped typing and looked up from his phone, smiling. 'Sure.'

Rice clearly didn't look the happiest with Riddick's nonchalant attitude; mind you, he never really did. Snarling disgust was kind of his default.

'Would you like a coffee?' Blood rushed to Rice's cheeks, and he suddenly looked as if he was choking on something.

Really? 'Are you taking the piss?'

'Just trying to be sodding hospitable. You and that chuffin' chip on your shoulder. I—'

Riddick couldn't resist a laugh.

'Why're you laughing?'

'Can you blame me? It's just... well, *you*... hospitable? Someone must have put you up to it? Marsh?'

'No one...'

'Bollocks. Is that how you've held on to that assistant SIO role despite being impossible to work with?'

'A pot and a black kettle spring to mind. Fine, if that's your attitude, stick your coffee up—'

'It was me,' Gardner said, stepping up behind Rice. 'I told him to offer you coffee. Seems that time hasn't helped either of you move on from your pissing competition. I should've known better.'

She moved alongside Rice and looked between both men with hands on her hips. She was trying to look authoritative. Riddick wondered if it was an act. If she felt the same way about seeing him as he felt about her, she'd be a quivering wreck inside.

He opened his mouth to speak, but simply stared, completely lost for words. For so long, he'd been desperate to see her, but now he was looking at her, it felt as if no time had passed at all.

Gardner looked at Rice. 'Get our guest a coffee please, Phil? Two sugars.'

Rice sighed and turned.

'Actually, just the one sugar now, Phil. Been cutting down,' Riddick said.

Rice threw him the birdie over his shoulder.

Fortunately, Gardner didn't see him do this. Her eyes were firmly on Riddick.

'Can I sit?' Gardner asked, nodding at the chair beside him.

Riddick shrugged. 'It's your incident room.' He grinned awkwardly, trying to hide his nerves. 'You just made that abundantly clear. I reckon Phil is currently pouring arsenic in my coffee.'

Gardner sat down. 'Maybe you deserve it.'

Riddick laughed. 'I think we all know that I probably do.' He looked at Gardner's profile and felt a growing sense of warmth inside. He saw a familiar gentleness hiding behind that stern expression. A tenderness.

'I've missed you,' he said.

It didn't thaw her. If anything, her expression grew sharper and more rigid. 'You didn't.'

He rolled his eyes. 'I'm lying then.'

She looked at him. She didn't need to voice her response. He saw it in her eyes: '*Well, it wouldn't be the first time you've lied, would it?*'

It was fair. He forced down a surge of irritation. He'd still plead his case, though. 'Do you check your messages? If you did, you'll have seen that I've tried tonnes... and tonnes... of times to contact you.'

'I saw.' Gardner sighed. 'But was it because you missed me, or because you needed me?'

Riddick lowered his head. Another fair point. 'No... I *missed* you, boss. That's why I kept trying.'

'Even if that was the case... it wasn't a good idea. And you know that.'

'Do I?'

She looked away from him again. 'Have you completely forgotten about our last week together?'

'Of course not, but I also remember that we were friends.'

'Yes. *Were.*'

'Are,' he insisted.

'Come on!' she snorted. 'Friends don't betray each other like you betrayed me.'

'What I did' – he stopped himself short of saying Ronnie's name – 'had nothing to do with you.'

'Like hell! I'm your partner... your superior. You compromised me. It's not just about you. The consequences of your actions affect others, which is why you can't possibly be my friend.'

Riddick shook his head. She hadn't looked at him in a short time. It was tearing him apart. 'Please... boss... look at me.'

She did, albeit with a raised eyebrow and an unconvinced look on her face.

'When I saw you come into this room a moment ago, it felt like we'd never been away from each other. And now we're talking again, I feel absolutely convinced of that.'

'You call this talking?'

'Yes. This is normal. You were always bloody stubborn.'

At first, she looked stunned, then she appeared horrified for a moment, before her face suddenly melted into an expression of disbelief. She shook her head. 'You can't be serious... Jesus, you are, aren't you? I'm stubborn!' She pointed at herself. 'Me? Please tell me this is a joke. You're the most stubborn person I've ever met.'

'It wasn't me who decided that our friendship was null and void.'

Gardner turned away, shook her head and sighed. 'Give me strength.' She stood, made to walk away, but then looked back instead. 'Why do you care so much about this friendship anyway? You've moved on. You're happy.'

'Moved on? Happy? Why do you say that?'

'You've met someone else.'

'I didn't know that you knew.'

Gardner's face reddened. 'Well, now you do. So, you should be happy.'

'I probably should.' He recalled Claire's note the previous evening. *Instead, of always working so hard to mess things up.*

'And not always dwelling on the past!'

Easier said than done. 'Does the fact that I'm with Claire bother you?'

'Ridiculous!' Gardner waved her hand at him and walked away. Two metres from him she swung back. 'Of course it doesn't bother me! I'm happy for you.'

'You were married, remember? Back when I was here—'

'Bloody hell – what's that got to do with anything?'

'I don't know,' Riddick said and shrugged, confused. Because this conversation genuinely confused him. He wasn't sure where it was heading. 'Just going to stick to my guns here, boss. I missed you. I still consider you a friend. We're quite similar...'

She stepped back towards him, pointing. 'We're not. *Not* at all.'

He sighed. She was just too disappointed in him. Ashamed of him. Time hadn't softened her stance. Or healed it.

Rice came in, holding a cup of coffee, putting them both out of their misery. He handed the coffee to Riddick. '*Two* sugars as requested.'

Prick.

Riddick stood and looked between them. 'Have we got twenty minutes before the briefing?'

'Yes,' Gardner said. 'That's fine.'

'Brilliant.' He tried to sound enthusiastic, determined to appear professional and unfazed by the reunion with Gardner. 'I wondered if you could both talk me through where you're up to in Operation Red Cascade. The personal touch will help. I can then refine my piece for your troops on the Mansters and Bradford.'

As they filled him in, Riddick realised he was lying to himself.

He was completely fazed by the reunion.

Revisiting this conversation later felt as inevitable as sunrise.

42

During the briefing, Gardner fought to focus – her interaction with Riddick had thrown her.

Had she just made a complete fool of herself?

You've met someone else.

Does the fact that I'm with Claire bother you?

She inwardly groaned. *I must have sounded like a jealous, lovesick teenager.*

And that wasn't what I'd meant at all!

Was it?

She'd also been distracted by the response of the room to Riddick's return.

It'd been mixed to say the least!

Prior to Gardner's arrival, one of Riddick's cases had involved a teenage suicide. His handling of the investigation had come under intense scrutiny, and a scathing report by brutal freelance journalist Marianne Perse had been the nail in the coffin. The DI's reputation had been in tatters, both inside HQ and outside of it.

Some of his former colleagues saw through the smoke to the real man and had, today, welcomed him home with firm hand shakes and some back slaps, while those who'd always considered him a loose cannon, and had been glad to see the back of him almost a year back, gave him a wide berth.

Still, regardless of people's views of Riddick, including her own, here he was, delivering the goods, as he'd so often done in the past.

Riddick revealed that the victim, Ralphie Parks had, indeed, been on the Mansters' pay roll for the past month. He showed the team photographs of Ralphie meeting members of the Mansters, including the now-dead Nathan Cummings. There was also one image of Ralphie holding the duffel bag that looked remarkably like the one recovered from his late girlfriend's room. Keyboard-happy Matt Blanks threw this into HOLMES 2 with his usual loud clacking flair.

Rice said, 'Makes sense. It's been over a month since Ralphie was last seen in his halls of residence or in any lectures. It seems he'd ditched uni without telling anyone – even his parents. If you believe what they say. Seems he's been a busy boy.'

Had Vivianne known?

Had this perhaps been the cause of their argument reported by Toby Brundle – the teenager who'd opted not to walk alongside the murdered couple en route to that cemetery?

Barnett had his hand in the air. 'Maybe Ralphie stole from the Mansters? Skimmed profits? We *know* he was using the drugs, personally. Was he paying for them?'

'Of course, it's possible,' Riddick said. 'Although, there's been no indication on our end that Ralphie went rogue with the drugs. And even if he'd been skimming from the Mansters' profits, killing both him and his girlfriend would be a little extreme even for them. Not that you should rule it out.'

When Riddick went into more detail over who these Mansters were, Gardner recognised something in Riddick's eyes and tone of voice. If you didn't know Riddick like she did, you would probably consider it passion.

But she knew better.

She recognised his obsession immediately.

Gardner didn't need to hear much more of this narrative to know that the existence of Nathan Cummings and the Mansters had consumed Riddick over the past year.

Just as so many others before had consumed him.

When it came to those who were a scourge on the vulnerable, Riddick was there. Whole-heartedly. Admittedly, an admirable trait in an officer of the law, except, perhaps, when you'd no limits.

She thought of the destruction that Riddick's relentlessness had caused to himself and those he loved. All in the name of what was right.

At what point did the lines blur?

When Riddick showed a photograph of the carvings in Arthur Fields' chest, she wasn't looking at the grotesqueness of the image, she was looking at the tears in his eyes, and how quickly he turned away to brush them from his eyes before anyone noticed.

Oh, Riddick...

She lowered her head. *Don't go there, Emma. Don't you dare.*

Riddick then talked everyone through Keith Fields – Yorkshire's equivalent to a Kray twin during the seventies and eighties. 'Or so he'd have you believe,' Riddick had added with a sneer. 'And I don't buy that he's an exile from the underworld. I think this life of poverty is a front. He's involved, somehow, in all of this. I'm certain of it.'

Having recovered from her embarrassing conversation with Riddick, Gardner took the floor and made suggestions on how these dots could be connected.

'I think it'd be a monumental surprise now if these murders didn't turn out to be drug related.' She pointed at a photograph of

Ralphie on the board. 'One of our victims dropped out of university, to work county lines. He stored a large bag of unicorn tablets at Vivianne's house. He was also dealing them to the youth around Knaresborough, and further afield, in Harrogate and Boroughbridge, I imagine. I'm not buying that Vivianne didn't know about her boyfriend's involvement. Great character reference, yes, but love does funny things to people. Also, there are suspicions he was emotionally abusing her. Mary Gill said that he'd been critical of her weight. Okay, so let's think... the night of their deaths, they lied to their parents, and headed to Ethan Williams' party here at about 7.15 p.m.' She pointed out the location of the party on the map.

'Fifteen revellers in total. All enjoying some of Ralphie's Bradford-sourced product.' She pointed at the list of names. 'Stories are consistent but vague. Potentially because they were off their heads or potentially because they're hiding something. One thing they all stressed, suspiciously I might add, is that Vivianne and Ralphie were getting on like a house on fire.'

She looked between the faces of her team. 'An ambulance is called for Charlotte Hughes and Adam Briggs at 11.35 p.m., and everyone left. The reports *then* get even more bloody hazy. It seems most of our teens *claimed* to walk in a different direction to Vivianne and Ralphie. Apart from Toby Brundle. Toby went against the grain by indicating that the couple weren't seeing eye to eye. Was Vivianne pissed off over her boyfriend's double life as a drug dealer? It was a fifteen-minute walk to the graveyard. Toby lost sight of them because he went deliberately slowly because of the awkwardness of the situation. Presumably, they, Vivianne and Ralphie, went straight to the cemetery and were murdered between 12 a.m. and 2 a.m....'

She pointed at the list of the fifteen students at the party. 'I don't like this. I don't like the vagueness. The ambiguity. The emphasis on our victims being loved-up in the house. It feels manufactured. Someone is hiding something. What's Toby let out of the bag here? We need to go *at* the students again and again; force long and detailed statements from them until someone spills. Get *everything*. What songs did they dance to? Who did they talk to? How often did they go to the toilet? We need to turn it into a school assignment. Drive them crackers if necessary. Someone must know something. And...' She pointed at all the roads between Ethan's home and the cemetery. 'As emphasised yesterday, we pound these doors until they come off their hinges.'

She looked at Riddick. 'If the Mansters were involved... did they follow our victims? Did Toby see anyone following them? Maybe Paul, another gang is involved? Maybe they met Ralphie in the graveyard, and the Mansters gatecrashed that clandestine meet? You've informed us of how violent and explosive the clashing of rivals can be.'

Riddick nodded. 'It's possible.'

'Could our killer and Nathan's killer be the same?'

Riddick didn't look convinced.

'Assignments on the board. I'm working with Paul on the Mansters' angle.' She'd just decided this off the cuff. It felt sensible. She caught Rice's eyes. He looked stormy.

Yep. That might be an issue. Give him some kudos.

'I'm keeping DI Rice central to this. If these kids know anything, if the families know anything, if Sebastian bloody Harrington knows anything, it won't get past DI Rice.' She offered him a wink. He looked a little less stormy. *Good.*

The thought of Sebastian sent a shiver down her spine. Should she mention his connection to the strange man, Neville Fairweather, who may or may not have been to her house yesterday? She decided not to. It all still felt *too personal.*

'And, finally, it's becoming more and more apparent that

Howard Walters' murder and the excavation of Penny Maiden's body aren't linked to Operation Red Cascade. Just a horrible coincidence. Ecstasy was used recreationally in the seventies, but it wasn't widespread until into the eighties – after Penny's death. I think the drug angle clearly distinguishes the two cases now. So, unfortunately, we'll be losing DS Barnett this morning as he returns to the Howard Walters' investigation.'

'Great,' Barnett said and sighed.

She nodded at him sympathetically. 'We'll miss you.'

She then looked back at Riddick and inwardly sighed. *Working together again.*

And if it was anything like last time, there'd be fireworks.

Lots of them.

43

Speaking of days to remember... well, this was certainly promising to be one.

Earlier, the conversation between Riddick and Gardner had been spontaneous and passionate; their interaction now just felt wooden and cold.

'How are Rose and Ana?' Riddick asked.

'Good.'

'Settled?'

'Yes, I guess.'

'And you?'

She indicated left off a roundabout. 'Am I what, sorry?'

'Settled.'

'I'm fine.'

'That's good.'

She caught Riddick nodding out of the corner of her eye. He probably thought she was being a right cow.

Am I?

Probably.

Should I care?

She sighed inwardly as she moved into the first lane of the motorway. 'And how's Claire?'

'You know her name?'

'You mentioned it earlier.'

'Ah, yes, I remember.' He nodded again, and then ran a hand through his hair. 'She's... well... she's not great.'

Gardner flicked a look at him with a raised eyebrow. 'Oh, why?'

'Not happy. She just left me.'

'I'm sorry.' She offered a forced, sympathetic expression.

'She needs time to think.'

'No need to tell me anything.' Gardner indicated to change lanes.

But if you do wish to elaborate... feel free... I'm all ears.

'You asked.'

'Being polite. I don't need details.' *I'd like them, yes, but you don't deserve to know I'm interested.*

'Okay, no details then.'

Shit. Gardner changed lanes. They sat in an awkward silence for a minute.

Sod it. 'So, you think you'll get back together?'

Riddick smiled at her. She conceded defeat and shrugged. 'We were friends... once.'

'We were... Look, concerning Claire, I don't know.'

'What was the reason you split?' Gardner pressed.

'The usual. Need to get myself in better shape, again.'

Out of sorts, eh? She looked at him. *Story of your life, isn't it?*

Gardner indicated to come off the motorway.

'So, anyone in your life?' Riddick asked.

She snorted. 'Blunt!' But fair play. Not like she'd been holding back.

'Being polite,' Riddick said, echoing her earlier excuse.

'Yes... except you couldn't sound any less interested.'

'Bloody hell, boss. Okay, I'm *interested* to know if there's a significant other.'

'Now, you sound smarmy!'

Riddick groaned. 'Do you know what? Just leave it. You were the one who just drew attention to our friendship.'

There was another awkward silence for a minute. Riddick tapped his fingers on the door and stared out of the window.

Irritating.

Sod it again!

'I'm not seeing anyone. Okay? Happy now?'

He turned from the window, appearing very confused. 'Why would that make me happy?'

'No... I didn't mean happy over my being alone, happy that I answered your question!' She felt her cheeks filling with blood.

'Well, yes, I like talking to—'

'For the record, I'm not lonely.'

Riddick raised his eyebrows. 'I never said you were.'

Her cheeks burned now. 'Music.' She reached forward and switched on the radio. The sound of a Take That classic filled the car. 'Until we get to Bradford, probably best.'

Riddick sighed. 'I agree. But before Bradford, I want to show you something to give you context, okay?'

'Okay... guess that's why you're here. Where exactly?' she asked, wanting the ground to open up and swallow her.

44

Gardner stood back in the hospital room and watched as Riddick clutched the hand of the vulnerable young man and brushed limp, greasy hair from his eyes.

At first, it surprised her to see Riddick being so tactile with a man pushing twenty, but it quickly became clear that he was only really an adult physically. He spoke with limited vocabulary and was childlike in his facial expressions and tone of voice.

From the earlier briefing, Gardner already knew that this was the young man who'd been severely injured by the Mansters, which had filled Riddick with guilt. She also knew about the lad's father, Keith Fields – the Yorkshire Kray twin.

Seeing Riddick so enamoured by this vulnerable young man was both heart-warming and terrifying.

Her mind flicked back to her earlier concerns in the incident room. This was classic Riddick. He was too emotionally involved.

'Where's this change of plan come from anyway?' Riddick said, laughing. 'Aren't you supposed to be Antman? Antman's nobody's sidekick!'

'Please... you're just better at it. I can learn... from you.'

'No, fella, you're not being my sidekick. You're the superhero, and we both know that I'm *no* superhero.'

'You saved me yesterday.'

'I'll think you'll find that was the paramedic. To be fair, they're the true superheroes in town. Sorry, buddy.' He ruffled his hair, but after doing so, had to move hair from his eyes again. 'You're the main man. Antman.'

'I don't mind being a sidekick. I could be Wasp?' Gardner said, stepping forward.

Riddick smiled up at her.

She nodded at him. 'Yes, I've seen a few of them, you know?'

'Didn't doubt it,' Riddick said, still smiling. 'I can certainly see the wasp in you.'

'I'm going to take that as a compliment, being that she's a rich, famous, attractive movie star.'

Gardner approached, so she was standing alongside Riddick. 'How are you doing, Arthur?' she asked.

He grinned. 'I'm always happy when Paul is here.'

Gardner raised an eyebrow. 'Mustn't be the jokes.'

'You'd be right there, boss,' Riddick said. 'Arthur is the comic genius round these parts.'

Arthur laughed and then winced, one of his hands jolting to the bandages on his chest. 'It hurts.'

Gardner exchanged a look with Riddick. The sadness in his eyes was clear. Her own heart dropped.

Riddick clutched Arthur's hand again. 'Easy there, big man. You know it'll settle. Like last time.'

Arthur nodded. Tears from the pain crept from the corners of his eyes. He looked up at Gardner. 'Are you Paul's girlfriend?'

Gardner blushed.

Out of the corner of her eye, she saw Riddick put a hand over his eyes and shake his head. 'Oh, Arthur, you never stop, do you? It's my boss – I told you before.'

Arthur laughed and winced again. Whether he meant it as a joke, or he'd just forgotten what Riddick had told him earlier, was uncertain.

'Yes, I remember,' Arthur said. 'Wait... wait... DSI Emma Garden.'

'Close enough,' Gardner said and laughed. 'But call me Emma!'

They talked for a while longer before Riddick announced that duty called'.

'It was lovely meeting you, Arthur,' Gardner said.

'Bye Emma!' He gave her a thumbs-up. She'd seen Riddick do that a few times and wondered if he was emulating him. 'Enjoy the *garden*!' He laughed at his joke.

They both laughed too. It was hard not to – the boy was so childlike and sweet.

She winked. 'I'll be in touch about being your sidekick!'

'Thanks!' Arthur said and grinned.

She waited outside while Riddick said goodbye. She watched him through the glass window as he kissed Arthur on the forehead as if he was his own child.

Outside, back in the car, they sat in silence for a moment.

A few times she glanced over at Riddick and saw that sadness in his eyes. That *familiar* sadness that she'd seen so many times before.

She felt an urge to reach over to him, squeeze his arm, but fought it off. *No way I'm letting you back in again.*

She started the engine, shaking her head. *Why Paul? Why do you do it to yourself?*

'I wanted you to see what you're dealing with,' Riddick said. 'I want you to appreciate what Nathan and those other monsters did.'

'You think I don't appreciate what we deal with?'

Riddick nodded and looked out of the passenger window. 'Sometimes we forget. Sometimes there's no time for the humanity—'

'You don't think it's enough for me to *know* that these bastards, these Mansters, carved a vulnerable man up?'

'He's like a child.'

'I'm aware, and—'

'Nathan... his people... they *tortured* a child.'

Gardner sighed, looked in the rear-view mirror and reversed from the parking spot. 'Well, I get it... you don't need to show me any more examples of their dirty work. If this case helps stop them in their tracks, go for it. Like I'd have ever stood in your way!'

She drove towards the car park barrier. Riddick was yet to respond. She glanced nervously at him. His shoulders were quivering – was he crying?

She pulled over just before the barrier. Unable to hold back any longer, she reached over and squeezed his upper arm. She left her hand there. 'It's kind of you, Paul. So very kind of you to give him friendship.'

He turned and looked at Gardner. His eyes were damp. 'No boss. It was him. It was him that gave me his friendship.'

45

Following the doctor's visit, Dean Maiden felt better than ever.

Rather peculiar when you considered the doctor's prognosis. His ticker was on the decline. A couple of months at the most.

About bloody time. He laughed. *It's been over forty years since I lost everything I ever gave a flying—*

His laugh suddenly melted into a cough. As it always did. He pinned the mask to his mouth and took a couple of breaths of oxygen. Once the coughing had settled, he climbed out of bed, walked over to the window and gazed out over the empty green fields.

A couple of months, you say.

Well, I won't be taking it easy until the finishing line, I'll tell you that.

A couple of strolls out there, sun on his face, hair in the wind. An absolute must.

Sod my breathing and sod the chest pains.

He looked around his room. *Rather keel over tomorrow and die in the grass, than fester for two more months in this sterile room.*

Dean went over to his dressing table, sat down and looked in the mirror. 'Hello old man.'

He fastened the top button on his striped pyjamas to make himself look smarter, straightened his back, as much as you could straighten an arthritic spine shaped like a pretzel, and smiled at himself.

He'd never been good looking, but once upon a time, he'd not been *bad* looking.

His heart condition had taken the colour from his skin and aged him beyond his years.

I look like a sack of spanners.

Add to that the empty left eye socket, which made his lid sag.

No sir, it doesn't add up to a pretty picture.

He reached over to the table and popped in his glass eye.

Better, but you ain't getting onto the cover of Men's Health.

He looked down at a framed photograph of all three of them together around a birthday cake in a restaurant. Penny was wearing a yellow floral dress. It'd been a birthday gift from him and Estelle on her seventeenth birthday. She'd never reached her eighteenth.

He traced his daughter's face and smiled.

So unfair, my girl. You deserved to have your life.

He hugged the frame to his chest and closed his eyes. *Listen to that, my girl, listen to the winding down of your old man's heart. I could be with you soon enough.*

He sighed... So, so unfair...

If not for Neil Clark, how would everything have turned out, eh?

If not for Neil Clark...

And then he was back in that night again, sprinting up that road, unemployed, half-cut, down on himself, a fool for forgetting to pick up his daughter from the church and...

Mike Crawley... Harry Rhodes... good men... good police...

unable to look him in the eyes, and that gurney... *oh God, that gurney*... that plastic sheet... that plea not to look...

The blood being diluted by the thrashing rain...

Washed away down the hill.

Penny.

His daughter.

Washed away.

He opened his eyes, placed the frame back down on the desk and traced her face again.

I'm sorry.

He could feel his daughter's eyes on him. A hint of condemnation in them.

'I really am sorry. I was a mess. I failed you, Penny, and if I'd the time again I'd be at the church door, right on time.'

Rubbing at his temples, he closed his eyes once more. Headaches. Another bane of his life. Usually, when he was neglecting his oxygen. He often tried to weather it to see if he could adjust. An impossibility. How did you adjust to a failing heart? You didn't. He always headed back to the mask and the tank – his dream of independence again shattered.

He opened his eyes and looked over at the tank. *Sod you. I'm dead in two months, anyway.* He looked back at his daughter.

And there's nothing to hang around for. Doesn't look like they have a clue who took you from your spot, Penny, and left that old hound dog in your place.

He already knew who'd killed his daughter. *Neil Clark.* The digging up of Penny, and the murder of Howard Walters, was a mystery he could die with. After everything he'd been through, he could handle that. Besides, Penny was back at rest, now with her mother... and Howard was no skin off his nose, not really. The man hadn't really been a good friend.

He rubbed harder at his temples; the headache was worsening.

And don't worry, Penny. The whole truth will come out when I've gone.

He'd already penned a note – hidden in his belongings. It revealed the facts behind Penny's death... Keith's intimidation... the brutal murder of Neil.

Keith, you'll face justice. But for now, I'll leave you to fester in the hell hole you've dug out for yourself.

Because he knew all about that. Dean had spent most of his life keeping tabs on Keith Fields. If he hadn't already fallen into poverty and disgrace, he'd have shopped him to the police sooner. But his suffering was clear for all to see. And Dean, joining him as an accomplice, dying in a prison bed, instead of walking those green fields? Well, if it wasn't necessary, it wasn't necessary. Keith's miserable end was a certainty following his passing, anyway.

Headache now threatening to split his head in two, Dean rose and moved back to his bed and the oxygen tank which would offer him relief.

After lying back down, he closed his eyes and reached for the mask. He found himself falling into a pained blackness before he got the mask to his face.

A spanner flashed through the air.

'Keith, stop! That's enough. Damn it. You've knocked his bloody eye out of his head...'

Dean recognised the voice.

Unbelievable.

What was he doing here?

Dean's eyes bolted open in the here and now. He pinned the mask to his face and sucked as hard on the oxygen as he could. His chest burned, and he clutched at it with his available hand.

Don't give up on me now... damn you... not after what I just saw... what I remembered.

That moment of unconsciousness, sleep, or whatever it was, had revealed a memory to him.

It hadn't merely been a questionable dream. It'd been a truth. A truth buried by Keith's violent blows over forty years ago.

The pain started to ease. *Thank God... thank God...*

But *this* memory... *this* fragment... what sense did it even make?

If he told anyone else, they'd assure him it was just a dying man's brain playing tricks on him.

But it's not! It sure as shit happened.

'Keith, stop! That's enough. Damn it. You've knocked his bloody eye *out of his head...'*

Their MP. Sebastian Harrington.

Dean eased himself up into a sitting position and stared over at the picture of him and his family.

How easy that investigation into Penny had died. So quickly.

The day Neil Clark had disappeared from the face of the earth...

But the police had never known about Neil Clark. For them, the case was unsolved. So, why had the investigation into Penny died such a sudden death?

Why didn't the likes of Mike Crawley and Harry Rhodes carry on pulling up trees? For a few more months at least? Looking for the bastard who mowed down an innocent, young woman?

Unless...

Had someone leaned on them?

A politician. One of the most powerful politicians of that era. *Sebastian Harrington.*

And why'd he do that?

To protect Keith.

Unless...

And this really filled Dean with dread: unless Keith had been protecting Sebastian?

From what?

He steadied his breathing and then climbed back out of bed.

It was time to leave the home.

This was one mystery that couldn't wait until after his death.

46

After spending the best part of an onerous morning recalling evidence from storage, DS Ray Barnett sighed over the boxes containing Howard Walters' belongings.

Barnett wasn't confident, but then who was during evidence reviews? After all, it'd already been scrutinised to the minutest detail, and the results fed into HOLMES 2, meaning it could be recalled at the touch of a button anyway.

Still, Barnett believed that there was no substitute for getting your fingers on the raw evidence. As time passed, and an investigative web thickened, tired or potentially overlooked evidence could suddenly become the link that completed the chain. And, after Operation Red Cascade had reared its ugly head at the same cemetery, there was no better time for a crack of the whip.

He dived into Howard's world. The photographs of him with many women. A lady's man according to Dean Maiden. These snaps didn't suggest otherwise. There were also a lot of photographs of cars – and it seemed like he'd spent a lot of time at shows and conventions. There were old tickets for concerts, and Barnett enjoyed touching them – especially the stub for a Floyd conference and a Bowie one. Old passports, driver's licences. Jewellery.

Nothing triggered him.

He groaned when he moved on to the business records; daunting, dull and a far cry from the music memorabilia.

He separated out the records: receipts for products, handwritten tax declarations, VAT claims etc. All the time having painful flashbacks to the last time he did this...

It was still like looking for a needle in a haystack!

Hours crawled past.

What the hell am I doing?

Finally, he moved on to Howard's business logbook. He focused primarily on 1978–1981, covering the year before, during and after Penny had died.

Fortunately, Howard had been a neat writer. Barnett ran his finger down the bookings.

His eyes closed. He groaned again and took five minutes for a strong coffee. It seemed to invigorate him.

He moved through the list and paused over one booking: 21 June 1978. SAH.

Howard rarely used initials for his customers.

So why didn't I flag it last time?

He mustn't have paused for a coffee. Never underestimate the power of caffeine.

He wrote SAH down in his notebook and continued down the list quickly, looking for another booking made for the initials SAH. 20 June 1979. Made sense. A yearly service.

He jumped ahead to June in 1980. There he was again, 22 June.

He moved ahead to June 1981, but found no record of this person here.

Did you find a new mechanic, SAH?

Well, you did at least three years on the bounce...

Barnett looked through his notes for the date of Penny Maiden's death.

The 24 June 1980.

He returned to the initials on the 22 June 1980.

SAH had taken in his car two days before Penny's death...

He continued running his finger down the page until it stopped on the 25 June 1980.

SAH...

And he'd taken his car in *again* the day after Penny's death.

Highly unlikely to be having two services three days apart.

What did this mean? Who the bloody hell was SAH?

Why are you protecting your identity?

Barnett assumed the customer must have asked Howard to do that.

Who'd want to be so secretive? Someone famous... high-profile... concerned about having their name seen in a book out in the open...

S?

A thought occurred. Barnett hit Google and searched.

Shit.

Sebastian Aaron Harrington.

Filled with adrenaline, Barnett grabbed his suit blazer and darted out of the office.

47

The doorbell woke Sebastian.

He raised his head from the desk and looked down at the photo album in front of him. It was open on its usual page.

A picture of her eating ice cream on her father's shoulders.

He'd one just like it in his *own* photo collection. Except, in his version, his daughter had been dripping the ice cream into his hair.

The doorbell sounded again.

He closed the photo album and, groaning, rose to his feet.

Stiff from yesterday's goal-scoring exploits at the youth centre, he stumbled out of the office and onto his winding staircase. Trying to put as much weight on the winding banister as he could, Sebastian worked his way down the stairs.

The doorbell went a third time. *Okay... okay... hold your horses...*

He increased his speed, grunting and groaning, shaking his head over his attempts at football in his seventies.

Breathing deeply, he reached the bottom step and hobbled over to where the monitor was on the wall. *Bloody hell!* His legs felt like they were on fire.

He stared into the monitor.

Breath catching in his throat, he took a long step backwards.

It can't be!

He rubbed at his eyes. Grogginess, surely?

It just couldn't be...

He took a deep breath, looked into the monitor again and, forcing back a rising tide of nausea, welcomed in a most unexpected guest with the touch of a button.

48

Manningham.

Gardner stared out of the car window at three crumbling terraced houses sandwiched between two derelict shops.

One shop had been a nail salon and, despite the smashed windows and the litter strewn around it, could be kicked into life again by someone eager to do so. The sign, *Nailed On*, was still just that – nailed on, while it'd been painted recently.

Unfortunately, the other shop had no such hope – the front had been torched, and with it, any clue as to what it used to sell there.

'What the hell happened to that shop?' Gardner asked.

'Used to be a pawn shop. Someone took offence at the small offering for his mother's wedding ring.'

'Selling a family heirloom. Guess it was desperate times.'

'Indeed – very desperate – especially when the mother and father were still alive and married.'

'Shit.'

'Yes... let's just say they've yet to visit him in jail.'

'Quite a trade for you, eh? Knaresborough for this. You and Devon spend a lot of time out here?'

'Too much.'

'You and her... get on well?'

'I don't know. I think I irritate the hell out of her.'

'I *don't* believe that!'

'Piss off.' He smiled. 'Anyway, we sit in places like this regularly. But there are a lot of places like this... and most of the time, it's *bloody* slow. They rarely slip up. And when they slip up, it must be monumental, otherwise, you're wasting your time breaking surveillance. It must be conviction worthy.'

'Sounds like a blast.'

'It was an opportunity.'

Gardner nodded. 'Do you miss home?'

Riddick eyed her. 'Are you suggesting I come back?'

No. She quickly changed the subject. 'It's quiet.'

Riddick had promised to bring Gardner to the Mansters. 'It's *always* quiet. Low profile. Nathan's two right-hand men are known to occupy that one.' He pointed at the central house of the three sandwiched between the derelict shops.

'And that's the one you saw Ralphie Parks going in and out of?'

'Yes.'

'How do we know they're in?'

Riddick pointed out some vehicles. 'The Kawasaki Ninja bike is Geo Bennett's, and the pimped-up Audi A3 is Harris Mitchell's.'

'Geo?'

'Short for George... well, kind of; sounds nothing like it, I guess. Must have taken a liking to Neo in *The Matrix*. We could always ask him.'

'I'll leave that to you... with it being your territory.'

'Good idea. They can be rather feisty with people they don't know.'

'Doesn't sound that safe.'

Riddick cracked the door. 'It's not. If you opted to stay here, I'd understand.'

She opened her door. 'Are you trying to dissuade me, Paul?'

'No.' Riddick leaned over and smiled. 'I want you to come... be just like the good old days.'

The ones full of fireworks? Yes... that's what I'm afraid of.

49

Rice stopped his car behind Barnett's. 'What're you doing, man?'

Barnett was at the gated entrance to Sebastian Harrington's property. The gate was open.

'Get yourself in there!' Rice said, wishing Barnett could hear him.

Several minutes passed. Frustrated, Rice exited his vehicle and jogged up alongside Barnett's vehicle. He knocked on the window and Barnett opened it.

'What's the hold up?'

'The gate was already open.'

'Great. Jog on in then!'

'I think we should wait for more back-up.'

'You do, eh? Why?'

'Why'd he leave his gate open? No point in having security if you're not going to use it. And to be fair, this man has quite a few people who dislike him. Something untoward is going off. I've already called it in.'

Rice rolled his eyes. 'Listen... fella... the people who suffered under Thatcher and disliked Maggie's minion here to the point of murder are surely too long in the tooth to be of any danger now. You're going overboard. Now, get in there, or if you really are concerned, shift out of my way, so I can get in.'

Knowing that Barnett would oblige – he outranked him, after all – Rice returned to his car. He was certain he heard Barnett mutter an obscenity. Directed at him, no doubt.

Water off a duck's back.

Rice wasn't just discovering he was unpopular. He'd known this for most of his career. And it didn't seem to work against him. He'd made detective inspector less than a year back. Besides, being a stubborn, caustic bastard had hardly affected his father's career – he'd risen right to the top.

'Attaboy,' he said, smirking, as he followed Barnett down the long gravel drive.

Barnett waited for Rice to exit his car, and then they ascended the steps to the door together. Barnett's silence spoke volumes. A little nod at the door suggested he was happy to let Rice knock.

After four knocks, and some further lengthy silences, Barnett turned and went down the steps.

'He's probably just gone out and left the gate open,' Rice said. 'How long before back-up arrives, anyway?'

'Four minutes.'

'Okay.' Rice descended the steps, reaching into his pocket for his phone. 'I'll let the boss know.'

When Barnett didn't respond, Rice looked over his shoulder to see the DS looking in through the living room window.

Knock yourself out, Rice thought, returning to his phone and scrolling through it for Gardner's number.

'Shit!' Barnett said.

Rice swung in time to see Barnett slip past him and back onto the steps. 'We need an ambulance. He's down on the floor.'

Rice made the call while Barnett tried the handle. 'It's open!'

With the phone pressed to his ear, Rice followed Barnett through the door. The man was fast, but he kept up with him.

Rice requested the ambulance, while Barnett knelt beside Sebastian, who was face down.

Barnett checked his pulse and shook his head. 'Shit!' He turned the man over.

Rice felt his blood run cold.

Sebastian's face was pale, and vomit was around his mouth.

Barnett started CPR.

50

At first, the young Mansters, Geo and Harris, didn't want to let the two detectives in, but Riddick was his usual charming and subtle self. 'So... let me get this right, Harris and Neo – apologies, Geo – rather than answer a few questions in the comfort of your living room, you want me to arrange a warrant and drag half of North Yorkshire constabulary through your establishment. What a pair of dickheads.' He tore his phone from his pocket. 'Suits me just fine.'

Harris said, 'You can't speak to us like that—'

Riddick held up his hand to signal that he was now on the phone. 'Yes. Detective Inspector Riddick here, I need to arrange a warrant.'

Complete bullshit, of course.

'Okay, whatever,' Geo said, taking Harris's upper shoulder and turning him. 'Come in if you want!'

'I'll take a raincheck on that warrant... for now,' Riddick said into the phone as they both followed the Mansters in.

Riddick slipped the phone into his pocket and smiled at Gardner.

'Forgotten how subtle you were,' she whispered.

'You think these amoebas possess the intelligence for subtlety?'

Gardner inwardly sighed. If she closed her eyes, she could very well be with Rice right now.

Still, there was one major difference here. Riddick behaved like this because he was driven by sympathy and justice. Rice behaved like this because he was an angry alpha male, raised and often ignored by another angry alpha male.

Although it made Riddick the most endearing of the two, it also made him the most dangerous by a country mile.

She could've put a stop to him that day she'd found out about Ronnie Haller.

Would she come to regret deciding against it?

As they approached the lounge, Gardner saw a young and attractive Asian woman coming down the stairs, dressed in leggings and a tight blouse. The girl paused midway, stared at them and then turned to walk back up the stairs. Gardner looked at Riddick. 'You see that?'

'Yes. I recognised her.'

'From where?'

He shook his head. 'Not sure. Maybe I saw her coming in and out of this place on one of my evening shifts.'

'Shall we go and speak to her?'

Riddick considered. 'Let's stick with these two numpties first.'

In the lounge, Geo and Harris were already on the sofa, playing *FIFA* on a large HD screen that took up nearly a full wall.

Gardner recalled their heated debate outside as they approached the house:

'They're a right pair of scrotes,' Riddick had warned her.

'Of youths failed by society,' she had argued back.

Right now, seeing them blanking two officers of the law for *FIFA*, made Riddick the grandmaster of debates.

'Is this how you grieve the loss of your dear friend?' Riddick asked.

Geo and Harris leaned forward, gritting their teeth, working their joypads.

'Hello?' Riddick said. 'Nathan. Your boss? Has it hit you that hard that you don't remember who he is?'

Without looking at Riddick, Geo said, 'This was his favourite game.'

'Yeah,' Harris said. 'It's a tribute, like.'

Riddick walked over to the large television and tapped the top. 'Nice box, this. Take me the best part of a year to save for that. What's it you do again?'

'Finance,' Geo quipped, not taking his eyes from the screen.

'Online investment,' Harris said.

Riddick and Gardner exchanged a smile.

Hardly amoebas.

'I admit,' Riddick said out loud. 'They've more wit than I gave them credit for.'

Harris, who was cultivating some kind of beard from random splashes of bum fluff, cheered. 'One-nil!'

Geo responded with a colourful choice of language.

'To business, boys,' Riddick said. 'Ralphie Parks.'

Gardner watched the young men for a reaction. There wasn't one. Their eyes remained trained on the screen.

'Did you know Ralphie Parks?' Gardner said, speaking for the first time, and with a slightly raised voice.

'Never heard of him,' Geo said. 'Shit...' He rose from the sofa, working his joypad, teeth clenched. 'Don't you dare... don't you... ha ha! Piss off clown.'

'Still one-nil, dickhead.' Harris snorted.

Riddick and Gardner exchanged a glance.

Riddick sighed and shook his head. 'Kids, eh?' He pulled the plug from the wall.

Geo glared at Riddick. 'What the—'

'Listen, *boys*,' Riddick said. 'I don't have teenage sons, but I imagine this is how it sometimes works. Unless you play nice, you aren't playing.'

Geo threw his joypad down on the sofa. 'What do you want, pig?'

Riddick smiled at Gardner. She didn't smile back. Sickened by the aggressive tone of this interaction, she felt the urge to cut it short. Take the young men into custody if necessary. But, right now, she felt like she was on Riddick's patch. She'd carry on respecting his lead in the hope he knew what he was doing.

For now, anyway.

'Now, now, little man,' Riddick said, taking a step forward. 'I don't do tantrums.'

'I don't know a Ralphie Parks,' Geo said. 'So just piss off!'

Riddick waved his finger. 'That still sounds like a tantrum to me. Now, unfortunately for you, being childless, I've developed no patience for young'uns.'

Gardner flinched when she heard the word 'childless'. It hadn't always been that way for Riddick. But these young men didn't know that. To hear him say it, though, felt so tragic to her.

'Why'd we talk to the filth?' Harris said. 'If you'd anything, you'd arrest us.'

'Actually,' Riddick said, 'I could educate you on this. I'm happy to take you to the station and waste your time.'

'And you'd be wasting your time too,' Harris hissed.

'Undoubtedly,' Riddick said, nodding. 'You'll have a suit next to you encouraging you not to answer a single question. I get that. But I'm patient, as is DCI Gardner, so we'll get the entire day off you. Then, after a day of "no comments", I'll find a reason to come back and pick you up for another day... and another... and another... A waste of everyone's time. The difference is' – he pointed at his chest – 'we carry on earning our money while you'll have to rely on others... and you know what they say... when the king's away, the servants come out to play...'

Gardner was certain he'd just made that expression up. It seemed to have some effect, though. Geo and Harris were suddenly looking a lot more serious.

Riddick walked over to the coffee table, pulling a photograph of Ralphie walking into this very house out of his pocket. 'Whether you like it or not, you two are persons of interest...' He threw the picture down next to some empty pizza boxes. 'Nathan is dead. As is Ralphie Parks. And the thing is, *lads*, Ralphie ain't really one of you... not really. Posh and privileged. You know his uncle is an ex-Tory MP!' He shrugged. 'I know, I know, I hate it as much as the next person... but these are the cards we've all been dealt. If I want to make your lives a misery for the next week over the death of a former Tory MP's nephew, do you think I won't get the backing?' Riddick snorted, looked at Gardner and then back at the boys. 'So, it's your call... boys... song and dance... no time to work... no time to stop those underlings plotting against you' – he nodded at the television – 'no time to pay off the finance on this bad boy or... you give me ten minutes of your time, right now... and then, *Geo*, I'll give you a chance to equalise in your game.'

The kids looked at each other.

Gardner already knew Riddick had them.

He'd a talent for taking control... no question. Even if it felt completely wrong.

'We didn't kill that arrogant little toff dickhead,' Geo said. 'And we didn't kill Nathan...' He looked at Harris, clearly weighing up how much he could say. 'That's all we have.'

Riddick walked over to Gardner. She could see the frustration on his face. He whispered so Geo and Harris wouldn't hear. 'You want to wait outside?'

She narrowed her eyes. *Why? So I don't have to witness more of this unacceptable behaviour?* She shook her head. *No, do what you must do, Riddick. This is your turf. I'll accept the rules are just different here... at least for today, anyway...*

Riddick turned back. 'Just interested in Ralphie Parks, lads, nothing else. I know what you do here, but that's irrelevant to me for this moment alone. Whatever you tell me is off the record. One last chance... Talk to me, and I'll let you get on with the game.'

51

While Barnett repeatedly tried to get in touch with Gardner, Rice stood at the cordon blocking off the front gates of Sebastian's home.

Inside, Rice conceded that Barnett had been right about the open front gate – that something untoward had indeed occurred. Still, Rice didn't do admissions, or apologies, so Barnett could sling his hook.

The empty sleeping pill bottle on the table beside Sebastian's sofa suggested suicide, but the open front gates nagged. Sebastian had switched the automatic option on the gates off, so they had to be opened and closed with a press of a button. It implied someone had been here prior to Sebastian's death. Sebastian could've just forgotten to close the gates after they'd left – *unlikely* – or he'd been dead and so unable to hit the button after the murderer had left...

Rice let the SOCOs do their work while he mulled over it. He saw someone familiar approaching, on foot, alongside the line of vehicles. *That's all we bloody need.*

Marianne Perse and her cameraman stopped on the other side of the cordon.

'Bloody hell, that was quick!' *Shit!* He eyed the lens pointing at him. *Less of the expletives, Phil.*

Marianne pointed at the line of vehicles she'd just walked alongside. 'What can I say? You draw attention to yourselves!'

Rice smiled and raised an eyebrow. 'Is that camera on?'

She returned his smile. 'Is Sebastian Harrington okay?'

'Someone will be along to talk to you in due course.'

'Is this anything to do with the *still* unsolved murder of Howard Walters?'

She really was a bloody cow of the highest order! He stared at the camera pointing at him, and smiled again. 'Someone will be along in due course. If you could step back from the cordon, please?'

Marianne tapped her cameraman on the shoulder. He lowered it. 'Off the record?'

'No. You're too negative... about us.'

'With good reason.'

'Seriously, though... how did you find out so quick? Police scanner? Is someone feeding you from inside our department?'

Marianne smiled. 'Very accusatory, DI Rice. Tell you what' – she tapped the cameraman, who raised the camera again – 'let's keep it all on the record.'

Rice felt his blood boil. The lens was pushed further in his direction, *over* the cordon.

'I'm going to ask you to step back for a second time, ma'am, back from the cordon.' He pointed over at a vehicle. 'Over there should suffice.'

'Is Sebastian Harrington home?' Marianne asked.

'Ma'am, I'm sorry if this isn't clear, but if I must ask a third time, I'll have to make a call. You're interfering with a police matter,' Rice said.

Marianne smiled at him again. She tapped the cameraman, who again lowered his camera.

'We'll have it your way, DI. Maybe, we could catch up *alone* later... off the record?'

Rice raised an eyebrow. Now, that wasn't an offer you got every day. He briefly wondered what it'd be like to date Marianne. He wasn't completely averse to the idea. She was certainly attractive and far more glamorous than anyone he'd dated before. Completely out of his league, his colleagues would banter. Maybe that was what made her so appealing.

Still, he'd other fish to fry right now. 'Thank you, ma'am.'

He waited until Marianne was several metres back before turning and walking towards Barnett. 'Is the former MP hurt?' Marianne shouted from a distance.

He reached Barnett, who was pacing with frustration. 'Can't get in touch with the boss.'

'She's with *him*, what do you expect?'

Barnett shook his head. 'What's that mean?'

'You never noticed how they get lost in each other's eyes?' Rice said and smiled.

'Can't say I have...' Barnett said.

'Maybe you should open your own bloody eyes then,' Rice said.

Rice noticed how anxious Barnett looked and felt a rare moment of guilt. 'Go try in there,' Rice said. 'By the way, with Maggie's minion, there was nothing else you could've done—'

'Could you not call him that?'

Rice shrugged. He could hear Marianne still kicking up a storm and he thumbed over his shoulder towards the irritating, but attractive, journalist. 'She's a right one, isn't she?'

Barnett nodded. 'How did she get here so fast, anyway?'

'I know… makes you wonder…' Rice raised an eyebrow and looked down at the mobile in Barnett's hand. 'Makes you wonder, indeed.'

'What're you implying?'

Rice shrugged. 'Relax. Nothing. She'll be in touch. I'm going to see if we've any progress.' He turned and saw Marianne had wandered right back over to the cordon. He sighed.

Bloody woman. He wondered if she liked pizza. There was a new Italian on the high street.

'Phil!'

Rice turned to see Fiona Lane charging over from the front of the house.

'We've managed to get access to the—'

Rice interrupted her by placing a finger to his lips, and then nodded over in the direction of Marianne. He leaned in. 'Loose lips sink ships.'

Lane's expression quickly morphed from one of excitement to irritation.

Do I really have this effect on everyone? 'Go on then, Fiona.'

'The cameras. We have access to all the cameras around the property. We can see who came and went.'

52

Dean Maiden stepped into the lift, put the bag for life down, pressed the button for the fifth floor, and, as the doors closed, he gasped for air. He pounded the centre of his chest with his fist. *Come on... stick with me... not much longer...*

He'd survived the taxi journey to Bradford and – he glanced down at the bag for life – he'd even survived the pit stop for the necessaries.

To die now would be a bitter blow.

As the lift ascended, he put his throbbing head against the wall, closing his eyes, trying desperately to take back control of his breathing...

Howie's Garage.

He saw it with such clarity.

Burnt engine oil.

The smell was overpowering.

Screaming.

The noise of a young man's death.

A boy.

No older than Penny had been.

Had he been innocent?

Did I stand back and listen to an innocent boy burn?

The lift door opened.

'Keith, stop! That's enough. Damn it. You've knocked his bloody eye out of his head...'

Dean opened his eyes and lifted his head from the wall. He picked up his bag for life.

A young Asian couple stood there – barely into their twenties.

How long had it been since he'd last left the nursing home?

Years.

He didn't know how to respond to anyone any more. 'How do?'

'Are you okay?' the lad asked.

'Yes, son... thank you.'

As he staggered from the lift, the girl put a hand on his arm. 'Do you need help getting to your flat?'

He shook his head. 'I'm fine. Just need a sit down. Price of age, dear.'

Dean thanked them before walking away. He worked his way down the corridor, pausing every now and again to lean against the wall and catch his breath.

Not much further... now...

When he reached the right door, he pounded his chest again. *Be strong, Dean. Be strong one last time...*

What did you say, Stell... no backbone?

I'll show you. Better late than never.

He knocked and placed the bag for life on the floor just behind him. He didn't want Keith seeing into it. Spoil the surprise.

The door opened.

Keith looked emaciated; he also had a heavy stoop in his back.

'The years haven't been kind to us, Keith.' He coughed.

Keith eyed him up and down, struggling to recognise him.

'Really?' Dean asked between coughs.

Keith shrugged. 'Memory like a sieve, you know?' He started coughing, too.

'Does this help?' Dean said, pointing at his glass eye. 'Or this?' He turned his finger towards the scar on Keith's cheek. 'I still remember the sound that made. And the smell of burning.' He gulped back some air. 'I think about it often... It shouldn't give me pleasure... but it does.'

Keith's eyes widened, and he smiled. 'Look what the cat dragged in! Dean Maiden. As I live and breathe! Shit... old age doesn't suit you.'

'I'm not alone in that.' Dean steadied himself against the door frame and took some deep breaths.

Keith laughed, coughed and spat into a tissue in his hand. 'No, you're not. Although, at least I can still draw breath, once I clear out the sacks.' He patted his own chest. 'Whereas, you fella, you look like you're into the last minutes of your ticking clock.'

'I don't need long. Just five minutes.'

'How did you find me?'

'I made a point of always knowing where you were and what you were up to... It was nice to hear you'd fallen on rough times. It's been worth the effort.'

Keith smiled again. 'All these years, eh? Following me. Jesus, haven't thought about you... for...' He pointed at Dean's glass eye. 'Well, since I popped that sucker.'

'I remembered something. I want to know what it means...'

'Now you've my attention. What do you remember?'

'I remember someone stopping you. You were hitting me... and someone stopped you. I remembered today who that was.'

Keith nodded, smiling. 'Wow! You really forgot that until now. Shit, who'd have thought? I was ready for you to pop up again, cause a problem, and when you didn't, I just thought you'd seen sense. I assumed you'd realised you were out of your league.'

Dean coughed and took some mouthfuls of air. 'That bastard puppet for Thatcher and her brave new world. What did he have to do with anything?'

'Apart from saving your other eye? Your life?'

'I don't believe it... That man was a monster... everyone knows—'

'Don't believe everything you read. I'm telling you, he *saved* your life. If not for him, I would've taken the most sensible option.'

'So, why did he save me?'

Keith raised an eyebrow.

'I need to know,' Dean persisted.

'Do you?'

'Yes. I'm dying.'

'No shit. I'm surprised you've lasted this long in the conversation. You sound like Darth Vader.'

'Talk to me, Keith.'

'You won't like it. Dying in ignorance would be better for you.'

'It wouldn't. I died a long time ago. The night Penny died. I just want to close this.'

Keith nodded. 'I tried to give you closure once. You remember?'

'Neil Clark? Your closure was a lie, wasn't it?'

'Why didn't you just go to see Sebastian – ask him? Seems more logical.'

'Because I only have it in me for one trip. And this is about you. It's always been about you.'

Keith turned and took a step. 'Come on in then, Dean... but be warned' – he looked back over his shoulder – 'I still smoke... a lot... so if it kills you, then I won't be held responsible.'

53

'Well, that was a blast from the past. Although, I don't remember it ever being quite as bad as that,' Gardner said, climbing into the driver's seat, and closing her car door.

Riddick shrugged as he climbed into his side. 'Do you want my help or not?'

'Well, witness intimidation isn't something I signed up for.'

Riddick snorted and closed his door. 'Intimidation! Really – Geo and Harris just wanted shot of us so they could finish their game of *FIFA*! At what point do you reckon they felt intimidated precisely?'

'You're a lot more powerful than you realise – and they're practically children. You've got worse, Paul.'

Riddick narrowed his eyes and turned to Gardner. 'Children? Give me a break. What do we do, speak to their parents and suggest stopping their pocket money?'

'There's a right way and a wrong way. And you're long enough in the tooth to know which is the better option.'

'Look at the streets!' Riddick pointed out of the window at the derelict shops. 'Newsflash: this isn't Knaresborough! You think there's more than one option available here?'

'You think I've not worked areas like this before?'

'Maybe you've forgotten. Think about your investigation so far... you've interviewed the Parks, the Gills and Sebastian bloody Harrington! Privilege central! It's just a case of knowing your audience. It's you that's slipping, not me.'

'Even when you were in Knaresborough, you were too heavy-handed.'

'Whatever.'

'And that didn't end well.'

Riddick glared at her. 'Here we go.'

'Leave it.'

'No... go on... doors closed... no one can hear. Get it off your chest.'

Gardner started the car.

'Go on, boss, please, I'm all ears.'

Gardner shook her head.

'I killed a man,' Riddick said.

Gardner sighed, closed her eyes and shook her head. 'No... you paid for it.'

'Is there a difference?'

No. 'Yes.'

'Really?'

She hit the steering wheel and looked at him. 'This isn't the priority right now. What've we learned in there?'

Riddick sighed. 'Barely anything... but I think they were telling the truth. Ralphie Parks was doing a good job for them. What reason did they have to kill him?'

'Do you buy that they don't know who did it?'

'Yes. You think if they were at war, they'd be sitting playing *FIFA* and answering the door to coppers? I think they're as stumped as we are. They've got the feelers out though. We'll come back every day until they know more.'

Her phone beeped. She took it from her pocket and saw that she'd several messages on voicemail. Reception must have dropped out at some point in the Mansters' house. She was just about to catch up when she noticed, out of the corner of her eye, the front door of the house open. The young Asian woman that had turned around on the stairs earlier strolled out.

'Look... it's the girl that was familiar to you,' Gardner said.

Gardner dropped her phone into the door pocket.

When the young woman reached the gate, she looked up. Her eyes widened. She'd seen that Riddick and Gardner were parked on the opposite side of the road.

'Shit...' Riddick said. 'I remember her now.'

The girl turned and started to run.

'Who is it?' Gardner asked.

But Riddick was already diving from the vehicle. 'Follow us.' He slammed the car door behind him.

Gardner tried her best to follow alongside Riddick as he sprinted; fortunately, there wasn't currently any other traffic coming from either direction.

Riddick was still reasonably fast, but she could tell he hadn't been looking after himself and had put on some weight. The young woman he was chasing was tall, slight and had about twenty years on her pursuer. The gap between them was growing far too quickly for Gardner's liking.

The young woman took a sudden right down a ginnel.

Shit...

She looked up at the main road that she'd have to turn on and access the parallel street. There were vehicles on that road, but it didn't look ridiculously busy.

Accelerating, she hit her indicator to turn right, and sighted

Riddick, out of the corner of her eye, heading down that same ginnel.

There was suddenly a small line of cars occupying the left lane on the main road she was targeting. She hit the brake. 'Shit!'

She tapped her wheel. 'Come on... come on...' God, she wished she had her blues and twos!

Finally, thank Christ, space...

She swung her vehicle out and gave the engine a burst of fuel.

Her mobile phone rang.

She indicated right again, and turned off onto the street parallel to the one she'd just left. She hit the dash to answer the call on the hands-free.

'Yes...'

'DCI Gardner?'

'Yes... who's this?' No sign of Riddick on the street ahead, and no sign of another ginnel opposite the other. *Where the bloody hell are you?*

'It's Doctor Rodgerson from the Rosecamp Home.'

Doctor Rodgerson? Rosecamp... *familiar...*

She stopped the car at the end of the ginnel that Riddick and the young lady had entered from the other side. 'Sorry... I...' Gardner said, a churning sensation kicking up in her stomach. *Paul, are you still in there?* 'Can I phone back...?'

'Sure thing. There was a note on Dean Maiden's file... that was all.'

Dean Maiden. Shit. Of course. Rosecamp Home.

She'd had that note attached eight months earlier after interviewing him, asking that she be contacted in the event of any significant happening.

But Paul. Her heart was thrashing in her chest now, and she'd barely moved. 'What's happened to Dean?'

'He left the home an hour back. No one saw him leave. No one saw where he went.'

It was most certainly relevant, but right now, she'd visions o Riddick down on his knees, clutching his stomach, and that young woman, holding some kind of weapon. 'I'll phone back.'

She pounced from the car and ran towards the ginnel.

A tree branch and its foliage drooped over the entrance, so i was difficult to see as she drew close. She could hear something though.

The closer she came, the more recognisable the sound became Moans of pain.

54

Lucy O'Brien ate her cereal bar. Reminded of that moment in which Gardner's fingers had brushed her own when accepting that cereal bar in the incident room yesterday, she smiled.

Had that been accidental or intentional, Emma?

With Gardner on her mind, O'Brien opted to phone and check up on her sister. Everyone, including Gardner's children, were just fine.

Then, she exited her vehicle and approached the Brundle household.

Rice had phoned her with this gig after both he and Barnett had become preoccupied with Sebastian's suicide.

Toby Brundle.

The only guest at Ethan Williams' party who'd reported a spat between Vivianne and Ralphie.

And the only guest, *apparently*, who'd walked the same direction as the murdered couple, albeit at a safe distance – due to the awkwardness of the situation.

Rice had already tried this morning, but Toby had been out walking the dog.

'He does this most days – he grabs a book, takes the dog out and heads off somewhere to read,' his mother had said. 'Should be back early afternoon.'

O'Brien knocked and the door opened to reveal Toby's mother. 'Hi, ma'am. DC Lucy O'Brien. My colleague was here earlier. I was wondering if Toby has returned.'

Mrs Brundle's face paling, she took several steps back and steadied herself against a radiator in the hallway.

'Mrs Brundle, are you okay?' O'Brien said, following her into the house. She could suddenly hear the yapping of a small dog from somewhere deeper in the house.

'No...' Toby's mother said. Her eyes darted around anxiously. 'Ten minutes ago, Amy, our dog came back...'

She broke off and clutched her mouth.

'So, where's Toby, ma'am?'

'I don't know... Amy came home... *alone*.'

55

Heart thrashing, Gardner swerved the drooping branch and entered the ginnel.

She saw Riddick was working his way towards her. The young woman had her arm around his neck and was limping.

Sighing with relief, Gardner backed away to allow them out, pushing the overhanging branch away.

'I think I can manage now,' the young woman said, taking her arm from Riddick's shoulder. 'I'll just keep the weight off it.'

Riddick sighted Gardner's car against the kerb and ran to open the door for her. The woman limped in, and Riddick closed it.

They talked outside of the car.

'Who is it?' Gardner asked.

'Not one of the Mansters that's for sure.'

'I just watched her walking out of their house, and then run away...'

'Trust me,' Riddick said. 'She's not *really* one of them. From what I made out in her panic and pain back in the ginnel, she's been fooling them and has gained access to their lives. So, she didn't want to be seen talking with two coppers for obvious reasons.'

'Is she undercover?'

'Not in any formal capacity,' Riddick said and sighed. 'She's a civilian.'

'Jesus... what in God's name is she doing?'

Riddick leaned in closer to Gardner, so he was whispering. 'I didn't tell you the entire story about that night... the night when Arthur was scarred.'

'Now why doesn't this surprise me?'

'Bloody hell, boss. Give it a rest. Do you want to know or not?'

Gardner nodded, keeping the frustration trapped in her gritted teeth.

'Rafiq Khan, the shopkeeper who was attacked to distract me and Devon, has brain damage. He's still hospitalised.' Riddick nodded at the rear car window. 'And that's his daughter.'

'Jesus wept.'

'Samantha Khan. I recognise her from her father's bedside. We didn't speak long, hence the reason it took me a while to clock who it was.'

'And she's put herself into that drug den to spy on those scrotes?'

Riddick grinned. 'I'm sure that's my word.'

'It is, but I'm disliking them more and more.' Gardner looked at the girl through the rear window. 'Poor girl. What the hell was she thinking?'

Riddick sighed. 'Trying to get evidence. Hang them out in her dad's name. I've yet to get the finer details of how she pulled it off and what she knows. So, shall we talk to her?' Riddick nodded at the car.

Gardner recalled the call from Doctor Rodgerson at Rosecamp Home. *Dean left the home an hour ago.*

Was that important?

It'd certainly be important to Barnett, who'd been flung back into Howard Walters's murder, but was it relevant to Operation Red Cascade? They were yet to draw any connections between the two investigations...

Didn't stop it feeling bloody relevant though. 'I have to make a call, first. You start speaking to Samantha.'

Remembering she'd left the phone in the car, she opened the driver's door and plucked it from the pocket. She caught the young woman's eyes. 'Hi Samantha. I'm DCI Emma Gardner. You're safe, now.'

'Sam, please.' She wiped tears away.

'I'm sorry about what happened to your father.'

She looked down.

'Is he improving?'

'A little,' Sam said. 'Sometimes he remembers me now. He's unlikely to ever speak again, though.'

'I'm *so* sorry, Sam.' She held up a phone. 'I'm just going to make a phone call while Paul speaks to you. Then, we'll get you to the hospital—'

'It's just a sprain...' She looked up. 'I'm sure it won't be neces-sary... Maybe, I could just go home?'

We'll see, Gardner thought, smiling, and withdrawing from the vehicle. She closed the car door as Riddick opened the passenger side and climbed in.

She was about to phone Rodgerson back when she noticed the notifications for missed calls on her screen.

Of course! Just before we saw Samantha coming out of the house. The voicemails...

She listened to the first message from Barnett.

Barnett had discovered Sebastian Harrington's initials in Howard Walters's appointment book.

No connection, Emma? Think again. Here we go!

Howard had worked on Sebastian's car and the dates corre
sponded with the week of Penny Maiden's death.

She held her breath as she tried to think through it.

Had Sebastian driven the car that killed Penny?

And then taken it in to be worked on by Howard Walters after th
hit-and-run?

'Bloody hell,' she said, breathing out.

Is this anything to do with Penny's father, Dean, suddenly leavin
Rosecamp? Had he just found this out too? But how?

She recalled the leak from her station that had plagued severa
of her other cases here.

Had someone let Dean know?

It can't be. It's too sudden, too quick... it had to be a coincidence...

Regardless, truths were now bubbling to the surface and Dear
was out there, doing God knows what...

She shook her head. *Behave, Emma. Dean is a dying man and i*
in no fit state to do anything.

The voicemail had her reeling, but the next one really knocke
the stuffing out of her.

Sebastian dead? Suspicious suicide?

Jesus, maybe Dean Maiden has it in him, after all. A dying man'
last waltz...

But Dean wasn't responsible for Howard's murder. He'd bee
cleared, having been at Rosecamp Home that night. He'd bee
seen by multiple nurses and carers.

Maybe Sebastian had killed Howard for working on his ca
back in 1980? For knowing the truth? But if that was the case, wh
had Sebastian waited forty-three years? Unless Howard had onl
just come out of the woodwork to blackmail him, perhaps?

But Howard had been financially comfortable prior to hi
death. Why bother putting himself in so desperate a situation?

Her phone started ringing. Marsh. 'Yes, ma'am?'

'Emma... we need to talk.'

'I know, I've heard the messages. Sebastian took his car to Howard's garage on the week that Penny died. And now Sebastian has committed suicide...'

'There's more.'

Her heart raced. Had she been right? 'Was it Dean Maiden?'

'What makes you say that?'

'He's left Rosecamp Home...'

'What? Shit! No... it wasn't him. But someone was with him prior to his death—'

'Who?'

Silence.

'*Who?*'

'Listen, before I tell you, Emma, I want you to promise not to panic. Cameras show that Sebastian welcomed his guest like an old friend. Foul play isn't suspected. Sebastian can be seen clearly showing his guest out of the door, so I don't suspect he'd just been force-fed tablets. And it all may be coincidental...'

Gardner knew.

If Marsh was worried about her, it could only mean one thing.

Gardner's heart thrashed harder still.

'The guest was—'

'Neville Fairweather,' Gardner said.

'I'm sorry, Emma.'

56

Dean put the bag for life down on the floor beside him, while Keith eased himself into his La-Z-Boy, groaning, and then adjusted the seat so he could recline into a horizontal position.

'I'd offer you a seat,' Keith said, smiling. 'If I'd another.'

Dean surveyed the smoky room. The walls were yellowed and blistered. The ashtray beside the La-Z-Boy overflowed with fag ends.

Squalor.

Good.

It was just what the old bastard deserved.

Keith groaned as he reached over to the table beside himself for a fag and a lighter.

'How are you still alive?' Dean asked.

'Ha! Is that concern or regret?' He fired up his cigarette and took some hungry drags. 'Doctor tried to get me to quit. A useless endeavour. Mind you, to his credit, he convinced me to use filters. So, you could attribute my longevity to him, I suppose.' He laughed. 'And you know, that dickhead died from a stroke at fifty-three and never smoked a day in his life!' Keith's chuckles were gravelly, and it antagonised his clogged chest. He coughed aggressively for about twenty seconds, before leaning over and spitting into the ashtray.

'You're disgusting,' Dean said, wondering if his own heart would hold out under a coughing fit that violent.

'Ha... says you with that eye.' He took another puff. 'Can't you wear a patch or something?' He blew out a cloud of smoke. 'And what's in that bag? A gun? You planning to kill me, fella?'

'It's not a gun.'

Keith snorted. 'I'm not surprised. The Dean I remember... wow... now that man wouldn't hurt a fly.'

Dean took a step back to avoid the billowing smoke clouds at their most concentrated. He doubted it made much difference – he could barely breathe these days. 'Maybe you forget? When I came to you that night...' He forced in some air. 'If I hadn't been drunk, disorientated, I'd have had the better of you.'

'Bollocks.' Keith waved him away. 'You were down on your knees, snivelling, like you always were. You were pathetic and weak.' He took a puff, held the smoke in for a minute, tilted his head back and blew it out in a stream. 'Ha! Eye hanging out your chuffin' head, it was!'

Keep the adrenaline under control, old man.

If Dean lost control of his temper, he'd lose control of his breathing and then his heart. He had to remain calm. Stoic. Fulfil his duties, *his duties as a father*, before dying.

'Things are different now,' Dean said. 'When a man loses everything, as I did, he adapts...'

'Ah, yeah... that's right... she died too, didn't she? *Stell.*' Keith took another drag and blew out a smoke ring. He pointed up at it. 'Look at that! I've still got it.'

The anger inside Dean was like a coiled snake.

Keith was doing it on purpose. He'd spent his whole life antagonising others and now, with his life in the state it was, it was his default – the only thing he knew how to do.

The thought of Keith's deterioration offered him some comfort and helped to keep the snake calm.

'She couldn't bear to live any longer,' Dean said.

Keith smoked greedily. 'Death of a child will do that to you. Or so I'm told.'

'I heard you had a child.'

Keith laughed. 'Well... half a child...' He tapped his head. 'Not fully there if you catch my drift. But still, a man has responsibilities – you know what I mean? He's with his mother, anyhow. Now, there's a bitch if there ever was one. A real bitch!' He stubbed out his fag and reached for another. 'God, she's forever been an anchor around my neck.' He lit his fag. 'Seems you got yourself a lucky escape—'

'*Enough,*' Dean said. The coiled snake twitched. He felt a pain in his chest. He forced in some air, wishing he'd a tank of oxygen with him. Just enough to keep him going... until... 'I need to know. Neil Clark... the man *you* burned... did he kill my daughter?'

'*We* burned,' Keith said, smoking.

'Was it him?'

Keith smiled and coughed. It wasn't a coughing fit this time, but he still brought something up for the ashtray. After spitting it out, he looked up at Dean. 'I think you already know the answer to that one. If you didn't, why bother coming here?'

The snake's tail flickered.

'Did you kill an innocent man?'

'*We.* How many times? And no, Neil Clark wasn't innocent, don't you worry about that. Raped a girl, you know? Sixteen-year-old Katy Jones. *We* did the world a favour. Boy needed putting down.'

Dean felt a succession of sharp pains in his chest as the snake opened its eyes. 'Penny... did Neil kill Penny?'

Keith closed an eye and shook his cigarette in Dean's direction. 'Now, that Stell. You know, I sometimes think about her to this day. She was a card, wasn't she? If she'd stuck around, got over that depression, she'd have put all this together long before you, old man...'

The snake raised its head. 'Did *Neil* kill my daughter?'

'Stell was a right little vixen in her day. But I guess you'd know, Dean, eh?'

'Or was it Sebastian Harrington?' Dean clutched his chest and gasped for air.

'Easy now, tiger, don't be dying—'

Wincing, Dean fought the pain in his chest and the lack of oxygen to reach down into his bag for life.

'Shit, really?' Keith said, laughing over what emerged. 'Now this I've got to see.'

Rather than reply, Dean sucked in some air, pulled his hand from his chest and unscrewed the cap on the five-litre petrol container.

Keith's hand reached over to the controls of his La-Z-Boy.

'Don't...' Dean leaned over Keith with the container raised slightly. 'You've a lit fag in your hand.'

Keith drew his hand back. 'I tried to give you peace of mind, Dean. Neil was an opportunity for—'

The snake was wide awake now. Surveying. Slithering. Searching.

Dean coughed. The pain was intensifying. 'Peace of mind?' *Blood on the road... washed away.* 'What peace is there? There's only emptiness.' The snake raised its head again. 'Sebastian Harrington?'

'Rich. You know how it goes, Dean. You *knew* the world we lived in.'

'You helped him... protected him...' Dean felt a flash of pain. He staggered backward slightly. *Not yet. Damn it! Not yet.* He took a deep breath and steadied himself, just in time to give Keith second thoughts about reaching for the controls. 'Didn't you?'

'I made sure I got something back for the working man.'

The snake bared its fangs. 'Bollocks... he helped you build a sodding empire!'

Keith gestured around the room with his eyes. 'Some empire!' Keith held up the cigarette – there was a long stem of ash. 'I need to flick it.'

Dean felt another blast of pain, and this time a wave of dizziness. He didn't even realise that he'd staggered back this time. But after realising it, he said, 'Move your fingers another inch, Keith, and you'll burn...'

Keith drew his hand back.

'Seems I was wrong about you after all this time, eh? Wasn't Stell who was the card...'

The snake weaved its head. Dean knew his body was close to giving up.

Keith pointed at his raised feet at the end of his La-Z-Boy. 'Guess I'm at your mercy. Is this how it ends?'

Dean nodded.

'Wow... and all because Howard, the pissed-up dipstick, did such a shit job on Sebastian's brakes!'

Howard... is that why he was killed? Had Sebastian finally taken revenge?

Dean was desperate to ask more questions, but his pain, his breathing, his coordination... he was failing. It was now or never...

'You know none of this was intentional, don't you? And now what? I pay the price for that pair of dickheads...'

Dean nodded again. 'You *knew* the truth.'

Keith quickly put out his cigarette and grabbed his lighter. He threw it across the room. 'I'll be out of this chair and onto the back of you, old man, before you get to it. Those breaths are getting more and more strained by the second. I'd get yourself an ambulance before it's too late.'

From his pocket, Dean pulled out an old Ronson Varaflame lighter.

'Shit... I didn't know they still made them that way.'

'They... don't. You gave... me this.'

'Jesus. From that night? From the night when that gobshite was on his knees?'

Dean used his last remaining dregs of energy to tip the petrol container over. The fuel rained down on Keith.

A dizzy spell...

Then, Dean was on his knees by the La-Z-Boy.

He heard the motor kick in; Keith had the handle.

Dean looked at the clunky silver lighter in his hand and then pressed it once.

Twice.

Three times a charm.

57

As Riddick talked to Sam Khan, he watched his former boss pace back and forth on the pavement outside. She looked like she'd seen a ghost.

Riddick was annoyed with Sam for putting herself in such a precarious situation, but she was sad and desperate, so he worked hard at keeping any hint of tone out of his voice.

'I just couldn't wait any longer. You hadn't made a single arrest,' she said.

Riddick inwardly sighed. Sam was right of course.

They were still nowhere near finding the person who'd struck her father and Devon. And eight months was a very long time to wait. Resources had been allocated elsewhere.

Riddick himself had been too distracted with his vendetta against Nathan Cummings and concern for Arthur Fields.

He looked at the lost young woman in the rear-view mirror and felt the guilt searing him.

Who could blame her?

To be angry with her would be hypocritical. Roles reversed, as if Riddick wouldn't have taken matters into his own hands!

Riddick turned around in his seat and looked back at her. 'You're right – it's not good enough. The problem is, the person who attacked your father was just a kid. The powers that be don't want to chase after kids. Nothing ever sticks. It's not an excuse, just a sad fact. Kids like this are manipulated by people like Cummings... and that's a strong defence. Then, it becomes the kids' word against the manipulator, so we can't even get the bastard puppeteer locked up.' He shook his head. 'What am I saying? These are excuses. *I* should've done more though, Sam. I'm so sorry you put yourself through... through... *that*.'

'That' was a relationship with Harris.

The whole thought of it repulsed Riddick, and the guilt burned hotter.

She looked away. She was clearly disgusted with herself.

Riddick empathised. He, too, had committed repulsive acts, from a feeling of necessity.

'I didn't even get to the truth.' She wiped a tear away. 'I still don't know who the kid is who ruined my life. Our lives... My mother, she's a shell... barely eats... sleeps... and, after all that, I failed. From the moment, I approached Harris in that bar, I haven't been able to look at myself in the mirror. I kept imagining it was happening to someone else. And yet, after all this, the dickhead didn't even give me what I was after.'

'It was Nathan Cummings. He set it up. That's who's really to blame. And he's dead.'

'Yes, but—'

'I'm sorry.' He touched her knee. She looked at him. 'It was him, *Nathan*, and he's dead.' He pulled his hand back.

'I *still* want to know.'

'You can't go back to those men. That's final.'

She narrowed her eyes. Clearly, she didn't like being told what to do. But, right now, she'd given him little option. 'Do you understand?'

She sighed and nodded. 'Don't have a choice now, do I? They might've seen you chase me. They might be suspicious.'

'Precisely. You need to go back to your family.' A thought occurred to him. 'They don't know where you live, do they?'

'No... my father made enough to move us from Manningham years ago. He kept our shop here, but he wouldn't let us have anything to do with this place. I got a cheap room round the corner, so Harris would think I'd just moved into the area. It's disgusting... *I'm* disgusting... And now I don't even have the bastard responsible.'

Riddick turned forward in his seat again, glancing out the window at Gardner. She was *still* deep in conversation, *still* pacing, *still* looking as if she'd seen a ghost.

We're quite a pair, aren't we, Emma?

Sometimes, it felt like they were good for each other; other times, it felt like the most volatile combination since Bonnie and Clyde...

There didn't seem to be any in-between.

'Those *bloody* worms,' Sam said. 'I suffered for nothing. Drugged up, sweating pigs. Nathan Cummings was a monster, but they couldn't even stay loyal to him. Scum, absolute scum—'

Riddick turned his head so quickly that his neck cracked. 'Come again? What do you mean by loyalty?'

'Just that they didn't have any. I'd to listen to them banter over who'd take over Nathan's role. Give them enough time and these kinds of animals always turn on one another... you can tell.'

'Do you think they'd anything to do with what happened to Nathan?'

'They definitely *knew* it was going to happen.'

Riddick took a deep breath and his heart fluttered. 'What makes you think that?'

'We were all in the club the night Nathan kicked off with that bloke at the bar. After the fight, we stayed back in the club, while he was outside with the police, then we all went back to the house without Nathan, so it couldn't have been them... but...'

Riddick leaned in. 'Go on.'

'But when we got back, that's when they started joking about who'd be a better leader. Although they didn't mention Nathan getting killed at that point, they must have suspected something was going to happen; otherwise, why bring it up? They either knew or arranged it. That's all I know. I'll be happy, actually, *more than bloody happy*, to give a statement. The more of these you can lock up, the better. I wouldn't be surprised if Pasture was behind Nathan's death.'

Pasture?

'Who the bloody hell is Pasture?'

Sam stared at him like he was a fool. She raised an eyebrow. 'Their boss?'

Riddick's mind whirled. He suddenly felt like Gardner looked outside, pacing back and forth on her phone. 'Nathan was their boss! I've never heard of *Pasture*. It sounds like a bloody codename. Maybe it's a surname... did Harris or Geo mention a first name? Ever call him Mr Pasture by any chance?'

'No... just Pasture as far as I remember—'

'There must be something else, Sam!'

The car was suddenly silent, and Riddick worried that he may have come on too strong. 'Sorry, I—'

'No... it's okay... I'm thinking... It was hard to ask questions.' She paused for a moment to think. 'In my head, I pictured Pasture as an old man.'

'An old man? Did Harris or Geo say he was old?'

'Not exactly. I don't recall that word being used. But they did discuss his experience, their faith in him. That's it, I remember Harris told Geo that they could trust Pasture because he'd been around the block many times and knew what he was doing. And this was when Nathan wasn't with them.'

'Round the block?'

'Yes! Have you really never heard of him?'

'Still, no,' Riddick said and sighed. 'Keep thinking, Sam, please Pasture. Potentially old. Definitely experienced... is there anything else?'

She thought. 'They did talk about him a lot. Geo and Harris Pasture wants this... wants that... you know, that kind of thing. I seems they revered him or were terrified of him. Probably both. only heard Harris bring up Pasture once in Nathan's presence Months ago. Harris remarked that Pasture had finally put the Mansters on the map "good and proper". Nathan didn't like that He went apeshit and shouted Harris down, saying Pasture wouldn't last forever.'

'I bet Nathan resented it. He was arrogant. This is the first I've heard about him taking orders from anybody, actually. I bet it ate away at him.'

'So, maybe it was this Pasture who killed Nathan in the end?'

Makes sense. If the shadow boss knew Nathan was gunning for him probably via Harris and Geo, then that outcome felt inevitable. 'Possible... Are you sure you never saw him?' Riddick asked. 'An older man, perhaps, coming through that door?'

Sam shook her head. 'I've seen plenty of scummy idiot coming through that door, but they were mainly young, testosterone pumped, aggressive, ticking time bombs.' She looked off thoughtfully. 'I was always in the background just trying to work out which one of the bastards hit my dad.'

Pasture.

Potentially old.

Experienced.

Pasture... Pasture...

Riddick could feel the truth dawning on him, but it felt unbelievable... or was it just unacceptable?

He hoisted out his phone and hit Google. He punched in 'pasture synonyms'.

Grazing land, grassland, range, paddock, meadow...

His breath caught in his throat as his fear was confirmed.

Field.

Riddick's eyes widened. Deep down, he'd known it all along.

The old bastard had never retired to die from lung cancer in a bloody La-Z-Boy.

Keith Fields was still pulling the bloody strings.

58

After they'd dropped Samantha off with her mother, Gardner pulled over on a quiet street so Riddick could explain everything.

Gardner tried to focus on what he was saying, but her mind remained preoccupied with the other set of revelations involving the mysterious Neville Fairweather. Although she was making sense of her former assistant SIO's words, his news seemed to be taking place outside of this reality, as if she was watching it on a television screen.

She felt completely disconnected from the world.

As they drove to Keith Fields' flat, Riddick probed her on her phone calls outside the car. She tried to brush it off, simply not ready to let him in on that strange loop.

'You looked like you'd seen a ghost,' Riddick persevered.

'Let's speak to Keith first,' Gardner said. 'And then I'll explain.'

But explain what? In her own mind, it sounded too incredible to be true.

Neville Fairweather – the man who came to her house yesterday with a picture of Willows and was *supposed* to be out of the country – was suddenly connected to Operation Red Cascade?

And, worse still, may even be responsible for Sebastian Harrington's death?

What the hell did it all mean?

In a way, she'd be glad to have Riddick's take on this. But she wouldn't hold her breath for an explanation. Really, how could anyone be expected to join those dots?

She had texted O'Brien's sister earlier, asking if everything was okay. She'd got a prompt reply. Her kids were currently having the time of their lives on an outdoor trampoline in the garden.

She had sighed, vowing to treat her kids to their own outdoor trampoline when this shit show was finally over.

Gardner parked outside the block of flats and Riddick opened his car door.

'How convinced are you that it's Keith?' Gardner said.

Riddick looked back at her. 'It's Keith, all right. Deep down, I've probably known all along. A bastard like that never lays down to die until he's forced too.'

'Fine, not disputing it... but doesn't that make him dangerous?'

Riddick thought about it. 'We're not in danger. He deliberately keeps this low profile. An old man on the bones of his arse. Everything is done with this now.' He pointed at his mouth. He then turned and gestured up at the flat. 'That's where we find him most vulnerable.'

'What you going to do – arrest him?'

Riddick looked back at her, and Gardner could tell he'd not thought this part through.

'So, he denies he's Pasture, and we walk away empty-handed?' Gardner asked.

Riddick didn't respond.

She could tell from his eyes he was going up there for a confession, no matter what.

'Do you want to stay in the car?' he asked.

'And risk watching you and an old man rolling off a top-floor balcony?'

'I've forgotten how dramatic you can be,' Riddick said, exiting the car.

She climbed from the car, shaking her head. *Dramatic is your middle bloody name, Paul.*

She followed him as he approached the entrance. *My life is so much easier without you in it.*

He turned back and gestured for her to catch up.

Why then, am I so happy to see you?

The block of flats was a mess. Her mind whirred as it tried to drive her back to the moment when she'd seen Collette Willows lying at the foot of a similar block in Wiltshire. She took several deep breaths, and then forced herself back into the moment.

Riddick was looking over his shoulder at her, his eyebrows raised expectantly.

She held up her hand to suggest she was okay and caught him up beside a horrendous battered lift. As they entered, she said, 'Can't remember the Kray twins slumming it like this.' The lift doors closed.

'Bollocks, isn't it? I knew this place was a front. I *should've* dug him out before now.'

Gardner noticed Riddick was clenching his fists.

Here we go.

'What?' He'd caught her staring.

'Nothing.' *Except you're a broken record. Everything is your fault. Is anything ever going to change? But what's the point any more? You never listen.*

The lift pinged.

Floor five.

The door opened.

Smoke. Burning. A stench like burnt meat.

'Why's there no bloody alarm?' Gardner said as they sprinted down the corridor.

'You sound surprised!'

A smoke sensor out of action wasn't an uncommon occurrence in impoverished areas with a parasitic landlord.

Riddick slammed his elbow into the glass of a fire alarm, and a wailing kicked up.

They swung around a corner.

The smoke was thicker here, emerging from an open doorway, knotting into darker clumps beside someone sitting against the wall. Their chin on their chest.

'It's his flat!' Riddick said, breaking into a sprint, opening distance between them. He looked down at the fallen man. 'This isn't him.'

Gardner caught up with Riddick and looked down at the withered form of Dean Maiden. His eyes were closed.

Dean Maiden? More dots. Reaching out to one another. Trying to connect.

She'd never felt so disorientated by an investigation, but now wasn't the time.

Riddick, who'd stopped dead at the open flat door, shouted, 'Shit... I need a blanket!' He plunged in.

Jesus! 'Wait,' Gardner shouted, turning her back on Dean and sprinting through the open flat door.

Her stomach turned. She grabbed her mouth.

There was a man on fire.

As were the arms of the La-Z-Boy he lay back on.

The victim was still.

Coughing, Riddick burst from a room alongside her, trailing a blanket. She pinned herself back against the hallway wall as he charged forward into the lounge, raising the blanket. He threw the material, and himself, onto the burning man and the chair.

Riddick frantically banged on the blanket and rolled his body weight over it. Gardner, also coughing now, stepped forward to help, but after seeing that Riddick had extinguished the flames she held back.

When Riddick pulled the blanket free, he swore and kicked over a petrol container on the floor.

She'd known already after seeing the state of Fields that he was past saving. It was an image that'd never leave her. Another image to join the others this accursed job had thrown at her over the years.

'Call it in. I'll check on the other guy.'

She returned to the corridor. It was less smoky here, so she got her cough back under control.

She knelt beside Dean, expecting him to be dead. But even though his chin was on his chest and his face was pale, she could see his chest tremble slightly with shallow, fast inhalations. Close still, she could hear a faint wheezing sound.

'Dean?'

His eyes fluttered open. He attempted to lift his one working eye to see Gardner. She lowered herself so he could. A thin line of saliva dangled from the corner of his mouth. He tried to smile, but his lips merely trembled. Then, he began slipping to one side, so Gardner quickly slid down beside him, so his head came back into her lap.

He looked up at her, wheezing.

She was desperate to ask him questions. *Why kill Keith Fields? What had he done to Penny? Was he connected to Sebastian Harrington too? Had Fields protected him? And, if so, why come for him now? Today? In the last seconds of your life?*

So many questions.

But, looking down, she knew there was no point. Dean was too frail to engage. She could hear Riddick on the phone to the emergency services.

When they arrived, there would be two bodies.

He murmured something. She leaned closer to hear his words. They were weak, slurred and lost in the sounds of wheezing. She leaned closer still, her back burning.

'Penny...' He finally managed a smile as he stared up at Gardner. 'My baby... girl.' His working eye rolled. His eyelids quivered. 'I knew... always... knew...' He wheezed. 'Everything... everything... you ever wanted.' She had to lean closer still. Her middle-aged back screamed in dissent.

She opened her mouth to question him. It was for the best, surely. Knowing the truth before he passed.

And then she recognised something in his face. Something she'd seen in her own parents' eyes the day she'd started her career. A miracle following a turbulent upbringing alongside a sociopathic brother.

Pride.

In his final moments, he believed he was looking at the face of his daughter. Grown up and successful.

Could she take that away from him?

No, she couldn't.

The truth of everything could wait. Here was a man who'd lived with an unthinkable experience for most of his life.

Yes, the truth could bloody well wait.

She stroked Dean's hair.

'I'm... sorry...' Dean managed.

She closed her own eyes, and she thought, momentarily, about Willows, smiling, on that final day just before they had visited that flat in Tidworth. 'I'm sorry, too.'

When she opened her eyes, a tear ran down her cheek, and she could see that his eyes had closed. Assuming he'd passed, she stretched her back out, but then noticed Dean's eyes flicker open again, his lips quivering. She leaned back in, wincing to hear if he had anything more to say before he slipped away.

She listened.

It may've been one final ragged breath, or it may also have been, 'I love you, Penny.'

She couldn't be sure, but she'd like to think it'd been the latter.

So, that was what she thought.

59

In the company of two bodies, Gardner and Riddick desperately tried to process the experience.

They unloaded information onto each other, keen to fill in each other's blanks, and join up the dots.

Could there be any sense to be found in this chaos?

After some discussion, and no real conclusions, the emergency services arrived, and the world around them erupted into activity.

Back in the car, Gardner could see Riddick was chewing hard on something. It was unsurprising. She assumed it was his failure to get here in time. It wasn't.

'You should've told me earlier about this Neville Fairweather.'

'Why? I didn't know it was connected.'

He shook his head. 'No, not because of the investigation... just because...' He looked at her. She saw the concern on his face. 'Just because.'

Her phone rang. The caller was unknown. 'DCI Gardner?'

There was weeping.

'Sorry, who's this?'

'Kiera McLeod.'

The young woman who worked with Sebastian at the youth centre.

'Are you okay?'

'I don't know...' She paused and sniffed. 'I know what happened to Sebastian. I know *everything*.'

60

All eyes turned to the screen as the projector flared into life, and Incident Room 2 fell into deathly silence.

Operation Red Cascade had been a peculiar ride to date, but nothing had prepared anyone for today's turn of events.

Gardner forgave herself for not working harder to connect Operation Red Cascade to Howard Walters' murder. Not only had Marsh been averse to the idea, but both investigations had completely different contexts. One linked back to a tragedy in 1980 and a collection of now-jaded old men, while the other involved county lines and a party of hedonistic middle-class teenagers. They both had very different cast lists!

Had.

Not any more.

The Conservative MP from 1980, Sebastian Harrington, was the dead uncle of the murdered Ralphie Parks. Barnett had discovered his link to the murdered Howard Walters via the mechanic's logbooks.

Dean Maiden had murdered Keith Fields, aka Pasture, the shadow leader of the Mansters.

Victim Ralphie Parks had been working for the Mansters.

Then throw in Neville Fairweather, a rich, powerful man who had been connected to Collette Willows – and a man who'd taken a keen interest in Gardner...

Gardner was struggling to link these areas. She was struggling to find the words.

Fortunately, Sebastian Harrington *had* had some words to offer.

Words he'd recorded on camera for his suicide and then sent to Kiera McLeod.

On the screen, Sebastian looked assertive and calm, which was odd considering what he was about to do.

But wasn't that the mark of an adroit politician?

A presentation that didn't quite reflect the inner turmoil. And sometimes, especially in this case, the inner quagmire of deceit and corruption.

'Kiera... sorry to send you this. You're the only person I really know these days who I can trust. You're kind and filled with integrity. Qualities I was ambitious for but fell well short of! I know you'll use these last words responsibly and right some wrongs with these truths I give you.

'Looking back, my life seems brief. Seems odd, considering my mistakes could fill a thousand lifetimes. Still, I aim to keep these last words fleeting... I don't disagree that a catalogue of disaster and missteps might make interesting listening, and cause saliva tion in some of my more ravenous critics, but, if I give you a complete autobiography, then I fear it'll come across as self-obses sion and then self-pity. That's not my intention. I'm an irrelevance and deserve to die as one. So, although the media will revel in yet another disgraced politician, which they've every right to, I hasten to add, I hope that the genuine message comes across here

Because there's something else here so much more important than one more stuck-up liar.'

For the first time, Sebastian's veneer threatened to crack. His top lip trembled. After picking a glass of water up, he turned momentarily from the webcam to take a mouthful. Then, he put the glass down, turned back and IR2 again felt fixed in the stare of a dead man.

'I want to tell you about Penny Maiden. A young lady. Like you, she was warm-hearted... in her prime... ready to give back to a world that had brought her into existence. An important life.' He put a fist to his mouth and squeezed his eyes shut. He must have been inches away from breaking down and starting again.

Who knows, Gardner thought, *maybe this was the two hundredth version he'd recorded?*

He opened his eyes. 'I took her life on a rainy June evening in 1980. It mightn't have been intentional, but I took her life all the same. And there cannot be, shouldn't be, excuses for that. But I made those excuses to myself, and I abstained from taking responsibility. I've been a coward. And I'm still a coward. Now that my nephew has died, and the investigation into Howard Walters' murder is under the spotlight again, I suspect it will only be a matter of time...'

It wasn't your nephew's death that shone that spotlight, Sebastian. It was Ray, diligently scouring old evidence. If not for his spotlight this whole sorry affair would still be languishing in the dark. Dean, himself, departed this world, leaving us nothing. So, something must have spooked you into this confession, Sebastian. Into this suicide.

Neville Fairweather?

Did he put pressure on you? Why?

'There's no defence. None. There can only be a heartfelt apology for what I've done. To the family. To my old constituents. To you, Kiera. To the whole world. But please don't accept it. Any of you. It's fitting as a last punishment that you don't. I'm a disgrace. I wish to die a disgrace and be forever known as a disgrace – until that last memory of me wilts away.

'For years, the excuse to myself was Howard Walters. I'd him to blame for his incompetence – the poor service on those brakes. I later learned that it was his drinking that led him to such poor workmanship. His negligence was becoming more than just a rumour. And I'd discovered that firsthand! Yes, in the years after the incident, Howard turned it around for himself. Got himself back on the straight and narrow, built himself quite an excellent reputation over the years, but it was too late by then, wasn't it? At least for Penny. So, it became easier for me to use the bastard as an excuse.

'And it ate me up... inside... like a cancer. Still, I tried hard to believe in my arrogance... that I was important to my community... that I could make amends by serving my constituents. Believing that I could pay my penance by improving the lives of others! Another cowardly excuse. Besides, we all know how my attempts fared, don't we? It never seemed to matter how many people I helped, I seemed to fail so many more. And now, looking back, did those I helped even really need me? Did they? The people I helped always fall on their feet, anyway. Those that fail, well, I realise now, too late, that the ending of their stories is often quite different.'

He turned away for another mouthful of water. Gardner wondered if a quick flick of Sebastian's right hand had been him brushing away a tear. He turned back.

'People witnessed what happened that night. Can you believe it? Three separate people. MP Harrington's beamer on Bond End! No one else would've stood a chance. But I used my power and influence, and the power and influence of another, to bury the truth. Keith Fields. A man with so much control. A man like me, I guess – just in a different echelon of life. He helped tidy up the situation. I provided the money to the witnesses for their silence, and he provided the fear needed to maintain it. Keith also had contacts inside the police, so the case died away, and Keith pacified Dean and Estelle Maiden with a scapegoat. One of his men who died accidentally doing God knows what! I didn't ask too many questions. Didn't need to.'

So, that was why Dean hadn't spent his whole life pursuing his daughter's killer. He must have believed Keith had served up that justice...

Without the parents hounding the police, then the investigation would've quickly cooled.

Somewhere down the line, Dean must have discovered the truth, but why leave it until today to strike?

She'd a chilly feeling inside that there were some questions that'd never be answered.

Sebastian continued, 'In 1980, I thought Keith was a scab on humanity. A worm. But... I now know that me and him weren't any different... not really. We're both scabs.' He picked up a bottle of pills and shook them. 'Needing to be picked off. I expect one day the same will become of him.'

Sooner than you thought, in fact. She thought of him crisping over in the La-Z-Boy. *And painfully, too.*

Sebastian opened the bottle and tipped the pills into his mouth. He took a large mouthful of water and swallowed. Gardner winced, feeling the urge to call an ambulance. *Ridiculous!* Sebastian was already ice cold in the morgue.

'I'm sorry you had to see me do that, Kiera, but I need you to know, *everyone* to know, that I did this to myself. This is *my* decision.'

Was it? Gardner thought. *Or were you coerced? Did Neville Fairweather threaten your family, perhaps?*

He smiled. 'Kiera... those children where we work... every

single one of them, I see – I don't know how to word it, I see such hope, *potential*... yes, that's right... *potential*. For so long, I believed in privilege and God-given rights. Not an excuse, but I remember the bastards drilling it into us at school every single day. Our potential was justified, no matter what we did – others had to earn it. We had to condemn others for not having aspirations, when we didn't either! Not really. We didn't need any! We were given whatever we wanted. It was all bullshit. I look at those kids now, with you, Kiera, and I know it. Understand it all. *Properly.* I just couldn't see it back then.' He turned away from the camera and used a tissue on his eyes this time.

He leaned over to the floor, and when he rose back up, he was holding up a photo album. 'This was potential here.' He held it up and pointed at the smiling Penny Maiden, standing next to her suited father.

How the bloody hell had he got that?

Had he been in the family home, while Dean and Estelle had been out, then left with a keepsake?

More bloody questions that may remain forever unanswered.

'She's celebrating her O-levels,' Sebastian continued. 'Look how proud he is. He wore a suit for his daughter's results.' After putting the album back down on the floor, he took a deep breath. 'I didn't just snuff out her potential, Kiera. I snuffed out the potential of thousands all those years back. Please, don't see any good in me after you watch this... please, don't justify anything that happened. For so long, I wasn't that man you know from the youth centre. Hear me now. I know you, Kiera. I know you'll be at my funeral, but try not to cry, try not to say anything about me. In fact, I forbid you to speak. I'm a scab, always was. I've been picked off... and that's a cause for celebration... not sadness.'

He took another mouthful of water.

He raised an eyebrow. 'I can hear you, Kiera. I can still hear you trying to justify! My dear, you're such a gentle soul, Kiera – a blessing in this world. Still, the tale doesn't end here... so, prepare yourself. I think I've just enough to kick out any doubts you have.'

Answers... please, Sebastian, give me answers...

'For years and years, the guilt ate at me until I felt hollow and, when it became clear that I wasn't healing the world, that my *potential*, my *justified* existence, had been a lie, manufactured by our institutions, I vanished from the public eye. It was at this point I should've taken these bloody pills. Instead of living in retirement, a ghost filled with self-pity and guilt...' He shook his head. 'And then, less than a year ago, I started to dream of atonement. Before I knew it, the dream had become a commitment. And I became determined for it. How ridiculous thinking back to it now! Believing that I had the right. As if I could somehow atone by distributing justice for Penny to others. What kind of arrogant, narrow-minded hypocrisy is that?

'But that's what happened. I thought I could fill myself again. It wasn't hard to arrange either – knowing the people I've known for so long. Keith was never the worst of them, and that's saying something. I spent a lot of money to have Howard Walters taken from this earth, and I spent a lot more to have him buried where that poor girl, Penny, had been laid to rest. I asked for her body to be placed with her mother! Just saying it all now – it's surreal! My mind wasn't right. Not at all. You may think that by taking the pills now, it still isn't right, but honestly, this overdose is probably the most rational thing I've done in my whole sodding life!

'Giving Penny and Estelle some kind of justice while I still roam free? Ridiculous, eh? Howard may've been culpable, but so was I. I was driving the car, for pity's sake! Yet, here's me, playing the vigilante. The people I paid are irrelevant. They may be para-sites, but I'll leave them to natural justice now, and not give you their names. I've learned my lesson in that regard. How dare I play judge and jury?

'It feels good to confess to all these things, Kiera, especially to you. You're the one person who maybe saw a glimmer of what could've been. After Howard's death, I was genuinely happy for a time. I don't know if this was because of what I did, or rather because I was part of helping those children. Yet, is this just more evidence of my selfish nature? The false belief that my survival and freedom are justified if I can help others?

'Anyway, I've been brought back down to earth with a bang by another of my failures. Ralphie. Yes. Jesus... Ralphie! That boy deserved better. Deserved better than to be born into this accursed family, and to have me as his bloody uncle. He obviously died because he got mixed up with the wrong people. I should've helped him more, rather than simply using my influence. I could've taken him under my wing. Guided him. But I didn't. I couldn't even save him...'

He put his face in his hands and was silent for a time. Gardner wondered if the sleeping pills had kicked in. No doubt he'd wanted to send this before he went under, and of course, he had done, but she guessed he needn't have been too worried. Forensics would've recovered the video, regardless.

Eventually, he looked back up at the camera, looking more bleary-eyed.

Yes, they're taking effect.

'There isn't anything left for me to say except sorry. Sorry to the Maiden family, and sorry to all those people I've failed for so long. No one will mourn me, and no one should. Don't make that mistake, Kiera. Everything is going to you. I need you to use that money to do what you do best... help people. It's been a pleasure to know you. It's the only pleasure I've ever really known.' He mimed doffing a cap, and the screen went blank.

61

The identification of Howard's hired killers would be near on impossible. They'd be well-paid professionals, summoned from the shadows of the dark web. And would've sidled back there, seconds after their work was done. So, bar this frustration, the long, unsolvable investigation around Howard had reached some kind of conclusion.

However, the room remained flat. Not only because of Sebastian's tragic story of selfishness and greed, but because one victory wasn't enough for celebration. They remained no closer to the truth behind Ralphie and Vivianne.

O'Brien, who recounted her day's experience with partygoer Toby Brundle, helped wake the docile crowd.

Toby, who'd told an interesting story about the night of the murders, had taken his dog, Amy, for a walk this morning. Amy had returned, but Toby hadn't. He wasn't answering his mobile phone.

It'd been too soon to panic, and it was frustrating more than anything, but Gardner felt it was time to begin looking for him.

After the briefing, Rice came over wearing an out-of-character expression of sympathy. He looked pathetic. 'Must have been tough... having Maiden die like that...'

'In my arms?'

He flinched. 'Aye... that.'

She glared. 'Just leave it, okay?'

Rice's false expression morphed into a stunned one that looked very real.

She sighed. 'Sorry... uncalled for... just on edge.'

Rice stared at her for a moment. Fortunately, he didn't go for the exaggerated display of sympathy this time. 'Dean was a murderer. He didn't die innocent. You know?'

I feel on top of the world now, thanks, Phil. She turned and headed for the exit where Riddick was already standing.

She felt a surge of irritation. She wondered how much more she could stand today. 'Fifteen minutes, my office, please.'

He nodded.

As she walked past him, she looked back and hissed, 'We've been on your territory, Paul, most of the day, so I've let you rule the roost. Now, you're back on mine, you follow my lead. Got it?'

Riddick nodded.

'Fifteen minutes. Don't be late, or you can go back to Bradford.'

* * *

Back in her office, her phone rang immediately.

Unknown.

She answered. 'Hi, DCI—'

'Hello DCI Gardner.' The voice was familiar, and as irritating as ever. 'Would you like to make a comment regarding the deaths of Sebastian Harrington, Dean Maiden and Keith—'

'Jesus wept, not now,' Gardner interrupted.

'Is that your comment?'

'*No.* How did you even get this number? Look, Marianne, Officer Bridge will talk to you about Harrington, and the incident in Bradford. There's nothing I'm going to add to that.'

'I was hoping you could give me something on your *conduct*?'

'My conduct! What the bloody hell are—'

'Check my blog.'

The phone went dead.

* * *

Exiled judgemental DCI strikes again...

Gardner sighed as she began the article.

As with many, my default has always been to sympathise with a fish out of water. Even one exiled from her own backyard down in Wiltshire. Like many, I wanted to believe in second chances, and hoped that the flapping fish would prove her southern doubters wrong. Hoping, praying, in fact, that she'd offer something to a community that's laboured under false promises of justice, and security, for almost a decade!

However, I felt the writing was on the wall following the debacle of the Howard Walters' investigation and now, unfortunately, I've been proven right. Like the next person, I'm always willing to help someone understand the unfamiliar community they find themselves in, and support them at every turn for the cause of the greater good, but when someone approaches our delicate and unique world with such ignorance and arrogance, how much patience are we expected to have? DCI Emma Gardner...

Gardner sighed again. *Piss off, Marianne! You're so bloody predictable!*

Marianne Perse had made a successful career out of character assassination and needed a new target since Riddick was no longer available. Gardner read on through the blog, sighing, keeping her reactions nonchalant and appropriate to the drivel. However, her eyes soon started widening.

Marianne had interviewed Max and Evie Parks! At their request. *Surely, bullshit?* The scavenger had probably gone sniffing around their doorway.

She was probably one of their bloody guests at a sex party...

'Chuffin' hell,' Gardner said, using one of Rice's favourite expressions.

Max and Evie Parks had chosen some strong adjectives to really stick the knife in.

Unsympathetic.

Judgemental.

Overly suspicious.

Apparently, Gardner had *swaggered* in the night Ralphie had died, while they'd had guests staying over.

Guests staying over? It'd been a bloody orgy!

A direct quote from Evie:

She looked down on us because of our wealth and high status. I mean, we've worked for everything we have!

And from Max:

A working-class lass from the south with a chip on her shoulder. If she'd thought to look, she'd see we give generously to charity.

It was tripe, of course, so Gardner had no choice but to ignore it. It could be a problem, though. Marianne had a wide readership, and it could sour community relations further.

Really, she should've killed it dead there and then, but curiosity was a powerful thing...

Gardner read through the many comments posted by readers and was both stunned and disheartened by the sheer number. Most were anecdotes from disgruntled locals, explaining how the police were failing the community. Barking dogs out of control, rubbish in the park, children stealing sweets from the local store.

'It's a warzone,' Gardner said, shaking her head.

More appropriately, some readers had chimed in with their views on the murders, which was the blog's focus. Still, the comments remained unhelpful. Under-resourced police unable to solve murders – apparently – and modern policing was more focused on recovering money through fines.

Gardner kept telling herself that this was just a snapshot of a certain demographic and didn't represent the majority. At least, she hoped it didn't!

The comments seemed to become more bitter. There was a lot of aggression in the discussion of how the police treated the Parks. Talking about their vital contributions to society, and how Ralphie had been an example of the future – a talented lad with so much to offer.

The evidence suggests otherwise.

Her phone rang. *Unknown again.* She answered. 'DCI—'

'So?'

'Can I help you?'

'A comment?'

'I think you've got the wrong number.'

'Arrogant. I'll print that as an example.'

She hung up.

Go ahead. Seriously, this is reality television, opinion-inviting bull-

shit. I've got other things to think about.

Her eyes fell to another comment that stood out from the rest and she straightened up in her chair. *Shit...*

Riddick came to the door and poked his head in. 'Any better?'

'No.' She didn't look at him – she was too busy rereading the comment. 'I still need fifteen minutes.'

'Boss, I—'

'Shut the door, Paul.'

She re-read the comment for a third time.

Ralphie Parks was a nasty little bastard. He bullied other kids at school. He made my son's life a living hell. Community? He was no part of any decent community! He got everything coming to him.

The comment had been posted anonymously.

* * *

It seemed like Ralphie had made a career out of bullying peers at secondary school.

The head teacher, Paula Bradford, insisted that they'd gone about it the right way. They'd investigated all incidences and completed reports. He'd been on the verge of being kicked out in Year 10, but managed, at the last, to turn over a new leaf. Gardner asked how many kids had to go through hell before they excluded someone. Paula didn't take too kindly to the suggestion that the influence of Sebastian Harrington had kept him enrolled.

'We followed all processes. Ofsted judged us outstanding in safeguarding.'

Here's another process for you to follow, Gardner thought. 'Could you email me the documents on every incident please?'

She then contacted the IT department to see if they could track the person who wrote on the blog. They could, so long as the keyboard warrior hadn't used a proxy server.

She then sat and waited, drumming her fingers on the table, and turned Riddick away for another fifteen minutes. This time, he spat the dummy out and told her he was off.

She didn't want him to go, but she was in no mood to argue. And she wasn't leaving the office – not until she found out who thought Ralphie Parks had it coming to him.

* * *

When the list came, it was long, and again, Gardner wondered how Ralphie had survived in his educational career for so long. She also wondered if Ofsted had seen this list before dishing out an outstanding judgement.

Hard to believe. Ralphie Parks had attempted to wreck more than a few childhoods. He should've been excluded from this school long before Year 10.

What was interesting were some of the other names involved in bullying.

There were a reasonable number! She sensed a lot of legwork on the horizon.

Near the end of the list, she saw one familiar name.

Toby Brundle.

The partygoer who'd not returned home with his dog.

Apparently, he'd been involved in a stone-throwing incident as well as three others. He didn't feature as frequently as Ralphie by any stretch of the imagination, but he'd contributed to Ralphie's reign of terror.

She picked up her pad of notes and headed back out to see who was available.

Finding Toby suddenly felt like the number one priority.

62

'You should've phoned me when it happened,' Riddick said.

'There wasn't any time to think,' Roni said. 'And once they'd sedated Arthur, well, I didn't want to bring you flying back to the hospital… and then I heard about Keith, and kind of just got distracted.'

'He's definitely *still* calm?' Riddick said, phone pinned to his ear, drumming his fingers on the roof of the car.

'Well, yes,' Roni said. 'He hasn't woken since the sedative.'

Riddick sighed. 'What did Arthur say while he was freaking out?'

'Incomprehensible. He just went for his chest… like last time. He got some dressings off. But I was there.' She broke off to cry.

Riddick squeezed his eyes shut. *Damn this…*

'The nurses helped,' Roni continued. 'And we stopped him doing any more damage.'

'Can't they put mitts on him or something?' Riddick asked.

'I can ask.'

Riddick ceased his drumming on the car roof to rub at his temples.

Nathan bloody Cummings. *You really left your mark on Arthur, didn't you? You may be dead, but you're going to keep haunting this poor lad forever.*

'When he wakes up, Roni, please don't tell him about his father. Just call me immediately. Okay?'

'I was hoping you'd tell him, anyway.'

'That's fine.' Although it felt anything but fine. How would the poor boy respond?

'And about Keith, Roni... how do *you* feel?'

Roni snorted. 'Better than I expected. But then I've hated that man for a long time. He was a leech, and the worst kind too. Not content to feed until full, he'd suck you completely dry, like a sodding vampire. Arthur is better off without him in his life. And Arthur is all that matters.'

'Okay... remember to keep me updated,' Riddick said. 'I'll—'

'Sorry, Paul, it's the nurse... she wants me to go back inside.'

Riddick tried to listen to the conversation, but it was too muffled for him to make anything out.

Out of the corner of his eye, he saw Gardner coming towards him at a pace.

He doubted she was coming over to bollock him, as she'd simply do that by phone. The manner in which she marched suggested something of importance.

As she drew nearer, he clocked the serious look on her face.

Something's coming...

'Roni?' he said down the phone.

'I've got to go,' Roni hissed.

Gardner was barely a metre away. 'We've to go now, Paul,' she said.

'Roni?' Riddick said. 'Is everything all right?'

The phone was already dead.

He lowered the phone, confused by the rather abrupt end to the phone conversation. 'What's going on?' Riddick said.

'We've found Toby Brundle. You drive.'

63

Riddick advised Gardner to park in Henshaws, as it'd be quicker to get to the Horseshoe Field behind Conyngham Hall.

Toby had used his phone to contact his mother. He'd wanted to tell her he loved her, and that he'd not let Amy wander home alone as it'd first appeared. He'd returned home and dropped her off in their front garden when no one had been looking.

Toby's mother was obviously beside herself. What did this mean? Was her son in any danger? Was he, God forbid, suicidal?

Fortunately, cell tower triangulation had come to their aid and roughly pinpointed his location. When Gardner had presented his rough location to his mother over the phone, she'd suggested that it was likely to be Horseshoe Field, one of Toby's favourite spots. 'He particularly likes the sandbanks by the Nidd. Amy wading about in the Nidd is a sight. He's always been fond of the peace and quiet, too...'

Sandbanks... walking his dog... peace and quiet. He didn't cut the usual profile of a school bully, who enjoyed raving and ecstasy tablets, but then, people were capable of a great deal when manipulated – and it seemed Ralphie Parks had been quite the manipulator.

After parking, Riddick and Gardner jogged to Horseshoe Field. Between the dog walkers and the nettle bushes, they had to watch their step.

Despite the peculiar nature of returning the dog home, and then the melancholic phone call, Riddick and Gardner hadn't spoken about the possibility that Toby was a suicide risk.

Rice, if he'd been here, would've been quick to voice it... referring to cases where the mobile phone was found abandoned on a riverbank as the victim floated downstream.

But Rice was someone that enjoyed spicing up conversations with doom and gloom. Gardner and Riddick preferred to keep the worst possibilities inside, stewing, until they either became a reality, or were delightfully disproved.

They jogged along the edge of the field, glancing in at some sandbanks. Some dogs were swimming, and older owners relaxing.

They reached the final sandbank, which was empty, and Gardner felt the cold stab of doubt in her chest, not too far from where she was stabbed in Wiltshire many years earlier.

Are we too late?

They crested a small mound and worked their way down to the stony edge of the Nidd. Gardner scoured the ground for a mobile phone, hearing Rice's irritating voice in her head. *Told you...*

The Nidd was moving gently and wasn't too deep at the edge this time of year. She couldn't imagine anyone coming a cropper in the cold waters.

She looked left.

A young man, barely out of his teens, was sitting hunched up in front of a tree on the bank.

'Toby?'

She saw the blood on his forearm.

64

Toby groaned.

As she approached, she saw that he'd rolled up a sleeve and was cutting himself with a sharp rock.

Closer still, Gardner inwardly sighed with relief when she realised Toby wasn't working into an artery. It bought them some time.

Gardner held up her palm, gesturing to Riddick to stay back. Her stare would hopefully deliver the message: *This is my patch now, remember?*

He gave a swift nod to show compliance.

Not that she feared Riddick's interaction with Toby. She knew her ex-colleague could be sensitive with younger people – she'd recently seen him in action with Arthur, after all. She just felt that the sudden presence of two adults would be far too overwhelming for a youngster in the process of self-harming.

'Toby?'

He didn't respond, so she got to within a metre of him.

He was trembling, and his face was red and damp from tears.

This close, she could tell that the bloody lines he was drawing into his arms weren't the first – there were old scars there too.

'My name is Emma. I'm with the police.'

Had his mother known about this? Unlikely. She'd have surely said something when they'd spoken just before on the phone.

Beside him, she lowered to her haunches.

The tip of the sharp stone was currently penetrating the skin; blood bubbled from the wound.

She winced and looked at him, his face now screwed up and his teeth gritted.

'Toby, I'm going to take that stone away.'

She placed her hand firmly on the back of his, stopping the movement. Then she lifted his hand, slipped her palm beneath it and worked the stone from his grip. She threw it away behind her back.

She glanced back at his face – which was no longer screwed up. He stared down at his messy forearm, weeping.

After double-checking that he'd not nicked an artery, and that the bleeding wasn't worsening, Gardner allowed him a moment to collect himself, while she continued to hold his hand.

Eventually, he spoke. 'Is Mum okay?'

'She's fine. Just worried about you.'

'I told her not to worry.'

Gardner moved her hand from his, and held his shoulder gently instead. 'She's your mum, Toby.'

Toby nodded slowly as tears ran down his cheek.

'Do you want to go home and see her?'

Toby shook his head. 'No... not yet. Can we just stay here for a while?'

'Of course. We could also get a drink at some point if you'd like?' *At the hospital*, she thought, looking down at his wounds again.

She took her hand back from his shoulder and allowed him some more breathing space. Eventually, he nodded down at his arm. 'Sometimes... well, sometimes... it gets out of hand.'

'That's okay,' Gardner said.

'I don't deserve your help though. I don't deserve anyone's help.' He fixed his eyes on Gardner's for the first time.

Gardner could hear Riddick drawing closer to them. She wanted to tell him to stay back, but she didn't want to break the connection she was making with Toby. 'How so?'

Toby looked down at his arm again.

Shit.

He rolled down his sleeve, blood soaking through the light blue material.

Had Toby killed Vivianne and Ralphie?

By his own admission, he'd been the only one heading in their direction after the party... He'd also claimed to hear them argue, breaking the story of the others.

Was all this a cry for help?

Had Ralphie coerced him into something in his earlier years?

Manipulated the boy who liked nothing more than walking his dog, and sitting in the peace and quiet by the Nidd?

She looked up at Riddick to her left, who was alongside her now.

He looked impatient, so she narrowed her eyes, warning him back.

Gardner put her hand back on Toby's shoulder. 'Is there anything you want to tell me? Anything you want to say?'

He didn't respond, and simply fastened the button on his sleeve.

'You told DS Barnett that everyone left the party at 11.40 p.m.?'

Toby nodded.

'Apart from Charlotte and Adam, of course, who left in the ambulance?'

Another nod.

'You said that Vivianne and Ralphie were having an argument as they walked away?'

He didn't nod this time.

'You walked in the same direction as they did, the direction of Knaresborough cemetery. But you didn't want to get too close as they were arguing, and it was awkward. Is that right?'

Nothing.

'Can you not see how that looks?'

He shook his head gently.

'Did you have anything to do with their deaths?'

'No,' he said.

'What were they arguing about, Toby?'

He shook his head more vigorously now.

Gardner glanced up at Riddick. He was pointing at himself to suggest that he could have a run at it. She shook her head.

'They argued... and you were the only other person there. You need to give me more.'

'No... no!' He looked at her. 'I don't know what they were arguing about!'

Gardner swallowed and took a deep breath. 'I don't believe you.'

He opened his mouth and then closed it again. A moment later, he said, 'I can't... I just can't... I'll betray everyone. All of my friends. We all agreed never to talk about it.'

'Talk about what?' Riddick asked.

Gardner glared up at him, but his attention was firmly on Toby.

'What they were arguing about. What *we* all did at the party,' Toby said.

Gardner's eyes fell back down to Toby's as her heart raced.

Toby put his hands to his face and shook his head again.

'It's time, Toby,' Gardner said. 'I think you know that now.'

He let his hands fall away, and looked at Gardner again, eye full of tears. 'We hurt him. *Really* hurt him.'

'Who?' Gardner's phone started ringing.

Bloody hell!

She fumbled in her pocket for her phone and saw that it wa the IT department. She knocked it on silent. 'Who?'

He shook his head. '*I* hurt him. *Me.*'

'Who did you hurt?'

'He *made* me do it. Just like *every time...*'

'Ralphie?'

'Yes. I'm glad he's dead. He always made me do these things. He does it to everyone. People have always followed him lik bloody sheep.'

'What did he make you do?'

He shook his head, crying harder now.

'Tell me, *what* did he make you do, Toby?'

'You can watch.' He reached into his pocket for his phone pulled it out and fiddled with his screen.

Gardner's phone lit up in her hand. IT, again. *They must hav the person who commented on the blog.*

Shit...

'I need to take this.' She stood and eyed Riddick. *Don't you mes this up.* She answered, 'Hello?'

'Boss. We've a name for you on the IP address.'

'Okay, shoot,' Gardner said, taking a few steps away an turning in time to see Riddick kneeling and watching Toby screen.

When Gardner heard the name of the person who

commented, the world jolted, and she had to close her eyes, fearing it may come off its axis. 'No,' she said. 'It can't be.'

'I'm sorry, boss, it most definitely is.'

She let the phone drop to her side. *Oh God... Paul...* She opened her eyes.

Riddick was on his feet now. Taking the phone from Toby, pacing back and forth with a deep frown that almost completely folded his eyebrows over his eyes.

She slipped her own phone in her pocket and started forward.

She could hear laughter and whooping coming from the phone in Riddick's hand.

'Paul,' she shouted.

He ignored her and carried on watching.

'Paul, give me the phone.'

Riddick turned to her. He was pale. His hand fell to his side and the phone slipped from his grasp and fell to the ground.

She knelt to retrieve it, all the while the name of the person who'd commented on the blog echoed in her head.

Roni Fields.

'What've you seen, Paul?' she asked, her hand settling on the phone. 'Paul?'

When she looked up, Riddick had already made a move.

Ah shit...

She rose and charged, but she was too late.

Riddick had Toby pinned to the tree by his throat.

65

Riddick could hear Gardner's shouts and Toby's pleas.

But neither steadied him.

The sight of Toby pushing a unicorn ecstasy tablet into Arthur's mouth was replaying through his mind.

Riddick drove his fist into Toby's stomach.

He closed his eyes, and in the gloom, saw Arthur's face. Long... pale... drawn. And those eyes... those swollen black hollows.

Riddick's eyes bolted open. He grabbed the winded lad by the collar and threw himself into a spin.

The pleading and shouted continued, but what he'd seen on that phone screen pummelled his mind.

The party. The sofa. Toby tilting Arthur's head back by the chin, pressing a beer to his lips, forcing him to swallow the ecstasy tablet...

And another...

All the time, chants of 'swallow... swallow... swallow...' coming from the other wasted teenagers.

He released Toby. There was a splash.

Riddick put his hands to his face. 'No... how *could* you?'

More images from that video pummelled him:

Toby peeling Arthur's shirt off so everyone could read the scar on his chest.

Mansters.

Arthur attempting to speak, but simply dribbling, and mumbling incomprehensibly.

A teenage girl, wearing next to nothing, kissing Arthur on the cheek, before looking at the camera and stroking his scar. 'Can I join your gang?'

Riddick let his hands fall away and refocused on Gardner helping Toby out of the Nidd. Toby, drenched, leaned on Gardner, mumbling, 'I'm sorry...'

Riddick went in again. Gardner intercepted.

He looked into her narrowed eyes. 'Emma, move. I can't be—'

'Get control of yourself. Get. Control. *Now.*'

Riddick shook his head. 'But you don't understand!' He reached over Gardner's shoulder for Toby, but the boy evaded his grasp.

Gardner pushed her face closer towards his and hissed, 'Damn it. *Control yourself* or I'll have to call in support.'

Shit. Riddick turned away, scrunched his eyes shut, let out a stream of loud obscenities. Then he bent over, clutching his knees and taking several deep breaths before turning back. 'Let me hear what he has to say for himself!'

'With this aggression, Paul? How can I risk it?'

'But you haven't seen the bloody video! You haven't seen what that bastard did! He force-fed Arthur drugs. *They* laughed at him. Mocked him. *Shamed* him.' Riddick glared at Toby again. 'You expect people to feel sorry for you after that? Pathetic. Don't make me laugh. The day after you drugged my friend' – he put his hand on his own chest – 'Arthur scratched his chest to ribbons again. He's in hospital because of you.'

'I didn't know,' Toby said. 'I didn't—'

'So? What's that got to do with anything? You did it... and if you've damaged him in some way, I swear I'll—'

'Riddick, stop threatening him,' Gardner said.

He saw the frustration in her eyes, but it was nothing compared to the liquid fire running through his own veins right now.

Riddick shook his head and looked down, knowing he should rein it in, but, in the same way that sometimes the drinking took complete control and dominated his every thought, it was just too hard to take back control of his emotions.

He took some deep breaths.

Thinking it might be helping, he chanced a quick look up again, but the sight of that weasel made him flare again.

He turned away to try and remove the temptation to charge. He managed a few steps but he was unable to keep his thoughts in. That was a bridge too far. They came out at a loud volume. 'Treated him like a circus animal. What sodding year do you lot live in? You're educated... you're *all* educated. What the hell were you playing at? You could've killed him.'

'No one was in control,' Toby said, raising his voice now. 'No one wanted to hurt him. He was like a local celebrity. With what happened with the Mansters.'

'They *branded* him. Would you like to be branded?'

'That's awful... yes... but at the time, with us, he seemed to enjoy the attention.'

'Is that what you call it? He looked like he was on a different planet to me.'

'That was the problem... I think we all were.'

Riddick leaned against a tree, shaking his head. At least Gardner was giving him some wiggle room for now and allowing him to speak. No doubt, like him, she could sense the truth reaching the surface. He just had to stay calm enough until he had it.

With his back to both of them, he forced the volume of his voice down and spoke over his shoulder. 'No... no... you don't weasel your way out of this. You don't get to do that. You brought him round to parade him like a freak. Was it you? Did you drive around to pick him up?'

'No. Me and Ralphie saw him earlier in town. Ralphie convinced him to come to the party. Shit. I never believed for a second that he'd turn up!'

Riddick brushed away tears before turning from the tree into Toby's direction again. 'He's vulnerable. *Vulnerable.* You need me to spell it out? Invite someone to a party who's desperate to be liked, desperate to have friends... what did you think he'd do? Stay at home?' He shook his head again. 'You took advantage.' *You vicious little shit.* He held his breath. It was all he could do to keep in the comments that would most antagonise Gardner.

'God, I've watched it a thousand times,' Toby said. 'A thousand times! I just can't believe I'm doing it. I was off my head. I mean we all were. *Completely.* It was like nothing you've ever tried before. These unicorns. Super strong. Everyone just lost their shit.' He lowered his head. 'And when Ralphie says things, people listen. I listen. Everyone always does what he says.'

Riddick grunted. 'And if he told you to jump into a fire?'

'He had this way... I really wish I'd never met him.'

Riddick could feel his adrenaline spiking again. 'So, this is all about you again, is it? Poor little Toby with his scarred arms.'

'Right, I'm calling time now,' Gardner said. 'Go back to the car. I'll get Ray to collect us.'

He held up his palm towards her. 'No need. I—'

'Ralphie bullied me, too, you know?' Toby said. 'Never gave me any space.'

The sound of Toby's voice caused another flare-up. Riddick edged forward again. 'You and your privileged upbringing. What kind of life do you think Arthur has had, eh? You know about his dad, right? About the things he's experienced. And you think your issues even compare?'

'We all have issues,' Toby hissed.

Riddick took another step. 'I'll give you a *bloody* issue.'

Riddick felt Gardner's palm land firmly on his chest.

He narrowed his eyes as he stared at her. 'You want the truth? At least he's coughing up the truth, unlike his spineless friends.' He snorted and looked over Gardner at Toby again. 'When you were conspiring to keep your treatment of Arthur a secret, did you not think the video evidence on that phone might prove a problem?'

'I kept it on purpose...' Toby lowered his head. 'I kept it because Ralphie told me to delete it. Said it might bring problems. Affect his work. Dealing and that. I wanted to keep it. Destroy him. I *hated* him at this point. I think I've always hated him, but I don't know – I've always wanted him to like me... like me more than he ever did...'

'Is this a sexual thing?'

'No.' Gardner started to push him backwards, hissing, 'Paul, he's practically a kid.'

'More of a kid than Arthur?' Riddick hissed back. 'I think we know where the balance of power is here. Have you not been listening to what's coming out of his mouth?'

'Yes. And I understand your pain. But your judgement is clouded.'

'My judgement is clear.'

'If it was clear, you'd turn and walk away.'

Inside, Riddick could feel the rage boiling within him. *How How can I do that?*

He met Gardner's eyes, and they looked at each other for a time. He didn't see the disappointment there that he'd seen before, and so often feared. Her frustration was also gone. Now, he saw compassion. Sympathy. A desire to help him.

It was soothing.

And then she placed a hand to Riddick's cheek.

An indescribable feeling surged through him. He closed his eyes. 'Stop... please...'

She didn't.

He knew he should pull away, but the pressure of her hand was firm, and he didn't want it to end.

He heard Gardner whispering in his ear. 'Paul, listen... please. This needs to stop.'

The tears from before returned to the corners of his eyes.

He nodded gently, enjoying so much the warmth of her palm on his cheek.

'You've every right to be upset. You're emotionally involved. Go and be with Arthur. I'll handle this. Do you trust me?'

He sighed.

'Do you?'

'Yes.'

'No one will get away with anything.'

'It hurts so much, though,' Riddick murmured. 'I don't know why. Arthur's not my son. I've only known him for a short time, but I feel broken...'

'We'll put it right, I promise, but first give me a little space. Please.'

Riddick sighed again. Soothed by her hand, he imagined Arthur now. In the hospital bed.

He'd go there. Hold his hand. Be there for him for the truth of his father's death.

He'd build him back up from all of this. The possibility of doing so felt good.

He looked at Gardner, who had her eyes on his, and he suddenly felt that warmth from her palm rushing through his entire body. 'I... I...'

'Go, Paul. Take your car. I'll get Ray to collect us.'

Riddick nodded and turned away.

She was right.

And, to be honest, he just couldn't bear to look at that weasel again.

66

After parking at the hospital, Riddick didn't run, but went at a fast enough pace that he was out of breath by the time he reached Arthur's ward.

Now that he knew the actual reasons behind Arthur's mental deterioration these past few days, he was desperate to get to him, to reassure him, to help him.

As best he could anyway.

The receptionist in the ward was busy, so he bypassed them, holding up his badge. They'd probably recognise him from his previous visits. And, if they didn't, let them send security. He'd cross that bridge when he came to it.

His eyes widened when he looked in Arthur's room.

Empty.

He leaned against the doorframe, catching his breath, and sighted Roni's handbag on the chair beside the unmade bed.

A walk, perhaps? A toilet visit, maybe?

He returned to the reception. The receptionist was now free and she stared at Riddick with a pale, stunned face. He recognised her, and she surely recognised him, but the terror didn't leave her face.

Something was wrong.

He turned his head towards the sound of commotion in one of the hospital's main corridors to his left.

Some hospital staff were running down the corridor.

He looked back at the receptionist.

And he knew...

67

Toby, wet from the Nidd, shivered as they made their way to the car park where Barnett was already waiting for them.

'DI Riddick was the one that found Arthur, you know,' Gardner said. 'After the Mansters had scarred him.' *Not an excuse for his behaviour, but hopefully something that'll steady your hand in making an immediate complaint.*

She looked at the shivering youngster, awaiting a reply. He looked to be deep in thought, and he prodded his blood-stained sleeve as they walked. 'What I did to Arthur was disgusting.'

Yes, it was.

He prodded his sleeve harder now and winced.

She reached over and took him by the wrist, gently, to move his hand away. 'You'll make it worse.'

He stared at her. His eyes said it all. *Good. I deserve it.*

'You weren't in control of yourself. The drugs you were taking were strong.'

'Feels like an excuse.'

Yes. But sometimes it's all we have, Toby.

'Maybe DI Riddick is right. You should've let him drown me or something,' he continued.

'DI Riddick cares a lot,' Gardner said. 'About people.' *Sometimes too much for him to do his job.* 'He'll see your side of the story in time. Right now, he's just thinking about Arthur.'

'I wish I'd thought about him.'

'Help us, Toby, then. That's how you make it up to Arthur, as best you can. Tell me what that argument between Vivianne and Ralphie was about. I know you know.'

'Isn't it obvious now?' Toby said and took a deep breath. 'What happened with Arthur horrified Viv. She was calling Ralphie disgusting for being involved in it. He's always treated her like shit, you know? She was far too good for him. He manipulated her like he manipulated everyone.'

'Did she ever say anything to you about how she felt? I mean, how did she feel about being with a drug dealer?'

'Viv was always so quiet. Whenever I was alone with her, she'd only say positive things about him. In fact, she barely said anything about their relationship. It really stunned me when she confronted him about Arthur. It was *so* awkward and unusual for her.'

'And that's why you hung back?'

'Yes.'

'And you didn't see them go into the cemetery?'

'No. As I said, I turned off before we reached the graveyard.'

Gardner didn't want to get her notebook out as they walked, so she made a mental note of the street name he then gave.

'Would you be willing to give DNA samples?'

Toby nodded. 'Waste of time because it wasn't me...'

'Before, you told me you hated him?'

'Yes.' He stopped and looked down. 'I also loved him.'

Funny how that often happens, Gardner thought.

He sighed. 'I'll give you DNA samples.'

They continued and, as they neared the car park at Henshaws, something unanswered took centre stage in Gardner's mind. 'Where did Arthur go? *After?* Did he leave when the ambulance arrived, or before?'

'He left when everyone else did.'

'And which way did he walk?'

'Actually, in the same direction as Ralphie, Viv and me, but—'

Gardner stopped this time. 'You said it was just you *three*. In that direction.'

'No, I never. Did I? Sorry. He didn't walk with any of us. Ralphie and Viv walked on ahead, and I followed at a distance. Then, behind me, also at a distance, I noticed Arthur coming in the same direction. Obviously, I didn't want to say before, because, well, you know...'

Gardner shook her head. Her heart was pounding. *Jesus.* 'Where was Arthur going?'

'I don't know. Home, perhaps? I guess that direction would take him to York Road. He could get a bus or an Uber...'

'And you didn't think to help him get home?' *After torturing the poor kid?*

Toby flinched and looked away. 'He was behaving oddly.'

Was it any wonder? She really had to hold back the surging anger. She didn't want him clamming up, and she didn't want him self-harming again. 'Define oddly?'

'He was in a right state, banging off walls and stuff. Talking to himself.'

Probably because of all the bloody pills you force-fed him.

'I should've gone to help him,' he continued. 'But I was out of it, too. And Ralphie and Viv were arguing and I just wanted out of the whole thing. I felt sick. I felt shame. So, I just turned off down the street—'

'And Arthur?'

'Just carried on. I could hear him mumbling as he crossed over behind me.'

Gardner's eyes widened. 'Continuing in the same direction as Ralphie and Vivianne? The direction of the graveyard?'

Toby nodded, but then his own eyes widened, and he shook his head. 'But that's ridiculous. If you're thinking... *no... no chance.* He's not capable of something like that... is he? He's too gentle. Simple-minded. And he was out of it. Completely.'

Gardner felt a cold sensation spreading throughout her body. 'Yet, you just said he was behaving *oddly.* Enough to intimidate you?'

'Yeah, but that's different. I didn't feel threatened by him. Not physically. It's more the shame and guilt. Look, Arthur hasn't got it in him to harm anybody. He's still the same frightened kid that we first met in Year 7.'

That you all bullied...

'He couldn't kill two people,' Toby continued. 'He's not capable.'

Everyone's capable, given the circumstances, Gardner thought, reaching for her phone.

As she drew the phone from her pocket, she saw Rice was calling.

'Phil?'

'Boss... have you heard...?'

'Phil? Heard what?'

'I'm on my way to the hospital now...'

As Rice explained, Gardner drew back away from Toby, sucking in air, suddenly feeling like someone had punched her in the stomach.

68

Riddick's legs burned. 'Police!'

He barged past a small gathering by an open door off the corridor and hit a stairwell. He threw himself up the steps, between people, and around them, their angry words disappearing in Riddick's own haze of adrenaline, confusion and despair.

Lungs fit to explode, he reached the last floor and burst through the door onto a flat roof.

So many people... doctors... nurses... security guards...

He weaved among them, disorientated, confused.

Someone grabbed him by the arm, stopping him dead. 'Watch your step.'

Riddick looked down over a straight drop into the heart of the building. Falling down there would have ended him. Shrubbery, a bench, some curious folks looking upwards, and some glass windows portioning out the several floors.

He gulped air. Sweat stung his eyes. He turned from the drop, seeking the source of the chaos.

Anxious whispers ahead of him led him in that direction. Someone seized his arm. 'Hang back... the police are coming.'

He caught sight of what was happening ahead before he could respond.

Then, his mouth simply hung open, while his blood ran cold.

Arthur paced the edge of the roof.

No, Arthur. God, no...

Arthur shook his head, muttering, repeatedly banging his chest with his own fist.

Riddick edged forward and someone grabbed his arm.

'I'm the police. Get your hands off me.'

A large man in scrubs removed his hand and, after making eye contact with Riddick, backed away, palms raised.

Riddick approached the roof edge.

Four or five metres back from the edge of the roof, Roni was on her knees, her head lowered. A suited man knelt beside her with his arm curled around her shoulders. His grip looked tight.

Was she being held back?

A woman, also dressed in a suit, was a couple of metres closer to Arthur, obviously trying to talk him down.

If he could hear her over the repeated thumping of his chest and his mumbles, it wasn't apparent.

Arthur paused. He turned, shakily. Unsteady...

Heart in his mouth, Riddick moved alongside Roni and the man restraining her. *Please... Arthur...*

Arthur resumed his pacing in the other direction. Riddick sighed.

Riddick could now hear the woman's pleas. 'Talk to me, Arthur. I'm here to listen... I can—'

Suddenly, Arthur increased the velocity and ferocity of his chest punches. His eyes moved upwards to the heavens. He stumbled.

'Arthur, no!' Riddick lurched forward.

Arthur regained his footing and glanced right towards the woman and Riddick.

He heard me.

Riddick moved alongside the negotiator. Arthur, still now, was looking right at him. But his eyes remained wide, and tears ran down his face. A rabbit caught in headlights.

Riddick turned, snatched his badge out and held it up. 'Police. Get *off* the roof. Get *off* now.'

The members of the gathering crowd exchanged glances.

'Now!'

Onlookers sidled away.

When he turned back, he saw that Arthur's wide eyes were still in his direction.

'They're going, Arthur.' He glanced at the negotiator. 'I'll take it from here.'

'I think I'm getting through,' she said.

'No, you weren't. He *knows* me.'

'I'm trained.'

'So am I,' Riddick lied. 'Now, move away.'

The woman looked between Arthur, Riddick and Roni, before sighing and nodding. She backed away.

Riddick saw some of the fear leaving Arthur's eyes. He looked over his shoulder to see that the crowd had thinned considerably. There were just a few people, including the woman, yet to exit.

Clearing the chaos had obviously helped.

Double-checking again that Arthur was no longer pacing or punching himself, he took a step back so he was within earshot of Roni and the suited man.

'Roni,' he said.

She didn't respond.

He looked in her direction. She was trembling, weeping, and

had eyes only for her son. He knelt, keeping his eyes on Arthur, who was, *thank Christ*, looking calmer by the second. Riddick needed to know what had caused this before making his move.

'Police. What happened?'

The suited man restraining her spoke. 'I'm security. They triggered the alarm on the roof door. I saw it on the video feed...'

'Wait... they?'

'Yes... she brought him up here. Didn't you, ma'am?'

It made no sense. 'Why'd you do that, Roni?'

Riddick kept his eyes firmly on Arthur as he waited for a response from Roni. She didn't give one.

'When I made it up here,' the guard explained, 'they were both standing near the edge, but not right up on it, like the lad is right now. I approached... quietly... they didn't see me... I heard her assuring him they'd be together—'

Roni suddenly pulled against the guard. Veins were standing out on her face like ropes.

The guard clenched his teeth as he restrained her more firmly.

'Arthur... go... before it's too late,' she screamed.

Jesus. 'Roni, what're you doing?' Riddick hissed.

Roni sagged in the security guard's arms.

Out of breath, he said, 'There's no reasoning with her. I had to grab her before she took them both off the bloody roof!'

'You can't...' Roni was crying hard. 'You must let him go.'

Riddick shook his head. She'd lost her mind.

He considered going straight for Arthur, but it may end badly. He worshipped his mother. She was surely the best option to put an end to this.

He moved around the guard and in front of Roni. He took her limp hand. 'Roni... *please*... listen to me. He needs our help. You need to *tell* him to get down from the edge. You're his mother, Roni. And you're not thinking clearly!'

She squeezed her eyes shut hard. 'I've never been clearer about anything.'

He tried to keep control of his frustration, but he could feel himself losing it. 'What is it then? For God's sake, talk to me.'

Her eyes opened and fixed him with a stare. 'You're not putting my son in a cage... it'll tear him to pieces.'

'I don't understand.' And he really didn't. 'I'd never let that happen. Someone gave him those drugs. Forced him to take those drugs. He's done nothing wrong. We've the facts.'

She stared at him and grimaced. 'No... you don't. You don't know what he's done. You just don't know—'

'He's done *nothing* Roni. Listen, he's done—'

He broke off.

The world suddenly seemed to spin around him.

He closed his eyes to stop himself falling backwards, but his stomach churned... and then came a familiar sensation.

A horrible, vicious sensation. One he'd felt many times before.

Burning.

A raging inferno.

Consuming and destroying everything inside him.

Eventually, to be left hollow. Empty. And without the physical pain. But not without agony.

Loss.

Here it is again.

'He *told* me what happened,' Roni said. 'About that bastard, Ralphie, and his poor—'

'No!' Riddick said, standing. 'No!' He looked down at her. 'If you won't get him down, then I will.'

'Paul... Imagine. Imagine him in a cage.'

Riddick looked at the guard. 'Put your hand over her mouth.'

'I can't—'

'Do it,' Riddick said. 'It's the only way. I'll take responsibility.'

'Please…'

'Now,' Riddick said. 'Or I can't save him.'

Riddick turned, shaking, not waiting to see if the request was fulfilled.

Arthur was still on the edge, staring at him. He *still* looked calmer than before.

Riddick held out his hand and approached. 'Arthur, that's enough now, buddy. That's enough.'

'Paul… Paul…' He repeated his name several times. 'Paul…'

'Arthur,' Riddick said firmly, trying to snap his friend out of it. 'Are you my sidekick?'

'You said that I couldn't be…'

'Forget I said that. You want the gig or not?'

'I don't know.'

Shit. That wasn't good. Riddick stopped a metre from Arthur with his arm out. 'My sidekick? Surely, you're not turning that down.'

'I trusted you before… I *keep* trusting you… It keeps going wrong.'

Riddick flinched. The carving in the poor boy's chest, the abuse he received from those ridiculous nineteen-year-olds at the party.

'No more mistakes, Arthur. I promise. No more mistakes.' He moved closer and proffered his hand.

Behind him, he could hear muffling. The guard must have come good on his request.

Arthur smiled. 'I guess superheroes need to be allowed to make some mistakes…'

Riddick returned the smile. 'Yes! As can the best sidekicks. Then, we can learn from them—'

'I'm not sure…' Arthur rubbed his chest. He winced. 'Everything hurts. Everything *feels* broken.'

'Everything can be fixed, pal. *Everything.* Step forward, take my hand, and I'll fix everything.'

'But this dream, Paul.' He suddenly pounded his chest twice. 'Why would superheroes have dreams like that? I don't think I can be a sidekick any more.'

'Dreams trick us. That's what they do.' Riddick pointed at himself with the hand he wasn't offering up. 'Believe in what you can see right now.'

'But I can't get it out of my head. It feels real.' He pounded his chest. 'Real.' Arthur opened his hands and looked down at them. 'I was angry... I kept hitting them and hitting them and hitting them.'

Riddick fought hard against the burning. The inferno. Later, he'd also have to fight against the hollowness. But, for now, he needed to stop this escalating.

He sucked in a deep breath.

'They gave you drugs... they *forced* you. Trust me, you were in no fit state to do anything. The chemicals are playing with your mind.'

Arthur smiled. 'They looked beautiful together... before. After... I sat them up together... tried to make them look beautiful again.'

The bodies had indeed been found in that manner. Propped up. Like two lovers on a bench.

Riddick clenched his teeth.

God, it was true.

The unthinkable was true.

Fight the despair, Paul. For crying out loud, fight the despair.

'Arthur, take my hand.'

'I just wanted them to like me,' Arthur said.

Riddick flinched again. 'I know, Arthur.'

'But they were just like everyone else. I wish people would *like* me like they like each other.'

'I like you,' Riddick said, forcing back the tears, desperate to keep up the illusion of control for his friend.

'Please... Arthur...' Roni called. 'Before it's too late. The cage. Remember the cage. I'll follow—'

Back to muffling. The guard was surely regaining control again.

Riddick nodded at his outstretched palm less than a metre from his young friend. 'Come and take my hand, sidekick. I've got you.'

'I don't want to go into a cage.'

'You won't.'

And if anyone tries to put you in one, son, I'll pull them to pieces.

'You promise?'

'This is one promise I won't let you down on.'

Arthur reached out for Riddick's hand.

Riddick moved closer to take his hand, relief spreading through him.

'Paul?'

The voice was familiar, but Riddick ignored it, the wonder of his fingertips meeting Arthur's surpassing everything.

'Paul... *listen...*'

Phil Rice.

Jesus, Phil not now.

'Listen to me, Paul!' His voice was growing in volume. He must have been coming quickly across the roof towards them.

'Who's that?' Arthur asked, pulling his hand back slightly.

'It doesn't matter,' Riddick said, edging forward so their fingertips were touching again...

'Paul, listen to me. Step back.' Rice was close now. His voice was even louder than Roni's had been.

Phil, what're you doing? Riddick closed his hands, trapping Arthur's fingertips in his palm. *Good.* 'Come forward, Arthur.'

'Don't get too close,' Rice shouted.

'Not now...' Riddick said. 'Not now, Phil.'

'But you don't understand. The boy is dangerous!' Rice called.

'Dangerous?' Arthur said. 'I'm not dangerous.'

He yanked his hand away and fell backwards off the roof.

69

While Gardner and Barnett sprinted through the hospital, she tried Riddick's phone repeatedly, but he wasn't picking up.

Barnett kept trying Rice, also with no success.

'Police!' Gardner shouted.

A crowd of people in the corridor parted to allow the pair through.

Gardner led the way up the stairwell to the top floor and, gasping for breath, opened the door.

She immediately heard the screams and shouts from people far below, reminding her of that fateful day when Collette Willow had fallen to her death.

We're too late.

She moved out onto the flat roof and looked left towards the edge.

Bloody hell! *Paul, what the hell are you doing?*

'Ray, quick!'

Riddick was mounted on top of a motionless figure, throwing punches downwards.

She charged, and shouted, '*Paul*, get the hell off...'

It didn't stop him.

Metres from Riddick, she identified the man receiving the pummelling as Rice.

Whether he had fought back to begin with, she'd no idea, but he certainly wasn't fighting back now.

She grabbed Riddick's left shoulder and attempted to pull him away, but he was rooted down and immoveable, and his right fist continued to make a mess of their colleague's face. 'You're going to bloody well kill him!'

He threw his left hand backwards. She backed away, clutching her gut. Again, she tried to steady Riddick, but she was winded and could get no words out.

She sighted a man in a suit, standing on the edge. *What the—*

Barnett launched past her, threw his arms around Riddick's waist and took him to the floor beside Rice.

Rice groaned, coughed, spluttered and rolled onto his side.

Barnett was much bigger than Riddick and had him pressed down to the floor under his weight.

Riddick wasn't giving up easily. He writhed, shouting at the top of his lungs. 'He's gone... Arthur's gone... get off me...'

Gardner took a deep breath, recovering from her winding, and looked up at the suited man at the edge. Annoyed that he was just standing there, and hadn't come to stop Riddick from committing murder, she marched towards him.

Behind her, she could hear Riddick shouting, 'I had him... don't you understand... I *had* him...'

From outside the hospital, she could hear the shouts and sobs of those below, looking at the body of a nineteen-year-old boy.

The suited man watched her approach.

'DCI Gardner,' she said. 'Who are you?'

'Miles Becker. Security guard here.' He looked pale. His eyes twitched.

'What're you doing here? At the edge?'

His eyes filled with tears. 'She got away from me.'

'Who?'

'The mother...' He held up his hand. There was blood on the back of it. 'She bit me and then, well, then... she was just gone.'

God, no...

She looked over the edge, sighted the two bodies and the panicky crowd, and then looked back towards her colleagues.

Rice, thank God, was already sitting up.

Riddick was still pinned beneath Barnett.

He'd his head raised and was looking directly at her.

She considered shaking her head to deliver the bad news.

But what was the point?

He already knew.

He lowered his forehead to the ground and wailed.

70

TWO WEEKS LATER

It'd been Marsh's suggestion that Gardner take some leave.

It wasn't like the superintendent to show a compassionate side, so Gardner had just assumed that her boss was sick of constantly seeing her prize detective with a faraway look in her eyes, as well as being regularly on the phone checking in on her children's safety.

Still, whatever the reason, the breathing space was welcome. And, having the opportunity to spend several hours with her children daily at Cathy O'Brien's home every day once they'd finished school was bliss.

On leave, she'd tried, daily, to contact Paul Riddick, suspended after Rice's accusation of assault. Rice's stance had softened in the last week, and he'd suggested to Gardner that he may just drop the charges, and claim it was half a dozen of one and six of the other. Rice had even made out to Gardner that he was sympathetic to Riddick, but Gardner was suspicious. Rice would probably enjoy having one up on Riddick, and the bragging rights behind saving his career.

Riddick's last words to Gardner had been, 'You're better off without me in your life.'

The stubborn fool was trying his best to prove this by never answering the phone to her.

To be honest, she was probably better off!

Probably?

Undoubtedly!

But, regardless, she continued trying anyway.

She had also spent a large chunk of the two weeks researching Neville Fairweather.

Fairweather was an enigma.

Whenever she tried to contact him, he was outside the country on business. UKVI and Border Force would always back this up.

Still, he'd clearly not been officially in the UK when he'd visited her home and left that sodding photograph. Neither was he out of the country when he'd visited former MP Sebastian Harrington on the day of his suicide. Although then, it was later claimed, he'd returned the previous evening on an impromptu flight.

He'd also been interviewed and cleared of any involvement in Sebastian's death. Not by Gardner, of course. But someone lurking in the shadows far up the chain of command.

DCI Michael Yorke, her former boss and now confidante, had also come up empty in his investigations down in Wiltshire. Yorke carried some clout these days after being appointed head of SEROCU, so if he came up empty, that made Fairweather even more of an enigma.

Gardner's anxiety grew daily.

What was Fairweather's connection to Collette Willows, and why had he felt the need to make his presence known in such a sinister way?

Her kids couldn't come home until that question was answered. And it was an answer that felt light years away.

A day before her return to work, Gardner was mowing the grass around the back of her home when there was a knock at her rear gate. She assumed that someone had approached the front door, and she'd missed them. Probably a courier company. She shielded her face as she approached the gate in case an over-eager driver flung the parcel over it.

She opened the gate to a strong-looking man in his thirties with tidy, cropped hair. He wore a black suit and tie.

You're missing an earpiece and a pair of shades, she thought.

If Riddick had been here, he'd most certainly have just come out and said it.

'DCI Gardner. Are you available now, please?'

'Depends,' Gardner said, eyeing up a pair of garden shears buried in the soil around the garden edge, 'on who you are and whether it's safe to do so.'

'You're safe. It's you who has been insistent on this meeting. Mr Fairweather is happy to speak to you now.'

'Oh, he is, is he?' Gardner said, feeling a surge of anger. She wondered if she should take the shears, regardless.

'Yes, ma'am.'

'Is he at the front of my house in a stretch limo with shaded windows?'

The man couldn't resist a smile. 'Ma'am?'

'Let's not keep him waiting, eh?'

Gardner followed the suited man to the front of her home.

There was no stretch limo. Just a rather sporty-looking Mercedes. And no shaded windows.

One of the windows was lowered, and she saw Fairweather in profile.

'Shall I let someone know that I'm getting in there before I do?' Gardner said, loud enough for her visitor to hear.

'No need,' Fairweather said, cracking the door and stepping out.

She felt another surge of anger. Still, who wouldn't? This man had come to her home wielding a photograph of a friend who'd died because of her careless actions and left her terrified enough to move her children.

'I didn't know you were in the country.'

'I arrived home earlier today. DCI Gardner... Emma... would you like ten minutes of my time?'

'Would I like?' She snorted. 'Well, it depends on whether you're going to tell the truth... and you're insane if you think I'm getting in your car.'

He closed the door behind him, a ghost of a smile on his face. 'Shall we walk then?'

She leaned against the railings at the front of her home while he exchanged words with the suited man. It seemed they'd be walking alone, as the driver, bodyguard, or whatever he was climbed back into the car.

Fairweather walked ahead. He glanced back over his shoulder. 'Coming?'

His West Country accent was strong. It reminded her of home.

'You've been trying to get in touch... I believe?' Fairweather said when Gardner drew alongside him.

'Look,' Gardner said, stopping dead. 'Cut the crap. You came to me twice. You claimed to be house-hunting the first time. Why?'

He nodded and grinned as if he was recalling a fond memory. 'I remember it well. Rose. Spirited. Very spirited. Not unlike you.'

'Let's leave my child out of this.'

'Jack's child, you mean?' He looked to the side at her with an eyebrow raised.

She felt a sudden rush of adrenaline. *Jack?*

'I never told you his name.'

'Are you sure?'

'Yes,' Gardner hissed. 'Who *are* you?'

The ghost of a smile broke into a grin for the first time. 'I'm not your enemy. You don't have to fear me. And you certainly don't have to send your children to stay with Cathy O'Brien.'

Gardner steadied herself against a wall behind her. 'Shit. Is there anything you don't know?'

'Stop, please.' He held the palm of his hand up. 'I'm not that man. That person. If you were in any danger from me... we'd never have got as far as this conversation.'

'Who are you?' Gardner asked. 'A spook?'

'No.'

'Just a powerful man, eh?'

'Of sorts.'

'Of sorts! It seems you control the Home Office.'

'Let's not exaggerate.'

Gardner sighed. 'I wish I was. I need to warn you I've put powerful men behind bars before. There's only so far power will take you.'

'I won't be going to jail, Emma. I serve the greater good. I'm necessary.'

'Forgive me. But those powerful men I just told you about. They offered similar justifications. Corruption, abuse, even paedophilia... I've heard it before.'

His smile fell away, and his expression turned to disgust. 'I agree. There are many that feel entitlement. And you, Emma, have proven adept at stopping people like that. But do you really believe it a one-person crusade? Do you really think that you would've succeeded without the support of others?'

'No, of course not.'

'Support, perhaps, from people like me?'

'Ah, I see. Sebastian Harrington. Did you have a hand in that?'

'Sebastian was an old friend. I came to pay my respects.'

'Just before his suicide?'

'Alas, his actions were his alone.'

'Did you talk him into taking those pills?'

'That's absurd.'

'How about talking him out of it? Did you try?'

Fairweather shrugged. 'A person has to make his own decisions. What I'd consider the right choice of action would be entirely irrelevant.'

'Out of curiosity, what would've been the right choice of action?'

'As I just said, irrelevant. Sebastian had reached the end of his road. He didn't want to live with disgrace. He chose his own action.'

Gardner took a deep breath in through her nostrils, turned from the wall and continued down the street. She exhaled as she shook her head.

A car drove past, and a neighbour she recognised waved out of the window. She didn't wave back.

She sensed Fairweather walking alongside her again.

'What the hell do you want from me?' Gardner asked.

'Two things. Both things you'll be happy to give me.'

She snorted. 'Happy? That's quite a leap.'

'Before I get to these two things, there's something you should know. Or, maybe, a few things you should know. All the subterfuge that's unnerved you, well, I'm sorry, but it's necessary to take precautions, considering the importance of things. And the Sebastian issue, please rest assured it's unrelated to our relationship and merely a coincidence.'

'You come into my life, scare me half to death and leave a

picture behind of Collette. She was a wonderful girl who lost her life tragically. Yet, you antagonise me with my guilt and trauma. Now you want something. Actually, you want two things.' She snorted again.

'You're right about Collette. She was wonderful... and...' He stopped. 'She was my daughter.'

Gardner stopped and looked at him. She wasn't shocked. 'I saw a photograph of you together. But she told me her father was dead.'

Fairweather looked sad. 'Actually, Collette never knew.' He sighed. 'She resulted from my union with her mother, just before she became attached to the man who'd take on the role of Collette's father. I stayed a family friend, and Collette believed the man was her real dad. It was the best I could offer, anyway. A person like me wouldn't have the time for such a great responsibility. I was happy to be a friend to her, but I could never provide for her day to day.'

'So, why leave the photograph with me? Do you blame me for her death or something?'

'No, of course not. I know the circumstances around what happened. It was an accident. A tragedy caused by two driven people doing their job. No. I *simply* wanted to establish a connection with you.'

'By scaring me half to death?'

'I needed your attention. So, now I have it. And now I'm here to tell you about the two things I need.'

Gardner shook her head. 'This is all too peculiar—'

'First,' Fairweather said, holding up a finger. 'I want you to bring Rose and Anabelle back to your house and allow them to crack on with their lives! You're in no danger. Never have been. Never will be. In fact, you're far safer just knowing me than you probably ever have been in your life.'

She hadn't expected that. 'But how can I really—'

'You're *safe*, Emma. Now, the second thing is important too...'

Gardner raised an eyebrow. 'Which is?'

'One day, I may ask you for your help. I cannot tell you why just yet, and it may not even come to it, but be aware it could happen. And, if it does, you must give it without question. You'll understand, anyway, that it's *necessary*. But it must be without question. There may not be time for questions.'

'I'd never exploit my position in the force. You've come to the wrong place—'

'No, you misunderstand, Emma. I don't want you to use your position in the force. I'm not some gangster. Besides, I'd be asking you to use your position as a family member.'

'Sorry... come again... what? Family member? Of who?'

'Your brother... Jack.'

'Jack? What's he got to do with anything?'

Fairweather didn't respond.

'What could you possibly want with my brother? He's a sociopath. A bloody criminal.'

'Yes. Partly. But maybe you don't know Jack as well as you think you do.'

'I know him well enough.' She pointed at the scar on her head. 'He tried to brain me when we were children, after all. Anyway, how is Jack relevant? I don't understand.'

'It's too soon to explain that. Just be ready. And know that there is more to him than meets the eye.'

Gardner opened her mouth to again deny this claim, but the words died in her mouth. Hadn't Jack proved her wrong once before? He'd cared about Rose – he'd been desperate for her to live with Gardner, sacrificing himself so she could have the life he couldn't give her.

But it remained irrelevant. She still had no idea what this man wanted. 'I won't help you unless you tell me more... Also, I won't have anything to do with Jack, anyway. I'll warn you of that in advance.'

'You'll have to help, Emma, and, to emphasise again... help without question.'

'And what'll you do if I don't?' She sneered. '*Exactly*.'

'Nothing.'

'That makes little sense.'

'No, it makes perfect sense. Because if you don't help me without question then, unfortunately, your brother, Jack, will die.'

71

Following a stint in the incident room, Gardner slumped back in her office chair.

She'd only been back at work a week, but she was already feeling completely shattered.

It'd be easy to blame the suspicious death up in Boroughbridge that had her and her team chasing their tails, but it certainly wasn't the truth of the matter.

The truth was it had been that peculiar visit of Willows biological father, Neville Fairweather, and his references to her brother, Jack.

It was this that kept her mind alert until the early hours every day and, if she was lucky enough to sleep for over four hours dreams that'd test the hardiest of horror film addicts.

She sighed, looked at her watch, and decided it was probably time for her daily phone call to Paul Riddick. She'd love to refer to it as a check-in, but he'd *actually* have to answer the phone for it to be termed that...

After making the call and leaving a message – how many was

this? *Thirty*? – she sighed, put the phone down, leaned back in her chair and rubbed her temples.

Closing her eyes, she took three deep breaths.

Sod this.

She grabbed her phone and stood up.

Yes Paul, you may be right. My life may be better without you in it. But surely that's my decision to make.

She left the office.

* * *

She drove to Riddick's rented property on the outskirts of Bradford.

After pounding on the door for an eternity, she had to accept that he wasn't in, or just wasn't prepared to speak to her.

She knelt, pushed open the letterbox and shouted in, 'Don't you think it's about time we spoke?'

When she was certain he wasn't going to reply, she let the letterbox clatter shut and stood up, irritated.

You stubborn, bloody idiot.

She circled the house and glanced in a few windows. The place looked dead. Maybe, he was out. *Hopefully.* Better that than moping around in the shadows doing God knows what. Drinking probably.

She returned to her car, knowing what she had to do next.

It was going to be awkward.

But what choice did she have? She was starting to get worried.

* * *

Gardner sat in her car outside Riddick's house as she contacted Claire Hornsby.

She stared at Riddick's house as they spoke, recalling the night she'd driven up to see Riddick and Claire kissing on his doorstep, before making a quick exit.

Consequently, she expected this conversation to be awkward. It wasn't. It was just very sad.

Gardner began by apologising for acquiring her phone number without her permission, before offering her excuses. 'I'm worried about him.'

'That's what we do a lot, isn't it? The people around him. Worry about him. A great deal.'

He's been through a hell of a lot.

Claire was a grief counsellor, and she'd know this more than anyone – she was obviously feeling very bitter. She didn't need to say that they were no longer in a relationship. This came across clearly.

'He's not answering his phone,' Gardner said. 'He hasn't done for three weeks.'

Claire sighed. 'I find that strange. He's fond of you. He spoke about you often. Said you were the best officer he'd known – that you always listened.'

Gardner took a deep breath, forcing back the emotion. She wasn't going to lose any control here.

'He always beats himself up for not being a good listener,' Claire said.

'He's not that bad,' Gardner said. 'When he's not distracted.'

'When is that?'

Gardner smiled. 'Good point.'

There was silence on the phone. Both of them were clearly reflecting on their personal connections with Riddick.

Get to it, Emma. She was just building herself up to ask when Claire had last seen him, when she got there first. 'I haven't seen him, you know... I don't know whether he told you before Arthur's death... well, I'd already packed up and left.'

'No, he didn't...' Gardner said. 'I'm sorry to hear that—'

'Don't be sorry. *I* left.'

Still, sometimes we don't have a choice, do we? She looked at Riddick's house again. *Sometimes they don't really give us that choice.*

'I've been contacting him by phone, though.'

'And he picks up?'

'Usually.'

Lucky you.

'And how did he seem?'

'How you'd expect. Distant. Distracted.'

Gardner nodded. 'Lost.'

'Yes, but he didn't want me coming over. He was adamant. I think he was drinking. So, I sent his sponsor, Daz Horne.'

'Could I take his number?'

'Of course.'

Gardner wrote it down. 'And what did Daz tell you?'

'Not much. He did tell me to stay away for the time being, which does make me think that *yes*, he was drinking again. This was over a week ago. I've only spoken to him once since then... about five days back... and, well, I kind of made up my mind that it'd be the last time.'

'I see. Do you mind me asking why?'

Silence. *Obviously, she did.*

'I'm sorry, maybe it's none of my business. I was just worried—'

'No... you're right. Look, something happened... something unpleasant.'

More silence.

'I understand if it's not a good time... if you—'

'I *was* pregnant.'

Gardner put her hand to her mouth.

Pregnant.

Was.

'I lost the baby.'

'I'm sorry...' Gardner rubbed her forehead. 'I really am.' She fought against the emotion.

'It happens, doesn't it? But I needed him. I was devastated. I phoned him, I told him, but it was like it barely registered... it was as if he was numb.' She broke off, crying.

After the call, Gardner sat and stared at the house, wiping tears from her own eyes.

Riddick may be suffering, but so too, was that poor woman, Claire.

This was the problem with being in so much pain. It made you selfish. Turned your eyes from the suffering of others.

She wanted to contact Daz Horne, but she simply felt too overwhelmed to talk right now, so she sat in silence.

* * *

Eventually, she did call Daz Horne, but he didn't want to speak to her on the phone. He arranged to meet her on Riddick's doorstep. 'I've a key,' he said. 'See you in ten.'

He was there in eight minutes.

Gardner shook the large man's hand. His face was lined and weathered. She introduced herself again.

'You don't need to tell me who you are,' Daz said. 'He was always on about you. I feel like I already know you.'

Claire had said something similar. *He spoke about you often.*

She flinched. The guilt she suddenly felt was overwhelming.

Three weeks, Emma. Three weeks it's taken you to get to his doorstep.

She recalled her earlier thought that pain made you selfish

and ignorant to the suffering of others. Had she been too preoccupied with Neville Fairweather and her own issues to seek him out when he most needed her?

And now what?

She gulped when she thought about how eager Daz had been to come to meet her.

Was she too late?

He held the key up. 'I haven't spoken to him in two days.'

Claire had claimed not to have spoken to him in five.

Two days was a long time when someone was in trouble.

It was a lifetime.

'It couldn't be helped,' Daz said, sighing. 'I've been visiting family in the south for the past week.' He rubbed the back of his hand as if it was cold out. It wasn't. 'Look, I phoned him every day. He seemed a bit better, you know? Picking up, slightly. He didn't answer yesterday, so I came home today. Been back less than an hour.'

'Maybe you should've called someone?' Gardner said.

'Who?' He sighed. 'Does he have anyone left? And, if I'd called you, he'd have never spoken to me again.'

Gardner shook her head. Suddenly feeling ashamed, she couldn't make eye contact with Daz. 'I used to be there for him. We were close... once.'

'You still are. I think that's the reason he won't talk to you. He now believes he's a danger to everyone he knows. Bullshit, of course. The way he tells his story, you can kind of see why he believes it. He almost had me convinced once.'

Gardner nodded at the door behind Daz and forced herself to make eye contact. 'Do you think he's okay in there?'

'Yes. It's not the first time he hasn't answered his phone to me. The other times, I found him at the bottom of a bottle.' He held up his key. 'That's why he gave me this. To clean him up when needs

be. It's not my fault you're here. He can't blame me for that. But I'l
ask you seriously, do you want to go in here? You may not like wha
you see.'

'Open the door, please. I need to see that he's okay.'

* * *

The place wasn't tidy by any stretch of the imagination, but i
wasn't as bad as she'd suspected it'd be. There was no build-up o
mail or strewn beer bottles and cans in the hallway for a start.

She expected Daz had been helping Riddick keep it clean.

Daz was already away, working through the rooms, calling
Riddick's name.

Gardner had never been in the home he'd shared with Clairc
before. Watercolour paintings of various spots around the UK
patterned the walls, and she gazed into a well-decorated loungc
with a picture of the Boulevard of Broken Dreams hanging abovc
the fireplace.

It certainly had a homely feel.

At this point, Riddick was still to answer the call of his sponsoi
and she detected the agitation in Daz's voice.

Until now, she'd managed to keep her own concern fo
Riddick's safety reasonably in check, but when Daz startec
bounding up the stairs, shouting, 'Paul, where the bloody hell arc
you?' she felt her adrenaline levels soar, and her heart begar
thrashing in her chest.

You be okay, Paul, she thought. *Do you hear? You be okay...*

She turned into the kitchen.

'Oh Paul...'

Here there was evidence of Riddick's decline.

Empty spirit bottles on the worktop, pizza boxes, unwashec

plates. The place appeared as if it'd been the epicentre of a house party rather than the home of one person's despair.

Upstairs, she could hear Daz bounding about, still calling for Riddick.

At least he hadn't yet found anything that'd cause him to fall to his knees in despair.

Stomach turning over, and heart crashing against her ribcage, she turned her eyes to the kitchen table. There was a collection of beer cans at the head of the table, and a couple of whisky bottles in the centre, but apart from that, it seemed to be the cleanest part of the kitchen.

She imagined him, night after night, sitting there, drinking himself to death, communicating with those he'd lost.

He'd done this before. *Imagined them there. Spoken to them.* For hours, days, sometimes weeks on end. He'd told her the stories.

She could hear Daz running down the stairs. 'He's not here. He's not *bloody* here.'

Gardner approached the kitchen table and placed her hands on the chair she believed Riddick would've sat in.

Five photographs were spread out around the perimeter of the table.

One for each place at the table, positioned where you'd expect the cutlery to be set.

Daz was at the door. 'He's gone. Where the bloody hell has he gone?'

Gardner circled the table, touching the photographs one by one.

His wife, Rachel.

His daughters, Molly and Lucy.

His mentor, Anders.

And finally, his young friend.

Arthur.

ACKNOWLEDGEMENTS

It seems no matter the circumstances, Riddick and Gardner always seem determined to find each other again! This is not always intentional on my part; the characters, themselves, have started to make a lot of their own decisions, leaving me an interested bystander. But nothing is always straightforward, is it?

I enjoyed writing this novel for many reasons. Most notably, the opportunity to revisit the eighties, when I was a youngster and, of course, the graveyard setting. I always had an ambition to write a story centred around a graveyard. They have so much character and mystery.

A massive thank you to Boldwood once again, and my wonderful team of editors: Emily Ruston, Candida Bradford and Susan Sugden.

My children, who grow ever more restless and determined to read these novels. Not happening for a good few years!

Thanks to my ever-supportive wife, Jo.

Everyone in my wonderful ARC group. Fantastic supportive bloggers: Donna M, Sharon R and Kath M.

I look forward to seeing you in the next Yorkshire Murders, which begins on a wintry night at Christmas at a local tavern where a storyteller prepares to engage his audience...

ABOUT THE AUTHOR

Wes Markin is the bestselling author of the DCI Yorke crime novels, set in Salisbury. His new series for Boldwood stars the pragmatic detective DCI Emma Gardner who will be tackling the criminals of North Yorkshire. Wes lives in Harrogate and the first book in The Yorkshire Murders series was published in November 2022.

Sign up to Wes Markin's mailing list for news, competitions and updates on future books.

Visit Wes Markin's website: <u>wesmarkinauthor.com</u>

Follow Wes on social media:

𝕏 x.com/MarkinWes

facebook.com/WesMarkinAuthor

ALSO BY WES MARKIN

The Yorkshire Murders

The Viaduct Killings

The Lonely Lake Killings

The Crying Cave Killings

The Graveyard Killings

DCI Michael Yorke thrillers

One Last Prayer

The Repenting Serpent

The Silence of Severance

Rise of the Rays

Dance with the Reaper

Christmas with the Conduit

Better the Devil

Jake Pettman Thrillers

The Killing Pit

Fire in Bone

Blue Falls

The Rotten Core

Rock and a Hard Place

THE

Murder

LIST

THE MURDER LIST IS A NEWSLETTER DEDICATED TO ALL THINGS CRIME AND THRILLER FICTION!

SIGN UP TO MAKE SURE YOU'RE ON OUR HIT LIST FOR GRIPPING PAGE-TURNERS AND HEARTSTOPPING READS.

SIGN UP TO OUR NEWSLETTER

BIT.LY/THEMURDERLISTNEWS

Boldw⊙⊙d

Boldwood Books is an award-winning fiction publishing company seeking out the best stories from around the world.

Find out more at www.boldwoodbooks.com

Join our reader community for brilliant books, competitions and offers!

Follow us
@BoldwoodBooks
@TheBoldBookClub

Sign up to our weekly deals newsletter

https://bit.ly/BoldwoodBNewsletter

Printed in Great Britain
by Amazon

39784494R00225